RHYS FORD

BLACK
DOG BLUES

DSP PUBLICATIONS

Published by

DSP PUBLICATIONS

5032 Capital Circle SW, Suite 2, PMB# 279, Tallahassee, FL 32305-7886 USA
www.dsppublications.com

Black Dog Blues
© 2019 Rhys Ford.

Cover Art
© 2019 Chris McGrath.
www.christianmcgrath.com
Cover content is for illustrative purposes only and any person depicted on the cover is a model.

Trade Paperback ISBN: 978-1-64405-318-8
Digital ISBN: 978-1-64405-317-1
Mass Market Paperback ISBN: 978-1-64108-179-5
Library of Congress Control Number: 2018962535
Trade Paperback published March 2019
v. 3.0
First Edition published by Rhys Ford, June 2013.
Second Edition published by DSP Publications, February 2015.

Printed in the United States of America
∞
This paper meets the requirements of
ANSI/NISO Z39.48-1992 (Permanence of Paper).

Readers love
The Kai Gracen Series
by RHYS FORD

"Kai is my favorite type of character – the tough, scrappy, outcast, snark-monger extraordinaire."

—Gail Carriger, Author of The Parasol Protectorate Series

"Heart-pounding action, dramatic betrayals, and creepy backstories are all in a day's work for Kai."

—AudioFile Magazine

Black Dog Blues

—Library Journal Best Books of 2013
—AudioFile Earphones Award winner

"Awesome book that I'll absolutely recommend to fantasy lovers."

—It's About The Book

"This story is everything a fantasy should be."

—Love Bytes

Mad Lizard Mambo

—Paranormal Romance Guild
Reviewers Choice Award: Best Novel

"*Mad Lizard Mambo* is an outstanding sequel. Once again we are drawn into this crazy world author Rhys Ford has so lovingly created and carried away on an adventure beyond our imagination."

—Joyfully Jay

DEC — 1 2020

By RHYS FORD

KAI GRACEN
Black Dog Blues
Mad Lizard Mambo
Jacked Cat Jive

INK AND SHADOWS
Ink and Shadows

Dim Sum Asylum
7&7: A DSP Publications Anthology of Virtue and Vice
Devil Take Me Anthology

Published by DSP PUBLICATIONS
www.dsppublications.com

This one is for Elizabeth—who has given Kai a new home.

This book would be nothing without the Five. Tamm, Lea, Penn, and Jenn. As always. Also, my sisters in all but blood—Ree, Ren, and Lisa.

Haato and snookies to you all.

ACKNOWLEDGMENTS

SO MANY people to thank and where to begin? Let's first start with Terese, Suzhang, Brooke, and Ericka, who have always wanted Kai to hit the pixel and page.

Major kudos to Elizabeth North because, really, this journey into print and pixel started with her and her reading *Dirty Kiss*… and liking *Dirty Kiss*. Thank you. So many thank-yous. And also to everyone at Dreamspinner who really make me look good.

Lastly but not leastly (yes, I am a writer), much love and gratitude goes out to the Dirty Ford Guinea Pigs who keep me sane… and insane. A select group of fantastical, wonderful people whom I am ever so thankful to know.

Oh, and thank you Metallica, Anthrax, Tool, and a number of other bands too numerous to mention for giving me music for this book as I wrote.

GLOSSARY

THE WORDS contained in *Black Dog Blues* have a base in current language and serve as representative words in Singlish, a polyglot common tongue spoken in the book. While many have retained their original meaning, some have experienced a lingual drift and have developed alternative definitions.

Áinle—multi-use word, can be hero, champion, angel or if used in certain context, wild cat (Gaelic)

Ainmhí dubh—black dog (Gaelic)

Ampulla—vial, blister; slang: piece of shit, waste of a person (Spanish)

Arracht—monster (Gaelic)

Bao—an Asian-centric bread, usually a soft white yeasty bread (Chinese origin word)

Bebé—baby (Spanish)

Bonito—handsome, masculine pretty (Spanish)

Chi wo de shi—slang: eat my shit, damn it (Mandarin)

Chikusho—slang: damn it, fuck, or crap (Japanese)

Deartháir—brother (Gaelic)

Diu nei ah seng—fuck your family (Singapore slang)

Gusano—worm (sometimes found in tequila) (Spanish)

Hibiki—resonance, echo (Japanese)

Hondashi—dried bonito (fish) flakes, mainly used for soup stock (Japanese)

Iesu—Jesus (Hawaiian)

Indios—indigenous Austronesian peoples living in the Southern California/Mexico regions

Jan-ken-po—rock, paper, and scissors (Hawaiian slang of Japanese phrase)

Kimchee—spicy cabbage pickles, national dish of Korea. Also spelled kim chi or kim chee. (Korean)

Kuso—crap (Japanese)

Malasadas—deep-fried yeast doughnuts rolled in granulated sugar (Portuguese)

Meata—gone bad, turned rotten (Gaelic)

Miso—soybean paste, commonly used in soup (Japanese)

Muirnín—beloved, sweetheart, darling (Gaelic)

Musang—wild cat, civet, feral cat (Filipino-Tagalog)

Nori—seaweed, usually pressed into sheets (Japanese)

Paho'eho'e—rough, crumbly lava (Hawaiian)

Peata—pet (Gaelic)

Pele—goddess of lava, volcanoes, passion and general badassery. Not someone to be fucked with. (Hawaiian)

Saimin—local Hawaiian word for noodle soup dish based on Japanese ramen, Filipino pancit, and other Asian noodles. Possibly based on Japanese word *ramen*/*sōmen* or Chinese words *xì* and *miàn*.

Shoyu—soy sauce (Japanese)

Siao liao—crazy, out of your mind, insane (Singpore slang)

Sidhe—fairy folk, also Seelie. Considered the "good" court of the Underhill faerie/elves. Pronounced she. (Gaelic)

Sláinte—health, salute (Gaelic)

Sucio—filth, dirty things (Spanish)

Tik-tik—bulbous triangular taxi cab, single-driver car with wide back to accommodate passengers, suspended above roadways by upper rails and trolley lines, resembles a rounder version of a 1976 Ford Pinto (word of Indian origin)

Unsidhe—fairy folk, also Unseelie. Considered the "evil" court of the Underhill faerie/elves. Pronounced un-she. (Gaelic)

RHYS FORD

BLACK DOG BLUES

CHAPTER ONE

IT WASN'T a great day to be me.

The nick below the tip of my right ear itched, and when I scratched at it, the itch fled, traveling down my stomach and into my crotch. I willed it to go away, and after annoying me for a few seconds, it disappeared. I was cold, stinking of blood from the three elfin shadow dogs I'd already killed, and grumpy because there was still a live one out there I had to hunt down.

I smelled the last dog before I saw it. Nothing can mask the stench of an unsidhe cur. They reek like a week-old herring rolled in the juices of a bloated corpse left out in the sun. I checked the thunder gray sky for rain and sniffed for any water. Wet black dog could make a dead man vomit, and the smell would soak through the metal bed of my truck.

"Come to Kai, baby." I snuck a peek at the thing, peering around the tree I'd hidden behind. "I need some groceries."

The black dog looked like a mange-infested mastiff that'd fallen into an iguana's gene pool and was about twice the girth of the others I'd already taken down. It appeared to be male, but gender didn't matter if a dog got a lot of meat to eat, and this one looked like it ate well. Its long lizard tail doubled as a weed-whacker when it stomped through the brush, taking out huge arcs of grass with each step, and its belly dragged on the ground, a fat, happy lizard-dog bastard out for an afternoon snack.

Even though it was close to me, its forehead and short snout wove in and out of view behind boulders along the hillside's slope, keeping me from a kill shot. The coarse ebony fur on its body ran to thick, wrinkled gray flesh on its legs, long claws growing out of its reptilian paws. One of its smaller back horns was broken, probably from a mating fight, but from what I could see as it opened its maw to scent the air on its tongue, all its finger-length teeth were intact.

Good thing, because I wouldn't want to be only half-chewed when the damned thing ate me alive.

I pulled up my shotgun, cracking it open one last time to check its slugs. With the hound coming around the trees, I would have to wait for a

1

clear shot. Dempsey liked a knife or a bow. *Stalker should hunt like a man,* he grumbled in my head. I liked having a sawed-off shotgun or a pair of Glocks I could reload.

"Fucking Dempsey and his crossbows. I'd have to shoot the damned thing five times with a bow when a damned slug can do it in one or two." When it came down to it, I'd rather be alive with gunpowder on my skin than have my picture hanging up on the Post's tribute wall to the manly Stalkers who died taking something down. "Crossbows are shit."

"God, that thing stinks." My eyes watered from the smell. Resisting the urge to check my ammo again, I waited as the wind shifted and sent a brief thanks to the slaughtered god when my nose cleared of black dog.

The dog was almost in full view, and the change in wind direction helped me more than the hound as the breeze stole my scent away. Its broad chest vibrated as it laid its head back and howled, the piercing keen of its eerie song echoing across the area as it called for the others in its pack. If I had any luck, it would soon be joining their dead bodies in the back of my truck.

The thing was going to be a bitch to drag down to the road. Bounty laws said I couldn't leave the body behind, mostly to protect wildlife from eating a black dog's acidic meat, so I'd have to drag out every pound of its dead body to the truck after I killed it. Carry out what you kill, Dempsey beat into me.

"Or find some stupid elfin kid to do it for you." I snorted.

The hound didn't have to worry about dragging me off the mountain. If it got me, it would eat me on the spot, probably spitting out the zipper of my jeans and my earring when it was done. With luck, I'd get the chance to pee myself first, because my bladder began complaining loudly, and the itch returned to my bits.

It turned, and a flicker of a red eye gleamed in the black of its face. Holding its head lower than its massive shoulders, it skulked across the ground, hitting on my scent. I couldn't hide from its nose. Damned things could track prey over anything.

The dog snagged my trail, growling as it moved its head back and forth to scent. I held my breath, letting the scent-trail draw it closer. It crept quickly over the forest floor, making a slithering sound through the leaves. If it wouldn't have given the dog the drop on me, I would have laughed. The thing was nearly as large as a tik-tik cab. The only way it could hide was if a lorry dropped down in front of it.

With its sloping body tucked down, the black dog stilled; its wide nostrils sniffed at the air. A curl of its tongue lapped around the brush of teeth, long strands of milky saliva roping down to cover a clutch of weeds. The leaves shriveled and burned when the hound's spit struck, tiny wisps of smoke rising around the black dog's head as the acid ate through the greens. The wind shifted again and caught my scent, carrying it to the dog. It turned, found me staring at it, and leaped straight for me.

Singlish is really an ugly language. It has its toes in many lingual puddles, from old Britain to Cantonese with hot dashes of wasabi Japanese, but there were times when only the ugly gutter back street Nippon would do.

This was definitely one of those times.

"*Kuso!*" I brought the shotgun down as the black dog barreled toward my hiding spot. The wind shift carried something of me on it, and the creature found me as easily as if I'd jumped out into the open and waved my arms around.

The hound smelled the death of its pack on me, and it was pissed.

My first blast hit it between the eyes, jerking its head around. I took the recoil, easier for me than a human, but the gun bead shook, and I had to resight. For a long scary moment, I thought the shot went wide. The black dog kept coming, its earflaps laid back and its mouth opened wide enough to pop my head off with a single bite, but a trail of black gore spit up behind its head. It was hit, but not enough to bring it down.

Bringing the shotgun back around, I let loose the second round, aiming for one of its eyes. Its head jerked back again, and its cheek shattered, the eye popping into a wet mess, but the damned thing kept coming. I dropped the gun and grabbed for the Glock lying in the grass as the black dog's paws dug into the ground in front of me.

It went over me just as my hand closed on the grip. Twisting to get another shot off, I ate dirt when the black dog's weight shoved me into the ground. It hit hard, and I choked on my wind, coughing to pull enough air into my chest to inflate my lungs. Flipping over, I couldn't breathe. At nearly five hundred pounds and as fragrant as whale puke, the hound covered my legs and torso, pinning me against a bed of pine needles.

My brain told me the thing was dead, but my mind wasn't what needed convincing. The dog's mouth snapped and tore at the air near my head and shoulders as its body twitched frantically. Lines of foam polluted its pink-rimmed lips, acidic ropes of spit that burned my skin, and I placed the barrel against the creature's flat skull and pulled the trigger.

Bone chips stung my cheek, and I tasted powder before I could get my mouth closed. The blast blossomed out of the dog's head, and its skull spat out furred chunks and scaly skin. I fought to breathe as its spasms slowed, its legs stiffening out behind its body. Slowly, the glow in its eyes dimmed, turning the vivid red lights to a dull gray. It twitched once more, then went still, as dead as the rocks digging into my back.

"About time you died, damned thing." Exhaling with relief, I tried squirming out, but the dog's weight settled hard on my shins, trapping me against the forest floor.

Leaning back into a bed of dried pine needles, I stared up at the sky and sighed. "Ah, fuck me. Oh no, we're not doing this shit." Growling at the shattered head, I kicked the thing in its belly. "I am not going to lie here like some fricking bed of cabbage under sashimi. You are getting the hell off me."

It was a strain to bend forward, but I reached behind my legs to scoop out handfuls of needles from behind my knees, hoping I could give myself enough wiggle room to slide out. The ground sloped up sharply behind my shoulders, and I kept hitting my head against forest debris when I tried to get leverage. A few flailing tries and I cursed the damned thing again. The dog had me pinned, and the not-so-great day went straight to shitty when one of its enormous paws dug straight into my already strained bladder.

"Hey, mister, why'd you shoot that dog?"

It sounded like a kid, and from the silhouette I could make out when I twisted my head to the side, it looked kid-shaped. It moved into the light, and the shadowy thing turned into a dirty-faced child wearing a pair of white briefs and a thin T-shirt. Like most children under knee level, I couldn't tell if it was a girl or a boy, especially since it was wearing what looked like generations-old hand-me-downs.

"Hi. You're not out here alone, are you?" I smiled, keeping my elfin canines hidden. Sharp incisors do not a warm, welcoming smile make. I hoped the kid hadn't wandered off from some campsite. The last thing I needed was to have a lost bawler to deal with as I dragged the dog back to my truck—if I figured out a way to get out from under it. "There's a mommy or daddy around, right? Please tell me you come with someone bigger attached to you."

"Yeah, we live right there." S/he pointed behind us, up the ridge. "All of us. Mama, Daddy, and everyone."

"Is someone home right now? Maybe someone really big who can help get the big dog off me?" Someone once told me to talk to kids like I was excited to see them, told me it was easier to convince them to do things if children heard the things in a happy voice. Every kid I'd ever met had always made me a liar, but I was using as happy a voice as I had. I'd buy the kid anything it wanted, but it looked too young to bribe.

"Daddy's big!" The runty human studied me. "Bigger than you. Stronger!"

"Good," I replied. I'd be glad to lose in a size-pissing contest if it would help me get the feeling back in my feet. "Can you go get Daddy?"

"Jaime! Where did you get off to?"

Craning my neck to stare up the slope, I sent a belated thanks to Iesu and Buddha when the short cliff above me suddenly sprouted another person, taller and definitely a woman.

I kept the happy voice up, but by now it was less happy and more badly-needing-to-pee. "Who's that? Someone you know?"

"That's Mama!" The child beamed, waving its arms above its head to get the woman's attention. "Mama! It's one of those pointy-eared people! Can I keep him? He can sleep next to my turtle!"

"YOU KNOW what I miss, boy? The blood," Dempsey said around the cigar stump in his mouth. "I miss the blood the most."

Up to my elbows in said blood, I spared the human who raised me a look and offered him my knife. Isolated, Dempsey's place was a good spot to dispose of black dogs' bodies, and laying down a slab table with runnels to catch the gore into a cistern made the job even easier. "If you want to, I can leave this to you. That leg of yours is bad, but your hands still work."

"You're not too big for me to wipe my ass with." Spitting a chunk of loose tobacco off his tongue, he hitched himself up onto the bed of the truck. "And the moment you say that's because I have a big ass is the second I break that pretty face of yours with a backhand."

He'd always been a big man, with coarse features and a grizzle of beard no matter how often he shaved. A run up the coast had brought him to his knees, a swipe of a giant scorpion's tail blowing out his leg. Despite the fierce limp hobbling his walk, Dempsey hadn't changed much, even if his days of being a Stalker were done.

I'd give Dempsey this—he might have retired from the Stalker business, but he was as mean as the day he'd taken me as winnings in a card game. I didn't have any doubt that he could hand me my ass, so I kept silent, having learned from experience how quick the large man could move, even with his gimped leg. I might be stronger and quicker than most humans, but Dempsey was meaner than anything I'd ever met. Keeping my mouth shut was usually the wisest thing to do.

When he was retired out, Dempsey looked for someplace to live and found a few acres in Lakeside that were cheap. A couple of battered storage containers had been easily converted into a large home, and after a few burns from the cutting torch, I'd gotten the hang of making windows while Dempsey welded the metal rectangles into place. A few coats of paint and a deck made the place almost homey, although the gun racks in the kitchen put a serious dent into the suburban image the place struggled to put up. We'd left most of the sage and brush around the perimeter; the brambles were a natural barrier for anything large to plow through.

"Spent a lot of money and time feeding and teaching you, boy," he'd growled at me across the kitchen table, biting back a snarl as he took a shot of Jim. Too banged up to do the job, he'd had to turn over his license, and his mood roamed from mad to mad drunk. "Time to pay up for that."

Being a retired Stalker didn't come with a pension plan, and Dempsey never had been smart with his money. Most of it was spent on whiskey, poker, and women, so when the time came for him to step back from jobs, he looked to me to support him. I gave him a third of my earnings in exchange for a place to burn black dogs' bodies. Since I lived in the city, it was a cheaper way to dispose of the useless meat. The incinerator at San Diego Central Works was expensive and too often down for maintenance.

I could think of a thousand things I'd rather be doing than dragging around skinned carcasses of black dogs while looking for a place to burn them. Sitting on a fire-ant hill covered in honey came to mind.

"Took down four, then?" He stepped closer, inspecting the large alpha male I'd killed last. "Good job, that. Skulls are ruined, though. Don't know why you can't make a kill without shattering the skull. Used to be a Stalker was known by the skulls he'd collected."

"Because I'd rather be alive than have a trophy? If it makes you feel better, I waited until I could spit on it before I shot."

Bringing the dog down from the mountain hadn't made it any smaller. If anything, the thing seemed bigger, nearly impossible to get out of the bed of the truck and onto the cutting slab. The mound of black dog lying out on the concrete was the last one I had to do. The others were already skinned for the bounty, and the carcasses piled up to be burned. I'd already put charcoal into the pit. After a brief discussion with Dempsey, we both agreed the dogs weren't worth wasting any precious gasoline. They'd have to burn with good old Kingston like the others before them.

"We'll get a good bounty on these." He nodded at the furs stretched on the rack, the raw skin sprinkled with salt to soak up the excess gore. The Post didn't need them tanned, but I disliked carrying decaying skins through the city, and ocean salt worked quickly on dog flesh. I appreciated him doing the salt. My skin was still tender from the acidic blood. Getting salt on the burns would be hellish. "Should get what? Five hundred for the smaller ones? Maybe more?"

"Probably more," I agreed, gripping the male's paw and slicing up around its shoulder. "The Post's offering a hundred for every hand length now. It went up last week. Lots of the dogs in the area. SoCalGov's getting flak for all the packs roaming in the farmlands. Dead people don't pay taxes."

"True. Government would want to avoid that." Dempsey walked around me, avoiding the line of blood filling the cement channels. His hand came up to scratch his nose. I flinched a little, unable to stop myself from jerking back. Growing up with Dempsey sometimes meant my lessons were given with a hard fist as much as rough words, and my body seemed to instinctively remember that, although I couldn't remember the last time he hit me.

Working my fingers under the cut skin, I separated the pelt from the black dog's body, ignoring the burn of its blood on my hands. Being elfin, I'd heal from the poison-ivy-like rash within minutes of pulling my hands from its carcass, but it still stung. Gloves were more of a bother than they were worth. Latex melted and stuck to flesh, and leather ones were too expensive to replace after every dog skinning. Even Dempsey, when he could be bothered to help with a skinning, went barehanded.

7

With the fur off in one piece, I began the task of taking the carcass apart. A black dog bounty paid per handspan, measured carefully by the clerks down at the Post. Bounty was paid not only for the pelt but also for the kill. Stitching together a pelt that had been cut meant waiting for the money to be released while the Post determined if the fur came from a single animal or had been cobbled together from separate pieces for a bounty. Trying to pass off strangely cut dog pelts brought in short a leg or haunch usually meant a yanked license.

A real Stalker knew all the tricks and never played them. Having a firm reputation for being reliable and honest was nearly as good as being a keen shot. Dempsey might be an asshole, but he never shorted anyone or ran off on a job. He'd left Stalking behind with his head held high, and people still spoke about runs he'd done along the coast. Other than a warm woman at night, it was all he'd wanted. Well, he also told me he wanted to die in his bed at the age of ninety-eight from being shot by a jealous husband, but a warm woman at night would be good enough.

Dempsey took over shoveling chunks of dog meat into the pit with his bare hands. He worked quickly, keeping his contact with the acid down to a minimum. Grinning unevenly, he stopped long enough to ruffle the hair at the back of my head, getting gore and guts on my neck. "You can hose yourself off outside. You stink like the dog-hugger you are, and that black mop of yours is all dusty, like you were rolling in a barn. There's some of your clothes in the back room. I'll bring 'em out for you."

I didn't argue. I'd spent the night in the truck's cab, parked under one of the tall trees, after getting to Lakeside at nearly three in the morning. The sun was barely up when Dempsey knocked on the truck window to wake me up with a cup of coffee as pitch black as the dogs I had lying in the truck bed. The tarp I'd spread over the truck's seat wasn't very comfortable to lie on, but it kept the fabric clean. I had a crick in my neck and stank from cutting open gullets filled with rotting meat. The coffee in my belly was a distant memory, and I still needed to drive back in to San Diego. A shower would go a long way in shaking me awake.

The outside shower's water was cold, leaving me with pinpricks on my skin and shivering when the wind hit my bare ass. The dog's weight left me sore, and I was covered in purple and black bruises. Moving to the side was a bit painful, and I was sure my back had suffered as much as my legs had, perhaps even more, from being rubbed against the rocky hillside. A few spots of dog blood had made it through my jeans, scorching the two hand-size Asiatic dragons tattooed on my hip and back. The blistered skin didn't look like it had lifted up any ink, but I'd have to wait a few hours to see if it healed smoothly or whether I'd have to make a trip down to the Flying Panther to fix it.

"That last damned dog was a bitch to move. Must have been an escapee from a Wild Hunt. Damned elfin can't keep track of their own hunting packs, and we always got to go out and wipe up their messes." Dempsey gave me a once-over as he handed me a worn towel, frowning at the bruising on my thighs. "What the hell did you do? Ride the damned thing to death?"

"If I'd ridden it to death, I wouldn't have been under the damned thing when it died," I said, taking the towel and trying to use its sparse pile to soak up the water on my naked belly. The air whistled between the outdoor spigot and the trees around it, catching on every icy drop on my skin. He stood staring at me for a moment too long, and I started to wonder if he'd switched the side of the street he walked on. "What?"

"Haven't really looked at you in a few years. Grown up a bit. You're not as skinny as you used to be. Muscled up nice." He moved his cigar from one side of his mouth to the other. "Finally got some meat on that stick body of yours. Hell, I could have waited a few years and pimped you out for money instead of teaching you to Stalk."

"Nice of you to have a backup plan in case the job gets too hard for me," I muttered, grabbing at the clothes he held out for me. I looped the wet towel over a branch then slid on my jeans, shaking out the water from my hair as best I could.

"Not like I didn't have offers for you before. That face of yours and those purple-blue eyes," he scoffed, leaning on the tree. "Lots of folks thought you were tasty, even with you being elfin, but whoring's too much work for too little. Stalking's easier, and you don't have to worry about someone not paying up. Well, not as often."

I couldn't help but laugh. Part of being a Stalker meant having to take private jobs when Government Issue was lean. We'd both been burned too many times to count after a run.

"'Sides, not like you wouldn't have stabbed anyone who pissed you off," Dempsey said. "You cut enough people with your teeth when I first got you. Savage little cat-bastard."

Dempsey's words didn't bother me. We'd been down this road before. He'd been suckered into taking a mostly wild elfin in a poker game, calling a bluff that resulted in the bluffer passing me over the table as payment. I hadn't understood a word of Singlish, and up until that point, I'd spent more time bleeding than eating. Over the years, I'd heard him wonder if it wouldn't have been more profitable just to sell me to whoever would give him a good price. But sponsoring me as a Stalker was one of his better ideas, especially on those mornings when his fondness for drink kept him in bed. I was more motivated by the hunger in my belly, where Dempsey needed only a fifth to survive on for a week.

Considering where I'd come from, Dempsey was a godsend, no matter which god sent him.

"Not that I don't want to bask in the warmth of your undying love, Dempsey, but I should head in and drop off the furs, then get some sleep. I'll have the Post drop your share into the fund," I said, pulling on a faded red T-shirt. "The account's the same, right? They can do a transfer."

"Yeah, same account," he replied. "Stay a bit. I'll bring out some food. Might as well feed you before you head back into the city. You can always eat. I've fed that damned stomach of yours long enough to know that. You probably need some more coffee in you too."

"Yeah, I could eat." I was hungry. I was always hungry, but I didn't expect Dempsey to invite me in. The woman he was with hated elfin with a passion. She refused to be in the house if I stepped into it, calling a priest to bless the place whenever I crossed the threshold. It was easier to eat on the porch with him and afterward toss my paper plate and wooden chopsticks into the fire with the burning dogs.

He gathered breakfast quickly, and we sat eating rice, cold Spam, and wet eggs as the flames burned through the dogs' bodies. I tossed my plate into the fire when I was done and lit a clove cigarette, filling my lungs with the kretek's husky sweetness to wash away the stink of burning dog.

Dempsey's plate joined mine after a few more mouthfuls. Standing next to me, he put his chewed-on cigar stump into his mouth, lit the end, then drew it back to life with a few pulls. Blowing out a stream of smoke to battle the dogs' reek, he pursed his lips and stared off into the distance.

"You could have just sent me off with some food, you know." I spotted the sun behind the gloom in the sky, surprised to discover it was only midmorning. Dempsey must have woken me up after only a few hours of sleep.

"Nah, that wouldn't be right," he growled. "You know it's not good to eat on the run, and a Stalker should always have his man's back. Be a shame if I'd spent all that time beating some sense into you and left that bit out."

CHAPTER TWO

I DROVE the truck into the city. By the time I hit El Cajon, the landscape had changed from rural to tall steel and concrete, but bits of the elfin world poked up in places. When I approached the city proper, the Merge between Earth and Underhill was more apparent. Cracked fingers of wide freeways jutted out of old sage canyons, and the newer roadways fought against the spread of rolling green hills dotted with haunted cairns brimming with ghosts. Some places, like the Mission, were perpetually shrouded in fog, and some areas of the understreets were filled with slithering things eager to suck out the brains or eyes of a wayward warm body. San Diego tried its best, but the Underhill was stubborn, refusing to give up anything it took over.

I ran my way through the Eight corridor's traffic, slipping into the express access lane toward the city and across the wide bridge stretching over the remains of Mission Valley, spanning the Merge-formed inlet. The ocean water pouring into the corridor mingled with the clear fresh water coming down from the snowy mountains, creating a brackish tempest in the city's guts. Another chasm, thinner than the Eight corridor, cut down past the old park, and the Balboa River raged past the elfin forest, crowding into the area. Set aside as sidhe territory after the Troubles, it lay empty, its enormous old trees shoving at the remains of old San Diego museums. The area squatted like an undead raccoon in the middle of a pristine lawn, waiting for something to reanimate it so it could dig through the garbage.

It gave me the creeps every time I went past it.

Along the corridor, San Diego sprawled over canyons and mesas, lined with walls of converted storage containers like the ones we used to build Dempsey's place. Following the Merge, people flooded into the city, coming from far-off neighborhoods and across the border to a place they felt safe. We'd come to San Diego after Dempsey's accident and I bought my own place near the Bayshore.

My link beeped at me from around the truck's shifter, reminding me I had messages. I'd taken the thick leather band off when I'd gone up the mountain because I didn't want a beep to draw a dog's attention and didn't put it back on afterward because I had to skin the dogs. No matter how good the tech was, its electronics couldn't hold up to black dog blood.

The blue call light winked at me, and I snapped the band around my wrist, hitting the call buttons to listen to my messages.

"*Hello, Kai.*" The voice was familiar, but I couldn't place it until he said his name. "*This is David. I know we haven't seen….*"

"That is why you don't sleep with anyone you know, Kai," I reminded myself, deleting the message before it went any further and forwarding to the next one. "They get your phone number and call you."

"*Hey, you!*" Her voice was bright, too sunny to be for the likes of me. I could almost see Dalia's grin, and my heart did a little twist. "*I'm going to be working later, but I'll stop by for a bit. You better have been a good boy.*"

"Hope she remembered to feed Newt," I murmured, turning down the ramp and into the Presidio, sitting on its isolated green hilltop near the shore. "Or I'll have hell to pay."

The old Presidio's adobe walls were painted Navajo white, and the buildings stood alone on their peak, surrounded by grassy hills and gardens. Once an old Spanish fort, the Presidio housed the Office of Reclamation and Mercantile Services, which paid out bounties for runs or hunts. Old-timers called it the Post for short. The only thing that mattered to the Post was that I brought in bounty and completed all the jobs I took.

It was probably the closest thing I had to a mother.

I pulled into the lot next to a battered Rover I knew belonged to a Stalker named Jonas Wyatt. Like all SoCalGov buildings, weapons were forbidden inside the Post, so I locked my guns up in the truck's cab, grabbed the roll of pelts, and headed in.

The Presidio was half-full of people, their conversations low, as if their secrets could only be told to the person taking in bounties. When I walked into the Presidio, Jonas spotted me and greeted me with a nod, the sunlight from the open windows gleaming on his shiny head. Like me, he'd brought in a few skins, thin nylon ropes binding them into a tight roll.

"How you doing, Kai?" Jonas slapped me on the shoulder when I edged up against him, and I tried not to whimper, taking the hit to my bruises like a man. Curious, he peeked over my shoulder to see what I'd brought in. "Lord, boy, what the hell do you have there? That sack looks like you've got a whole dog."

I wasn't short. I stood a bit under six feet, but I had to crane my neck to look at Jonas's face. A balding man the color of ebony and with an easy smile, he'd been one of the first Stalkers Dempsey had brought around me. Despite having half-moon scars on his thigh from my sharp teeth, he still appeared to like me. I liked him in return, especially after he'd given me my first taste of hot chocolate on a run to Montana.

"There was a small pack in Julian," I replied. "Four big ones heading toward the village. If I'd known there were that many, I'd have called you."

"I'd have been busy," he said, toeing the bundle. "Got three myself, but from the looks of it, smaller than yours. Out by Spring Barrio. They were picking off old ladies going to church. Can't have that. Catholics don't like the competition."

"No, definitely not a good thing." Usually weeks went by without a black dog making an appearance. Seven in a few days seemed like a threat. "Think someone's running a Hunt?"

"Haven't heard about any Dusk Court cat-bastard losing their dogs, but who knows? Someone could have lost his hounds and slunk off with his tail between his legs," Jonas said. "Sorry, kid. You know I don't mean you."

"It's all good," I said, shrugging. "And you whipped my ass enough to know elfin don't have tails."

There was a large Dusk Court below the border. They usually stayed down there, picking off the locals instead of heading into the city, but I wouldn't put it past a Dusk Court unsidhe to bring a barely trained Hunt to the city. The unsidhe weren't the most responsible of the two elfin races. Without strict control, a black dog could break free of its master and do some major damage. I'd seen entire packs running through major metropolitan areas because a Hunt Master couldn't control his dogs.

Both intake windows had lines up to them, people shuffling back and forth as they waited their turn to lodge a complaint or file a job with the clerk. Sarah, one of the older workers at the Post, was paying out a young man who seemed to be giving her trouble. My money was on Sarah.

Sarah Marks had been at the Post since I'd first come in with Dempsey. At the time, my Singlish wasn't very solid, so I didn't understand everything she said, but I could make out most of it when she asked Dempsey if he thought he was going to turn me in for a bounty. She was a beefy woman who liked to dress in loud floral shirts and had dyed her curly poof of hair various shades of ginger over the years. Her broad face was tanned, freckles darkening the bridge of her nose. She was as much of a fixture in the Post as the bells hanging in the tower.

"Take your money and leave before you find yourself breathing out of a new set of nostrils," Jonas whispered into the man's ear, clamping one hand on the young man's shoulder. His fingers dug into the new leather, crumpling it. The man turned, raising his hand to slap Jonas away, but common sense won out. Somewhere in his lizard brain, it registered that striking a man nearly seven feet tall and three feet wide could possibly be the last thing he'd do in his life.

"She's cheating me. I've got three skins, and she's only giving me money for two." He gave me a hard look. I recognized it. It wasn't the first time someone looked disgusted when they noticed my elfin face and pointed ear tips.

"One looks like it's been through a chewer," Jonas remarked, looking over the skin. "She's got to check it through before you get any money for it. Just give her your account, and they'll process the money that way."

"They can keep it." He risked dismemberment by spitting on the counter next to Sarah's hand, and I stepped back in case she decided to respond in kind. "I don't need the money anyway."

Jonas led the boy away from the counter, giving me a smirk and a wink as he passed by. "Kai, you go on first. I want to see how much you get for those monsters you brought in."

Sarah watched Jonas herd the leather-clad newbie to the door, his hand still firmly gripping the young man's shoulder. Her hands were below the counter, probably gripping the shotgun clipped underneath. Her icy blue eyes remained pinned on the young man's back until he left the Presidio, and only then did her hands come up, a thin smile curving her tight lips.

"Hello, Mr. Gracen," she said, patting the counter. "Roll them out for me, please."

"Hey, Sarah." I put the burlap roll on the counter and undid its ties.

"Hay is for horses, Mr. Gracen." I got one of Sarah's patented cold glares, and I smiled, watching her face soften. "But then, how can I expect more from you, considering who raised you?"

"Dempsey sends his love, ma'am." He hadn't, but I often extended courtesies for Dempsey. Through me, he'd become much more pleasant over the years than he'd ever been in person. "He hopes you're doing well."

"Humph," she grunted. "Let's see what you've got."

I did the pack leader first, stretching the pelt over the counter. Measuring tics were etched on either side of the counter, marked off per handspan, but those were mostly for show. An electronic reader scanned the skins as I placed them, marking off the length and width for each. The dog's haunches and legs draped over the side a bit, and moving the pelt ruined the reading. Sighing, Sarah arranged the skin for me, flattening the wrinkles out. The reader beeped, and a green line of light ran through the counter's pane, gridding the pelt into sections.

"Did you save the skull on that one?" Jonas asked, towering behind me. "It must be a glorious thing."

"Um, no. It sort of broke apart when I shot it."

"Damn it, boy! When are you going to hunt proper?"

"Funny, Dempsey said the same thing," I replied, poking at Jonas with my elbow to edge him back. "I like shotguns. You're just pissed off because you can't handle them."

It didn't take long to scan the rest of the pelts, especially after I left the arranging to Sarah. The bounty brought a whistle to Jonas's lips, a low trill of admiration. Shunting a third of it into Dempsey's account, I signed off on the chit to surrender the pelts, agreeing to their destruction.

"Don't go yet, Kai," Sarah said, reaching for a transparent sheet with a marker dot. My name and license number ran along the top of the sheet, the illuminated symbols flashing red as they scrolled from left to right. "I've got a job tagged for you. It came in this morning."

"Let me read it while you measure up Jonas," I said, stepping back from the counter. "I don't know if I want to take a job right now."

"You don't have much of a choice," she replied, waving Jonas forward. "It came over as a special. Government requisition. I'll help Mr. Wyatt, and then we can talk about the details."

The marker dot gave under my pinch, activating the job listing. I scrolled through the specs, and Jonas was gone before I finished reading the plasma sheet. Sarah was waiting for me at the counter, and I grumbled as I approached her.

"You weren't kidding. This says I can't refuse the job or I get points off my license." I slid the sheet across the counter. Sarah slapped it down before it could go over the edge, reached for her glasses, then settled them on her nose. "Last time I looked, I'd say I wasn't owned by SoCalGov."

"You are not owned, Mr. Gracen," she pointed out. "But you are a licensed Stalker, and you jeopardize that license in refusing a special chit. It's an easy enough job. Go to the Los Angeles border with the contractor and bring back an additional passenger. Simple."

"Jobs are never that simple," I said, frowning at the sheet she placed back in my hands. "And it's for… a sidhe lord? Why isn't someone up in LA bringing the passenger down?"

"They asked for you." Sarah shrugged, creating ripples in the purple hibiscus shroud she wore. "You could make the run tomorrow if you wanted to. It shouldn't take you more than a full day."

"How far into LA do I have to go to get them?" I scrolled down the sheet, looking for the pick-up point. "Anaheim. That's deep into sidhe territory. I'm not a tour guide, Sarah. Why the hell do they need a Stalker for this run?"

"It didn't say. The run will pay out four times as much as your bounty did today. That's nothing to turn away for an easy ride up."

"A shot through Pendle isn't an easy ride up."

"It's not pretty when you whine, Mr. Gracen."

Before the Merge, the area north of Carlsbad was home to a military base and residences. Above that, a nuclear power plant and more homes. After the Merge, it was all gone, consumed by Underhill wastelands. The black lava fields and desolation made Pendle a hard ride between Orange County and San Diego. Most Stalkers chose to circle around, making the four-day trip through Brawley and passing into Palm Springs before heading into Los Angeles proper. A day run through Pendle meant risking encounters with things far worse than a black dog, providing a vehicle could make it in the cooking heat coming up from the ground.

"Why not go around?" I asked, thinking about what I had to do over the next few days. With the pack in Julian taken down, I was mostly free. Dempsey didn't have any projects he needed help with, especially after we'd just laid down the rest of the fencing along his back acre.

"The passenger is a pregnant young woman, a human." Sarah held up her hand at the snorting noise I made. "Hold up and listen to me. She's due in a few weeks and needs to be down here. The trip through Palm Springs is hard on a woman in that kind of condition and would take too long. The mountain pass isn't good for a baby that far along."

17

"And going through Pendle is?" I muttered. "What the hell am I supposed to do if the baby decides to poke its head out on the way down? Duct tape her legs shut and tell her to think about unicorns?"

"She's good for a month or so," she said. "It's easy money, Kai, and money you don't have to split with Dempsey."

That's really what it came down to for Sarah. She had an odd hatred for my mentor. He'd never said one word against her to my knowledge, but Sarah had carried her dislike for the man for as long as I'd known her. She dealt with him civilly, but any warmth she had she saved for other people. When asked, Dempsey would just shrug his shoulders, but I knew there was more to it than either one of them was letting on.

"If she pops on the way down, I want more money," I said, blowing my breath out between puffed cheeks.

"I can negotiate that," she said, sitting back with a smug expression on her face. The chair creaked and rocked back a little. "From what the intake worker said, the girl's parents aren't very happy about her pregnancy."

"How unhappy can they be to let her head here? What's down in San Diego for her?"

"Sanctuary."

"No, really...."

"Really," Sarah replied. "The sidhe lord is paying...."

I leaned my hands on the counter. "And since when has the sidhe started handing out charity to humans? Especially the sidhe down here?"

"I thought you'd know by now." There wasn't a flicker of innocence on Sarah's face. She knew damned well I had no idea what she was talking about. I kept as far away from the few elfin in San Diego as I could. "There's a sidhe lord here. He's formed a Dawn Court. I believe they'll be taking over the land SoCalGov set aside for the sidhe. He probably was the one who asked for you, since you're both elfin."

"Yeah, because we all love one another so much." I felt about as reassured as a turkey being thrown from a helicopter. "Wait, why doesn't he fly her down?"

"It's the start of mating season," Sarah reminded me. "The skies aren't going to be safe for another four months. And even then, you know the dragons like that area. It's not worth the risk to fly something through there right now."

"Shit, I forgot about mating season." Glancing at my link, I scanned the scroll for the date. Sarah was right. Pendle would be in full aggressive bloom about now.

"On the plus side, you don't have to worry about any sea monsters crawling up the coast to chase after you. They'd be eaten by the dragons."

"Great, thanks." I snapped the listing out of her hands.

"You are quite welcome, Mr. Gracen." Her smile reminded me of the black dogs I'd brought in, cunning and sharp. "The sidhe is going to want to talk to you about it, but do you think you can do the run tomorrow night? It's on a short leash."

"Thanks for letting me get some sleep," I muttered. It was hard to extract myself from the conversation without looking like a fool. "Yeah, tell him I'll talk to him after I've gotten a few hours in."

"You're a good boy, Kai Gracen." Sarah patted my cheek, her palm soft against my skin. She smelled of powder and cigarettes. She gave me crap about smoking kreteks but secretly snuck a few sticks in when she was on break. "Go home. Get some food in you and sleep. I'll see you in a couple of days to pay your chit."

CHAPTER THREE

BEFORE HEADING home, I stopped to swap out the fuel cells in the truck and then got groceries. It was nearly dark by the time I pulled into the cul-de-sac where I lived. When I'd first started looking for a place to squat, I found a small area by the Port that still had warehouses for sale. Most were slated for demolition, but a few were considered salvageable. Long and thin, they'd been used for storing printer spools and other water-sensitive materials, so the buildings were nearly airtight, with banks of frosted windows slanting down on the south ceiling. I'd bought one without seeing the inside, caring only that the docking bay had been enclosed so it would serve as a garage.

After I'd been given the keys to the front door, Dempsey had declared me insane and sworn off ever coming into the city to visit me. It was smack dab in the middle of the hub, nearly on top of the SoCalGov building complex and not far from the Post.

It suited me perfectly and gave Dempsey hives. He'd stayed a few weeks to help me empty the place of debris and erect a stairwell up to the roof of the docking bay so I could use it as a bedroom. I painted the walls white where I could and left the honey brick alone, ignoring Dempsey's grumbling when I insisted on enclosing a space for a bathroom. I heard more disgusted snorts when I hauled in a large bathtub with lion's feet I'd gotten from salvage, because apparently bathing wasn't as manly as scraping dirt off while standing under an outdoor shower spigot with no hot water.

Dempsey welded the last of the railings into place around the upper level I wanted for a bedroom area and called it the final trip he'd take into the city. With that, he left me to haul the mattress up by myself and drove off. I'd added things since then, combing through swap meets for furniture. I didn't need much—a couch and some rugs to cover the poured concrete floor, mostly to take off morning chill. I didn't bother trying to scrape off the splatters of paint and glue left from years of workers' spills. It seemed a sacrilege to wipe them away with a sandblaster.

I backed the truck up against the rolling door of the bay, making sure I could reach the hitch without hanging it up on the steel panes. I grabbed the bags of food in one hand, then headed around to the front of the building toward the door, keeping my shotguns tucked up against my body.

A woman stood in front of the entrance to my place, her hand on the keypad. I stopped for a second to admire the curve of her body, her long legs visible through the thin fabric of her skirt where the beams from the building's floodlights hit her. She'd tucked her riot of cherry red hair up, fastening the strands with an odd clip thing that only women understood.

"Dalia Yamada, does your mother know you're breaking into a man's house?"

"I didn't even hear your truck." She turned, and her almond eyes were almost wide enough to swallow her features. "Don't sneak up on me, Kai."

"The truck doesn't make that much noise anymore." I kissed the top of her head in hello. "I fixed the alternator and the coils."

"I wasn't sure if you'd be back, so I was going to feed Newt." She keyed the door open and swung it clear to let me in. I slid past her, ordering the lights on as I dumped the bags onto a low table by the door. She stood at the threshold, lingering behind me. "And then leave a note because he'd tell you he was starving."

Dalia was gorgeous, plain and simple, a petite Irish-Nipponese woman from up North. Her hair color changed as often as the wind did, and she snorted when she laughed, but she drove me nuts when I saw her. Her hips made waves in my self-control, and the smiles she gave me sometimes led me straight to a cold shower. I could tell anyone who asked that she had twenty-four dark brown freckles over the bridge of her nose and a tiny divot of a scar next to her right eye.

And she was firmly off limits. Dalia was a friend and someone I could count on to stitch me up when I came off a hunt sliced to ribbons. She also fed my cat when I was away. That was something I needed more than a good time in bed.

"Did you find a car to go around that engine yet?" She pointed at the 455 motor I had sitting on a rack in the living room area.

"No, not yet," I admitted. "Hard to find a GTO with a clean body close by. I might have to go up to Oregon. I hear there's one in a barn near Eugene." I rustled around in the bags, then found the cardboard flat I'd picked up at the market. "Here, I got these for you."

"Kai, you shouldn't have." She lifted the lid, inhaling the sweet scent of strawberries. "They had to be expensive."

"You're worth it," I said, turning away before I saw her lift one of the succulent red berries to her mouth. I was sometimes an idiot, but Dempsey didn't raise a fool. Craning my head back, I yelled, "Newt!"

The cat poked his head out over the edge of the upper loft. He screamed a hoarse welcome and scrabbled down the stairs.

I acquired Newt when I noticed him on my truck bed during a pouring rain, shivering as he chowed down on the giant newt I'd cornered at a mall. I'd spent a good five minutes with my arm down the reptile's gullet, hunting for a shoe it swallowed when it tried to consume a little girl. I'd dragged the child free before I blew its head open, but the shoe'd been a favorite.

No matter how tough a Stalker is supposed to be, there's nothing like a little girl's tearstained face as she holds up a ribbon-covered pink shoe to make someone dig into a newt's guts.

With his mouth full of newt meat, the kitten growled at me, standing on his three good legs over the tear he'd made in the creature's shoulder. He was ugly, with matted short fur the color of vomit and concrete and holding a paw up against his body…. There was a notch missing from his left ear, like the one in my right, and his other ear wasn't much better. When I plucked him from the newt's shoulder, he bit me.

An ugly lame kitten is much worse than the tearstained face of a little girl.

Newt's paw eventually healed, although it was shorter than the rest. His fur became glossier, but the color remained a hideous blend of grays, blacks, and white. Only a few pounds heavier than when I'd found him, Newt still made a racket coming down stairs. I've heard quieter bison stampedes.

"Hey, baby." I leaned over, scratching under his chin. "Come on, I got something special for you."

Dumping a can of whitefish into a bowl, I placed it on the kitchen floor and stepped back. Newt fell on it like he'd been starved for a week. I left him to his food, staying out of swiping distance as he growled a warning with a full mouth.

"Can you do me a favor and feed him over the next couple of days?" I took one of Dalia's strawberries. She growled in a good Newt imitation but let me bite into it. "I got tagged with a job I can't turn down."

"Sure." She sucked the fruit juice from her fingers and bared her teeth at me. "Any seeds? I've got a half shift down at Medical."

"No, you're good." I made a pretense of checking her nostrils. "Nothing up there either. And yeah, a Pendle run of all things. They want me to leave tomorrow night. I should be back down the next night, but no telling sometimes. I'll call you at Midpoint if things get hairy."

"You're going during mating season?"

"Everyone likes bringing that up," I said with a grimace. "I'm trying to let it slip my mind. Something about mating dragons makes me shudder."

"Probably because it stinks of a commitment," she teased, poking me in the side. I winced as her fingers found one of the remaining sore spots on my ribs. "And if there's one thing that scares the big bad Stalker, it's anything that smacks of commitment."

"Hey! I have a cat!" I pointed toward Newt, who responded to my declaration of love with a throaty rumble to keep me away from his food. "That's commitment."

"That's not a relationship," Dalia scoffed. "He's enslaved you. You're his pet."

Her words sent a chill into my bones, and I shifted my face into a schooled mask. It had been a long time since I'd been called pet, and to hear it from Dalia shocked the silly out of me.

"It was a joke, Kai." Her fingers were cold and sticky on my bare arm, jerking me back to the present. "Don't look so serious."

I smiled it off, and she agreed to feed my monster, even promised to spend a few minutes giving him a belly rub if he demanded it. He demanded them frequently, sometimes by throwing himself at my feet while I walked by.

I closed the door behind her, ignoring Newt's mewls for more fish. He stepped into the bowl, either to keep it steady so he could lick the final drops of juice from it or to keep me from having any. I bravely stepped over him, avoiding the paw aimed for my ankle.

"Brush your teeth before you come up," I shouted at Newt as I stripped my clothes off. "You're not climbing into my bed smelling like a bait shop."

Despite my admonishment about brushing his teeth, Newt reeked of fish. He grumbled when I turned over, dislodging him for a moment, but he curled back into a ball on my hip, and I fell asleep to the sound of his tongue, my mouth tasting of strawberries and the memories of my own blood.

CHAPTER FOUR

To hear Poe tell it, doom gently raps on the door. In this case, I'd have to say Poe got it so very wrong. Doom did not rap-rap gently on my chamber door. Instead, it pounded furiously on the carved door I'd gotten at a street fair in Borrego, and from the sound of it, aimed to shatter the delicate knot work I'd grown fond of.

The cool of the sheets had worn off, and the breeze coming from the open jalousies above me kissed at the sweat on my belly. Blinking, I found the world still steeped in dark, familiar sensor lights shining up from the lower level. Lying there in the dark, I waited, hoping the pounding was something I'd dreamed or even some domestic dispute across the street, although only a few of the warehouses had been converted for residential use.

"Squatters, maybe," I reasoned, listening carefully for the familiar high-pitched screaming of a couple reaching for a disagreement. "Hell, visitors even."

The hard pounding started up again, rattling my door. Bleary-eyed, I struggled to reach the end of the bed, looking for something to put on without actually getting out of bed. I couldn't find my jeans at first, and Newt was in no hurry to move off my shoulder, where he'd sprawled. Wiping cat drool off my arm, I finally located a relatively clean pair of black denims under a blanket I'd pushed off the bed at some point. The dots on the wall cut into focus when I blinked, and I growled, sounding much like my cat.

"Is there some sort of conspiracy against me?" Buttoning my jeans as I walked, I nearly tripped down the stairs, grabbing at the wall before I slammed headfirst into the lower level. The pounding started again, making my head throb from the lack of sleep. "Hold on! Shit, I'm coming."

Being shirtless wasn't an issue. Being unarmed concerned me more. Snagging one of my shotguns from the rack next to the light switch, I held the muzzle down and peered through the privacy screen at the idiot determined to knock down my front door.

I'd gotten my first gun directly from Dempsey's hands. We'd been in an old camper truck and were caught unaware by a herd of nightmares thundering across the Arizona desert. Grabbing the shotgun from behind the seat, he told me to aim out the window and shoot anything that came near. I'm fairly certain he'd have told me to drive if my legs had been long enough to reach the pedals, but at the time, beggars couldn't be choosers, and all he could hope for was that I didn't shoot the engine out as he pushed the truck's motor to the limit.

My first kill was a nightmare stallion, his fangs clenched into the truck's door and ripping the steel. Close up, an iron slug does serious damage, even more so when the muzzle is placed directly above a creature's eye socket. I was too scared to close my eyes when I pulled the trigger, and the next thing I knew the stallion's head was flopping against the side of the truck, still attached to the door by the teeth, and I'd been blown back into Dempsey's shoulder.

"Keep shooting, boy," he'd growled, shoving me back over the bench seat. "We're not out of this yet."

I'd gone back to the window, understanding the shotgun was all that was going to keep me alive and if I didn't aim right, the devil horses would overtake us and eat us as we screamed for mercy.

That's pretty much how I felt when I saw the sidhe lord standing outside my door.

He'd made some attempt to tone down his lordliness, but if there was one thing that years of crawling around my father's boots had taught me, it was how to spot a sidhe lord.

There was some resemblance between us due to race: high cheekbones, almond eyes, and smooth ageless skin, but it wasn't much. He'd dressed down, wearing human clothes rather than the elaborate dress of a Court lord, but the arrogant air remained in the tilt of his head and the set of his mouth as he looked around the cul-de-sac, as if someone would come out of the shadows to open my door for him so he wouldn't dirty his hand on the knob.

A silver band queued back his gold-streaked light brown hair, indeterminate symbols running around the clasp. The brightness of his hair meant Dawn Court, with none of the telltale Dusk Court whites or blacks striped through a metallic or rainbow hue. I couldn't make out what the clasp said but guessed it was a token of his House. A brown leather jacket fit over his shoulders and fell to his hips, the skin much finer than I could ever afford. In the white of the door light, his buttoned shirt appeared to be sage, and his pants were dark, but neither looked like something bought off the back of a cart.

He was handsome and strong featured. Eons of fine breeding carved his face into the beauty an elfin was known for. A sensual mouth and strong aquiline nose provided a foundation for his deep green eyes. In a human, they'd be unnatural, a fiery emerald with flickers of opal and black set into the folds of his pupil. For a sidhe, they were nice enough but unremarkable, save for their thick dark lashes.

At that exact moment, I'd rather have faced the nightmares than open the door for him.

Newt patted my foot, letting loose a yowl that more than likely meant his belly was empty, but I took it for sympathetic distress. Nodding, I told him solemnly, "I'll open the door and shoot while you make a run for it. Save yourself, Newt. Head over to Dalia's. She'll protect you from the monster."

I held the gun loosely, ready to swing it up in case I needed to use it. Taking a deep breath, I opened the door and let the night air in.

"Yeah?" It came out sounding gruffer than I'd intended, and there was more than a small helping of Dempsey in my voice, but the sidhe didn't even flinch. Instead, he looked me up and down as if he'd never seen another of his kind before, a glimmer of surprise in his eyes.

"Kai Gracen?" He spoke with an elfin accent, sidhe tainted with a regional inflection I didn't know. It was fluid and bright, matching his mannerisms and looks. I didn't like the way he looked down my naked chest and belly or the time he took to come back up to my face, but his smile never faltered. "Stalker Gracen?"

The last time I'd been around another sidhe, I'd been a bit under the weather. Everything I'd heard about the tingle of sidhe when they met, the blood of our race singing, and the aching need to touch was true. He made me itch and want more than Dalia did. More than any whore ever had. I wanted to crawl into his mouth, down his body, and possibly under his skin.

If I hadn't already decided I hated him on sight, it would have made me start.

"Yeah?" I repeated, bringing the shotgun up to rest on my bare shoulder. Newt stood beside me, a tiny sentinel of fur and teeth. I didn't have much hope for his capabilities in a fight, but the gesture was heartwarming, if only I didn't believe he was just waiting for one of us to fall down dead so he could feast on our eyeballs.

What came out of his mouth next would have made me throw up if I'd had anything left in my stomach. His words were pure liquid gold, hammered soft and undulating. I'd not heard elfin in nearly a lifetime and had lost most of the language. There were possibilities that I could tell someone up or down; beyond that, I didn't understand anything the lord said. But the memories... the feeling of that language pouring over me sickened me, and I wanted to slam the door in his face, anything to shut out the images haunting me.

"Singlish." I needed to stop the elfin torrent picking at the scabs in my mind. The sidhe he spoke was too close to what I had heard in my past, and since I didn't want to see anything but the present, I needed him to stop flinging memories at me. "I don't do... elfin, sidhe or unsidhe. Speak Singlish, damn it."

"If that's what you prefer, of course. Sarah Marks from ORMS told me you'd picked up the listing." The lord cocked his head, switching easily into the common tongue. "May I come in to talk to you about the job?"

"What's wrong with uploading the specs like everyone else?" It was getting chilly, and the wind nipped at my bare chest. I never considered myself a proud or vain man, but I was fond of my nipples, and they were in danger of falling off from the cold. I needed a shirt. "You have any verification that Sarah sent you?"

He moved forward as if expecting me to give way and stopped short, unsure if he'd heard me correctly. "How many sidhe lords show up on your doorstep asking about a job?"

"Happens all the time," I replied, hoping I didn't sound as ragged as I felt. "Just last week, at least two."

"She said you'd be difficult," he said, looking at me as if he were measuring me for something. If I'd had to guess, I would have said a leash, but that was probably just memories whispering in the back of my head. "She also told me that you'd gone... native, I think was the term she used."

Native was Sarah's way of saying I was human. I'd heard her comment on my lack of elfinness over the years, joking that Dempsey beat anything of the Courts out of me. I could have told her that someone had gotten to me long before the old man did, but some secrets were my own.

"Come in." I stepped back from the door. "Let me get a shirt on. I wasn't expecting company."

I offered him nothing as I grabbed an old pub shirt off a chair and pulled it over my head, keeping my back to the wall so I could watch him. The elfin had odd customs around food. Human legends contained accounts of foolish people who ate something offered to them in Underhill and then were doomed to stay forever. Someone only ate at an elfin dinner table if they were allies, and it was considered a no-strings-attached courtesy to offer food and drink to visitors.

"I see you chose Dusk Court black for your hair. Interesting choice," he said, looking around the living room area and then back at me. His glance set me on fire. There was too much to read into what he wanted, and not all of it promised to be a good time. "Trying to distance yourself from the Dawn?"

"The black sort of chose me. It had nothing to do with the sidhe," I said, leaning against the back of the couch to watch him pace off my space. "You got a name? All I got on the listing was a jumble of titles."

"It's interesting how unelfin-like you are. I've seen others stray human, but there's always something that remains, their speech or how they move. Small things that we can't quite shake off, but you've nearly eradicated everything. It's nice you still keep to natural materials. Although this…." Another measuring, intense green look came my way, and then he stopped in front of the engine block. "Is this what I think it is?"

"If you think it's a Pontiac 455 V8 engine, then you're right. And if you thought that in specific, I've seriously misjudged you."

"Running a combustion engine is illegal," he said, squatting to get a better look at the piston assembly. "I didn't realize they were silver."

"If there was a car around it, then it'd be illegal," I said. "There's nothing unlawful about possessing an engine. Think of it as art. How about we get back to the original question—your name?"

"I'm sorry. I'm being rude, and I don't mean to be," he said, executing a brief bow, which I wasn't sure if he did to mock me or out of habit. "It's… just fascinating to see someone so immersed in the human culture."

"I'm still missing a name here, your lordship."

"Ryder, Clan Sebac, Third in the House of Devon." He chased his words with a smile. "And now I am High Lord of the Southern Rise Court, San Diego. Yourself?"

"Me what?" I knew what he wanted. I had no intention of giving it to him, even if I knew all of it. Newt joined me on the back of the couch,

28

sniffing curiously at our visitor. His white whiskers trembled as he opened his mouth. I gathered he was plotting which finger he would start on first.

"Your House?" Ryder finally stepped away from the block, joining me on the scramble of rugs I used to define my living room. "Your Clan? Or have you gone so deeply human that you don't share your bloodline anymore?"

"Yep, that's me. More human than human." Anything that I had been was gone, and I was going to leave it there. "This is a job, not a tea party. We don't need place holders to know where we sit at the table."

"All right, if that's how you prefer it." He pointed at Newt, unwisely moving his hand within inches of the pointy end of my cat. "Is that a gargoyle? I've never seen one so small before."

I stared at him, wondering if he'd just insulted Newt. I'd hunted down gargoyles, and most of them were fouler than a Wild Hunt dog. "Um, no. It's a cat."

"He's… rather, let's say, interesting." The lord examined Newt, who stayed the course of his disagreeable nature and hissed when Ryder brought his hand up to pet him. There was a flash of something sharp, and the sidhe drew back his hand, sucking at the puncture wounds on his thumb. "He bit me."

"He does that," I agreed. "Usually when he's hungry. Which is always."

"Ms. Marks was right." Ryder stepped toward me, avoiding Newt. He studied me, assessing what he saw. I was about ready to give the job back, even if it meant losing my license, when he nodded and smiled. "You'll do fine."

"I'll do fine what?" The lordship was beginning to get on my nerves, and every time Ryder came within a few inches of me, I felt like Newt did when he smelled raw eel. A pulse beat in Ryder's neck, and I wanted to bite down into it, filling my mouth with his skin. I muttered to myself as I swung over the couch to sit down. "Yep, definitely hate your guts."

He joined me, choosing a broad velvet chaise to perch on. Like most of the things in my place, nothing matched, least of all the furniture. But everything was comfortable and some of it now cat-colored after one of Newt's shedding sprees. The cat owned the warehouse more than I did, if possession was still nine-tenths of the law. All I did was sleep there sometimes, and even that unsuccessfully.

I wished I'd gotten something to drink, at the very least to wash away the scent of leather and sidhe from my mouth. "Hold up a minute."

I fetched a couple of cold water bottles from the fridge, then handed one to Ryder. As much as I'd wanted to ignore courtesies, I wasn't that much of an asshole to drink something in front of someone else. He thanked me, letting his hand close over mine. The touch was wrong, leaving me slightly shaken.

"Are these... iron?" He tentatively touched the curls of rebar and bolts lying on the table between the couches. Long and bent, they twisted into each other, some of the ends fused with rust. The red dust got on his fingers, and he jerked them back, blowing on the burning sensation over his skin. "You have iron pieces like these in your home?"

"Yep," I said, moving Newt's crocheted mouse before sitting down. "Got a problem with that?"

"No, it's just... unusual. You're not bothered by it?" He sat back, crossing his legs as he opened the bottle. The movement was too graceful, discordantly sinuous compared to the humans I lived around.

"Nope, not really. They're fine where they are."

"I'm sorry. I didn't mean anything by it." He was gracious with his apology, but a murmur of disquiet lay beneath it. "Not many sidhe would have raw iron in their homes. I suppose you've built up a partial immunity to it by handling it, but still, doesn't it burn a bit?"

"Maybe." Shrugging it off, I sat down. He continued to move about, settling for a moment, then pacing off the couch. "Tell me about the job. Why is a sidhe lord paying to bring a pregnant human woman down through Pendle?"

"I'm sure you've heard I established a Court...."

"No, actually Sarah told me when I got the job slip." I sipped at the water, the chill biting my teeth. "I don't really pay attention to what the elfin are up to."

"Noted," Ryder said, inclining his head. Newt bounced from the couch to the chaise then back again, and the sidhe eyed him suspiciously before continuing. "I started Southern Rise a few months ago but have just started gathering my people. I wanted a Court without the cloying politics or the backstabbing, someplace safer and more relaxed."

"Sounds like utopia," I said. "When do you start serving the Kool-Aid and passing out the tinfoil hats?"

"You're not the first one to mock me." He laughed. "My father said nearly the exact same thing. Well, in sidhe and without the tinfoil hats, but still, similar. You'd like him. He's... outspoken."

"I'm still working on liking the first family member I've met. Don't push it."

"Shannon, the girl in question, is friends with my sister, Ciarla. When she ended up in her current state, her family was displeased." Ryder ignored my snort, taking his first sip, and leaning into the chaise's curve. "The family's old-fashioned, very pre-Merge, so the situation's become stressful for Shannon."

"Her current state's so pregnant that she's about to burst like a peapod," I said. "And the family's more stressful than coming down through Pendle? What do they do? Eat their young?"

"Shannon's only eight months along. Hardly about to pop," Ryder said. "She's not a minor, so there's no complication of an illegal borderline crossing. She's coming of her own free will because I'm offering a fresh start."

"Where's the pickup?" I left Newt on the couch for a moment to retrieve the job contact sheet. "It says Anaheim. Which Court?"

"It's Beltaine Dawn in Elfhaine. They're hosting her until we get there," he answered. "They're originally from San Francisco, near my family's Court at Golden Gate. That's where my sister met her. They've been friends for years, good friends. Ciarla only wants to help."

"I'm usually suspicious when the sidhe offer to help," I commented, then jerked my head up. "The listing said I was taking a sidhe up with me. You're the sidhe I'm taking up with me?"

"How else did you think you'd gain entrance into a sidhe city?" He smiled, stopping before he took another sip. "So yes, Stalker Gracen, you might want to at least learn to tolerate a sidhe, because we'll be spending a lot of time together over the next couple of days."

CHAPTER FIVE

THE WAREHOUSE'S flat roof gave me a view of Mission Bay, its still waters daubed with floating lights from junks and houseboats. Behind me, glass towers dwarfed me, enormous spears made of glowing opaque panes and black connectors. Across the bay, Coronado was quiet, its rich dark forests surrounding the Del, the only structure other than the bridge to survive the Merge. The stars teased me through the cloudbank, and I'd gone through two cloves before I heard Dalia call to me from across the gap.

"Requesting permission to come aboard, Captain?" She'd changed from scrubs and let her coxcomb hair free of its ties. "Well, I'm giving *you* permission to cross, because there's no way you're getting me on that deathtrap."

"Hold on," I called back. "I'll be right there."

Our warehouses sat in wedges on the circle and at an angle; the separation between our two places was at most five feet. A thick rope bridge with wooden plank steps lay curled against the wall surrounding my roof, and it tossed easily over toward Dalia's roof, landing with a clunk on the other side. She gripped its end, pulling the ladder taut to secure it on a pair of hooks we'd fastened with anchors.

"Clear." She waved me over and held up a bottle of Primo's to entice me. "I've even brought the grog."

I didn't need the bribe. The sidhe left me unsettled, and I wanted someone sane to talk to. Newt was next to useless, not only mute but solely focused on filling his belly and sleeping. I pulled myself up, balanced myself with a stretch of my arms, then walked barefoot over the bridge.

"I can't watch you do that," she said, handing me the cold beer bottle. "It scares me and makes my feet itch."

"It's only, what? A thirty foot drop?" I peered over the side. "That's nothing."

"Maybe for you." Dalia snorted, popping the seal of her beer. "Seriously, people would think you're insane for doing that."

"Not when I have so many other things that could put me in a wraparound jacket," I said, clicking my bottle against hers before I took a sip. The yeasty bubbles tickled my nose, and I suppressed the urge to burp. "How was your shift?"

"Ah, speaking of crazy," she sighed, plopping down into one of the lounge chairs near the wall. I straddled the middle of one, close enough for our legs to touch. "Today was screaming at the doctor day, preferably done at the top of your lungs and usually about something crazy like the bugs are eating your eyes. What about yours?"

I told her about the sidhe, leaving out nothing, including the way he made me feel. Dalia listened, still and calm as I watched the boats in the distance and spoke about another man.

"There's something in our blood that sings when another elfin touches us. It's not always the same. Sometimes it's good. Sometimes it's nothing. I've had others… sidhe… touch me, and it's never been crazy under my skin before." I shrugged, unwilling to see the look on her face. I could feel her worry, the waves of it crashing against me. "He made me feel… like I wanted to crawl inside him and live there… or have him crawl inside me. And I can't do anything about it."

"Can't, or won't?" She sat up, turning to face me as she listened. Her eyes were enormous, soaking up the starlight, and she reached over to touch my leg.

"Can't," I said, meeting her gaze. "Won't. I can't give anyone… I'm not right. There's a lot inside me that's broken. Last thing anyone needs in their life is me."

"Baby, I don't know what to tell you," she said, putting her bottle down, reaching for me. Her hand seared my skin, even through my jeans. I swallowed another mouthful of beer, trying to clear away the sandy coating in my throat. I needed the splash of cold in my belly to work downward to quell the knot in my stomach when her nails traced over my knee. "Well, I do, but you don't want to hear me."

"Dalia." I put my hand over hers, stopping her before she could move her fingers again. "It is what it is."

She moved closer, leaving her hand under mine. Our legs touched, her shins wrapped around mine, our feet brushed, and she leaned in, her heat moistening my mouth. "We've known each other for what? Five… six years?"

"About that."

I didn't pull away. I should have. Every spark in my brain told me that sitting there with her legs curved around mine was possibly the stupidest thing I'd done since trying to eat a fuel cell. The other part of me whispered that the kick from the cell would be nothing compared to her mouth on mine. She stared up at me, an ivory and crimson doll that walked in my dreams, leaving bloody footprints on my thoughts and hardness in my body I couldn't shake. It would be easy to put the bottle down and cup Dalia's sweet face so I could drink those stars from her eyes.

I took another mouthful of beer instead.

"I've seen you troll the whores on the lower levels. Don't give me that look. Medical's right up against the red lantern district, and we step outside once in a while on break." Dalia stood and moved away, letting the cold in when she took her body away from mine. "I know you don't care if someone's human. You'd prefer it. Everything about you is human until you do something like skip across that rope. If someone can scratch an itch someone else can't, why not take the chance?"

"It's complicated." I joined her, walking across the rooftop to stare at the city. "Too complicated."

"I know that something's tangling you up inside." She came up behind me and wrapped her arms around my stomach, fitting her hips against the curve of my ass. "You take risks, and every time you walk back through the door, you're already thinking about how you're going to try to kill yourself next. Why not take the risk now?"

"I am not trying to get myself killed." Protesting seemed useless. I could feel her smile against the middle of my back. "I'm not."

"I think the only reason you're my friend is so I'll take care of your damned grumpy cat and those bits of machinery you play around with." She pinched my ass, making me yelp. "So what if you go out and get laid? Just be sure to come back home… and don't forget to bring me presents."

Turning, I held her tightly, rocking Dalia as she sighed. She hit me once with a small fist, then again when I laughed at her. When her giggles became hiccups, I pulled us both onto a lounge so she could lie down on my stomach. She stretched out, using my shirt to wipe her cold face.

"Thanks." I wrinkled my nose. "I'll treasure that forever."

"That won't be hard. When was the last time you did your own laundry?" She nestled down against me, and I closed my eyes, storing the feel of her into my memories. "Are you going to avoid me now that I know you're a red lantern troll?"

"Nah, you can't get rid of me that easy," I teased, trying to keep my voice light. "Who'd feed my cat?"

"God, I hate you."

"See, it starts already. Familiarity does breed contempt," I joked, but inside I felt hollow, a swelling emptiness I knew she could fill. It would break her, swallowing the sweetness of her soul until nothing remained but a husk and the bitter remains of a fantasy I'd concocted. "Who said that first?"

"It's one of Aesop's fables; once again, your poor education shows," Dalia corrected. "The fox is never contemptuous of the lion. The moral of that story is acquaintance softens prejudices. So maybe, my black fox, you've just met the one lion you've needed to meet."

"I think he's less of a lion and more like Typhoeus."

"Promise me you won't fall in love with your sidhe prince and ride off into the sunset." She poked at my nose, pushing the tip up until I was certain she could see the back of my skull. "Promise."

"I promise," I repeated, crossing my finger over my heart. "Besides, he's kind of an asshole."

I ORDERED Dalia to bed so she could sleep off the beer and her shift. She tossed the ladder back over to my side, and I waited for her to go downstairs, rolling it up and leaving it against the wall. Around me, the lower streets were beginning to come alive with the city's nightlife, the doors of bars opening for business. Unlike Dalia, San Diego was waking up, ready to drown its sorrows in whatever cheap vice it could find.

Being tagged with a job I couldn't turn down was more irritating than bad, but having a sidhe lord show up on my doorstep to look me over for that job was troubling. Ryder had accused me of "throwing" human, something I wouldn't deny considering I'd learned to be a person from Dempsey and other Stalkers, but he wasn't as haughty a sidhe as he should have been.

"Definitely didn't turn his nose up at drinking out of plastic," I said to Newt, who greeted me at the stairwell. "It bugs me that I don't know squat about someone I'm going to be stuck with for a couple of days. So, time to go sniffing around, Newt."

The couch creaked under me, and I pulled my legs up, grabbing my boots. The cat battled me for one of my socks, hooking his claws into the toe. He lost, and I tossed him a crocheted mouse as a consolation prize. He batted it around a few times, then promptly dumped it into one of his water dishes, stored for future retrieval.

"Don't open the door to anyone while I'm gone." I slid on a shoulder rig, tucking a Glock into the harness. Newt ignored me, licking his back right foot as I spoke to him and stopped at the door to put on my leather jacket. "And don't wait up."

THE NIGHT was cool, damp from the fog lingering in the air. Scents led me down to the understreets, the crackle of noodles hitting a hot wok at one of the corner stalls. My stomach reminded me about the last meal it'd had, something to do with rice and the taint of black dog blood in the wind. The beer I'd drunk earlier complained of loneliness, and I stopped at the kiosk, grabbing a small sleeve of cake noodles flavored with oyster sauce. I grabbed a pair of chopsticks from the bar, squirted a line of rooster sauce, and ate quickly. Chewing a mouthful of noodles, I found a short barrier wall to sit on while I ate. Cars passed by, interiors hidden behind glass smoked nearly black with concealing film. A few slowed, cracking their windows to take a better look at the men and women standing around the red paper lanterns strung up over the sidewalks.

No one stopped and took a look at me, but I was okay with that. I had work to do.

I tossed my trash into a blue bin and headed into the lower streets. A few yards in, the world went skyless, lit up with floods of neon and LEDs. The upper streets blocked out any view of the buildings, weaving concrete cats' cradles above me. It was a crazy jigsaw world, an Escher landscape turned upside down. It made some people dizzy, their minds trying to make sense of the truncated structures and swooping spans. Most of us just avoided looking up.

Split horizontally in two by a thick weave of streets, the city hub was a triangular wedge stretching from El Cajon to the ocean and divided into a well-to-do upper level of high rises and the grimy remnants of the old city under the cement tapestry divide. Originally the streets below were meant to be used for transportation and sewer tunnels, but that plan went the way of most urban renewal plans, balled up into a paper wad and tossed into a wastebasket. The poor and disenfranchised needed a place to live, and the relatively dank but vast undercity was cheap. Entire blocks of businesses and prefab residences sprang up before the city council could even blink. Other than a few riots and the occasional mutation crawling through, San Diego seemed quite fine with the arrangement.

Streams of water, filthy from running through the drains on the upper side, poured down on the street, thin and thick falls the locals dodged without thinking. "You can always tell a tourist by how wet they are," I'd been told. "A couple of drops, that's normal, but if you're walking understreets drenched like a rat, you might as well wear your wallet around your neck and beg to be robbed."

Since much of a Stalker's work was cleaning up messes the police didn't want to tackle, I needed to be able to get into the city quickly. The city or unified state would shunt local jobs to the Post, some small, like working a prison transfer, and some larger, which usually involved a lot of guns and some prayer. Private corporations and citizens also used the Post to log in jobs, sometimes skirting the line of illegal, and for the most part, paid much better than any government work.

Contract jobs ran a wide range of specs: missing teenagers, embezzlers on the run, and other various odd tasks. I'd taken a job once to protect a cow for three days. I didn't ask why, and the cow was pleasant enough company. I read and switched off shifts with Kinsey, another Stalker, so we could sleep. At the end of the three days, we were paid, and they slaughtered the cow for a sacrificial feast. Kinsey, being a vegetarian, was horrified, then refused the money. I signed for the account transfer, thanked them for the job, and took the twenty pounds of steaks they gave me.

The cow was as good to eat as she was to babysit.

Smaller jobs, however, usually required a lot of legwork, and being registered in a city let me take area-specific jobs. Locating a missing kid meant walking the streets and asking questions, sometimes even pushing someone up against the wall to ask a specific question, but it all required knowing the underside of an area.

So living on the edge of the red lantern district was perfect for me.

Most people who disappear don't know what they're doing. They'll take enough money to last a couple of days if they're adults. If they're suburban kids, then the common sense level drops dramatically. If you're born in the lower levels and go missing, no one goes looking for you. It's assumed that something or someone bigger and badder got you. People with enough money to hire a Stalker to look for a skipped-out husband, wife, or kid tend to be hysterical and say they only want news.

They don't want news. They want the Stalker to find their runaway and bring them kicking and screaming home so they can be yelled at.

I'd rather babysit cows, but groceries need to be bought and ammo is expensive, so I've taken more than my share of finding lost family members. And I've regretted nearly every single one.

The red lantern streets are the first place to look when someone goes missing. The clueless seem to be drawn there, as if the danger and grit will mask their scent. In reality, they stick out like a white egg on nori, and it makes them very easy to find. Ask a few questions and I'm usually led right to where the missing person is hiding out. Or directly to the person who's taken them in and is now working their ass on the streets.

Persuading someone to give back a meal ticket makes the job a little harder, but that's where bribery and ammo come into play. I keep track of my expenses and submit a detailed report when I hand over the family member. I try to be nice and use bribes first, but it's cheaper and easier to keep track of ammo, something most skin traders keep in mind when a Stalker knocks on their door to politely ask for the return of someone's daughter or son.

Since a lot of the work in the lantern district meant standing around waiting for a customer, there was ample time to gossip and pass information, making the lower streets the best place I could think of to find out about a sidhe lord.

Even having just eaten, the rows of cooking food set up under store overhangs made my mouth water. Like Newt, I always had time for a meal. Passing a woman pinching meat into white pockets of *bao*, I stepped around the line of people she had waiting, inhaling the sweet bread scent of the steam rising from her tables. A few stalls down, a man skimmed *malasadas* out of bubbling oil, then tossed the fried dough into a sugar vat, where a young boy gave them a light coat before serving them up.

Clouds of squat, sunburned people dressed in loud clothes wandered the main thoroughfare, some skulking into the side streets to look for local clubs or sex bars they'd read about. As I passed by Tiger Jimmy's, a sailor dressed in SoCalGov grays stumbled out of the tattoo parlor and hit me in the shoulder. A hot stream of Cantonese chased him out of the door, followed by a couple of his buddies, their faces glowing pink with alcohol.

"Bastard," the first one slurred under his breath. "Won't ink me 'cause I had a few beers. Risk my damned life on that boat every day. They should be proud to put something on me. Fricking bastards."

I sidestepped the drunk, but he grabbed my arm, staring up into my face. It took him a moment; then realization hit his marinated brain. Shock widened his reddened eyes; then anger narrowed them to pale blue slits.

"A frigging elf? Here?" He looked back at the shop, eyeing the small Chinese man standing firm in the doorway. "You'd give him a tattoo instead of one of your own? That's what this is?"

"He does not come in here," the tattooist said with a growl. "Sober up and then I'll ink you."

I tried shaking the sailor off, but he didn't take the hint. If anything his fingers got tighter. The tattooist disappeared back into his shop, letting the door swing shut behind him.

"My uncle died fighting shit like you, and here you are, walking around this city like you own it." His breath reeked, yeasty and hot.

"I'm sorry for your loss." I kept a close eye on the other two, but they seemed more interested in trying to untangle their arms from their jackets than what their friend was up to. "But I didn't kill him."

"If you ask me, you're the crap we should be fighting," he slurred, grabbing my jacket in his fists. "Instead, we're on the water dodging the blighted monsters you bastards brought with you."

He was taller than me, but being elfin, I was stronger. Sliding my arms up between his, I pushed out and broke his hold, stepping back onto the balls of my feet. I didn't have a lot of faith in a cop siding with me if one showed up. I was still outnumbered three to one, but I hated backing down. A fistfight wouldn't be bad, but my gun weighed heavy against my back. Shooting someone merely for being drunk and stupid was still against the law, and I couldn't risk one of them grabbing it.

"Hey, Shane, leave the guy alone." The larger of his two friends came up behind the drunken sailor and grabbed him by the shoulder. He smelled of beer too but seemed to be more on his feet. "If you get into something, the MPs are going to have your ass."

"You want me to stand here and do nothing while shit like him walks around one of our cities?" Shane spat as he spoke. "All of them should be dead and buried someplace deep."

"Yeah, yeah," the second one said, hooking his hand in Shane's other elbow. "But if you get into one more fight, you're in the brig."

"I'm coming back for you, you frigging shit," he shouted at me, leaning in close until I nearly passed out from the smell. "Next time I see you, I'll gut you, you freak."

"Looking forward to it." I grinned, letting my canines show. "Drop me a letter before you hit port, baby."

"That's what I love about you, sexy." Duffy's familiar voice tickled my ear. "You make friends wherever you go."

The evening was still young, but Duffy already smelled like she'd sold a bit of skin: sex, astringent, and a hint of plumeria. She smiled broadly and hugged me, smothering me against her full chest.

Shorter than me by three inches, she made up the height with five-inch red leather stiletto boots that hugged her long legs until they reached the tops of her thighs. A matching red minidress slithered over her curves, a small silver ring on each side draped a loose silver belt over her hips, and tiny bells jingled as she walked. Her thick dark brown hair made a severe line, angling from the nape of her neck down to her chin, but the smile she gave me warmed her strong face and softened the hard cut of her blue eyes.

"Hey, Duff." I winked at her, watching the crowd swallow up the sailors. "I was looking for you."

"Hi, baby," she rasped, her husky voice raw from inhaling the understreet exhaust. "Got some sugar for me?"

I let her kiss me, then felt the bite of her sharp teeth on my tongue. A dab of blood was all she got, but it was enough, and she pulled away, smearing the dot on her lip across her finger and licking it off.

"They're going to toss you in jail if you keep doing that. Blood sexing is dangerous."

"Says the Stalker. And I couldn't help myself. You're delicious."

"Got some time for me? Just to talk," I said, handing her some bills from my pocket.

"Sure, now that you're done chasing off potential customers. I was about to see if those little boys wanted to spend some time, but you took care of that." Duffy laughed, tucking the bills down into the pocket of her boot. "Come buy me a cup of coffee and tell me why you've got your hand out so early in the evening."

We found a coffee kiosk across from Medical, and I bought her something bitter and dark with lots of sugar. Cradling my own cup, I let Duffy take her time sipping at the cinnamon-infused brew. Her eyes hooded in delight when the caffeine hit her system. A couple of benches were open, and we sat.

"How's the stalking going, Kai?" She played with a rip in my jeans, teasing the hole with a long fingernail. "I hear you're doing well."

"I'm good," I agreed. My belly was still full from the noodles, but the cup's heat wasn't something I was going to shun. The understreets were beginning to get chilly, and it went a long way in keeping my belly warm. "You?"

"Really well. Nearly got enough for a farm in the Interior," Duffy said, stretching to pop her back. The move strained her dress, and I could see the rings of her nipple piercings outlined under the fabric. "Can't you see me farming?"

"I can imagine what you'd look like in cutoff overalls." I cocked my head when she laughed at me. "I don't think you'd get a lot of farming done, though."

"Tell me why you're here tonight," she said, patting the top of her boot. "Unless you've changed your mind about talking. In which case, why are we sitting here drinking coffee?"

"No, haven't changed my mind." I saluted her with my cup. "Nice, but that's not what I'm looking for. I need information on a sidhe."

"A sidhe?" Her wince pulled up the side of her upper lip. "Other than you, I don't really go that way. Don't like them. They give me the creeps." Duffy made a face but didn't apologize. I didn't expect her to.

"I got tapped for a job for him, and I need information or I'll be going in blind. I thought I'd start with you." I risked patting her leg. My nerves were tight, and the need for touch was growing, but Duffy was a good friend, and I wanted her to know I wasn't insulted. She'd been my first, a favor Jonas called in when he thought I was getting squirrelly. I liked to think she was fond of me, even with my pointy ears. I was certainly fond of her.

"I know someone you can talk to."

"Is this someone going to be willing to talk to me?"

"Oh, yeah. Seeing you will make him very happy. Tell him I sent you." Duffy pulled one of her business cards from her other boot. "Do you have a pen?"

I snagged a pencil from the coffee kiosk, promising to return it as soon as I could. Duffy scribbled on the back of the card, a sloppy mess of Korean written in light. Handing it to me, she tucked the pencil behind her ear. "Here. The guy you want to talk to is Orin Bennett."

I put the card into the inside pocket of my jacket. "Okay. Where can I find him?"

"Yeah, this is the part that you're probably not going to like." Duffy smiled at the kiosk owner, who glared back. "He owns the Diamond Kitty, and you, baby, are probably his kind of wet dream."

CHAPTER SIX

IF THE red lantern district was good for anything, it was satiation. The area lived, ate, and breathed to provide everything someone might want, no matter how decadent or deviant, because in the deepest black of the understreets, a person could find things they'd never known they wanted. Everything came with a price, and sometimes someone ended up paying with their soul, but it could be found. And sometimes the things someone wanted to avoid with every bone in their body dragged them kicking and screaming into one of their worst nightmares.

The Diamond Kitty was definitely on my list of nightmares.

"Oh, come on," I said, regretting that I'd not taken a shot of whiskey with my coffee. "That club is the last place I want to walk into. Wall to wall skin jobs? Are you crazy?"

"Sorry, kitten." Duffy shrugged. "That's the best I can do."

"No problem." I'd need not only a shot of whiskey but a couple of kreteks before I walked through that particular door. "You sure he'll know something?"

"Think about it, Kai." She snorted. "If anyone is up the elfins' asses, it would be someone who owned the Diamond Kitty."

I left Duffy with a kiss on the cheek and made her promise to return the las-pencil. I caught a tik-tik into the depths of the district. It took a few tries. Most won't stop for a tourist. Even fewer will stop for an elfin. Even years after the war, grudges held, and my face made a lot of enemies without my making any effort. I flagged down several empty tik-tiks in a row.

Two ignored me, catching a line to somewhere else, and the other flipped off his available sign as he passed me, refusing to meet my eyes. A third flipped me off, and another driver spat at my feet as he passed, not bothering to hide his license number behind a vent of steam. I was about to give up and head for the tunnel tubes when a battered light blue pod landed with a groan, its generating wheel slowly ticking off as it spun in place below the catch cable.

The driver lifted its wings and caught the line-hook with a smooth jump. The pod barely jerked as it lifted and joined the stream of auto traffic heading in. He shifted lines with a practiced ease, the trip only marred by a slight jostle when a modified cab bumped us with one of its fins. The men exchanged a stream of hot curses in pidgin for as long as they could see each other, and then we were on our way, my driver making apologies for the hit. I paid him in cash, dropping a large tip on the till.

"You want me to wait?" He looked around the area. The surrounding buildings were nearly faceless, only a few spots of light peeking out of slit windows. There was the barest hint of a thumping music coming from somewhere, but it was too muffled to make out the source. Small groups of people watched from the darkness, their movements hidden in the shadows. It wasn't the safest of neighborhoods, not by a long shot. Even if I asked him to wait, odds were he wouldn't.

"Nah, I'm fine." He didn't wait for me to say anything else. With a turn of a switch, he hooked onto a line and was off, the pod quickly fading into the distance.

The Diamond Kitty was easy to find. A sign featuring a giant purple neon feline holding a white gem was my first clue. The second clue was the pack of altered young humans hovering near the doorway, smoking tightly packed rolls of pot.

I wasn't sure what was more disturbing: their faces altered to resemble the elfin or them wanting surgery to look elfin. Nearly all of them had higher cheekbones, and a few had had their eyes altered, moving the fold of their lid higher and elongating the shape of their eyes. Mascara thickened the lashes of some until they were nearly black, while others looked as if they'd had ink done, darkening the lash line of their eyes. Contacts took care of the widening of their pupils and irises. One girl's eyes were nearly the same shade of green as Ryder's, the flickering neon catching on the silver strands running through the emerald ring.

"Hey, man, who did your cutwork?" one of the men asked when I approached the door. "Shit, how much did that run you?"

"Nothing," I said, grabbing the handle and pulling the door open. "My mother did it."

The club's soundproofing was excellent, because as soon as I opened the door, I slammed into sound. It took me a few moments to realize it was noise passing itself off as music. A jangle of poetry wove through oddly phrased guitar notes and sporadic drumming. Under it all played a sound that reminded me of the times Newt decided he'd swallowed some of his hair and it was time to eject it forcibly from his stomach.

I'd entered a small foyer, squares of white-speckled black linoleum covering the walls and floor. Strips of opaque plastic hung from a wide opening in the opposite wall, effectively blocking my view of the club. A large man sat on a stool by the strips, skin gleaming under the dancing lights. He paid me no attention, reading from a porno strip and listening to music through plugs in his ears. A purple shirt stretched over his wide chest, its hem tight across his round belly.

"Can I take your jacket?" A coat check girl sat in a booth next to the bouncer, her face as sculpted as the people outside. Her long hair was purple, crayon bright with streaks of black under it. I wondered if she'd been cute as a human. As an elfin, she looked unfinished, especially when she moved.

"No," I replied, speaking a little louder to be heard over the music. "Jacket stays."

"No weapons are allowed inside, sir." She pointed to the red scanning line above me. "I can offer you a lockbox to leave your gun in."

"Stalker." I dug out my wallet and showed her my credentials. "The gun stays too."

She scanned my badge number, checking the readout against my face, her features calm and collected, as if she took in armed Stalkers every night. Handing me back my fold, she smiled and nodded to the bouncer, who didn't even look up as he pulled the strips back.

"Where can I find Orin?" I asked.

"I'll have him find you, sir." She activated the slender link curving down from her ear. "Have a good evening. I hope you enjoy your time at the Diamond Kitty."

The supposed music didn't get any better behind the strips. If anything, it increased its grating and scraping at my eardrums. I took a few steps in and looked around, wondering what I ever did to the endless human gods to end up in one of their hells. The dance floor set half a story below had me trembling like a newborn.

If the group outside made me flinch, the dancing throngs under the flashing lights made my stomach churn. I couldn't imagine the money spent to alter the bodies writhing to the cacophony pouring from the speakers, but

I guessed it would run to the hundreds of thousands. Some were in a merged state of elfin and human, their chins or cheeks left undone, but the ruin of their natural features had already begun. Many had their lips plumped, and most hair colors ran to the rainbow of the unsidhe, with spots of the white or gold of the Dawn Court dotting the crowd.

I had to grip the railing to prevent myself from turning around and heading back outside. With the strokes of bright light playing over the dancers, it looked like a Dusk Court orgy.

It felt like I was back in the nightmare where I'd started.

A hand touched the center of my back, and I jumped, drawing my gun from its holster. With a growl, I shoved its muzzle up against the jawbone of the man behind me, clicking the trigger halfway before I realized it. Only the too-human eyes of the man's shocked face stopped me from pulling the shot off, and I backed away, holding the gun up. Breathing in the stink of human sweat and the smell of spilled beer cleared my head, and I stared down the man.

He was nearly sidhe in appearance. From the dandelion tuft of white hair down to his chin, the man looked like he'd walked out of a Dawn Court and into the understreets to play with the monkeys. His planed-down face was shaved bone, appearing smooth under his pale skin. I couldn't spot any implants above his cheekbones, usually a telltale channel under the lash line, and I wondered if he'd grown out the bone, an expensive and lengthy process. Strangely, his eyes were a too human brown, no threads or specks of color cutting through them, a jarring discordance in his elfin fakery.

"God, you are beautiful," he said in a voice shaky with shock. The man probably thought I couldn't hear him over the music, but he was close enough for me to make out his words.

"Bennett?" I shouted, tucking my gun back into the holster. I played it off, as if pulling a gun was a normal thing to do in a club, and hoped he didn't see my hand trembling.

"Marissa said you were looking for me," he shouted over the music, straightening the long frocked jacket he wore despite the heat of the lights. I looked down and found his height was the result of thick-soled boots, and his long legs were more of an illusion from a waistcoat rather than muscle and bone. Still, the result was scarily sidhe. "Let's go someplace we can talk."

I followed him to an alcove, waiting for him to sit down in the booth before settling on the other side of the banquette. He leaned forward and lit up a privacy screen, muting the sounds of the club to a murmur.

Under normal light, he was older than I'd first thought, certainly older than the young crowd outside the club's door. His skin was tight over his cheeks, and I could see the pores along his jaw where hair had grown before he'd lasered it off permanently. The effect was eerie, his face oddly sidhe with an undercoat of human.

"Welcome to the Diamond Kitty," he said, holding his hand out to me. I took it briefly, relieved to find the stroke of his skin on mine lacked the rush of blood I got from touching Ryder. "You must be Kai Gracen."

"Not many Stalkers come in looking for you?"

"There aren't many elfin Stalkers. I think you're the only one," Orin replied. "I've heard about you. I've seen pictures of you in some of the Post relays, but they're usually a blur. You're… much more beautiful than I'd imagined. If I'd known, I would have sought you out sooner."

"I don't think you and I travel in the same circles." I chanced a look around the club, watching the manufactured hybrids chatter and dance in the lights. "I can't imagine you'd have any business for a Stalker."

"Oh, it wouldn't be for a job." He flicked a finger wave to a waitress, calling her over to the table. "Can I interest you in something to drink?"

"A Coke, in a sleeve," I told the woman hovering near my elbow. "If they don't have it, then a bottle of water. Nothing in an open glass."

"I'll have the same," the faux sidhe said, smiling at me from across the table. "You don't trust me not to drug you."

"I don't know you," I said. "It's best not to start off on the wrong foot. You might like the elfin to obsession, but not everyone does. No sense in tempting fate."

"Ah," he said, making a steeple out of his fingers. "I can assure you that all my people share my… fondness for the Courts. It's a requirement to work here."

"People lie." I shrugged. Our drinks arrived, and I popped open the tab on the Coke.

He waited until the waitress left before asking, "What can I do for you, Mr. Gracen?"

"I need information on a sidhe lord who has come into the city," I said. "His name is Ryder…."

"Ah yes, Ryder of the Clan Sebac, High Lord of the Southern Rise Court and Third in the House of Devon. We're all very excited about his establishing a Court here." Orin's smile stretched his plump lips, leaving pillows of immobile flesh in the middle of his grin. "What would you like to know?"

"Anything I can get my hands on," I replied. "I'm doing a background check."

"And you came here? I'm honored."

"Someone suggested it. Seemed faster than digging through news briefs."

"Digging through briefs is sometimes… fun. It depends on whose they are."

I let that pass and stared at him from across the table.

"I've heard about you, you know," he said, moving his hands forward until our fingers almost touched on the small table. "I'd never pictured you with fully black hair. Like I said, the relays are often blurry and the color is sometimes off, but I like it. It's very Old Dusk Court. Do you have to touch it up often?"

"People seem to find the color of my hair fascinating lately." It was creepy to think of someone watching me on news relays. Even creepier to think that there *were* news relays. "How much for information on Ryder?"

"You're very direct for a sidhe," Orin commented, canting his head as he studied my face. "And your accent is barely there. It's only a purr under your words. Very curious. Is it true that you were raised among humans?"

"Here's how this goes," I said tightly. "I pay you some cash, and you tell me what you know about his lordship."

"I don't need any cash. I'd prefer something else." He smiled again, and I almost told him to get his money back for the cutwork on his mouth. "I'd like an exchange, really. Much more suitable."

"What? An exchange of information?" I balked with a shake of my head. "I don't think I have anything you'd want to hear…."

"That's not what I was thinking." His unnerving smile grew wider. "I'll tell you everything you want or need to know in exchange for a kiss."

"A kiss?" I was beginning to wonder if the man was insane. "You hoping a kiss will turn you into a sidhe? It doesn't work that way."

"It's a kiss, and I promise it will be quite chaste." Orin smirked. "Not anything else, although I wouldn't say no to that either. I've never tasted an actual elfin before. What harm can it do?"

I weighed my options, which weren't many. If I had another source of information, I'd walk out of the door, possibly still shooting Orin for the hell of it, but I was stuck. With Ryder in my car for two days, I needed to know more about him, and since I'd already taken the job I couldn't back out, not without losing my license and a healthy commission. The guy had me over the end of a very sticky rock, and he probably knew it.

"Damn it." I rubbed my face, wishing I'd ordered a shot of whiskey instead of a soda. "You go any further than that and I'll skin your sorry ass."

"I promise, nothing more." Orin stood up then came over to my side of the booth. He moved the table out of the way, the metal legs screeching over the floor. I pressed against the seat back, wondering what he was up to. Straddling my legs, he sat down, resting his hands on my shoulders as he leaned in, pressing his face against my neck and inhaling deeply.

"What the hell are you doing?" My hand was already on my gun. I didn't know when I'd moved it, but suddenly my palm was full of steel, and it was no surprise to me that I didn't mind it one bit. "I'm not a flower."

"I'm going to take my time, Mr. Gracen. This is… for me… a once in a lifetime opportunity. I'd be foolish to rush it," he said, his breath hot on my skin. "You don't mind if I call you Kai, do you? Considering…."

"Just get it over with," I growled. "And don't call me anything. Just get it done."

"Do you know how rare it is for a human to get this close to an elfin?" I felt his lips move on my skin as he spoke, skimming along my throat.

"Not very rare," I said, trying to dislodge his face from my throat with a wiggle. "Everyone I know is human. They're this close to me all the time."

"Lucky friends," he murmured. "You smell like… cinnamon and oranges. I knew the sidhe pheromones were pleasant to us, but this is… surprising. There's almost a spiced taste to you, like a brewed tea. Does everyone smell the same, or do you all have different scents?"

"Different, I think," I muttered, trying not to think of a green tea fragrance that sprung to mind. "I don't know. How long is this going to take?"

"Just a few seconds, I promise," Orin said, running his hands down my shoulders and over my chest. "You're more muscular than I thought you'd be. I'd like to see you without this jacket on."

"I'd like to see you with a hole in your forehead, but I'm guessing I won't get that either."

"And you're hostile to touch," he said, shifting on my lap. "I'd heard you aren't picky about what sex your lover is, but you're almost repulsed by my touch. The elfin love being touched. It's a part of their culture… almost part of their psyche."

"Psychotic," I corrected. "That's a part of their makeup too."

"Your eyes are so purple, almost black, but I can see the blue flecks in them, almost sapphire caught in amethyst." The back of his hand ran along my cheek and down my jaw. "It's amazing how smooth your skin is, absolutely no coarse hair, and golden under the pale. We have such a hard time mimicking that, you know? Those tones under the sidhe skin are so difficult to duplicate."

"I can't imagine anyone wanting to," I admitted. He wore pungent cologne, and it was beginning to make my nose itch. I would have sneezed on him if I weren't afraid he'd have taken my snot and tried to replicate me in some back-alley lab. "Look, I know what I look like. I don't need the refresher course. You going to do this, or what?"

He put his lips on mine before I could protest further. As a rule, I didn't like kissing, and the touch of his lips did nothing to change my mind. Orin slithered his tongue around mine, pressing into me until the taste of his mouth gagged me. He was sour on my tongue, and the sliver of silicon used to plump his lips moved like a cyst, rolling around under his skin.

I swallowed, trying not to pull away, but the tang of his body invaded mine, delving deep past my lips and into my throat. He sank his teeth into my lower lip, sucking the flesh into his mouth, and played with it using the tip of his tongue. His hands rose up and clasped the sides of my face. Then his tongue pressed in for more.

I gagged, gulping down the reflex before I lost the noodles I'd eaten. Shoving him away, I reached for my Coke to wash away the bite, not caring when Orin tumbled to the floor. He grabbed at the table, trying to catch himself. Too light to hold his weight, it toppled over. The metal hit the floor with a thump, and the other Coke sleeve rolled away, spilling the sticky soda over Orin's boots.

"You didn't need to do that," he said, staring up at me. "Why are you so cold?"

"Dude, you have no idea what cold is. And so we're straight, you ever touch me again and I'll kill you," I choked, getting my words out around a mouthful of soda. "I will fucking gut you and string up your intestines to hang lights from. Are we clear on that?"

"Crystal," he said as he stood. He righted the table, then smoothed his hair down and sat, his hands pressed on his chest and stomach. Orin looked shaken, taking a deep breath as he composed himself. "I'm satisfied with my end of the bargain."

"Good, because that's all you're ever going to get from me." I pulled out my gun. Placing it on the table next to my drink, I gave him my best Dempsey look, and he paled. "Now talk. Fast."

"He's been in the city for about five months and contacted all the elfin living here, even the unsidhe, or so I heard." Orin signaled the waitress for another drink, a very tall whiskey sour. Telling her not to bother cleaning up the spill, he waited until she returned with a brimming glass. He took a sip and met my stare. "Ryder's from a very old house, one of the oldest from Underhill. His family's ruled the Northern Court for centuries… it's near San Francisco… and he's the third of four children from two mothers who are sisters, I think."

"Four?" I drained the rest of my Coke, then opened the new one the waitress had brought me. I could still taste him in my throat. "Isn't that a lot for… them?"

"Their family line is exempted from any battle service because of their fertility. None of them fought in the Merge wars, although they're trained for it. I know they've had strong mages in their background, but I don't know if Ryder shares that talent." Orin reached for his pocket to pull out a cigarette case. He offered me one, then lit one for himself when I shook my head. "When I heard he was coming here, I did my research on him. I thought I might be able to offer some assistance—a human-elfin liaison."

"Why'd he come down here? To get away from his family?" I pondered Ryder's decision. What I knew about the elfin could fill my hand. Separating from a Clan wasn't unheard of, but there was always a reason, usually siblings fighting for political or social influence. "Who'd he piss off?"

"From what I understand, no one," Orin replied. "His mothers' family is very well thought of politically. They're known diplomats, and I suspect he's been trained as such. There was a vacuum of power down here in San Diego, and he was the natural choice to fill it. A Court existed here pre-Merge, one of the Devon House, so Ryder waited until the hostilities between our races died down, then stepped in to reestablish it."

The music shifted, becoming more lethargic. Smoke rose from the floor, nearly viscous with the heaviness of patchouli and vanilla. On the dance floor, the ghostly bodies behind the privacy screen slowed, their forms merging closer. The monsters were rubbing up against one another, some nearly fornicating through their clothes as they danced.

"There are some sidhe who followed him down, younger sidhe. Not anyone established in their Clan. Some of them are barely out of childhood. Maybe a few hundred years. Ryder's young. About four hundred or so." Orin looked at me curiously. "How old are you?"

"Old enough to drink and use a gun," I reminded him. "How many are here now? Five? Ten?"

"Thirty. Maybe more," he replied. The number surprised me. I should have been paying closer attention to the elfin movement in the area, but it hadn't been a worry before now. "They're very loyal to him. They're renting one of the Sun towers, but he's establishing his Court in the middle of Balboa. I think the Court will build there soon. There's been talk between Ryder and the Council about leaving the old human buildings intact and growing the Court up around them. I have a source that says he's been in contact with the Tijuana Dusk Court, but nothing's been confirmed."

"The Courts don't mingle. They hate each other. The only reason they aren't continuing to kill each other off now is because humans would outbreed them in a few generations."

"It's a rumor, but one that I'm working to substantiate." He fished a maraschino cherry from his drink then bit into it carefully. "If he is mingling the Dawn and Dusk, then I want to be there to see it. It's unprecedented in elfin history as far as I know, but then I could always use more information. I'd appreciate anything you can pass on to me. I can make it worth your time."

"I don't get this whole"—I waved my hand around—"obsession with the elfin thing that you've got. The two races don't mix between themselves *or* humans. Hell, the Courts can't even breed with each other. They'd spit on you and the rest of these freaks. Why the hell do you want to be like them?"

"Because the elfin are beautiful, and there is very little beauty in being human," he said, sucking his fingers clean. "And I noticed you said the races instead of our races. Why is that, Kai? You sound like you hate the elfin world you came from instead of embracing it as the beauty it is."

"Because behind that beauty lies something more rotten than black dog meat," I said, standing up and tucking my gun away. "If you were smart, you'd stay as far away from the Courts as you could. If not, well, hope you enjoy being eaten alive. Thanks for the soda. I think I've had enough."

"And thank you for the kiss," Orin said to my back. "If you need anything else, you know where to find me. Maybe I can help you work out that hatred of yours."

"You'll be the last one I think of when I get around to it," I promised under my breath as I hit the doors. Handing the waitress a tip, I squeezed past her. "You, baby, should get another job. Working for him? You might as well be working for the damned elfin."

CHAPTER SEVEN

WHEN I came out of the Diamond Kitty, they were waiting for me. As tails went, these three men were pretty crappy. A shuffle of feet on the dirt in the alley caught my attention even before I saw shadows against the wall. With a cough and a hissing scold, I made out there were at least two. The third became visible when he stepped into the light, and the other two followed him in a moment, outlined against the brick.

Stopping at the curb, I lit a kretek and sucked in the clove smoke, cupping the lighter I'd tucked into the box as I watched the men's shadows weave back and forth. Behind me, a couple of club kids chatted about pupil color and contacts. They'd seen me walk out, giving me the eye and probably under the impression I was one of their patchwork dolls. Both laughed and headed into the club, a much safer place for them than the gloom outside.

"Wonder how they think they're going to get jobs looking like that when they grow up," I muttered to myself, then laughed at the "old man" voice coming out of my mouth.

The fake elfin didn't bug me as much as the three lurking in the alley. I wasn't certain if they were looking for me in particular, but when I stepped into the street, they followed, making enough noise to wake the dead and drunk. Elfin hearing was only a little bit better than a human's, but Dempsey was one of the better Stalkers ever to hunt on the Left Coast. He'd toss me out on my ass if I couldn't have heard them bumble up behind me.

A squeaking keen rattled my ears. The sound of metal scraping along cement was distinctive, but I didn't want to look behind me to see what was being dragged along. A small flatbed truck loaded with boxes of chayote rumbled by, backfiring exhausts kicking gray-blue fumes into my face. I blinked and coughed, using the distraction to take a quick glance behind me, and groaned. I'd hoped for teens looking for a roust, or even college kids looking to haze into their fraternity, but the men following me were huge and thick-knuckled, definitely looking to kick someone's ass.

Better mine than those kids'. I shrugged, wiping the exhaust from my eyes. My ass could take it. I'd taken worse.

The men were nearly uniformly broad, close-cropped hair and blunt features. One tucked a length of pipe behind him, its end hitting the concrete every so often in a small singing chime. Another in a striped rugby shirt hefted a blackjack in his hand, swinging the weighted blunt leather-wrapped cosh at his side. The leather looked worn down, its weave matted with sweat and oil. The last one looked to be unarmed, but that usually meant he was going to be more trouble. There would be either a knife or worse on him somewhere, and he was keeping it on the sly until he was someplace that he could do some serious damage.

The cosh could hurt—would hurt—especially if I were hit in the face. I'd had one used on me before, and the weapon was mostly illegal except for law enforcement. I was authorized to carry one, but they were brutal to the flesh and hell on the bone. The guys intent on beating me were cops. I recognized one of them, and my gut told me if I stopped and flashed my Stalker credentials, my three shadows weren't going to grin broadly and invite me out for a beer.

At least not without smashing the bottle on something and cutting my face open.

Walking along the other side of the street, I looked for someplace a bit quieter than the sidewalk. Although it was late at night, small clusters of people hugged doorways and niches, dealing or smoking cigarettes. I was far from the red lantern district, but some of the more worn peddled their skin farther out. It always came down to a choice between less competition and more clients. A few grumbled as I passed, but no more than the usual mutterings. I was much more concerned about the trio lurking behind me. If they rushed me while I was out in the open, the people grumbling behind me could become a problem. I was going to be busy enough with the three. I didn't need more joining in on the fun.

The sound of boots pounding the pavement was all the warning they gave me. Unlike their tailing skills, these men knew what they were doing when they attacked. Silent except for the huff of their breath whistling past their teeth, they picked up their pace when I reached a stretch of boarded-up shops. I broke into a run, a closed wrought iron grate rattling loudly when my shoulder struck it. The hit turned me around slightly, twisting me about, and I used the momentum to push myself into a side street, catching the flat of my hand on the building's front wall. It stung a bit but faded under the adrenaline washing through my system.

Dodging a stack of wooden pallets, I sprinted past an old toothless man stinking of garbage and death. The reek of his unwashed body lingered with me for a moment, and I snorted, washing it from my nose.

"Bastards! Watch where you're going," he swore when the men caught up with him, his confused shuffle tangling them up for a moment before they fought past him. "Hey! Hey!"

A sewage pond poured out of an overflowing grate, and I splashed through it, scanning the area to look for some place to stand my ground. I could theoretically take the three, but it would have to be on my terms. If I were trapped in an open area, it would leave me defenseless on one side. As it was, my gun was a liability. I couldn't draw it without upping the violence, and if my instincts were right, the men behind me would have their own answer to even a warning shot.

The side street vomited me out into a crossover intersection. Traffic lights blinked red and yellow, warning nonexistent cars to slow down and stop before continuing. Far off to the right of me, a man called out to someone in a window above him. In the distance beyond, car tires screeched, but for the most part, the avenue was empty of people. Battered cars, some of them lacking tires, would give me some temporary cover. Between the three of them, it wouldn't take long for them to find me crouched against a vehicle.

Across the way, another alley crooked off to the right. I could make it across the waterlogged asphalt, but not before they spotted me, and I didn't know if it opened out into the street beyond.

"Always go left, Kai," I grumbled to myself.

Catching my breath only took a moment, and I headed into the street, dodging between the parked cars. One of the men shouted, a distant threat echoing between the buildings. I would reach the end of the block eventually, and with luck, someplace open that I could dive into. A bar wouldn't be bad, but a dance club was a better choice. In the dark, my features would be hidden, and they would have to search hard to find me.

I came to the corner of the street and slammed into the side of a sleek black two-seater pulling up to the light line. The car rocked when I hit it, the door handle digging into my stomach and taking my wind. The passenger window rolled down, and Ryder craned his head over the console.

"Get in the car!" he yelled, shouting to be heard over the rush of trolley wheels as the red line chugged over us.

It was a hard choice. Running to look for a strategic place to engage was one thing. Running away from a fight stuck in my throat, especially since I'd guessed the three men following me were San Diego's finest.

"Screw that," I growled back at Ryder.

A ping and a shower of glass on my head from a shot-up street lamp made my decision for me. They'd upped the stakes considerably, and no matter how good I was in a fight, I couldn't bring fists to the table when everyone else was laying guns down.

"Get in the damned car, Kai!" Ryder leaned over and grabbed my shirt, pulling hard. "Now!"

Not bothering to open the door, I went through the window, barely getting through the slim opening as Ryder peeled away from the curb. Powered by an electric motor, the car was slow to pick up speed, and I risked a glance around the seat.

A few feet behind us, one of the men raised his hand, leveling a wicked looking black pistol at Ryder's vehicle. He pressed the trigger and the boom of his shots rocked the street. One of the bullets hit the car's back end, cutting through the plastic-overlaid metal. Another hit the rear window, shattering the glass. Small clear pebbles flew at us, and the headliner sprouted a new smoking hole near the passenger window.

"They're shooting at us," Ryder said. "Keep down."

"Yeah, I kind of noticed the shooting," I said, trying to get the Glock out. Tumbling sideways, I caught my elbow on the door, hanging my jacket up. "Damn it. I can't reach my gun."

"Are you crazy? There are too many people around." He tugged at my jacket. I pulled loose, nearly sliding into the seat well. "Can you stop being stubborn long enough to hold on? I'm going to try to lose them."

Catching momentum, the engine kicked in and cycled up, shooting the car forward. Ryder kept it straight long enough for me to right myself in the seat, then heaved to the right and onto one of the main causeways. We traveled in the silence of my heavy breathing. Then he clicked on the overhead light, glancing at me worriedly.

"Are you okay? Did they hurt you?" His purring accent was thicker, drawing golden lines under every word.

"No, I'm good." I shook some remains of the glass from my hair, then stared at him for a moment. "How the hell did you find me?"

"I followed you from the pier," he said softly, ignoring my question. "I held back, but then I lost you in the alley. I tried to hurry to get around the block because they took off after you. Do you know them?"

"Nice guys," I sighed, resting in the soft leather seat. "And no, don't know them, but I'm pretty sure they're cops. They had that smell on them."

"Are you saying those are city policemen?"

"Yeah." Flicking glass from my lap, I secured the restraining belt around my waist. "Most of them are really good guys, but a few of them...." I shrugged. "Just bullies with badges. You hope for the first kind but don't ever depend on it."

"It's that way in some cities' sidhe districts," Ryder confessed. "I'd hoped we'd avoid that down here."

"Good luck with that," I said. "There's always crazy and mean in people. Doesn't look like it matters if they're elfin or human. Convenient that you were right there to haul my ass out of there. Like it was planned or something."

"You're welcome. I'm humbled by your gratitude," he said, quirking a sly smile at me. "And no, I didn't hire those men to beat you up. I headed back to talk to you and saw you leave the wharf area. So I got curious and followed you."

"You know the humans have a saying that curiosity kills the cat," I replied. "I could have taken them. I didn't need rescuing."

"How about if you hold off taking them until we come back from Elfhaine?" Ryder suggested, slowing the car down and moving into the far right lane. "I need you healthy and whole for at least a couple of days."

He took a ramp, and I found myself staring out of the window at the upper city, the level pass set in the windshield blipping green as the street sensors acknowledged his access.

Unlike the understreets, the city above bloomed with light. Tall wide-branched trees lined the avenues, tiny sparkles strung through the leaves to add to the brightness. Several couples strolled on the sidewalks, and a young woman ran steadily toward the docks, a leashed chipper brown and white terrier keeping pace with her stride. Open air restaurants were full, a few with lines to the door as customers waited for an open table under the clear night sky.

A chilly wind cut through the car's shot-out back window, but Ryder acted as if it were nothing to worry about. I guessed the expense of replacing the glass wouldn't hit him as too dear. When I'd lost the truck's back glass during a hunting trip, it took me nearly two weeks to get enough money to have it refitted.

The air changed, tinted with brine and a bit of an edge. We were getting closer to the docks and Medical. Its broad white spires punctured the causeway, thrusting up from below. One of the few buildings to span both upper and lower San Diego, it gleamed with a flood of light. Long strings of blue lights dimpled the heli landing pads flattening the lower towers, and a single red pinprick blinked on and off to signal the highest peak of each building. When Dalia worked in the ER and I'd popped in to take her out for food, I'd never actually gone inside the structure. There wasn't much chance they would have my blood type, even if someone were daft enough to admit me.

"So, why were you following me?" Asking outright was easier than waiting to be lied to, especially where the elfin were concerned.

"I thought I might owe you an apology. It seemed like I stepped on a few of your toes, and I was hoping to make it up to you. I didn't expect you to head underground. I thought maybe you were meeting someone, or I would have followed you into the club," he murmured, turning into a brew-house drop. "I need some coffee. Do you want some coffee?"

I waited until we'd pulled through the slot, and he handed me a steaming latte. Since a cup holder appeared to be an extraneous luxury in the car, I held his coffee until we reached the open end of the wedge. Ryder parked at a scenic drop above the warehouse district then took his drink and lifted it in salute.

"*Sláinte*," he said, smiling at me when he took a sip.

I licked the whipped cream escaping from the drink slit on the lid, sucking it into my mouth with a slurp. Ryder's green eyes were dark in the muted light, nearly black in the shadows and following my every move.

"What?" I grumbled, licking a stray drop from my thumb.

"Sharing a meal is the sharing of trust," Ryder replied softly. "Have you forgotten so much?"

"Want me to choke the whipped cream back up? Because I can if you want," I suggested, lowering the cup. "Food's just food, Ryder. Nothing else."

"You really have gone that—what was the word?—native that you've pushed aside everything that makes us... sidhe?" he said. "How many years have you been living with the humans? Thirty? Forty?"

"Don't really know. Don't really care." I shrugged. My stomach wanted something hot and sweet to calm it, and my nerves would appreciate the brew. "I'm drinking the coffee. You can take that any way you want."

"Did you desert your House? During the Wars, I mean. Do you need sanctuary from a blood debt?" The question took me a while to process, and I scowled at him, making him laugh. It was a hearty sound as bright as his hair. "I take that as no, then."

"No, I don't turn my back on my promises." Growling, I went back to sipping the too-hot coffee, hunching over in the seat. "You know what? I can find my own way home from here. Thanks for the rescue and the drink."

"Kai." Ryder reached out, grabbing my arm. I tried to shake him off, but he held on tight. He seemed fond of grabbing me, either pulling me along or holding me in place. It was becoming annoying, especially since he made my skin sing when he was near. "Please, stay and hear me out. I can't seem to win with you. Everything I say seems to hit a sore spot, and that's not what I want. You're a sidhe living in my city…."

"Hey, I was here first," I pointed out, lifting off the lid to blow the heat out. "Technically, you moved into my city."

"Fair enough," he conceded. "But I don't want to be at odds with you. You're in a unique position here with the humans, and it's one that I think could be very helpful to both the Court and the city."

"Ah, a liaison." I nodded, pursing my lips. "There's a guy back there who wants that job. Orin Bennett. You might want to give him a call. He's at the Diamond Kitty."

Ryder's opinion of the faux-elfin soured his face, his mouth twisting at the thought. "I've heard of him. I don't think that would be a good idea."

"You sure? I could introduce you," I offered. "Met him tonight, and he'd be very excited about working with you. Probably do it for free if he could lick your boots or suck on your toes."

"That's just disgusting," Ryder said, leaning back in his seat.

"Ah, but oh so true." The long day was wearing on me, and I wondered at the brilliance of drinking coffee so late in the evening. I'd be too wired to sleep, but the chase through the understreets had given my nerves a severe beating. Exhaling slowly, I said, "You don't owe me an apology, Ryder. I left anything elfin far back in the past. I couldn't even tell you which tree to hug on a high holy day."

"You should know we don't hug…." Ryder stopped, chuckling sharply. "Ah, that was a joke."

"Yeah, probably too human for you, but it's all I got," I said, shrugging. Holding up the coffee in thanks, I opened the car door. "I think I'll head down. I'll send you the meeting point for the run."

"Kai." Ryder's soft voice stopped me before I slipped from the car. "I meant it when I offered you sanctuary. If there's anything you're running from, you can count on me to protect you. Once you've been declared a part of Southern Rise, no one can touch you. Not without bringing down the wrath of all the Dawn Courts my bloodline belongs to."

"Yeah, thanks, but no," I refused with a shake of my head. "Appreciate the offer, though, your lordship."

"There's nothing that can't be forgiven, Kai," he insisted, leaning over to talk to me through the open window. "I mean it, nothing."

"What makes you think I'm the one that needs to be forgiven?" I tossed back, patting the car's roof. "See you tomorrow, Ryder. Don't be late or it won't be curiosity that kills you. It'll be me."

CHAPTER EIGHT

MY TRUCK'S tires kicked up tiny dust storms along the unpaved road out of Carlsbad, the hauling trailer bouncing around behind me as I drove around the larger holes and divots on the stretch. Purple sage dotted the hillsides, breaking the unrelenting drab gray brush leftover from winter. Soon wildflowers would spring up on the hills, adding delicate touches of color until the summer heat ate them away. I slowed down when I got to a grate across the road. An ancient cowcatcher hung loosely on its post, swinging back and forth in the light wind. Enormous palms lined the dirt road, dragging long gowns of ashy fronds onto the ground. The palm leaves swayed when I drove past, waving me down the road.

I'd left the Old Five Interstate, turning onto one of the back ways toward Pendle where a few remnants of old Carlsbad remained, low-lying buildings and rambling homes clinging to the uneven countryside. A hillside rippled, turning black and tan as a herd of wild eland darted up from a nearby canyon. Przewalski's horses kept pace with them, brush-maned stallions looking for a spare harem and keeping to the larger animals for protection. Farther inland, a wild animal park once corralled various species for conservation until a meltdown of the grid brought down its containments. A few generations later, the exotic animals spread out from the coastline to the interior deserts, their numbers thinned out by dragons, wild cats, and hunters looking to feed their families.

"Got to see how much of that impala I've got left in the freezer," I mused. "Maybe Jonas and Dempsey would be up for a hunting trip."

I had about an hour or so before sundown, the perfect time to make a run through Pendle. The heat coming up from the ground would leech into the cold desert air, and only the desperate scavengers would be out. With the dragons starting mating season, the night skies would be clear of any other predators; even thunderbirds hid when the flying lizards were out in force.

"Had to choose Pendle for your damned spawning ground. Entire damned land mass to choose from and you have to come here." I cursed the flying lizards. They made life hell sometimes.

More than twenty miles away from the Pendle borderline, I could still see specks of winged serpentine shapes circling in the fading sun. Many of the dragons flew long distances to mate, crossing continents to return to where they'd hatched and eaten their clutch mates before taking to the air.

Sparky's Landing looked exactly the same as it did a few weeks ago when I'd made my last run. Most of the storage buildings' rolling steel doors were open, and a pack of ill-bred mutts roamed the front, barking when I drew up, the hitched trailer jostling when its tires hit the cracked asphalt parking lot. Some people would question the wisdom of establishing a business based out of an old storage facility, but Sparky catered to all manner of customers. Everyone from local hunters to campers parked their vehicles at the Landing.

"Hey, Kai." Sparky came out of the office, tucking her hands inside the bib of her overalls. Her thin face was lined, burnished teak from spending hours in the sun. A mama dog growled protectively at me from behind Sparky's legs, her teats swollen and nearly dragging on the ground. Two wobbly-legged puppies fought over what was apparently a particularly tasty nipple. The bitch ignored them, following Sparky as she came to greet me. "You making a run?"

"Yeah," I said, handing her bags of fresh produce from the farmers' market. As isolated as the Landing was, the place usually was busy, and Sparky didn't always have time to fetch perishables. "Here you go. There's some strawberries in there and a couple of boxes of chocolate bars. Got a freeze-cooler of meat in the back for you too."

"How much do I owe you?" she asked. "Oh boy, green beans. Why'd you have to bring green beans?"

"Because they're good for you," I reminded her. "You can't live on red meat. It blocks up your insides. Makes you mean. Trust me. Dempsey raised me. I've learned from personal experience that eating only red meat makes you mean."

"Tell the old man 'hi' for me next time you see him. And that he still owes me a twenty from that poker game." Sparky set the produce down on a bench by the office's front door and took the cooler from me. She stopped, staring at the sleek silver car coming onto her property. "That looks like someone's lost."

I'd have agreed with her if I hadn't recognized the sidhe getting out of the car. "No, that's mine."

"Are you doing Pendle safaris for pointy-eared bastards now?" By the way she was eyeing the car, I knew Sparky was wondering how much she could overcharge him. "Easy money, but I never would have thought you'd go on dragon-watching runs."

"Nah, I'm heading up into Los Angeles. I'll need a bay for the truck and the trailer." I jerked a thumb at the foreign coupe dusted in the fine desert grit. "One for that thing too. That's the second one I've seen him with, so I'm guessing he's not hurting for money. Charge him what you want."

"Let me get you pass codes for the storage slots. You can take the south side under the trees. I'll put his toy into the one beside you." She handed me an old metal key set, the jangle distracting the puppies from their teat chasing. "Tank's full. Go on and take care of yourself while I go negotiate a storage fee. I'll send him 'round back when I'm done thinning his wallet."

Mesquite and pine trees spread cool shade over the south block of the storage units. Sparky reserved them for Stalkers and friends, anyone she felt deserved to come back to a vehicle cooler than an inferno. I'd known Dempsey was falling out of her good graces when she put him into the west end during one of our last runs together, changing him over to the south only when she saw me getting out of the truck.

I'd only just turned off the truck's engine when Ryder's coupe pulled into the unit next to me. I heard the roll of the door and the lock clang shut as I began taking down the tarp on the trailer. He walked out of the waning sun and under the overhang.

Once again he'd dressed human, but the cut of his black silk shirt and pressed slacks was at odds with the surroundings. Most of the Landing's customers' wardrobes ran to wife-beaters and dungarees that were new when someone invented denim. I'd dressed up for him by wearing a T-shirt without holes. I couldn't make the same claim for my jeans, but I didn't want to set high expectations.

Ryder joined me, crossing his arms over his chest when I pulled back the covering and unveiled our transportation through Pendle. His eyebrows disappeared under the brush of hair falling over his forehead. "What in the Morrígan's name is that?"

"*That*," I snarled, "is my baby. Watch your mouth when you talk about him or you're walking through Pendle."

He could insult Newt, who could defend himself, but Oketsu was off limits. I'd found the Mustang in an underground garage during a skip through old Downtown, and he was the only thing I was sure I loved, other than Newt and Dalia.

Back then, Jonas had hit me up for some help in chasing down an alligator grown too big for the city to ignore. We'd slogged through gutters and caught sight of its tail as it slithered through a drainage vent. We threw a quick *jan-ken-po* at a *T* in the sewer, and I'd lost the pick, throwing scissors to Jonas's rock. Being a bastard, Jonas pointed me down a tight open crawlspace as he went walking off, head tall, into the cavernous central hub.

He'd lucked out in finding the gator chewing through the rotting corpse of a homeless person it'd dragged down earlier. I emerged far away from the reptilian giant versus Stalker battle to the death and nearly on top of a battered zucchini green blacktop muscle car. He got the kill, and I fell in love hard and pulled every string I could, called in every favor or marker owed to me to get the battered Mustang out of the buried parking garage.

Most of my run money for the next few years went into the car, and when he rolled out of the spray booth, glistening and painted the deep red color of a black dog's eyes, I knew every drop of blood I'd shed to bring him to life was worth it.

The car gleamed. Even in the dank, shadowed confines of a gods-forsaken desert, he just… gleamed.

"This, your lordship, is a 1969 Ford Mustang Grande Coupe," I said, hopping up onto the car trailer's bed to flip down the glides. "His name's Oketsu, and he'll be taking us through the flatlands."

I popped open the hood and sprayed a bit of cleaner into the carburetor, readjusting the air filter when I was done. Sliding into the front seat, I inhaled the scent of leather and metal before pumping the accelerator once, then turned the ignition.

The roar made my heart flutter, the engine's growl reaching into my pants and cupping me tighter than anyone I'd paid for. I leaned back into the headrest, closing my eyes to immerse myself in the feel of the motor rocking the car's body, waiting for the kickback to settle the engine block into a steady rhythm. Oketsu bumped down, drowning out Ryder's shouts when I gunned the accelerator.

I eased the Mustang down the ramps, feeling the trailer give slightly under the weight shift. Staring at Ryder through the glass, I pointed to the side and leaned out the window. "Get out of the way, you fricking idiot. Do you want to get run over?"

I left Oketsu in idle, getting out and closing the bay door behind me. Ryder chewed on his upper lip, a frustrated curl to his mouth. "What?" I asked.

"I'm assuming that is a combustion gasoline engine. And since this one has a car around it, it is vastly illegal." He ran his fingers through his hair, tufting out the sides. It settled back down against the collar of his shirt, but a piece stuck up at his temple, softening the rigid perfection of his sidhe features. "I could point out the illegal nature of such an engine, but since I'm aware you already know that, my question is, do you also have your own personal oil rig and refinery? As far as I know, gasoline production is restricted to government use only."

"Yeah, Sparky's a petrochemical engineer." I locked the door down, using the pass code Sparky had given me. "Actually, I think she's got a few degrees in a bunch of other things, but I never really caught it all. What I do know is that she's got a high-octane fuel blend cooked up that Oketsu loves. No knocking. Not a rattle. So, unless you've got any other objections in that tight ass of yours, how about if we get into the car, get some of Sparky's juice, and go fetch that pregnant woman you're so concerned about."

He got in, taking two tries to close the heavy steel door. His knees bumped the front dash panel, and after a moment of repressed frustration, I took pity on him and leaned over, hooking my fingers into the latch.

"Push back with your legs." I looked up at him. My cheek brushed his thigh, and I swallowed, hoping he didn't see the flush I felt rising in my face. "It's not electronic. He's an old-school car. You have to use your weight to move the chair."

Ryder nodded, silent, as he used his shoulders to rock the seat back. He slid out from under me, increasing the distance between us, and lowered his legs, stretching them out under the dash. "Thanks."

I sat up, adjusting the rearview mirror to give me time to get my heartbeat under control. The next couple of days would be murder, but the bounty I'd gotten from the black dogs would only pay the bills for so long, and I'd need to plump up my account. The sun dipped, hiding behind a ridge, and the shadows lengthened around us, the perfect time to head into Pendle.

"You ready?" I asked, doing one last check on the shotguns I'd put into the seat racks behind us.

"Yes, most definitely," he replied, holding onto the armrest as I whipped Oketsu around the unit. "So, one question before we start this wild adventure."

"Shoot."

"Do you really think I have a tight ass?"

"How LONG have you been a Stalker?"

We'd just passed Avery Point, stopping long enough to grab some water out of the cooler in the backseat. Night had a full grip on the hour, turning the mountains to dark crags against a deep black sky. Far from ambient light, the stars came out in force, glittering and rich. The moon ducked back and forth as we drove, hidden behind dunes and broken landscape.

Pendle really showed what the Merge did to the terrain. Desert highlands were stitched together with rolling black lava hills, and the land was spotted with rusted geared elfin towers leaning on broken foundations, time crushed and forgotten. The structures were old before the Merge and now stood decaying in Pendle's extreme weather. Exploration of the area was nearly impossible, the rough stone hills hiding crevices and chasms under bleached tufts of grass. People stupid enough to wander around ended up either dying from a fall into a lava tube or had their innards sucked out like spray cheese by a hungry dragon.

The area stank of sulfur and decay; half-eaten cows and antelope from the outer hills rotted under the hot California sun. Even in the cool night air, the stink of rotting meat carried. Above the lava fields, mating dragons fed in the sky, swooping quickly to snatch their prey and continuing without missing a beat. Tossing their food into the air, they bit off what they could, letting the rest of the animal plummet to splatter on the ground below.

It made for an interesting road trip. I'd already swerved to avoid a water buffalo front and a couple of zebra halves, one head and one hindquarter, jagged from being sheared by dragon teeth.

"What did you say?" I took my attention briefly off the road to look at the sidhe lord. We were following the broken remains of an old freeway, connected only by stretches of dirt and cinder roads. When not on the asphalt, I slowed the Mustang down, keeping the dust to a minimum. The car's engine balked at being kept to a low roar, but off the freeway, dragons slept closer to the road, and waking one in the middle of the night was on my list of things I wanted to live through.

"I asked how long you've been a Stalker," Ryder repeated. He shifted in the seat, turning slightly to hook his leg up. I'd spent the past few miles trying to tell my body to ignore him. I even rolled down the window for a bit to drown out the green tea and vanilla scent of his skin, until the overpowering odor of dead cattle overtook us.

"Legally and on my own, about ten years." The road bumped and rolled, and I held the Mustang to its track. "But I ran jobs with Dempsey long before that."

"Is Dempsey the human who trained you?" He laughed when I glanced at him with narrowed eyes. "I asked around about you. It struck me as curious that a disaffected sidhe would take this job. Then I found out a human brought you into the business."

"Was this before or after you stalked me in the city?"

"After." He turned to grab another water bottle from the cooler then cracked it open for me. "It took a while for my person to find out anything about you, and even that was thin. I still don't know what House or Clan you belong to. Or what Court you came from."

"I don't belong to anyone," I said. "Just myself."

"Yet you give a cut of your earnings to the human...."

"His name's Dempsey." Another eland in the road, mostly intestines, and I slowed, trying to find a clean way around it. "Not that hard to pronounce."

"Why did you take this job if the sidhe are so distasteful to you?"

I'd been waiting for him to ask that question, and despite being in the middle of eland shit and guts, I answered as truthfully as I could. "I don't know. Maybe because I was forced to or I'd lose my license?"

We made it past the dead animal with a minimum of skidding of Oketsu's back tires. I'd have to hose out the undercarriage when we hit Anaheim, or the stink would stay until it burned off. He sat quietly as I maneuvered, watching the sky for any winged beasts.

"At least you're honest about it," he said finally. "I can respect that."

"Not like I was given much of a choice. They'll yank my license if I don't. Thanks for that, by the way." We found another stretch of freeway, and I gunned the Mustang, the blacktop eating up the noise of the engine. Oketsu flew down the straightaway, hugging the curve when we shot past the old border station where they separated San Diego from the rest of the old state. "Besides, the pay's good. I can always use the money."

"So you're doing this for money?"

"Why else would I be doing this?" I asked, watching the road unfurl over the hills. "Because I wanted to be stuck in my car with you for hours, then go knocking on the door of an old sidhe court to rescue a knocked-up chick who can't tell her parents to go screw themselves? Yeah, sounds like a fun night. On Sunday, I've got an appointment to have my toenails pulled out by a myopic three-year-old."

"You make yourself sound like a whore."

"If you'd said that last week, I might have punched you in the face." I thought about what I'd told Orin Bennett the night before. In hindsight, I should have argued the payment for his information, but considering some of the other choices I'd made over the past few years, it was par for the course. "Whore or mercenary. That's how life is."

"Life is about more than surviving," Ryder said, his arm drifting too close to my fingers on the shifter.

"Maybe yours is," I replied, moving my hand to the steering wheel. "For the rest of us living down here, it's about getting food, sleeping, and other nasty, dirty things."

I saw the lump in the road before Ryder shouted at me to watch out. Jerking the steering wheel, we skidded, catching the dragon's tail membrane. The flap caught at one of Oketsu's tires, spinning us around. The world flashed by, framed windows of jumbled hills and road.

Pulling at the wheel, I leaned into the spin, catching the rear momentum before we went any farther. Shreds of wet film lay across the road, mangled pieces of dragon tail trailing behind the Mustang. We were facing the wrong direction, ass end away from the dragon. I cranked the wheel, accelerating the car into a tight circle.

"What the Hells are you doing?" Ryder screamed, grabbing at the doorframe. "You're going straight for the damned dragon!"

"In a few seconds, that dragon's going to be on our ass." I leaned over and clicked Ryder's seat belt together with one hand. "Hold on and shut up."

CHAPTER NINE

THE ELFIN think dragons were born from blood magic festering too long over a fire. It bubbled and hardened, creating a red-shelled egg that grew too big and too hot for the cast iron pot that held it. The pot cracked, spilling the egg into the fire, where it warmed in the flames. Hatred, spite, and envy fed the elfin blood encapsulated in the shell, and when the embryonic foulness grew too large for the egg holding it in, it hatched, and the first dragon was born.

Legends are very pretty but rarely touch on the important facts of life. Things like whether a 1969 red Mustang powered by a 351 Windsor can outrun a seventy-foot reptilian predator.

It came at us hard, unfolding its coils and whipping up into the air. Delicate wings floated around it, gossamer-thin as they caught the wind, their spines rigid as the dragon came around. They acted as sails, a steering mechanism for an arcane creature held aloft by some bastard magic no one understood. Its tail lifted out behind it, thinner and capped by shredded frills, whipping about as it changed direction.

We were still a good distance from it, but its odor carried, a combination of pungent musk and fetid meat. Its last meal still clung to its teeth and beard, probably torn off the last carcass we passed. The wingless were carrion eaters, but it was mostly out of laziness than lack of ability. They picked at the larger dragons' dropped meals, although I'd seen them go after smaller prey, and they never backed down from fighting something larger once they had their hackles up.

At the moment we were definitely considered smaller prey.

With the road clear, I hit the gas, careening us under its undulating belly. The Mustang's headlights hit the surface of its body, transforming the metallic scallops from a dull gray to their full prismatic glory. I caught sight of its elongated crocodilian head, framed with battle-torn streamers. Its mouth opened, showing rows of glistening sharp teeth easily the size of my hand.

Two multipronged antlers arched behind its flattened ears, the horns a spotted dark brown against its titanium scales. Short legs pedaled through the air, a reflexive kneading in preparation for catching its prey. The talons could easily punch through Oketsu's roof, shearing off the sheet metal and exposing us to the dragon's mouth.

"It's gaining," Ryder shouted above the engine's growl.

"No shit," I grumbled back, pushing Oketsu harder. The car bucked and tossed, hitting the uneven road before leveling out. Its suspension took the punishment, absorbing the car's torque as I dodged a boulder in the middle of the lane. I risked a peek in the rearview mirror and found it filled with dragon. If I kept my eyes on it long enough, I was fairly certain I could count the rigid frills surrounding its head.

It hit the boulder full on. The dragon's momentum pushed the large rock up into the air, spinning it forward. It arced up and landed right in front of us, crumpling a few of the concrete freeway tiles paving the area. I pulled the wheel hard to the right, hitting the gas to push the rear tires into a spin. The differential I'd installed kicked in, and we spooled, drifting as I steered. We looped around the boulder, a slow pirouette guided by the front tires.

Keeping the Mustang steady with a firm grip, I reached behind the passenger seat and grabbed one of the sawed-off shotguns with my right hand, bringing it around Ryder's head. Using the door channel to steady my aim, I canted the gun up, partially squeezing the trigger. The dragon's head came into the frame, and I pulled down as Ryder's hands lifted up, spoiling the shot.

The blast took off the top half of the dragon's right antler, spraying velvet and brittle bone over the Mustang's hood. Crimson speckled the windshield, ambient spray from the shorn antler's weak blood vessels. Cursing, I righted the car and lurched forward, hoping for another shot.

I lost sight of it as it flew straight up and out of my view. Muttering, I debated using the second shell on Ryder but held it back for the dragon. The sharp whistle of its frills fanning out in the air told me it was nearby, audible even over the V8's deep scream.

"Where is it?" I held the car steady around a gap in the road, balancing my attention between the dragon and the freeway. "And what the hell was that back there?"

"Are you insane? They're sacred, damn it!" Ryder frowned, sticking his head out of the window to look for a serpentine shape in the sky. "The sidhe… even the unsidhe… don't kill dragons!"

71

"Well, hate to break it to you, but I've killed at least two. And I'm wearing the ink to prove it," I said. He contorted his body to give me a horrified look. "Get over it. I'd rather it be a dead sacred dragon than me being eaten."

"It's coming around." Ducking back into the car, he shook his head in disbelief. "We'll talk about the dragon thing later. Can't you just outrun it?"

"I can outrun anything that's dead," I reminded him. "Alive and flying, not so much. It's got up, where I've only got forward, backward, and sideways. That's kind of a disadvantage."

"You'll not shoot it," Ryder warned me.

The arrogance in his voice didn't go unnoticed. I still had the option of using the second round on something other than the dragon, but wiser thoughts prevailed. I had no place to dump his body, and I was in the middle of a run that would go a long way toward keeping Newt in tuna.

"I'm sure as the humans' slaughtered god going to blast it to hell if I've got a clear shot," I snapped back. "And keep your head down. You can't pay me if you're dead."

The whistling grew louder, keying to a higher pitch. I struggled to keep the Mustang on the pavement, ducking my head in the futile hope of spotting the dragon before it clamped its claws on the roof of my car. I felt a jolt, then we hit something large in the road, the undercarriage rocking with the impact, and we went airborne.

As we pitched forward, the dragon struck, slamming into the trunk with both front claws extended. I punched the gas before we landed, praying the Mustang would hit the ground at full speed. A back tire caught, burning a half circle in the road before the other hit. Catching the ground in midspin, we turned again and came to an abrupt stop, slamming back into our seats as the dragon overshot us, its damaged tail slapping at the roof as it went by. The slashed tendrils curled through the window, and I caught a smear of its fluids on my cheek, the membrane slicing my face.

The boulder I'd avoided was off in the distance, the Mustang's headlights playing over its rough surface. I stared at the immobile rock for a second and leaned forward, flicking off the lights.

"What the…? Gods…!" Ryder grabbed at the dashboard then held on as I hit reverse at full throttle.

"Hold. On. Shut. Up." I spun the wheel, working the Mustang around, and brought us to another stop. The brake lights flared on, creating a line of bright red on the road. I held my foot on the accelerator as I waited for the dragon to turn in the sky.

Under the starlight, it flew toward us, undulating with purple and green scales. I revved the engine, drawing its attention to our location. Screaming, the dragon flung its talons out and plummeted, aiming for us, its mangled antlers flattened against its lithe body.

At twenty feet, its breath steamed the windshield, and I let Oketsu have the run of the road. Sending an apology to any god that might have a spare moment, I winced when I felt the ground shake behind us, and smoke from the tires filled the air.

Drawn by the light, the dragon struck the road where I'd idled, slamming into the ground at its full speed. The crack of bone hitting pavement made my jaw hurt, the backs of my teeth aching from the sound. Ryder stared behind us, silent with numb shock as the dragon flailed in its death spasms, its head angled sharply from its long body.

I didn't look back after catching the last image of its writhing form convulsing in its death crater. Flipping the headlights on, I steered away from the dying beast, keeping my eyes out for any more surprises in the road.

"Well, at least you didn't shoot it," Ryder commented, turning around. His seat belt had twisted at some point in the chase, and he unlatched it, straightening the bindings. "I'm not sure that... I don't even know what I could call that...."

"Pancaking," I offered and shrugged when he gave me an incredulous look. "That's what I'd call it. And let's get one thing straight. I'm on the job because you needed me. If I think something needs to be shot at, it gets shot at. You ever risk my skin again because of your... ideas, then I'll leave your ass right there."

"So, we live and die by your rules, is that it?" Ryder bit back. "No one else has a say? Including the person paying you?"

"Especially the person paying me," I replied. "You hired me to get you through this. It's a stupid time to be going through the area, and what's worse, we'll be coming back the same way with one and a half more people. I don't care if you want to throw yourself out the gods-damned window in some sort of self-sacrifice to the almighty lizard; don't endanger me or the girl. And make damned sure that someone can pay me before you go serving yourself up as a blue-plate special."

The interior lights of the car were dim, but the disgust on Ryder's face was so familiar, I would be rich if I had a nickel for every time I saw it. "You have fallen so very far from what you should be."

"I didn't fall." There was something else in his voice, a sadness that I couldn't answer. "I was pushed."

"Are you planning anything else like that stunt with the dragon? Maybe something I should know about?" Ryder asked.

"Like what?"

"I don't know."

The tone in his voice rang like someone unused to being disobeyed or questioned. He was going to have a rude couple of days if we survived that long together.

"Pulling the wings off of faeries? Fornicating with *ainmhí dubh* and eating the stillborn puppies? Assassinating one of the sidhe lords in the Elfhaine Dawn Courts?"

"Nope, not off the top of my head," I said. The sheen of Anaheim's lights lit up the sky, and the sidhe Clans' towers filled the far-off horizon. "I'll let you know if we come across something I think you'd object to."

"Do me a favor." He exhaled sharply. "Don't talk about this to anyone we meet at Elfhaine. I have enough trouble to deal with without having to explain away a dragon killing."

"Not a word, promise," I said softly. "Hell, I wouldn't even be going near the place unless you were paying me."

"Do I have to pay you extra to keep quiet?" An elegant eyebrow lift mocked me.

"No, that I'll do for free," I replied. "Just stop trying to get us killed."

CHAPTER TEN

OKETSU MUMBLED a low complaint when I pulled off to the side of the road. It was as if he knew what was coming and had a few words to say to me before I popped open his trunk to activate the electric cells and backup motor I'd wired into his system. Running gasoline through his 351 was necessary to get through Pendle in one piece, but on civilized roads, it would mean a hefty jail sentence and a one-way trip to the crusher for the Mustang.

As dawn hit, we'd come out of Pendle near the Elfhaine limits. The off-ramp from the freeway ended in a gravel road, the coarse stones packed down into a fragrant soil. The forest smelled and felt old, a rich loamy perfume in the air, and the ground was clear between the expansive trunks. A light mist fed dribbles of water from dripping leaves, bursts of flowers dotted small hillocks, and a small rabbit popped out to look at us, its cheeks puffed up as it chewed on a blade of long grass.

It was an idyllic woodland scene filled with birdsong and the sound of a burbling stream nearby.

The place gave me the creeps.

"So you can run both?" Ryder asked, leaning against the quarter panel as I shifted the controls. "Why bother with the combustion?"

"Because a combustion engine can outrun just about anything but a fully enraged dragon, which, to be fair to Oketsu, I'd never had to do before," I said, clicking down the last connector. "An electric can't compete. For a long haul, it might be able to give good speed, but not right off the line when you need the power thrust. Besides," I said, grinning at him, "a motor sounds cooler."

"I'll clean off what I can of the dragon from the car." He splashed water from a bottle over the hardtop then wiped it down with some cloths from my trunk. "Not like we can find a car wash out here."

I used an old toothbrush and a mouthful of water to clean my teeth, spitting the slurry out and narrowly missing a small furry animal bouncing through a patch of dark red poppies. A handful of water took the sleep out of my eyes, and I used my shirt to dry my face, wondering if there was some place I could shower once we hit Elfhaine.

The Merge left much of Orange County in elfin territory. The cities vanished, and vast forests, craggy ranges, and Elfhaine remained. I'd seen the Living City from a distance, crystal white and copper towers emerging from the side of the Esgar Mountain. Still miles away, the snow-covered jag dominated the sky, rising high above the lower, darker ranges. I couldn't see Elfhaine from where I'd parked, but its presence was unmistakable. The ground thrummed and sang beneath my feet, an eerie shiver running through my spirit.

To my knowledge, I'd never been to North America's sidhe capital, but I couldn't say for certain. Dempsey swore he'd been up in NoCal when he bluffed his way through that losing hand, but he'd been known to misplace facts following some heavy drinking. For all I knew, I had blood kin in the Living City, and my gut told me they'd be none too happy to see me.

I didn't want to go walking into an elfin city, and certainly not one that housed one of the largest sidhe populations in the merged world. One gave me the shivers. I couldn't imagine how my body would react surrounded by them.

"Have you been?"

"What?" I started, pulled from my thoughts. "To Elfhaine? No."

"It's a beautiful city. Overpowering, but beautiful," Ryder said, wiping his hands. "My House has had a retreat there for over fifteen generations. We were considering relocating to Elfhaine, but the family decided to stay up north in Beltaine." I must have looked confused, because he continued, "You don't know basic Court history? When some of the Courts didn't Merge and the Houses decided to relocate to even out our numbers? Are you suffering from an amnesia of some sort?"

"Let's just agree that my sidhe education is lacking in some areas," I grumbled, slamming the damaged trunk shut. The paint was scratched to shit, and in some places the dragon's claws had pierced right through the metal. I added an additional ten percent to the bill I was going to hand Ryder just to cover my pissiness. "And I don't need it to drive you up to the gates, let you out, and wait in the car while you go get the girl."

"Are you sure you don't want to come with me?" he asked, stopping me in midstep.

A wild cat cried out in the trees around us, sending a flock of sparrows into the air. They darted and dove through the branches above our heads, the blue dots of their wings flashing as they beat a retreat to safer branches. I took a few steps around Oketsu, the gravel crunching under my boots. My brain began having a small meltdown, arguing with itself about whether I could leave Ryder in the middle of the road.

Years ago when I'd seen Elfhaine, it had rendered me speechless. Literally. I couldn't drag my eyes from the creamy white towers shot through with copper and brass, verdigris filigree work connecting the spires, and the rush of water flowing from seemingly impossible angles. Enormous trees rose and covered floating gardens, woven metal threads suspending impractically large platforms bursting with greenery and small buildings. The larger towers turned, slowly changing the views and keeping the shadows from consuming the buildings' interiors.

At the time, as I peered through my lens-scopes, I wondered why workers had abandoned a half-built sunroom. After a few minutes, I glanced back to the construction site. The glass panels were slowly growing into the metal frames around them, spindly shoots reaching out to form a larger web, giving the growth a framework to fill in. Smaller details came into my focus, the copper leaves unfolding from thick vines edging up around casements. A stony veil filled in behind other frames, firming into a hardened coral white and leaving spaces for doors and waterways. Cables wound down from other platforms, connecting to clamps and lifting to form walkways or tension bridges from one cluster to another.

And the little black voices in my head began to scream, terrified of returning to my rusted cage.

Leaning against the car, I spoke to Ryder over the hardtop. "You're here. Why do you need me to go in? You go in, and I'll stay and watch the car. Maybe knit a sweater. If I knew how to knit."

Avoiding the sidhe in general sounded like a very good idea to me, but Ryder was having none of it.

If his House was known for diplomacy, then it had skipped Ryder completely. He spoke to me slowly, as if enunciating the obvious for a dim child. "Because you're… a sidhe. Why wouldn't you want to go into Elfhaine?"

"You don't need two people to grab takeout," I pointed out. "Why do you need two to pick up a pregnant woman? I don't need to go into Elfhaine for that."

"No, you don't," Ryder insisted, running his hands through his hair in exasperation. "I know you don't think of yourself as sidhe, but I didn't think you were a psychotic anarchist."

"I'm not an anarchist."

"I see you're not denying you're psychotic."

"I don't even know what qualifies someone as psychotic, but if it's wanting to stuff the person who hired me into a trunk, then yes, I'm definitely psychotic." The prickles on my skin rubbed harder as I stepped back from the car. Esgar loomed, swallowing the sky with its whiteness.

The sidhe were as foreign to me as they were to Dempsey, and my questions had been answered with shrugs and grunts. What I remembered from before had no wonder in it, just darkness, pain, and blood. I couldn't remember much of the language, and he said I spoke none, communicating mostly with hisses and sharp teeth.

"One day from being sold to the red lantern district for meat," he'd told me later. "None of them would care if you knew what was going on. A few ropes or a shot of numb-powder and you'd make a profit. Meat is meat, boy. Don't you forget it."

Dempsey was a practical man, and I'd become much more trouble than I was worth. There was not a whit of teasing or joking in his tone. He was dead serious.

"Cloth and water aren't much help with this. All I'm doing is spreading it around," Ryder said, jerking me from my memories. He stared down at the Mustang's roof. "Give me a minute. I know a cleaning spell I think I can use."

There were other words, long syllables in his golden flowing tongue. For all I knew, Ryder could have been spouting centuries-old love poetry and declaring his undying love for a squirrel. The fluid elfin triggered something inside me, something dark and frightened, and I turned, emptying my stomach into the grasses growing at the side of the road.

Touch should be a reassuring thing. Countless scientists and nurturing mothers attest to that fact. For me, touch held its own horrors, a funhouse excursion through cloudy memories where all I know is sharpness and tears. Ryder's hands on my shoulders fed my embryonic fears until they grew and pressed me in.

I felt the gravel road beneath my knees, and the fragrant green forest whispered around me, drowning under the smell of my own sick. The mewling feral castoff Dempsey brought in awoke inside me and screamed, hammering at the civilized mask I'd built around its ugly face.

There were images, small flashes of faces like mine, shadowed and splattered with blood. I knew from my memories the blood was mine and would taste of cinnamon if I dabbed some on my tongue. Something burned, cooking flesh, then a keening echo, separated by blinding flashes of agony. The sensations roiled over me, catching me in their tides, slamming me back into my past.

"Kai." A drop of gold pierced the red and black, rippling outward. The light faded and then struck again, pulling me out. "Kai, come back. It's okay."

Blinking, I tried speaking and choked on the dregs in my throat. The sky stretched over me, edged in by long branches and Ryder's worried face. Moving brought pain, and I was ashamed to hear myself whimper when I tried to dislodge the rigidity in my muscles.

"No, just stay there. Here." He lifted me slowly, carefully supporting my shoulders against his chest. I lay between his legs, curled up and shaking. "Drink something."

Water hit my lips, the rim of the bottle resting against my mouth. He urged me to sip, cautiously spilling drops onto my shriveled tongue. My palate was dry, and when I tried to swallow, the water stung as it went down my throat. I let it trickle in, tilting my head back slowly.

The cool water tasted like Ryder, green tea and vanilla spiced with gold. He'd been sipping from the bottle earlier, leaving himself on its rim. I needed to pull back from the taste, but I needed the water more, so I let Ryder fill me.

"That's it." Soothing, he spoke softly, rubbing at my belly as I drank. "Just go slowly."

I caught my breath eventually, and the dark edges around my vision faded. Swallowing my last mouthful, I shook my head when he offered more. "No, I'm... good. Thank you."

"What the hell was that?" Ryder wet a napkin and wiped off my forehead and cheeks.

"I don't know." It pained me to admit it, but I was shaken down to my guts. If I'd had anything more than a few mouthfuls of water in me, I'd have pissed myself. "Maybe I'm allergic to dragon guts."

"Do you need me to take you to a healer? I can drive us...."

"If you think I'm letting you drive my car—" I choked on a laugh. "—you're crazy."

"Okay." Ryder got to his feet, helping me up. "Come on, maybe if you walk it off. You need to eat more. You're too light."

"I eat plenty." Grumbling, I stood and found my legs wobbling under me. "Okay, you might have to drive Oketsu, but if you get one scratch on him, I'll kill you."

"Then you won't get paid," he teased. I caught my balance under me, but the going was rough, as if I'd spent a night sucking at a bottle of rotgut whiskey in hopes of finding the bottom. "Remember?"

"Okay, later, then. After you've paid me." I sniffed. "Hurt the car, and as soon as we're back in San Diego, I will kill you dead."

CHAPTER ELEVEN

RYDER SLOWED the Mustang to a stop so I could take my first real good look at Elfhaine.

Staring up at the city, I forgot to breathe, only remembering to take air in when my lungs started screaming obscenities at me.

The city consumed the sky, rising up from the ground and eating up the white stone mountain looming behind it. Fog clotted the upper reaches, rounded tower caps threading through the feathery mists. Mica flecks sparkled along the plastered turrets, drawn out by the sun's rays, and a river poured from a keyhole in the mountain, coursing through an elaborate marble aqueduct and filling the city's winding, raised canals. Tiny specks floated on the causeways, punters steering triangular skiffs, pale-haired passengers stepping carefully into waiting water taxis along the way.

Small zeppelins bobbed past, their frameworks a complicated mélange of green and gold metals. The city's air seemed full, either with skippered cars rising or descending lead lines to different levels or bursting with tree canopies, tapered slopes of emerald and amethyst leaves brilliant against the pale, cream-toned buildings. Massive cogs turned, shifting some structures in measured clicks. The city felt alive, an organic, breathing creature nestling against a cold, protective mountain.

It made me feel awkward, a dirty smudge on a crystalline vase.

I knew the stink of a human city, had inhaled it deep into my lungs and entrenched its foul scent into my bones. If cut open, my marrow would bleed out sewage and plastics, discarded flotsam of a short-lived, savage people who gnawed off pieces of the earth to survive. The sidhe, in their beautiful golden city, were as far removed from me as the sun.

"Are you feeling okay?" Ryder asked.

"I'm okay." It was a lie. My body was sluggish, and my mind wasn't much better. Watching the city in the morning light was dizzying. There was too much to see, and the shifting dots of color kept drawing my attention away from what I'd been focusing on. "I could probably drive through the gates if they'd let me."

Ryder stared me down, his green eyes hard on my face. Shifting, I rested against the window, breathing slowly. It was an old trick, one I used while playing poker with other Stalkers. Lack of tension in the body meant a person was telling the truth or at least was oblivious to their surroundings. It was the perfect bluff and had raked me in more than one pot.

"You're lying," he said, snorting at me. "There are accommodations outside the city gates. You'll be able to take a shower in one of the pods and maybe sleep while I go in and get Shannon."

"Works for me. Just looking at that place makes my skin itch," I mumbled. We'd moved out of the forest and into the open road, leaving the weald behind.

A wall surrounded the city, sections of brass-inlaid white stone standing about thirty feet tall and running outward then back toward the mountain. The top of the wall had a walkway with patrols checking the span, their heads visible over the edge. Scalloped metal gates lay open, with the gravel road ending at the foot of the wall. Beyond the gates, Elfhaine's beige stonework laid out a wide street filled with midmorning foot traffic and the occasional car. Beyond, in the distance, one of the service canals sliced a dark ribbon through the gentle rise of the city as it climbed the mountain, the rock cut into tiers to support Elfhaine's upper levels.

A smattering of house pods sat next to the road, a few hundred yards from the gate. The mobile cabins were soft-shelled and could be broken down in minutes. I'd used them before while on longer runs in the wilderness, and while spartan, they were a damned sight better than sleeping on the ground.

"You were planning on driving Oketsu in?" I asked when he stopped at the pod closest to the gate.

"No. I don't want to run the risk of someone opening the hood to take a look inside. This thing you drive is a violation of the natural order." Getting out, Ryder reached for the jacket he'd tossed onto the backseat, then shook the wrinkles out with a snap of his hands. "If I leave the car out here, it'll be left alone, as it's your property. Besides, I'm not too sure I got the entire dragon off it. Even being a High Lord of a new Court, I'm not such a high rank that they won't seriously debate cooking me on a bonfire for that."

"You're serious?" I scanned the hardtop when I got out, looking for traces of the reptile's fins.

"It's a joke, Kai," he said, looking at me curiously.

"Just wake me when you come out." I waved him off, grabbing a pack from the trunk. "I'll be the one inside snoring. I've got enough time to get some snoring done, right?"

"Yes. You have enough time." He keyed open the pod, then left the door open for me. "There should be some food supplies inside, but if there's anything you need, let the gatekeepers know. They'll get it for you."

The guards at the gate watched us, keen-eyed sentinels dressed in black body armor. The city might be old, but it was obvious that the military or police kept up on technological developments. The chest casings the guards wore were newly minted, fresh off the lab racks if I wasn't mistaken. They also carried long-barreled automatics at their hips, and from the looks of the muzzles pointing down their backs, the sidhe encouraged the use of multi-shot rifles as well.

"That's a lot of firepower they've got there." I looked around at the pastoral scenery and back up to the fog-shrouded Esgar Mountain. "What the hell is there to shoot out here? Bunnies?"

"We just finished a war with the humans, if you recall," Ryder said dryly. "Tensions still run a bit high where security is concerned."

"That was years ago, and shit, you guys won." I was stacking up Ryder's curious looks pretty quickly and earned myself another. "Why bother?"

"A few human years, perhaps," he said, straightening his shirt and tugging his jacket down over his hips. "I've never heard a sidhe refer to his people as *you guys*, much less thinking that we came out of the war victorious."

"Okay, *their* side lost, what? A couple million, maybe?" I couldn't remember the exact number, but the casualties had been heavily skewed toward the human end of things. "The elfin, both Courts, lost only five hundred? Six hundred?"

"If you consider that a woman is deemed fertile if she has one child," Ryder pointed out. "Most marriages hope to raise one child among the whole group over their lifetimes, while humans reproduce quicker than bacteria. Those few hundred…. It was like every family bled for the war."

"I'm sure at least some humans mourned their dead too." I waved away any more conversation with a tired hand. Sleep dragged me down, and my thoughts were far from organized. "Go do whatever dance you need to do; get the girl so we can head out by nightfall. We'll need to hit Pendle as soon as it gets dark. I'll be good to go once I get some sleep in me."

Ryder gave me a curt nod, thinning his mouth into a tight line, then walked. I watched him approach the guards, stopping long enough to have a short conversation before disappearing into the city. The crowd sucked him in, and I lost sight of his tall form in the river of sidhe.

"I am never accepting another run to Anaheim," I promised myself, grabbing some clothes from a duffel bag. "Every sidhe is treasured, like the humans that died weren't someone's kid. What the hell makes the sidhe deaths more important than ours?"

Ours.

I waited until the cool darkness of the pod cabin enveloped me before I hiccupped with a choked-back curse. My reflection in the bathroom mirror surprised me, as it always did. I *forgot* I wasn't human. When I caught a glimpse of myself, I expected to see rounded eyes and flat-planed cheekbones. In my mind's eye, my face was squarer, rougher in features. The androgynous purple-eyed, black-haired *alien* I saw was a shock. It was the face of my nightmares, of the monsters that stalked me in the darkness when I was weak.

This is not my face, I'd cried once to Dempsey.

The bastard's reply stung, even now. *It's who you are, boy. Might as well accept what you are. You're elfin. You can pretend you're human all you like. But you know that's bullshit.*

"Maybe that's why that dick back at the club… what the fuck was his name… Orin. That's why he's screwed up," I said to the black-haired cat-bastard staring back at me from across the bathroom sink. "Maybe when he looks in the mirror, he's expecting to see this."

Muttering at the craziness, I stripped off my clothes and stepped into the hot water, using the spiced soap left in a toiletries basket on the counter. Fatigue made my bones heavy, and my hands dragged a scrub cloth over my limbs. Lathered, I stood under the almost too-hot water and let it pound my body, feeling the last of the bruises left beneath my skin by the black dog soften under the torrent. Turning my head, my neck clicked, popping back in place. Rotating my arm, I felt my shoulder blade shift and the knots release along the small of my back.

I soaped the cloth again, then twisted to scrub at my back. My fingers brushed along the edge of my shoulder blade, and I fingered the ridge of scar tissue there, unable to trace it to its end as it burrowed toward my spine and down my back. The smooth keloids ached, tender to the touch and hot under my fingertips, and I didn't need to see them to know what they looked like. I knew, because I'd studied their shapes in private, knowing where the tight spots were when I turned. The span restricted some of my movements, the thin skin tearing and weeping water when I overstretched. My body failed to recognize the tangled nerves and skin as an impediment and tore itself apart, reaching beyond what I could do… should do at times.

The elfin were supposed to heal quickly and without blemish, but then, my bastard father knew ways around that. My back would always wear his mark, and nothing I did seemed to budge one damned bit of scarring from my skin.

Dried off and dressed, I debated the pod's long, slender bed, not much more than a rack pressed against the one straight wall bisecting it in two, separating the space into a small bathroom and a larger sleeping and eating area.

Easily erected and soft-walled, pods were standard military issue and after the war became a camper's dream accommodations. Freeway underpasses and abandoned lots bristled with them, creating bubble cities underground. I'd spent more than one night in a rented pod, either on a run or sleeping on the floor while a drunk and snoring Dempsey slept off his week.

Yawning, I shoved a handful of dried beef-tofu strips into my mouth, softening the jerky with my saliva as I chewed. The rack was hard, and its thin mattress barely dented under my weight. I grabbed the pillows and sheet, then left the pod to unlock Oketsu's passenger door. A few latch presses later, the bucket seat reclined nearly flat, and I rolled the window down to let some airflow in. The black leather seat squeaked as I lay down, fitting around my body. Closing my eyes, I fell off quickly, shutting out the coppery cream city filling Oketsu's windshield.

A TAP on the window startled me awake. I had my hand on the shotgun resting between the door and the seat before my eyes were open. The sun nearly blinded me when I blinked, and I raised my other hand to block out the late afternoon light.

Two black-armored guards had come to rouse me. One lurked a short distance away from the Mustang's front end, and another stood by the door, the butt of his rifle resting against Oketsu's door. He'd raised the shield of his helmet, exposing his sidhe face. His features were broader than mine, coarser, and his eyes and hair ran to the amber gold of the Dawn Court. His mouth tightened, and he shifted, pressing his shoulders back as he stared me down.

Everything about him stank of cop.

Or asshole.

I was sure about the first from the uniform and the badge embroidered into the sleeve of his uniform. I suspected the second when he tapped the glass again, rattling it in its channel.

"Yeah?" I kept it short.

He said something to the one standing behind him, turning his sharp chin toward his companion. The sun hit the high gloss of his helmet, splashing a flare of white light into my eyes. I heard them laugh, a dirty, dark sound, before he turned back to me.

"I'm guessing you didn't come over to see if I was resting comfortably," I replied, sitting up. I pulled at the shotgun, bringing it up against my thigh. Nestled against the door, it would be invisible to the guard, but angled correctly, a blast from one of the cartridges would hit the sidhe in the face and embed most of the tempered glass into his skin. "Need something?"

"You need to speak 'uman to me?" The guard's teeth were white, his canines pointed and pressing against his lower lip as he spoke. His Singlish was horrible, and I barely understood him, but his intent was clear. "Bet between men. Dusk Court or 'uman, you?"

"Get out," the one behind him called to me. "See you. Now."

"See what?" I asked, taking a quick glance back at the gate. "Going to look at my ass for a tail?"

There were three more armored sidhe standing there, acting like they all had nothing better to do than watch the first two play bait-the-guy-in-the-Mustang. I understood him fine. They were bored, and since I was an outsider, I should be easy prey.

I suck at being easy prey. It puts a damper on my life.

"Get out car. Stupid? Can't hear?" Canines rapped the window again, this time with the business end of the rifle pointed at me. "Think unsidhe, not 'uman. Filth. Maybe have to kick it."

It's going to get ugly, I thought as I reached for the door handle. The shotgun only held two cartridges, and even with a good shot, the pellets wouldn't pierce the sidhes' armor. I'd loaded for meat and bone, not polymer-ceramic hardshell. I also wouldn't be able to reload in time to get the other three. Picking up one of the auto-rifles meant all hell would break loose, and I could guarantee I wouldn't be the one riding triumphant into the sunset.

Ryder would also kill me if I started something. I was sure of it. It would be almost worth it just to see the look on his face.

"Hold on," I said, opening the door slowly. "Just give me some space. Back up a bit."

He hawked, leaving a globule of spit on Oketsu's windshield. "Get out. Now."

Keeping a hold on my temper, I did a count and watched the viscous spit travel down the glass. *It's washable*, I told myself, *easily taken care of. Nothing to get into a fight over.*

Nothing a punch to his nose wouldn't take care of, the more feral part of my brain muttered.

Leaving my hand looped over the window, I held tightly onto the shotgun, hoping to keep it hidden in case I needed it. The guard bent forward, pressing himself into the hair at my temple, inhaling deeply. As close as he was, I held my ground, keeping my shoulders straight as he nudged into me. I had to look up at the sidhe, falling short of his height by several inches. I estimated he had a good fifty pounds of muscle on me, and the rifle he hefted promised to puncture a hole through me and Oketsu with one shot.

I didn't understand much of what he said after that. Mangled Singlish became sidhe, and I caught shreds of meaning, a comment on my smell and maybe my mother. With him pressed up against my body, I should have felt something other than disgust, even an arc of my nerves reacting to the presence of another sidhe like I'd had with Ryder, but there was nothing, just a slight hum, which receded after a few seconds.

His tongue touched me, rough on my bare skin.

And my world went red.

CHAPTER TWELVE

THE UNWANTED feel of another elfin tore me. I tasted blood, and I was unsure if I'd bitten through my cheek or tongue, but it sickened me—enraged me—as I held back the blackness rising inside.

Words floated to the surface of my mind, ebony liquid compared to the gold ribbon language Ryder spoke, but the similarities were uncanny. Power surged from someplace within, filling me with anger, and it ached to lash out, needing to savage the tongue that tasted me. The echo of hands roamed over my body, prodding into secret places and delving deep into crevices that hurt and ached. My head hurt, crackling noises interspersed with flashes of red, and I reeled under the pressure squeezing my thoughts together.

Conflicted, I wanted to both kill and die. Either, so long as it was with my bare hands.

Instead, I brought the shotgun up out of the car's deep wheel well between the seat and the doorframe, slamming its stock against his helmet and jerking his head back with a snap. Kicking the door so it flung fully open, I swung my legs out, keeping the shotgun pointed at his stomach. Oketsu's door hit him in the legs, pushing the guard back.

Wiping at the wet spot on my neck, I said, "Don't fucking touch me."

A rattle of gunfire filled the air when the second guard shot a flurry of rounds over our heads. I ducked, keeping the door open to hide behind as I grabbed shotgun shells from under the passenger seat, then shoved them into the pockets of my jeans. When I risked a glance over the doorframe, Canines was on me before I stepped away from the car, grabbing my shirt with one hand and hauling me over the metal, scraping my stomach on the door.

I let him drag me out, going limp to become dead weight in his hands. When he got me clear of the car, I twisted up, folded in two, and jabbed my knee into his unprotected throat. Surprised, he went down in a choking fit, dropping his rifle. Pulling free, I turned over and landed on my feet, then hooked the toe of my boot under the rifle's brace, tossed it up, and caught it in midair.

I brought the shotgun up to place its muzzle against his cheekbone, then stared at his companion, my finger pressed on the trigger. Flipping the rifle around, I pointed it in the direction of the second guard.

"Your choice. Back off, or I give him a new pair of nostrils," I said to the other one, digging my heel into the supine guard's crotch to keep him still. "His blood's the same color as my paint job. A couple cups of water will wash it right off. Shit, I'd even drink the water just to piss it off."

The whine of an autoglider rippled over the meadow, and it appeared, whipping out of the city's gates. It arced around the three guards running toward me, hugging the ground and kicking up streams of dust in its wake. Its pilot lit up its engine, closing the gap between the glider and Oketsu before I could even blink. A guard's helmet poked up out of the open cab, and I groaned, spotting an official-looking seal on the glider's side as it slowed to a stop, then settled onto the ground in front of the second guard.

"Stalker!" The pilot was out of the glider before it hit dirt, long legs eating up the distance. Husky voiced, the Singlish was muffled by the helmet's faceplate, blurring the words. "Drop the guns."

"Hell no." I shook my head, pointing the rifle's muzzle down. With the glider in the way, a shot to the second guard was out of the question, but I wasn't about to discount the three at the gate from joining in. "Sorry, I forgot. Hell no, your lordship."

The helmet came off, and I swallowed, man enough to admit I was awed by the woman behind the shield.

Willowy was a word probably used to describe her. I'd have chosen scary. It was hard not to notice her hard-set blue eyes or the utilitarian silver band of skulls she used to tie back her straight sunset red hair. Like the guards, she wore a set of black armor casings over black pants and a snug long sleeve T-shirt. Unlike the guards, she moved with great confidence, like running water across the dry dirt as she took command of the scene. Bone pale, her cheeks pinked with a flush, but it was anger more than embarrassment. I was fairly certain she'd chew my ass off if she had anything to say about it, but she was satisfied with cutting the guards down.

She was hot enough to send me to rigid only by looking at her.

"Excuse me," I said, giving a half bow. "Your ladyship."

"It's commander, Stalker Gracen. You there, get back to your post." There was no mistaking the sidhe woman for anything other than a soldier. She called off the guards with a single stern glance, disapproval curving her mouth. The guard behind the glider fell back. The one on his back under my foot shifted to move, and I pressed the gun muzzle down to keep him still. She said in Singlish, barking at the guards while keeping her eyes on me, "He's mine."

Moving closer, I saw her eyes ran with flecks of color, silver and black crystals set into the light blue folds. Not many would say she was gorgeous, even with the characteristic beauty of a sidhe in her bone structure. Her nose was slightly too long, and the arch of her eyebrows was too sharp, but the rich plump of her mouth hinted of a husky laugh, and her hands moved with a capable assurance as she removed the rifle from my grasp. She smelled like mint sticks dipped in chocolate, and the wink she gave me left me wanting a taste.

Gods help me, between Ryder and the redhead, I was going to be so tightly wound by the time I got back to San Diego, I'd lose half of the money I'd earned in the red lantern district.

"Let him up, Stalker," she said, drawing close. The mint-chocolate scent of her skin intensified, and my stomach growled, fighting with other parts of my body for attention. "I will guarantee your safety if you will guarantee theirs."

I stepped back, and the guard scrambled to his feet, barely catching the rifle she tossed at him. The guard clenched his teeth and hissed, crossing his arms over his broad chest, then glared at me. Shrugging, I wiped at my neck again, making sure I'd removed his spit from my skin before looking up.

"Hey, you started it," I objected feebly. I tucked the shotgun back into the Mustang then turned to watch the guard trundle back to the gate.

"My apologies," she said, a hint of a smile on her mouth. "They should not have bothered you."

"Not a problem. Thanks for pulling them off me."

"I think I was pulling you off them, Stalker Gracen." The sun left white streaks of light on her armor, its sheen polished highly enough I could see myself in her arm covering. "I am Watch Commander Alexa, Clan Sebac, House of Levar. My cousin, Ryder, sent me to fetch you."

"Fetch me? Whoa, wait a second." I stepped back, waving my hands in front of me. "I'm not setting foot in the place."

"Ryder sends his apologies about this, but our high-grandmother wishes to meet you," she said with a shrug. "He has no choice but to request you come in now."

"So? She's not my high-grandmother!" My protest fell on deaf ears as Alexa studied the Mustang's door.

"Your eye color is of a Dawn Court bloodline. For all we know, she could be your high-grandmother as well. And she is the matriarch of our Clan. She is the Sebac." Tapping the door channel, she glanced inside the car. "How does the glass pane come up? There is one, yes?"

I turned the hand crank, rolling the window up. "It's done manually. Or by that switch on the console if I have the power on."

"Manually? By hand?" The Commander played with the crank, turning it back and forth to watch the window move. "Interesting. This is an old car, then? Very old?"

"Very," I replied. "And let's get back to the going inside thing. I'm not. Going inside, that is."

"Ryder said you were beautiful even for one of us, and quite stubborn. And for once, I am inclined to agree with my cousin's opinion." She straightened and caught a chunk of my hair in her fingers. Its color made her skin look even paler, nearly translucent. "Your hair is so very black. So Dusk Court. In the sunlight, I can see the blue in it. If we had time, I'd have pleasures with you, but Grandmother does not like to be kept waiting. She is at a great age where even seconds matter now. Or so she says."

"Sorry. I don't have sex with anyone if I know their name." I shrugged. "Thanks, though."

"That was a Singlish joke, yes?" She trapped me against Oketsu's quarter panel, placing her hands on either side of my hips, and leaned forward. The brush of her mouth on mine flared a prickle of desire down my chest and into my belly. She tasted as good as she smelled, a rich darkness poured over white light. "And if not, I can make you forget my name, *áinle*. Give me a few minutes alone with you and I can make you forget a lot of things. Maybe even your own name."

"*áinle?*" I mangled the word, tripping over the pronunciation.

"It is... *musang*," she tried, laughing at me when I made a face. "Never mind, there's no time for it anyway. Grandmother waits."

"Suppose I don't want to go?" I looked at the city crouching behind its high wall. I'd faced down flaming salamanders, mutant sewer gators, and packs of rabid black dogs—and a city gave me tremors.

"Then I pick you up and throw you in," Alexa said confidently. "I don't disappoint Grandmother, and I don't let anyone else disappoint her either. You are getting into the glider, by yourself or with my help. If I get to help, then I get my hands on you. For me, it's a good thing either way."

She meant it. The playful tease of her voice was frosting on steel.

"I have ropes or leather ties. I have both, but I think the black leather." She eyed me experimentally. "That would look better on your skin. It's not my way, but I'm adaptable."

I grabbed the shotgun, daring her to object to my bringing in a weapon, but Alexa said nothing. She stood, waiting for me to mount the glider, checking the link at her wrist for the time. Pushing down on Oketsu's lock, I held the latch in as I shut the door, hearing the alarm click on with a chirrup. Grabbing the edge of the glider's open hatch, I climbed up the stirrup, then settled into the seat.

"Okay." I swallowed and took a deep breath, hoping I didn't shame myself by passing out at an old woman's feet. "Let's go meet Grandmother."

WE ZIPPED past the guards. The open gates were a haze of carved metal guarded by black blurs. Fearless, Alexa drove on, fitting the glider into a thin slot between two slower-moving vehicles. Bulbous spheres rolled under rounded chassis, carrying sidhe and cargo on the city's winding roads. At the glider's speed, it was difficult to make out faces, but it was easy to see we were drawing attention. Heads turned as we went by, the glider's electromagnetic coils screaming as it made a tight spin into a spiral.

Greenery and trees were as much a part of the city as stone and metal, old thick branches nearly five men wide supporting walkways or rooms jutting from tall towers. Spacious avenues were broken by an occasional garden, random drops of flowers blooming under a misty sky.

I looked up and lost myself in the spiraling towers above me. Sunlight and shadow wove in and out of the glider's cockpit as we passed under broad-leaved trees and floating platforms. The buildings I'd seen from far away swiveled and turned around us, shortening roadways as we drove.

The air was humid and fragrant, a cool breeze from the mountain rolling down into the warm gardens below. Mists rose from the damp soil, lacy clouds that wandered over walls and through courtyards. People were everywhere, tall elegant men and women dressed in flowing clothes. Red seemed a favored color, followed closely by shades of blue and various whites, with flowers and metal jewelry embellishing their garments' simple lines.

Elfhaine was beautiful. A city blended with nature, stone and metal. Gold and copper filigree supported a magenta and orange riot of flowers suspended against the stark white of grown stone. Color was everywhere, floral swags and hanging ribbons caught in the breeze—all against a marvel of spiraling buildings.

And there wasn't a child in sight.

There weren't any children in the pockets of sidhe we passed. There was no evidence of young sidhe, not a toy left on a lawn or a park set where filthy, grubby swings lay waiting for more dirt to be rubbed into chain links. The absence of chaos was unsettling. The world outside Elfhaine's walls was brutal, noisy, and messy. Blood and spit lubricated the gears of a human's life, with small spurts of joy adding the rush of speed to the journey. It was what I knew. The quiet was unnerving.

The glider's reckless speed pitched a low humming whine that should have been drowned out by the people around it, but an eerie silence hung around us. San Diego's crowded neighborhoods were a constant buzz of chatter, horns, and lights, where Elfhaine's spacious hills were empty, devoid of any sign of life, save for the golden and ivory mannequins walking through its streets.

"Where are the kids?" I had to shout over the wind to be heard.

"Kids?" Alexa slowed the craft and we dropped a few inches as the air pressure beneath the glider lessened. "Why would we have baby goats here? The outer districts of the city may have some."

"Not goats. Children." I made a rocking motion with my arms. "Baby sidhe."

"Ah." She nodded, her bright red hair settling about her shoulders and down her back. "I can tell you where each of them is right now if you like, but yes, most should be with their teachers."

"I don't think I need to know where they all are. Wouldn't that take a while?"

"Not long," she said, hitting a few buttons on the console. "There are fifty-one sidhe under the age of responsibility. One is in his nursery, and forty are in lessons. The other ten are older and doing independent study. Two are attached to my Clan." Alexa smiled. "One of the pre-adults is my daughter. She is very smart and quite fierce."

"Fifty-one?" I stared out at the seemingly endless city. "How many people live here?"

"One...." Alexa's Singlish failed, and she murmured a word in sidhe. "Million? Ten one hundred thousands? Million is the right word, I think."

"Shouldn't there be more kids than that?"

"We would always welcome more children. I would try having one with you. I like your eye color."

"Uh, no," I said, shaking my head. The thought of having a kid shook me. My genetics didn't need to go any farther than my own body.

"Providing a child to your Clan is an honor. Of course, she would belong to my Clan because I am the female, but there would be connections. Sebac is a good Clan, very strong. Very influential. It would raise your Clan status if it is poor."

"I don't think you'd want to get within ten miles of my bloodlines, honey. Believe me. You'd be better off mating with one of the dogs from the Hunt. The black dogs."

"The *ainmhí dubh*?" Alexa brought the glider into a side street. "Black creatures. You call them dogs? That kind belong to Dusk Court lords only."

"Yeah, they breed wild now," I said. "It's part of my job to hunt them."

"They kill if not controlled. They kill even when controlled. Very dangerous unsidhe things. *Meata*."

"Please tell me your grandmother speaks Singlish. I speak as much sidhe as my car does."

"I am thinking that somewhere, you ran away from being sidhe, or maybe it ran away from you," Alexa said, slowing the glider down as traffic crowded the street. "Ryder told me you are uncomfortable being elfin."

"That wasn't his business to share," I grumbled, moving the shotgun jammed into my leg. "Arrogant, controlling son of a bitch."

"He told me so I would take care with you." She risked our lives with a glance in my direction. A wall filled the glider dome for a split second; then it washed away under a rush of speed. "Ryder and I are close friends as well as blood. He trusted me with you. I promised to take care of you as if you were mine."

"That includes propositioning me?"

"If you were mine—" She grinned, giving me a wink. "—I would do much more than proposition, *áinle*. I've already said purple-eyed younglings would be nice. Trying for purple-eyed younglings would be even nicer."

Concerned eyes followed us, some wide with shock, and for a moment I wondered what they were seeing until a sidhe woman in an elaborate red hat made of feathers touched her pale ivory hair and stared at me as we went by.

Alexa saw her and reached out to touch my shoulder. "It's your hair, pretty. The black is not a color here. Golds and reds, yes. Sometimes a mink brown. But black—that is not seen here. They wonder why I'm bringing an unsidhe so deep into the city, but I'm thinking, with those beautiful twilight eyes, you are as much Dawn Court on the inside as you try to make yourself Dusk on the outside."

"Hey, people see what they want to see," I muttered, slouching farther down into the seat. The city had lost its glow, and I wanted to be in and out as quick as possible.

"We all only see that. It is nature, human or sidhe." She shrugged. "We are all the same inside. We anger. We love. And sometimes, we judge. It is not right, *áinle*, but it is a truth."

CHAPTER THIRTEEN

WE CIRCLED off the main road and into an open brick courtyard, then parked next to other gliders, all bearing different regal seals. Deciphering a sidhe household's complex crest made my head hurt, and even though Dempsey had tried to pound the basics into my skull, nothing took. A phoenix looked the same as a crane, and while I could tell a dragon from a drake, the subtleties of a rampant hound compared to a rampant dire wolf were lost on me. Add in the colors and ribbons and my eyes rolled back into my head. The calculus Sparky tried to shove into my ears made more sense.

Most of the parked gliders were a dark green with antique gold and black accents. Crests ran to the same colors, with a couple of deep purple streamlines mixed in. Alexa's was the only pure black vehicle in the place. I guessed it was a cop car, and the silver and blue emblem on the side was an official seal.

"Leave the shotgun," she said before I could reach for it. "No weapons are allowed inside the compound."

"I don't like walking into someplace naked," I muttered, but I left the gun in the cockpit. "It better be here when I get back."

"No one will touch it. Most sidhe prefer edged weapons or bows. We're simple creatures."

"Then they have a lot in common with the human that raised me."

I couldn't make sense of which turrets and spirals belonged to which building. The spires wrapped into one another, with spans connecting balconies made of woven metal. The only sign of an entrance was a small door with slender gold silk banners hung on either side. A thin whippet-like dog lay on a rug in front of the door, its long legs twitching as it slept. Alexa stepped over the animal and opened the door to let us in.

Inside was cool, and sconces threw circles of light against the red walls of a long corridor. From the fiery bird sculptures and tapestries, I guessed the bird I saw on the Sebac standard was a phoenix. The hallway floors were cut stone squares worn smooth after centuries of footsteps.

Now on the woman's front porch, I realized I knew nothing about how to greet an elderly sidhe. My social circles didn't run to hostess gifts, and extravagant meant a turn-tab on a bottle of cheap wine. I barely knew enough to take a hat off before I entered a temple.

"What am I supposed to say to her?" I asked Alexa's back. It was a nice back, and even if I was technically working, I took the time to admire her ass.

"Let her speak first," she said, stopping at a plain wooden door. "Grandmother will lead the conversation. She likes doing that. Don't eat or drink anything she offers, or you'll be beholden to her. This is a private chamber, so treat it like you would a dining hall. When she is done, come back here. I will be bringing Ryder here."

"Thanks."

"Thank me when you come back," Alexa said, wrinkling her nose. "We will be waiting here with some whiskey. You will probably need it. I know I always do when she is done with me."

I didn't know what to expect. Hallowed halls or a marble spa filled with overgrown exotic plants. Something more than the plain round stone room with a simple wooden chair set under a single window slit. The walls and ceiling were the same stone as the hallway outside, tightly fitted cream squares flecked with blue and green stones. Under my feet, the floor tiles were odd, a mosaic of shapes and grout. Light from the thin window crossed the center of the room, the late afternoon sun angling down through cut stone. The single wooden high-backed chair was placed across from the door. I suspected I was going to be spending the conversation standing.

Feeling like an extra from an old slasher movie, I stepped into the room. "Hello?"

The floor flared with light, blinding me with streams of cultured rays bursting up from the curved arcs of grout. I knew enough of the arcane to recognize magic, especially when it came pouring out of the ground under my feet. My skin burned where the light touched, sharper than when I'd gotten my koi inked on my hip, and I stepped around, trying to find someplace where I could stand without intersecting any of the beams. Spangled light blurred my vision, and I shook my head, trying to focus.

Crossing into the mosaic was a costly mistake.

Through the haze, I made for the door. I took four steps and slammed into something invisible, bashing my head against it.

"What the…?" Stretching my arms out, I tried to find the end of the field, walking half the circle before turning around to try again. The light was beginning to burn, a searing pain spreading over my eyes as I sought a way out. "What the hell is this?"

I couldn't get out of the circle. The light held me in, burning when I tried to cross it. I'd walked right into a web spun by a very old spider.

Opposite the door, a shape crossed the room. With my lashes wet with tears, I barely recognized it as a woman. I blinked, wiping at my face, and the throbbing light receded somewhat, leaving me with an echo of runes and lines across my sight.

She spoke in sidhe, as whispery as the mists outside. It startled me, even though I should have expected it, but I'd trusted Alexa when she said Singlish would be used. I was even more surprised when the rivers of words kept coming, waves of sound slamming into me as neatly as a stormy sea's tide. I couldn't escape the flood. Even placing my hands over my ears to drown out some of the words seemed futile, and I fell to my knees, my stomach turning inside out as I buckled over.

It was a spell, close to one I'd heard before, its silences punctuated with the rises and valleys of the chant. The echoing nothingness held more than the lack of her voice. It held a power capable of tying me fast to the stonework; each loop of words became another rope to anchor me in place.

It lacked the thorny prick of my father's voice but was effective just the same.

More words and the sickness hit again, punching through my abdomen and into my spine, closing over my groin and squeezing until I threw up the spoonful of bile I had in my empty stomach. The green smell of my innards fouled the floor, and the fluid began to smoke, boiling as the lit runes ate through my waste.

"Let me out of this thing." I pounded at the barrier, hearing it ripple with the blow. The twang reverberated, the echoes lessening as the sound moved away from me.

"It's no use." A leathery whisper penetrated the low pain of my aching eyes. "You won't be able to break free until I release you. I saw what you were from the towers before I came down. The spell is attuned to your kind—to your filthy blood."

"My blood?" Talking was hard, but I made the effort to speak, pulling myself up to stare at the woman now sitting in the chair. "What kind of sick game are you playing, old woman?"

I could see her more clearly after I wiped my eyes. She was ancient, a bleached, stretched woman with bones sticking out at her joints. Her triangular face was pointed, a cutting sharp skull under her ivory skin, and her deep-set gray eyes burned with a feverish glow. Long strands of white hair floated around her, falling from a center part and trailing on the stone floor at her feet.

A dark gold sheath covered her thin body, narrow straps leaving her arms and shoulders bare. Twin slats winged up over her flat chest, her collarbones overpowering the press of her sternum, her breastbone visible over the scooped neck of her loose dress. She gripped the chair's arms, skeletal hands heavy with signet rings and jewels, the blood gone from her knuckles as she bent forward to study me.

"Hello, darkling. Or are you used to being called changeling by your kin? Did they call you that? Or did they just call you what you are? Monster." Her Singlish was flawless, not a trace of an accent and spoken with a round tonal lilt that would not be out of place in a news broadfeed. "That's what you are. An unnatural monster."

"Bitch." I didn't care if Ryder was damned to sitting at the kiddie table for the rest of his life. My back burned along the hard ridges of the scarring on my shoulder blades, and my shirt clung to my spine, wet from sweat and possibly blood. Lifting my chin, I swallowed my pain. "Fuck you. I'm not the monster here."

"You will address me as the Sebac." Raising one hand, she clutched at the air, and the light flared, digging its claws deeper into my belly. "Or my lady, if you must speak."

"I'll stick with bitch for right now." I refused to give under the pain and swallowed my vomit, spitting out what I couldn't onto the floor. "I like how it sounds."

"Stubborn. And angry. Like all your kind." Stroking her cheek with a long fingernail, she followed my pacing with keen eyes. "You are so responsive to binding spells. Your master has a strange sense of humor, or perhaps it was the only way to keep you subdued."

"I don't have a master." I spat again, the yellow-tinged globule hitting the barrier between us. Instinctively she jerked her head back.

"Did he stitch you together? She cocked her head; a long slither of her hair fell over her spindly arm. "If I strip you, will I find your joints marked with black silk and punctures? I'm always curious about others' work. How did he animate you, monster? With electricity, like that human legend? I applaud the sickening of your body at being bound; it is ingenious. I'm impressed."

"Maybe it's not your damned spell making me sick. Maybe it's just you."

"Such a growling little puppy. Does my grandson know what you are, golem?" she asked, resting her chin against one fist. "Does he know he's brought an unreal creation to soil the ground at my feet?"

The pain subsided in my guts, and I stood up straighter, meeting her glare. "Let me out of this sorceress trap and I'll let you feel how real my hands are when I put them around your neck."

"And so violent. Did you kill your master, darkling? Is that why you're roaming free?" The Sebac waved away anything further I had to say. "Never mind, Ryder said he trusted you, even though he lied to me when he said you were sidhe. Now that I've seen you, I can understand why. You keep those secrets deep in your blood, hoping none of the Clans find you, or they'd kill you for what you are."

"Well, now at least I know why he wanted out of this hellhole," I responded. "Didn't quite understand it, but, oh, now it's really clear."

"Don't be ridiculous," she said derisively. "Ryder is one of my heirs. Once he tires of playing lord to his backwater court and pets like you, he'll return, leaving your kind behind him."

"My kind?" I said. Anger seemed to help push her magic back, and my blood burned less. "You don't know shit, bitch. You sit behind your damned walls and count the clouds or the stars or whatever it is that you do to pass the time until your body finally dries out. You know crap about me, but you can sit there and judge me on what? How I was born?"

"How you were *made*, darkling. You were not born," she sneered, peeling her thin lips back to show me her ground-down teeth. "There was nothing willingly given in your making. Your existence is repugnant. In this you are merely a tool, just like your maker intended. I can see that just by looking at you."

"So what? You brought me up here to let me know… what? That you know what I am?" I was running out of spit. My mouth was dry, and the anger I used to hold myself up was ebbing, but I'd be damned if I fell down at her feet. "Big deal. That you have more power than me? More magic? I knew that before I came through the city gates. I know what I am. I don't need something like you to teach me that. If it makes you feel bigger and badder than me, great. We're done."

We stayed like that for a heartbeat, or maybe an eternity. My panting filled the room, and it was a hard struggle not to start crying. Men don't cry, Dempsey always said. I couldn't count how many times I'd reminded him that I wasn't a man. I'd barely leaked a tear the last time I was skinned. I wasn't going to let the bitch see me weep over a few stabbing pains.

"Let me go," I finally said. "You brought me here to sniff my ass like some stray dog. You've done that, so there's no need to keep me here."

"I do," she said, slowly rising from her chair. "Have a need, that is."

"Couldn't find an eye of newt? Or wing of bat? Or do you need help pulling your broomstick out of your ass?"

"Is that some human insult? Because it's lost on me, monster." The woman sighed, staring down her nose at me. "I had you brought here to offer you a job of sorts, something that won't violate any word you've given to Ryder."

"You pull me into this, pull apart my insides to offer me a job?" I slapped the barrier with the flat of my hand. "You've got to be kidding."

"Ryder is having you transport a fecund human woman to the South."

"I think she's past fecund." I snorted. "From what I hear, she's ready to pod out."

"I need you to end that."

"End what?"

"The pregnancy. What she's carrying, monster." She stood, crossing to where I was stuck, trapped behind her spell. "I need you to kill it before she gives birth to something. Something even more of an abomination than you."

CHAPTER FOURTEEN

"Sebac!"

He was loud, bossy, and commanding, golden soft against the sharp pain in my head. Ryder sounded a bit out of breath and pissed, but his voice was steady, echoing around the chamber.

Strangely, I was on the floor, the stone digging into my back and the light pouring into my bones. Sebac's pain stretched me apart, peeled me apart. Dizzy, I tried opening my eyes, but something weighted them down, and I closed them again, taking a deep breath before making another attempt. The light drilled straight through my pupils, hooking into my brain, but I ignored it, snarling as I tried to get to my feet. There was blood in my mouth, and my tongue felt chewed on, shreds of meat catching on my teeth as I swallowed.

At some point during her ranting, I'd crashed, unable to stay conscious. I remembered snatches of words, phrases, and her anger—mostly I remembered her anger. The Sebac railed at me, screaming in her lizard-whispery voice about unleashed horrors and repugnant atrocities, but I'd stopped listening when I smelled my eyes cooking in my skull. A few moments later, I hit the stone floor and blacked out.

The stone was hard and unforgiving. My knees complained when I moved, and I silently told them to shut up.

"This doesn't concern you, Ryder," the old woman said. I couldn't see her through the haze over my eyes, but I could hear her breathing. "I am having words with… this thing."

"*He's* my guest." The golden voice echoed in my ear, and I turned toward it, peering up into Ryder's angry face. "Is this how you show our Clan's hospitality? Ripping his soul from his body?"

"You have *no* idea what you've brought into this House. Into *my* Clan."

"There's nothing I could bring into this Clan that is filthier than what is already here," he spat back. "*You've* made sure of that."

"Argue later," I mumbled, nearly toppling Ryder over when I grabbed at his shirt before I fell. "Leaving now."

"We're done, Sebac," Ryder growled, catching me under my arms. "Whatever you hoped to accomplish here, you've managed to sever the last of my trust."

They fell to arguing in sidhe, and the flow of words hammered cold and cut with an edge sharper than any of my knives. My vision cleared a bit, and the lights died down around us until only softly glowing glyphs remained, barely visible against the veins in the stone. I tried taking a step, but my legs wouldn't cooperate, folding under me.

"Lean on me, *muirnín*." Ryder slid his arm around my waist, as if suddenly remembering I was in the room. He turned to say one last thing to the ancient sidhe, and she spat back, harsh and brutal. I felt Ryder's skin flinch, but his face betrayed nothing, stone hard as he stared at her. Mockingly bowing his head, he said in Singlish, "Good-bye, Sebac. The next time I see you, it better be to beg my forgiveness."

Holding onto Ryder, I stumbled out of the room and into the hallway, wet with the sweat soaking my clothes. The corridor was dark, and I clung to the shadows like a drowning man to a pier. The stretch of stone was thankfully silent, devoid of the searing light that burned my marrow. Catching a snatch of dry heaves, I slid against the wall, curling into a crouch, and waited for the spasms to pass.

The last strands of the afternoon sun lit the end of the hall, and I closed my eyes, shutting it away. My *skin* hurt. My eyes felt like someone had taken a hot poker to them and touched the back of my skull with the burning tip, which was probably exactly what the Sebac had done with her little spell casting.

My hands sought out the plaster at my back, arms stretching backward to anchor myself on its rough texture. The birds outside sang, serenading the sun down into the ocean, and from what I could see framed in the far-off windows, a massive blue butterfly with black dotted wings sipped the last few drops of honey from a closing flower. I couldn't have been inside that room for more than an hour, but it felt like eons had passed.

A shadow fell across my legs, and I jerked back, hitting my head on the wall. "Gods, what has she done?" Ryder asked.

"Bitch," I swore one last time, choking on my own spit. "Whore bitch."

"Look up," Ryder said, squatting in front of me. "Let me see your eyes."

He was close enough for our shins to touch, and I swallowed, pressed up against the wall with nowhere to go. I was torn between wanting to shy away from his body and punching his face for putting me within the spider's reach. My mind whispered other options, but I ignored them, still pissed off at being played for a fool by Ryder's Clan members.

"Where's Alexa? Laughing her ass off? Is this what you guys do instead of having family picnics? Serve people up to that damned bitch?" Surprisingly, I sounded calm, steady even, as if having my core cracked open was an everyday event. "If Alexa's left, she's got one of my shotguns. I'll need it to blow your grandmother's head off."

"Alexa couldn't have known, or she wouldn't have let you go in," he insisted, turning my face with a twist of his hand on my chin. He pulled a silver flask from somewhere in his coat, and I wondered stupidly how long he'd been holding out on me. "Hold still, let me look at you. Stop fighting me. My cousin said you reminded her of an *áinle*. She's right. You're like that gargoyle you own."

"Bitch." I chewed on the word, liking it on my tongue. "Your grandmother is a bitch."

"You're not going to get any disagreement from me," he commented, unscrewing the flask and offering it to me. I took a tentative sip, feeling the burn of whiskey on my raw throat. The sidhe lord waited for my coughing fit to stop, encouraging me to take another swallow. My hands trembled as I tilted my head back, letting the liquor soothe my nerves. "I was supposed to go in with you. I told the Sebac to wait until I got here before seeing you."

"That definitely was not on her to-do list," I said. The whiskey warmed the parts of me she'd left cold and numbed my intestines, which were on fire. "Not so much."

"Damn her to all hells!" Ryder's handsome face looked apologetic, and he took the flask from me, taking a gulp before passing it back. "What the hell was she hoping to accomplish?"

"You'll have to ask her that." Sitting up took too much effort. My bones ached, and my stomach rebelled. I rested my head back, watching Ryder through my lashes. In the dim sconce light, his hair shone antique gold, blending into the darker brown streaks underneath, and I shivered, wanting to lick off the whiskey sheen on his mouth. Another sip from the flask and I was done, passing it back over. If I drank any more, I'd be useless for the ride down.

And there was no way I was going to spend another night anywhere close to Elfhaine.

"Can you tell me what she did or said?" His hands were warm, moving over my legs as if checking for breaks. Ryder was used to taking care of people; that much was obvious. He acted concerned, and part of me wished it wasn't a lie. "Why did she call you up here? I was told it was just to meet you."

"I don't think I stayed awake long enough to listen to it all. She's crazy, Ryder. Your Clan's led by a crazy woman." I shook my head. "I walked into the room, and she set my blood on fire. It hurt, and the bitch liked it." I glanced up, trying to meet Ryder's gaze, but I couldn't. I couldn't stop shaking, and the whiskey was hitting my empty stomach hard. "I passed out for a bit. When I woke up, you two were screaming at each other like angry iguanas."

"You were falling to the floor when I walked in, so you weren't out for long. Maybe a second or two." Ryder remained on his haunches while I slid the rest of the way down the wall, bringing my knees up. "Did you tell her to shove it up her ass before you passed out?"

"I think so." I rubbed my thighs, feeling the bruised muscles under my jeans. In a few hours, I was going to hurt more than I did now. "I just want to get out of here, Ryder. Out of here and into another shower. I can smell myself."

"Let's get you back to the pods. I don't want us here any longer than we have to be. Can you stand?" he asked, holding his hand out to me when I nodded. I gripped it, and he pulled me up to my feet, nudging me with his shoulder. "Shannon's ready to go, but I'm not done talking about this, Kai. I want to know what she said to you."

"It's not worth it." I shrugged, shakily finding my balance. The whiskey was potent, fooling my legs into believing I could walk.

"No, it is. I brought you in here and promised you safety. This is on me." The heat of his hand hovered close to the small of my back, but Ryder barely touched me, pulling back rather than herding me along. "She broke my promise to you."

"I'm okay. Just need a little time."

"I meant what I said, Kai," Ryder growled, keeping close behind me. "I never dreamed she would try to hurt you."

"She dreamed it. Very vividly. But I'm good. I've had worse." My throat closed up, and my mind welled with memories I'd left behind me. We passed a set of windows, and I skirted around the light, half expecting the yellow glow to reach out and slice into me. Cowardly perhaps, but I was at the better safe than sorry point. "Bitch."

"That's something we can agree on." Ryder laughed. It was a bitter sound, soured by experience. "Do you want to rest? If you're too tired...."

"Nah." I shook my head, opening the outside door carefully, holding it back before it hit the sleeping dog on the stoop. "Right now, the only way I want to see Elfhaine is in my rearview mirror. Go grab your human, Ryder. I'm going to go find my shotgun."

"SHIT, RYDER!" I hissed under my breath. "She's about to pop!"

He glanced at the woman, shrugging his shoulders nonchalantly as he loaded a satchel into the back of the Mustang. Alexa was helping the very pregnant Shannon out of the glider. The sidhe commander gave me a guilt-filled look before turning back to offer her passenger a hand.

I'd needed to wash the old woman off my skin, so I'd used the pod's facilities while Ryder waited outside. He'd shouted for me when he saw his cousin's glider clear the gates. I pulled on the last pair of clean jeans I'd stored in the Mustang's voluminous trunk and shoved what I wore into Elfhaine into a bag, wondering whether it would be easier to just burn the clothes rather than wash them.

"You can see her belly button! Through her clothes! That's unnatural." I poked Ryder in the ribs. "It's sticking out like one of those red things people shove into roasting turkeys."

"I never knew you could cook. Will wonders never cease?" he teased and turned, holding his hands out to the woman. "Shannon, this is Kai Gracen, our guide. Kai, this is Shannon, my sister's friend."

She gave me a tight smile, barely looking me over as she descended. Her belly shifted and swayed under her shirt. She was older than I'd expected and definitely did not look like someone who'd be cowed by conservative parents. Clearly a member of Frisco's turning-wheel movement, she wore a peasant shift made from green sari material. It fell from her shoulders, loose ruffles scalloping over soft, round breasts. A pair of leather sandals covered her feet, silver rings tucked on nearly all her toes.

Shannon didn't strike me as a woman on the run from her family. If anything, strip off her hippie clothing and dress her in a waitress uniform, and her hard face looked like she could sling hash at a truck stop with the best of them. Somewhere in the story Ryder told me, lying was involved. My gut told me something was off, but I couldn't be sure what. My experience with pregnant women amounted to picking up things for Jonas's wives when they craved something and he was out of town, mostly kimchee dip, but once in a while, something odd like peanut butter cups.

"Hey." I moved to take a small, light travel bag from her hands. "Let me shove this in the back. Um, unless you need it for something? In case you get sick?"

"Ryder, would you mind if I took the backseat?" She looked me over, lines wrinkling her forehead as she covered a yawn with her hand. Her lashes fluttered, too much to be only fatigue. "I'll probably pass out. Baby carrying takes it out of me."

"If you're sure you'll be comfortable back there, then I don't have a problem," he answered.

I moved the seat forward. "Probably safer back there. If something's coming through this much steel, then…."

"Nothing's going to happen," Ryder said, giving me an evil look.

"I can stretch out," Shannon murmured, rubbing her belly as she ducked her head. "It'll be nice for the ride down."

"Nice, she says," I muttered, sucking the last of the toothpaste from the roof of my mouth. "You know she's going to give birth on the way down, right?"

"No, she's not," he growled back at me. "She's not due for a few more weeks."

"Law of pregnant women, they always give birth at the worst time," I argued. "Jonas told me. He should know. He's caused enough of them."

A long shadow fell over me as I grabbed a few bottles of water from the trunk. The ground heat would still be rising as we crossed into Pendle, and we'd need to keep hydrated until the night cooled the ropy black paho'eho'e lava covering the area. I smelled Alexa in the wind, the unique bittersweet of her sidhe scent hitting me before I turned around.

"Stalker Gracen." Her fingers found the hair at the nape of my neck, stroking at the soft skin there. "I did not mean…."

"It's okay," I said, pulling away to look at her, and she moved in, pushing me into the car. "Hey, not like I don't like a woman against me, but I'm not in the mood for this."

"Please, Kai. I did not know…."

"Yeah, about breeding me like some cloned sheep? You'd better check with your grandmother before you make any plans for purple-eyed babies." I cocked my head. "She might have different plans."

"My grandmother does not dictate my life, Kai," Alexa replied. "I would not have taken you to her if I had known she… she trapped you, using your blood to hold you. At the least, it was rude."

"Rude?" I almost choked. "It felt a hell of a lot more painful than rude. She was trying to peel the meat from my bones."

"She has lost Ryder's trust." Alexa's mouth softened. "And mine. She has shamed me by hurting you, and I am sorry that my family caused you any pain. I am asking for your forgiveness, if you can give it."

"You have your arms around my Stalker, cousin," Ryder said, coming around the car. "I have plans for him, most of which involve him being in San Diego. With me."

She met my eyes once more, and I shrugged, unsure about practically everything since I'd gotten into my car and left San Diego. Whispering into my ear, she said, "I am very sorry."

"Yeah, okay," I replied softly. "You can't choose your family. I know that."

Alexa gave her cousin a look I couldn't read, then turned on her heel. Hopping into the glider, she gave Ryder either a sidhe salute or a suggestion about what he could do with his donkey. He stood there, nodding as she drove off, the glider kicking up a dirt storm into our faces.

"Let's get out of here." Ryder shut the trunk.

I tossed him half the bottles and replied, "That's the best idea you've probably ever come up with."

CHAPTER FIFTEEN

WE DROVE into Pendle on one of the northern roads, curving up toward the mountain range instead of hugging the coast. Ryder noticed the change in course, grunting from his slouching sulk in the passenger seat. I refused to let him drive, wanting to put as much distance between me and Elfhaine as possible, and he'd taken it as an insult.

There was no use telling him I needed to take some control over what was going on around me, especially since he seemed to be someone who expected others to hand their lives over to him without question.

"Why are we going this way?" He looked behind him, checking on Shannon.

She'd fallen asleep nearly as soon as we entered the forest, her round belly facing us. During the drive, her skirt rode up, and I was sure I saw a hand pressed up against the thin skin stretched over her womb. Ryder told me I was being silly, but he periodically glanced back to see if she was comfortable. I didn't believe him. It made more sense that he was checking on the fetus in case it decided to break from its prison and eat us alive.

"The dragon's body will still be across the middle of the road. It'll take days for scavengers to eat through its meat," I explained. "I won't be able to get Oketsu around that. This way is longer but safer. Last thing I want to do is drive past a lizard buffet."

"You could show some respect for them," he sighed. "Pretend there's some sidhe left inside you."

"I'd have preferred it had died off the road so we got down to San Diego quicker. As it is, we'll be crossing the border around two in the morning. Sparky's going to kill me for waking her up that late."

The paho'eho'e roped close to the road, covering a lane or two in some places. At some point, the military had bulldozed the center divide, opening up the old freeway a bit. Not as traveled as the main road, the northern route was rougher, crinkled in places from seismic activity. Moonlight shone bright, making it easy to spot the rock extrusions ahead of us. They rose from the asphalt, dark-rainbow hematite gargoyles, eyeless sentinels as we passed. I slowed the Mustang down as it banked into a curve. Unable to see around the bend, I didn't want to plow into something unexpected.

"Seems like a good time to talk about Grandmother," Ryder said softly, swiveling around in his seat to face me. Like the freeway, Ryder's words and face held unexpected dangers, and I risked taking my eyes off the road for a brief second, spotting the hardness in his green eyes. "Unless you want to talk about other things, like Alexa."

"Nope," I said. I wanted to drive, letting the Mustang carry me back to my life. I allowed the night to fill me, inhaling the smell of leather and the mountain air as I drove. There was serenity in losing myself in the soft hum of the road under the car's tires, and Ryder's incessant poking at sore spots wasn't what I had in mind for entertainment on a long drive. "*Siao liao*. Leave off, lordship."

"You can't keep avoiding me, Kai."

"No, really. I think I can." Shrugging him off got me a filthy green-eyed look. "Watch. San Diego's a big city. I can avoid you if I try hard enough."

"We live in the same city," he said pointedly. "And you're…."

"Sidhe?" I shook my head, watching for the freeway's crackled painted lines ahead of us. "Look, you want to talk about something, let's talk about that. The sooner you get it into your thick head that I'm not going to fall into step with the great sidhe empire you're building, the better off you'll be. I'll stay dockside with my cat, go out and eat noodles or a bean burrito. I'll go to strip clubs to watch humans take their clothes off, and sometimes I'm going to hit the red lantern district for a couple of hours of sweat and skin. Once in a while, the Post will drop me a line about a job, or I'll go out and do a bounty on some black dogs."

"That's not a life, Kai," Ryder said with a sigh. "You can do better than that."

"That's my life, Ryder. And that's the life I want to lead. Whatever you're doing or whatever you're thinking, that's on you," I said softly, trying not to wake Shannon up. "I'm not going to wake up one morning and suddenly decide dragons are holy. They're meat. The sidhe are meat, and so are humans. We're born, live dirty, and then die, but when it's all said and done, we're just meat. And I'm going to live my life the way I've always lived it, without the elfin, their politics or mind games. Got it?"

"I'm not trying to forge a traditional Court," Ryder replied, leaning back against his seat. The leather squeaked when he rolled down the window. Resting his arm on the door, he watched the horizon, the shadows on his face diving under his cheekbones. "We're in a different world, and I don't think we can exist without humans. If anything, humans are our only chance at survival."

"Humans don't even help themselves survive." I was being honest, or as honest as I wanted to be. "Do you really think they're going to hold a hand out to the elfin?"

"Who made you bitter? None of us can survive without one another," he said. His face grew distant, recalling a time when only the sidhe existed. "The unsidhe are our enemies, rivals for land and resources, and our Courts were constantly fighting humans when they weren't fighting with each other. Then suddenly we were here and everything changed."

"Yeah, there were humans to fight here," I said bitterly. "Who knew that was all the elfin needed to join the Dusk and Dawn?"

"It's not that simple." Ryder's open window let in the sulfur stink bubbling up from the steam vents along the freeway. "The elfin reacted. They're people too. No matter how long someone lives, they're still going to be… people. There's going to be anger, fear, and even irrational hatred. What we do with those emotions will define us. The Dawn hide in their cities, and the Dusk gather in the shadows until they feel safe. Divided, we are going to die out. We need to change."

"And you're the one leading the charge?"

"I'm going to be, yes." He nodded. "If people will let me."

I wasn't sure if he was naïve or delusional. "In San Diego? At this court you're making?"

"Yes." He laughed, a throaty sound caught in the wind from the open window. "At Southern Rise. We'll do our best."

"You think the elfin, either side, are going to let you tear down eons of stick-up-the-ass politics and war because you think it's time to gather around the fire and tell love stories?"

"No, they don't like it at all. Grandmother included," Ryder replied.

"Nice work-around there." I laughed. "I figured we'd get back to her soon enough."

"She's a problem," he said, smiling. It faded quickly, turning to dust on his lips. "I *am* sorry. I never wanted you to be pulled into this."

"See, the funny thing is, she wouldn't have pulled that kind of shit if I were human." The road shifted, and I banked to the right, avoiding a fissure the size of a rhino. "The sidhe are good at saying we're all equal, but today she just confirmed what I already knew: some are more equal than others."

"I'd like to disagree with you, but I can't." Ryder shrugged helplessly. "She hopes that I'll fail, spectacularly if possible, so she can look to the others and say 'Look what happens when we integrate with the humans.'"

"And you want to succeed because it'll piss her off."

"That's definitely a bonus in the plan," he admitted with a chuckle. "But more because I believe we need to."

"The sidhe can't breed with humans, so that's out," I said. "That would have been your best bet."

"It would have been," Ryder said. "But we're barely successful with each other. The humans have other ways, other things, to offer us. We just need to be able to listen and learn."

"And what are you going to give the humans?"

"Give to them?" He frowned. "What do you mean?"

"You want their help in fitting in? What are you going to give them in exchange?"

"Perhaps magical tutorage," Ryder explained. "Some of them have shown promise in that area, especially healing."

"Healing? Or the kind of shit your grandmother pulled? Because I can tell you, the last thing humans, or anyone really, need is another way to kill one another. That shit hurt."

"No one can dictate how someone uses a power. That's up to the individual. We can guide, but that's all we can do, Kai."

"Well then, your lordship, you might have a problem, because from what I've seen, humans like to see how something will kill before they want to see how it heals."

"Are you including yourself in that 'human' equation?"

"Yeah," I said curtly. "Because I'll be honest with you, if I'd had a way to slice open your grandmother's throat when she caught me in her trap, I would have used it. I don't care that she's the oldest sidhe or the head of your Clan. I would have cut her damned throat."

"If I had my way, Kai," he said before turning to stare out the window, "I would have given you something to use as a knife. It would make all our lives much easier."

A RED gleam amid the brush and the black stone was my first hint that something wasn't right. We were three-quarters into Pendle, our progress stopped by a small herd of antelope rabbits bounding across the road. I let them pass, much to Ryder's disgust. Unlike dragons, the antelope rabbits weren't trying to eat me alive, so I didn't feel like running them over. Since they weren't sacred to Ryder, plowing through them seemed like an okay plan to him. I was driving, so only my opinion counted.

And I thought they were cute. There isn't enough cute in the world. I take it when it's offered to me.

Shannon stirred when we stopped, sitting up and blearily asking if we'd reached San Diego. Her eyes widened when she spotted the antlered bunnies hopping slowly across the asphalt, pointing out the wee babies scrambling after their mothers. Too young to grow a full rack, their furry heads were dotted with tiny nubs, soft with protective velvet.

"Oh, they're cute!" She leaned forward, resting her elbows on the front seats. Her belly pressed between the space, bulging out over the center console I'd installed over the shifter. "I've never seen one. There must be close to a thousand."

"'Lope bunnies own the place, more than the dragons, really," I said, shifting the car into park to wait out the herd's migration. "You can usually see them at night. That's when most of their predators are asleep, and they can get down to new feeding grounds without having to dodge death."

"None of them are black," Ryder observed. "Just spots here and there. I'm surprised they survive out here in the flows."

"They're only passing through. They live down in the grasslands, up mountain, or ocean side. The flows are just a corridor. You can't really see them once they hit the weeds."

The furry migration was coming to an end. Spotting the wide branches of the male 'lopes rising above the hopping wave, I shifted the car back into drive, and the rear guards sat up on their haunches to stare into Oketsu's lights as the last of their charges bounded along, the yellow gleam of their eyes turning lime as they turned their heads. The remaining few lazily made their way across the road, closely followed by the sentries, and I let the brake off, pulling Oketsu forward.

We'd gone about four yards when a hillock of paho'eho'e blinked, tiny red gleams appearing over its ridge. They followed, popping up periodically as the Mustang roared along the road. I flipped off the high beams, dropping the headlights down to pick up the ground ahead of us. I knew those gleams and wasn't too happy to see them bobbing up and down behind us.

113

"We're going to have to see how well you can shoot, lordship," I said, reaching behind Ryder's seat to pull out a shotgun. I bumped into Shannon's belly with my elbow. "You might want to sit back a bit. Maybe even get down."

"What's going on?" Shannon pushed forward, and her jutting belly button brushed my arm.

"*Iesu*! Put that thing away," I muttered, handing Ryder the shotgun. "Right now, I don't know, but sit back, okay?"

"What's the matter?" Ryder took the gun. His fingers traced the pits on the battered metal barrel, touching the wood where my blood stained the stock. He handled it gingerly, as if the shotgun were an intimate part of me. "You sure you want to give this to me?"

"Look, I can't drive and shoot at the same time. Well, I can, but not as good as I'd like, and I don't have time to stop and switch places. All you have to do is aim for a head and hope for the best. Maybe I can lose them." Shannon's head popped up in the rearview mirror, her hair a dark, fuzzy shadow where the hills should be. "Girl, I'm going to tell you once. Stay down. I need to see out the back window."

She disappeared from my mirror with a yelp, curling down out of view. "Sorry."

Ryder frowned at me. "Do not speak to her like that."

"And I'm going to tell you to shut up. This is what I'm being paid for. I don't need any distractions." I curled around a curve, dropping over a hill and gunning the engine. The red lights twinkled and blinked out, reappearing to the right of us. "Shit. That's a whole pack."

"Shit what?" His frown grew. "Pack of what?"

"Don't really have time for this." I snapped the car to the left of the divide, hoping to break free of the crimson-eyed shadows. "Your grandmother got contacts in the Dusk Court? We've got a pack of black dogs on our trail. Big ones."

"Really? You think my grandmother would do this?" He craned his neck around and reached out to pat Shannon's shoulder. "Don't worry. Kai's just trying to be careful."

"No, Kai's trying to make sure we don't get eaten alive," I corrected.

"You can't outrun them?" Ryder asked, gripping the shotgun tighter. "This thing outran a dragon! It can't lose some *ainmhí dubh*?"

"Funny." I ground my teeth. Shifting in my seat, I glanced at the side mirror, keeping one eye on the road. The pack was moving closer, easily eating up the distance between them and the Mustang. Unhindered by the jagged lava hillocks, they cut over the curves in the winding road with an alarming speed. "Damned sons of bitches are fast."

One of the lead hounds leaped over a bend, landing on a section of road below us. It was waiting for us when we made the turn, body bunched in and head down. Oketsu rocked and bucked when the bumper hit the black dog rushing the Mustang's front end.

Blood sprayed over the windshield, blinding me, and I stupidly ducked, dropping my head below the dashboard before I realized the dog's body had gone up and over the roof. It bounced, hitting the asphalt, and began a long roll. I didn't stop to check on its well-being. Gunning the engine, I threw Oketsu into passing and drove the speed up. The suspension's dampeners kicked in, dropping the car lower to cut down on drag, and we ate away the road.

But not before the rearview mirror showed me the black dog wobbling to its feet and shaking itself off.

"It's only a couple of miles out of the lava from here. We'll hit the old freeway and lose them there. Shit." I glanced over to Ryder. A click of the wipers and a jet spray and the windshield was clean enough to see out of again. "Didn't even slow that thing down."

"Tell me the shotgun will help with that." He didn't sound convinced. With the Mustang hitting more than a hundred on the long stretches, I didn't have time to argue the finer points of weapon use.

"Can I ask something?" Shannon raised her hand, blocking my view again.

"No! Put your hand down!" I snapped. "I can't see a damned thing behind me."

"Sure," Ryder said, nudging my side. "Kai…."

"We're going to be chewed…." I took a breath, putting a wide smile on my face. "Sure, honey. What's up?"

"Stop that," he said crossly. "You look insane smiling like that."

"What's insane is that I'm having this conversation at—" I checked the speedometer. "—a hundred miles an hour with a pregnant woman while some stupid sidhe lord is aiming my shotgun at me. Point it down, you idiot!"

"Sorry," Ryder apologized, making a small attempt to look sheepish. "I forgot."

"Just remember, shoot me and you…." I didn't have time to finish my thought.

A mound of fur appeared on the Mustang's passenger side. Ryder yelped in surprise, and the shotgun went off, kicking the muzzle up into the roof seal. I swerved, trying to keep some distance between the car and the black dog pacing us. Gunpowder speckled my face, burning me in a dusty spray. The smell of cooked iron lingered, seeping into my hair and skin. Too close to the shot, the ringing in my ears pitched high, replacing the rumble of Oketsu's engine. It faded, leaving me with an ache in my teeth and the taste of shot in my mouth.

Another joined the first, and Shannon yelled over the roar of the engine, "I was going to say there's another one next to us."

"Gee, thanks." I gave Ryder a dirty look, working a finger into my left ear to pop it. "Maybe I've got the wrong person up here in front."

"How about if you keep the car steady so I get a good shot?" He rested the muzzle against the quarter window frame, beading in on the dog trailing the Mustang's back tire. "Steady."

I could imagine what he saw, staring down the barrel of a worn shotgun at the monsters drawn up from the shadows. With the windows wide open, the black dogs' odor made my nose itch, and I blinked, clearing the first dewdrops of water moistening my eyes. These dogs were huge, dwarfing the Mustang's rear. Their shoulders rose and fell out of view as they ran along beside the car. Every so often, a thread of acidic spit flung up, laying into the car to leave a smoking trail on the red paint.

"Oh, God," Shannon exclaimed loudly. Her hand pressed against the small side window, nearly popping the pane out of its channel.

"What? You see another one?" I craned my head around, narrowly avoiding a boulder in the road. The Mustang complained as I jerked the wheel, skidding on its wide tires and slamming into one of the dogs. It growled, gnashing its teeth. Rearing up, it lunged as I fought to straighten the car before we slid off the road. The ropy flow looked serene, but it would chew up the Mustang's tires before we went six inches across the black rock.

The car shimmied, shuddering as I fought to keep it on the road. When the black dog bit into its fender, the metal screamed as it ripped, shreds of red-glossed steel flying into the back window. I cringed at the sound of shrapnel hitting glass. Praying the Kevlar film would keep the back shield intact, I gasped when a slush of warm fluid hit me from behind.

"What the hell is that? Was Shannon hit?" I couldn't risk turning around to look. "Ryder, what's going on?"

The road went feral, fissures and creases folding the asphalt winding through the lava field. A few hundred yards away, the rock fell off and was replaced by grasslands and a road unbuckled by shifting ground. If anything, the prairie land would be easier for the dogs to run on.

Dropping the shotgun to the floor, Ryder reached behind the seat, doing something with Shannon. Liquid sloshed over the seat, and my stomach sank, waiting for the sidhe to tell me the bad news. I barely felt the black dog hit Oketsu's side with its shoulder, numbly swerving to avoid a second hit as the sound of Shannon's tortured breathing drifted to the front seat.

"I'm okay," I heard her say, shooing Ryder away with a slap of her hands. "We just have a small problem."

"What kind of problem?" I practically shouted into Ryder's ear, catching his hair on my lips. He smelled and tasted of gunpowder, an earthy taint to the sidhe tea scent of his body. I pulled away, removing him from my mouth so I could think. His body blocked my view, his once-crisp button-down shirt damp and sticking to his arm. "Ryder, what kind of problem?"

"We need to find someplace safe," he said with a worried look on his face. "We need to stop the car."

"Stop?" I veered, hitting the smoothness of untouched freeway. A few yards off the car's front end, the lead black dog faltered, his claws scrambling to find purchase on the smoother road. I pushed the Mustang as hard as I could, burying the gas pedal in the floorboard. The dogs faded into the distance, and I breathed a sigh of relief. "Are you insane? I just lost them. If we stop, they're going to find us."

"We don't have any choice," Ryder replied grimly as he sat down. "We're going to need to stop."

"For what?" I looked behind me, fixating on Shannon's flushed face and her half-open mouth. "Are you okay? Are you hit?"

"I'm fine." Her grunts concerned me, but nothing like what she said next. "It's just…." Another round of pants broke up her words, and she let go of a small, low keen that hurt my ears. "My water broke. The baby's coming. Right. Now."

"What?" I choked. "No, do something. Hold your legs together. We've… there's duct tape in the damned glove compartment. Shit, I *told* you something like this was going to happen. That baby *cannot* come right now."

"Just find us someplace. We can play *I told you* so later," Ryder said. "Because *ainmhí dubh* or no, the baby's coming."

117

CHAPTER SIXTEEN

RYDER SLID into the backseat to sit with Shannon, keeping an eye out for the dogs we'd lost when the road turned smooth, and I was able keep the Mustang at an open throttle. When a concrete centerline bisected the road, I steered to the right of the divide, praying for an off-ramp that was too stubborn to fall during the Merge. The Mustang ate away the miles, distancing us from the pack, but I wasn't reassured they couldn't find us again if we stopped.

I was concentrating on my driving when Ryder gave me a jolt, leaning over the front seat and nearly touching his lips to my ear. "She's got to let it go, Kai. She can't stop pushing."

"Sure, go ahead, push," I muttered. "There's already gunk all over my carpet and backseat. The side of my car is chewed up, and my back window is barely holding on. Why not push?"

"I'll pay you for that," he said. "The damage. Not the whining. Are Stalkers supposed to whine?"

"I'm one of the newer types. In touch with my inner child. We'll be slowing down a bit. Stuff up here changes a lot, and I've got to watch out." Spotting a swirl of cement pinned in place off the freeway, I moved the Mustang over, slowing it down in case there was a gap in the framework that I didn't spot. "Sit back. I'll need the mirror clear if I have to back up. The dogs can't cut across the fields like they can the lava. We've got some time on them."

Pendle stretched out for miles in all directions, covering the distance between the mountain range down to the ocean bluffs. At one point, a military base had squatted in the center of the region, with a sprawl of suburbs surrounding it. Although crushed under tons of liquid rock and shifting hills, the bones of the base lingered. Once in a while, an empty shell of a building rose as a ghost along the bones of a road, but nothing that would provide any kind of shelter. Hardly anything of the nearby houses and businesses remained, but toward the south end were structures defensible enough to squat in.

It was hard going. Between avoiding fallen chunks of stone and ground slides, my nerves tightened each time I heard Shannon ramp up. She'd fallen into a panting crescendo, ending each rise with a long hissing breath. We'd gone only two miles inland before a scream made me slam on the brakes and skid the Mustang to a stop.

"No, it's okay." Ryder put his hand up when I reached for the shotgun, jacked it open, and slid in two new shells before she finished her wail.

"I'm fine," she panted, hissing and grunting. "Screaming helps."

"*Iesu*, you're scaring the shit out of me." I righted the car, smelling the burn of brakes and rubber as I pulled away. "No problem. Ignore the screaming woman, Kai. Totally normal."

The inland freeway dead-ended, but other routes cut out from it, and the area held the promise of some shelter as we passed a smattering of oddly shaped buildings. A miniature windmill's broken sails turned slowly in the wind, and a sign promised the world's best pea soup in simple script, a remnant of a pre-Merge diner. Farther down, a fallen billboard announced the presence of a military surplus a few miles away.

"There we go," I said to myself, drowned out by another tight squeal from the backseat. "Let's see if there's any place left to hide in there."

The surplus store was a bust. Nothing but a cinder block wall standing amid brush and debris, tall grasses poked up from gutter openings and cracked sidewalks, some clumps almost as high as the Mustang's roof. A swath near a burned-out car shell lay flat in a nearly perfect circle, a telltale sign that something slept there, a wild and big enough something that it didn't care about predators.

A few side streets looked somewhat intact after the Merge's seismic activity, although there were more signs of cattle or antelopes about. A swift, dirty stream ran behind a row of shattered storage units, and the culvert was thick with leaves and branches, the damp ground on its banks riddled with hoofprints.

"What are you looking for?" Ryder asked in between Shannon's panting.

"Someplace with a roof. Doors would be good too. No one lives here— it's too far out, and the land's unstable—but scavengers have ripped up the area." A faded yellow plastic arrow, dislodged from a fast food chain sign, lay against the curb of the weed-infested street, its point aimed up at the gathering clouds. A dot of rain hit the windshield, rolling down the glass and sticking to a wiper. I peeked up and groaned. There were significantly fewer stars than when I'd first headed inland. "Great, now we've got rain."

"Maybe it'll pass," Ryder grunted over his shoulder. "If it rains, maybe the dogs will have a harder time finding us."

"That's a myth," I told him. Descended from Wild Hunts, black dogs fixed on a person's essence, making it nearly impossible to shake them off. Crossing running water was supposed to break their tracking, but it was a lie. If anything, traipsing through a stream merely slowed the hunted down so the dogs could catch up to their next meal. "It only works if the packs tracking you are actually dogs and not nightmares. If we stop for too long, they'll find us."

"Oh Gaaaaaawd," Shannon squealed, raking her fingers across the headliner, leaving deep grooves in the leather and ripping a section off at the seams.

Ryder visibly winced, mouthing an apology at me before he turned to help her.

"This one's not waiting."

"She knows a lot about having kids," I said to Ryder under my breath. He avoided my gaze, turning his head and scanning the side streets to look for anything promising. "Especially for someone being scared about what her parents would think."

"Not the time for that, Kai. Hold on. Back up," he ordered, angling between the seats to get a better look. "Go down that alley. Over there!"

Salvation came in the form of a decrepit Quonset, its battered round sides run orange with dried rust. Its galvanized iron walls would keep the black dogs out, and a thick coating of silicon paint covered most of the half-pipe hut, a half-made promise to keep the rain out if it poured, but it was something and a damned sight better than anything else we'd seen.

Oketsu's headlights grabbed at the lines of a rolling gate on the north side of the cylindrical structure. Leaving the engine idling, I got out and grabbed at the handle, praying the tracks weren't rusted closed. They gave slightly, then stopped. Ryder approached, holding the other of my shotguns, thankfully pointed down.

"Chained shut," he said, pointing to a loop of chain locking the door down. "I thought perhaps you would want to shoot it off."

"Yeah, thanks." I was careful in aiming. The rusted chain shattered under a single hit, and a piece flew, stinging my cheek.

"Here. Stop moving," Ryder said, holding my face to inspect the wound. "You're bleeding."

"You kiss it to make it better and I'll pop you one in the nose," I warned. "Just saying."

Cupping my chin, he stared at me. I'd known him for only a few days, and I could already see his mind working at the risks and advantages. Baring my teeth, I showed my canines, white, sharp, and ready to bite in case he decided my word wasn't good enough. Chuckling, Ryder wiped the spot, smearing my blood on his thumb, then sucked it clean, whistling as he headed back to the car.

"Asshole." The door rattled as I pulled it up, kinking on slightly warped tracks, but it held, rising high enough to drive the Mustang in.

"Want me to pull the car through?"

"Hold up. Let me check inside first." I waved him off, reloading the shotgun before I stepped in. "Toss me a torch from the middle console. I'll need some more light."

The place had been used for gardening storage or maintenance of some kind. Shipping pallets were stacked with large dust-covered bags near the other end, but the rest of the half-pipe hut was empty except for scraps of age-worn plastic sheeting. Windowless, the only other opening appeared to be a metal door on the far wall, but I spotted a cutout hatch in the ceiling and a steel-rung ladder anchored to the floor and wall beneath it. In the dry, high desert air, the Quonset's insides were free of rust, with only a few coppery spots at the upper tracks of the rolling door. A squeak echoed near the stacked bags, and then a kangaroo rat shot out, scrambling to get out of the car's headlight beams.

It was dank and musty, with a fragrance hinting of mold and rodent dung, but it was clear of anything ferocious. My light beam hit a stack of yellow paper bags, and I grinned. Someone had left stacks of deicing rock salt behind, and it seemed like there was more than enough of it to go around Oketsu.

I stepped aside to let Ryder bring the Mustang inside and rolled the door down. Playing the penlight over the car, I winced at the damage. Peeled steel and punctured fenders were a small price to pay for Shannon's safety, but it still hurt, especially the spider nicks in the back window. I could machine the steel, but the glass would be a bitch to replace.

Ryder stepped out of the car, leaving the door open. I could still hear Shannon's hissing breaths, but they were shorter now, more relaxed. "We'll need some light."

"Know any more useful spells? Like instant candle, just add air?" I asked, then took the keys and popped the trunk open. Switching the engine over was problematic if we were going to need speed, but the motor's battery could only power the lights for so long without running down. It was a case of damned once or twice.

"No, sorry." He peered into the trunk. "Tell me you have supplies back here besides water and jerky."

"Yeah, hold on. Let me lock down the fuel lines so I don't set us on fire. I'll turn on the electric so we can power up some lanterns." I'd mounted the flat engine up against the backseat after welding a piece of plexi-metal in to support it. The blue fuel cells hummed to life, brightening the headlights. With the reactants online, the engine could run for years without being maintained, especially since we weren't currently dodging unsidhe hounds.

Over the years, I'd learned what was useful for a run, stashing things away in the Mustang's trunk in case of emergencies. Slender vacuum-pack water bottles took up the space near the lock, but I stored other things in removable box crates. I popped a crate open, then grabbed an expanding lantern, its side folded down flat. I snapped it open, its slender, flexible LEC panels accordioning to lock into place along the wire frame. I plugged in the leader line connections, powering up one of the lanterns, then handed the rest to Ryder.

"Here. There's six more. If you can do the rest." I dragged out more lines and handed the ends to Ryder. "Watch your feet, though. They'll disconnect if you trip over the line. I'll grab the first aid kit. She might need something from it."

"You okay?" He nudged my side. "You look pale, maybe even a little sick."

"Yeah." Nodding, I dug around in the crates, wondering where I'd put the antibiotic packs I'd gotten from Dalia. "Woman things. I'm not very good with them."

"Well, if you've got anything hard to drink in that tesseract you call a trunk, bring it with you. I think she'd appreciate it afterwards."

"I might," I scoffed. "And screw her, I'll need it more."

Ryder's eyebrow jumped. "Your compassion warms my heart."

"Yeah, whatever. There's some rock salt stored back there." I jerked my chin toward the back. "If it's not packed solid from its own weight, we can use it to make a circle around the car. It'll at least keep the dogs out of here if they catch up to us while… well, you know."

"Now that I can help you with." He grinned at me and winked.

By the time I'd unearthed the antibiotics, Ryder had the lanterns up and two of the bags cut open. Lifting one, he tilted the bag, steadily pouring a stream of salt into a thick line. It took five bags to complete an uneven circle around the Mustang, and when we were done, I dusted off the fine, salty white powder clinging to me.

"I feel like a pretzel." I spit out a chunk of salt caught on my lip. "Taste like one too. All I need is some mustard."

"I think you taste more like a strong brewed chai." Ryder grinned at me, wiping a wet cloth over his face. "Can you activate it, or do you want me to?"

"Yeah, activating it? I don't know how." I rubbed at the back of my neck. "No one I know can fire up a salt circle. We just lay it down and pray it slows the bastards down."

"Do you have a knife in the car?" Ryder asked. "I can show you how to do it."

"Yeah? There's a couple of Ka-Bars and a Sheffield Bowie under the seat. Which one do you want?"

"I just need something sharp." He eyed the black blade I unsheathed and handed to him. "Thanks."

"What?"

"You should have taken one of these with you into Elfhaine. Grandmother would have been less inclined to mess with you."

"Alexa said no weapons. And I didn't think I was going to be asked in for tea and get my ass bitten," I said. "Even where I'm from, that's bad manners."

"It's bad manners where I'm from too," Ryder grunted as he laid the blade on his palm. "Damn, that's sharp. I didn't even feel the cut until it was through the skin."

"Yeah, I sometimes skin black dogs with those. I like them sharp."

"Thank you. I'm glad I rate the same knife as an *ainmhí dubh*." Holding his hand flat, Ryder let his blood pool in his palm.

"Everyone rates the same knife. I like them." I watched intently as he dribbled blood on four equidistant points on the salt, then crossed over to the diagonal spots, spacing out the pours.

"Stay inside the salt circle," he warned me. "Remember how you reacted to a spell when you were touching metal? I don't want the same thing to happen to you again."

I nodded, moving closer to the center. "So you think you can teach me this?"

"You can have dinner with me in exchange," Ryder suggested, looking up at me suddenly. "A date kind of dinner."

"I don't... date," I said, shaking my head. "Dating... complicates things."

"Maybe I just want to talk to you about joining my Court?"

"Yeah, sure," I grunted, crossing my arms over my chest. "If that's all you want to talk about, dinner's great. And I can tell you ahead of time that the answer's no, but hell, I'll get a free dinner and a way to keep black dogs out of an area."

"Do you like seafood?" He handed me the knife, sucking on the wound. The edges were already folding in, healing faster than I could. "I found a great crab place near Southside."

"Yeah, crab works. Steak too. Answer's still no to the court thing." I slid the knife back into its sheath, hooking it around a belt loop on my jeans. "Do you need anything else besides blood and salt?"

"No, the spell is simple, only a few sidhe words of protection," he said. "You might need help with pronunciation, but I can work on it with you."

"Funny thing, that," I said, leaning against the car's side. "Last person to teach me a language insisted her tongue needed to be in my mouth to make sure I was saying things right."

"I hadn't thought of it that way. Good idea." Ryder was bold and persistent. "I definitely could see the advantage in that."

I couldn't tell if he was teasing or serious. I went with serious. "You are not chasing words into my mouth with your tongue."

He stood over one of the bloody spots, placing a foot on either side of the salt. "It was worth a try."

"Shit." I drew the word out with a hiss, peeking in on Shannon. She gave me a smile and sipped at a water bottle. "You doing okay in there?"

"Yes," she said, pushing her hair out of her face. The strain on her body pinked her face, her cheekbones nearly as red as a coxcomb. "It's resting right now. I'm sure as soon as I fall asleep, it'll wake me up again."

"You don't even know what it is?" Most humans knew what they were going to have months before the kid actually made an appearance.

"No, it's better this way. It's good to wait," Shannon replied. "Besides, it's a sidhe tradition not to know. Ciarla wanted it that way."

"Huh." I kept my thoughts to myself, but I was certain Ryder caught the sound. Human or elfin, it was impossible for the three races to interbreed with one another, and Shannon looked too human to be like the kids at the Diamond Kitty, so it didn't make sense for her to follow a sidhe tradition.

"She and my sister are close friends, remember? Shannon follows a lot of sidhe paths."

Ryder lied worse than one of Jonas's toddlers. His eyes shifted back and forth, and the edges of his mouth tightened. I snorted, and he shot me a hard look.

Pointing down at the salt line, he asked, "Do you want to learn this?"

"Yeah. I'll record it on my link and see if I can memorize it."

"I can check your pronunciation later if you'd like, without the tongue of course."

"During that dinner, I suppose."

He grinned. "At least you're not threatening to shoot me anymore."

"Night's not over yet," I reminded him. "And I've got full loads of ammo."

"You're feral, but at least you come prepared." Ryder crouched over the blooded salt, placing his left hand flat on the line. "Ready?"

"Yeah." I clicked on my wrist link and moved behind him, adjusting the wide leather band until I had the piece angled toward Ryder. "Go ahead."

He opened his mouth, and my world fell away into black, the darkness choking my throat with strong, vicious fingers.

His voice hit me, slapping hard across my mind. My stomach clutched tight at the husky sidhe rasp he growled into the salt. I doubled over. My nerves cut free and dropped me to the ground. Each syllable drove me down, beating me with sharp hooks into my spine and guts. A searing ache spread across my shoulder blades, the skin slowly tearing as Ryder continued his mutterings.

I tried to push myself up, rocking on my knuckles, but the spell slithered around me, wrapping me tighter, and I could feel my skin throbbing with every heartbeat. Slow trickles of blood ran down my arms, parting at my elbows and flowing around my wrists. It pooled under my palms, and my shirt gave up trying to soak in the wetness coming from the split skin on my back. A pulse built, slow at first, then hardening to a steady throb along the keloids stretching over my shoulders, and my skin gave, parting down my spine. Sobs choked me, tears watering the red down to a liquid pink.

Shuddering, I rolled, fighting to take a breath. Razors filled my lungs, the air turning to ice as I sucked in deep. A few more words and I was done in, letting the darkness take me.

And still, I wasn't safe.

CHAPTER SEVENTEEN

STEWING IN the black, I cowered from long feline faces howling and laughing at my pain. Their voices echoed, becoming snatches of conversation filled with ugly words followed by even uglier fists. There wasn't an inch of my body left untouched—unbruised. I shivered, unable to move more than a few centimeters. My arms were useless, bound by something I couldn't see, but it didn't matter. The shackles were mostly for show. I wasn't going anywhere. There was nowhere *to* go.

Hands were on me, then inside me, lifting up the skin along my thighs, ass, and back. My voice was shot. There wasn't anything left in me to scream, and as for begging, I'd given that up a long time ago. I tried to blink, but the light poured into my eyes, burning away all my tears.

"Kai!"

The word sounded different, incomplete. I listened to it ripple out along my mind and found the sound empty and edgeless. Hearing it should cut, gutting me and letting my insides spill onto the floor. I listened for it again, fascinated by the change. It echoed again, reverberating in my ears.

Singlish.

I knew Singlish—pure, ugly, and simple. Its rough fatness suddenly left me weak with relief. The stop and start of sounds were crude compared to sidhe, but to my ears, it was a balm on swelling blisters. The world grew fuzzy, dotted with tiny uneven stabs of light that I guessed were the lanterns. Sparkling, the dots moved, attached to the flick of my lashes. More noises, words fading in and out, then I surfaced, understanding the language and hearing the panic around me.

"Goddess, Kai. Listen to me. Can you try to drink some water?" There was more, but I lost it in the echo. What I heard were different words, softer and inconsistent with the bleeding of me. I almost didn't want to answer, wondering where the tones would go, but the light tugged me back.

"Do we leave him? What about the babies?" A woman's voice joined in, a sharper keen pouring over me, velvet soft but with a firm push. She whispered, "How are we going to get out of here if he's sick? Can you drive the car?"

127

"Shannon, go back to the car," he insisted. "Let me take care of this. You need to rest while you can."

Ryder, my brain whispered. *Iesu*, *Buddha*, and *Gilgamesh*, he was a pain in the ass, or trying to be. He teased and mocked, lecturing me about dragons and sidhe. I knew Ryder. Shannon was easier to remember. Her body was going to explode, gurgitations of babies, blood, and water. My arm still needed washing where her belly button had touched me.

I risked opening my eyes wider, falling out of the familiar knifing darkness, and the light shifted, turning into dancing balls. The spheres were pretty, like cooked fish eyeballs bobbing around in a soup. I tried reaching for one, but my shoulder didn't want to work my arm, locking and clicking as I struggled.

"Don't move." The golden slither of Ryder's voice clung to me, holding me up from the shadows. "I'm going to cut your shirt off."

I mumbled something, but the cool metal sang so close to my flesh that I kept my mouth shut. Speaking would make jagged edges to his cutting, and it would be harder for Ryder to steal my skin from me. For some reason, this made me sad inside, and I stilled, wanting Ryder to have a whole skin when he pulled it free from my flesh. Some part of me mourned the silly thoughts I'd had about dinners and teasing. It was all the same. Everyone was all the same, and I numbed my brain, waiting for the anguished rush to hit me when Ryder made his first cut.

That was another time, my brain reminded me. *Now is different. Ryder is not doing those things to you. He is not one of those faces in the dark.*

"You're cold." He rubbed at my immovable arms. The touch stung, my nerves too ripe with sensation to stand his skin on mine. I felt a dribble of water on my mouth, and I gulped, trying to catch each drop. "Kai, swallow."

"Is he breathing?" She sounded distant. "It doesn't look like he's breathing."

"Bruugggh." There wasn't any hope that I'd sound coherent, but any noise coming out of me would at least assure Shannon that I was pulling in air. "Daaaaamn."

"See, he's breathing. You can tell. He's complaining," I heard Ryder say as he pulled my shirt apart. It stuck, then gave way, the drying blood stubbornly holding the fabric to my skin. His gasp sucked in so much air I wondered dimly how he held it all. "Morrígan help us. What have they done to you?"

What have they done to me? For a sidhe Lord establishing his own Court, that would be a good question to ask. For me, it was more of a *why*?

128

Why seemed much more important than *what*. *What* was the easiest thing to figure out. It only took one look at my back to see the answer to *what*.

The scars across my shoulder blades shocked them. They shocked most people, and I heard both Ryder and Shannon gasp. Awash in blood, my back would be horrific, carved out and lifted keloids shaping the skin into sweeping wings. It was the only thing my father ever gave me. His symbol. His black dragon wings carved out and scarred into my back.

"God, I'm going to be sick," Shannon murmured. "Why would he put bat wings on his back?"

"Not bat wings," Ryder whispered. Even with my ears ringing, I could hear the horror in his voice. "Those are black pearl dragon wings."

The wings were spread open, undulations along the scars more from the jagged rips of tearing skin than delicate knife work. Ridged rebar was used to form the metacarpus, the iron corroding and burning through. The curved rebar created phalanges, sweeping out from the main line. When I outgrew one length, the end of the scar was cut open and the bar removed. Then a longer, thicker bar was worked into the rusty scar sleeve to continue the process.

To form the flat of my wings, thin metal lifted and cut under my skin, spreading the hypertrophic slender scars. The wings' membranes were partially tattered and worn, edges curling in places, and other raised areas were formed by a burning stick passed back and forth over the wingspan. Varying ridges from the rebar loosely resembled the diamond pattern of a reptilian skin, but it'd been close enough to bring murmurs of pleasure. I'd lived for those purring dark signs of approval. Even in the deepest pain, the sound soothed me, a crumb tossed to my starving soul.

That was the *what* Ryder saw. He was wrong about the what, and the *why* was still a mystery to me.

"That's why you don't know anything about the Dawn Court. You're unsidhe. You're even wearing a Dusk Court's symbol on your back," Ryder murmured. "Why didn't you tell me?"

I hated the sound of betrayal in Ryder's voice. It should have soothed me, an assurance he wouldn't chase after my tail anymore, but something inside me broke. Ryder's assumption was natural. Why would I be wearing pearl dragon wings if I weren't unsidhe? *Because*, I wanted to scream at him, *the unsidhe mark everything, especially the things they own.*

"Doesn't matter." Mumbling, I tried to push him away, but Ryder was immovable.

"It does matter," he replied, wiping my face with a wet cloth. "I would have told Grandmother no. She must have known. That's why she insisted on meeting you. Kai, you're a fool for not telling me!"

"What does it change?" I felt stronger, but my insides were churning. "Other than I shouldn't have been inside that damned circle."

"I wouldn't have done the spell if you'd told me," Ryder growled. "I could have killed you."

"Wouldn't be the first time someone's tried. Get back. Going to be sick now." I heaved, folding in half. A gush of water tasting like rotten algae spilled out, but thankfully nothing else. Through the muddled recesses of my mind, I counted back to when I'd eaten last, only remembering some jerky before being dragged into Elfhaine. "Pele, I hate this."

"Don't move," Ryder ordered. He wet my back, and I caught a whiff of the antibiotic liquid from the first aid kit. He patted my skin dry with a towel, careful not to drag the scratchy pile over my wounds. "You should be healing faster. It must be something from the circle. I'm going to take you outside the salt ring."

"No." I swallowed my weakness, pulling back the rubbery feeling in my stomach. "I've got iron dust… under my skin. Can't get it out. Healing… takes longer for me."

"Iron dust? Are you suicidal?" He lifted me up, ignoring my growling protests and my hand pushing on his chest. "Stop fighting me."

"I didn't put it there. And leave off," I snarled, pushing to get to my feet. My throat hurt, and my voice sounded broken. Coughing, I spit up a wad of saliva mingled with bright blood. I'd not been this dizzy since lying at the Sebac's feet. The spell Ryder had used to activate his warding circle had taken me down hard, and my knees felt tenderized.

"Then who did? Who did this?" He didn't reach for me, letting me stand, however shakily, against the Mustang. Shannon hovered nearby, a hand on her belly. "Talk to me, Kai. Why would you have this on you?"

"Not important." I shook my head and set the resting woodpeckers off to resume their hammering. The rawness in my throat was easing, and the aches in my muscles were fading. I straightened my back and nodded at our passenger. "Don't worry about me. I'm okay. I need to walk this off. Besides, Shannon's gray. Really gray."

She'd gone pale, clutching at her stomach. Her mouth moved, breathless low-pitched gasps edging on a scream. Ryder got to her before I could take a step, catching her before she fell. Panting, the hissing began anew. Grabbing his shoulder for support, she waddled over to the car, sweeping her feet from side to side.

"Oh, it's time," Shannon said with a grimace. The expression on her face wasn't one of joy, more resignation than anything else, and she struggled to stay upright, her knees buckling with every step.

"Kai, are you going to be okay?" he said, easing Shannon into the passenger seat and giving me a worried look. "She's going back into labor."

"I'm fine." I waved off his concern. The truth was I wanted to crawl into Oketsu and drive off. It might not have been very hero-like, but it was what I wanted to do. Sucking it up was what would really happen. Besides, if the binding circle hurt me by being activated, I didn't want to imagine how I'd feel crossing over the salt ring. "Probably should give you back your money. Bad Stalker."

"No, and don't argue. We've got other things to worry about." He jerked his head for me to come closer. "Come over here. I need to keep an eye on both of you."

"Nuh-uh," I said. I tested my legs, carefully balancing on my feet. My equilibrium was almost back to normal, and the pounding of my heart was slowing. "Not watching that."

I wasn't a coward, but I'd heard from some of my male friends about how women went crazy while giving birth. Before he shaved his head down, the back of Jonas's head was missing a patch of hair after his last kid. His third wife, Najiri, grabbed his head and held on while she pushed and screamed. When the boy finally dropped, Jonas was scalped on one side, and Najiri swore he'd never touch her again. I'd suggested naming the kid Razor, but the wives overruled me.

Unfortunately, the name stuck, and in about twenty years, I was probably going to spend my time looking over my shoulder for Razor Wyatt when he came to kill me.

"This is a two-person job. I'm going to need help if you can give it." I could barely hear Ryder above Shannon's shrieking pants. "Grab one of your knives. Not the one I used."

"Not stupid." Muttering didn't help. He'd gone back to squatting between her knees. "You're just saying that to keep me close."

131

"Maybe," he admitted. "But right now, I'm worried more about you falling over than I am about Shannon giving birth, so get over here if you can."

Fetching a different Bowie, I then limped around the car, avoiding stepping on the salty ring. The line was black around the edges, leaving a thin white streak running down the middle, a skunk ouroboros meandering around to bite itself in the tail. I tried handing Ryder the knife, but he refused to take it.

"You're going to have to do the cutting," he said. "I'll have to hold the baby so you can cut it loose. Grab the knife, Kai. You're going to be an uncle."

BABY MAKING was fun. I liked it and was thankfully reassured that by having human partners, I'd never have to go through what Jonas did on a regular basis. I didn't even want to think about what Shannon was going through.

Baby birthing, however, seemed to take longer than any single sex session I'd had. And from what I'd heard from Shannon's profane mouth, it didn't seem worth it.

By the end of the hour, I'd gotten all the feeling back in my fingers in the hand she squeezed to juice, and my initial dizziness had subsided, leaving a small ringing sound behind I could faintly hear through the hissing and panting. I muttered some encouragement to Shannon, who huffed back at me with pressed lips.

Ryder helped Shannon get comfortable while I studiously ignored the squishy and grunting noises coming from my car. Turning around, I recoiled at Shannon's very naked lower half facing me, her heels hooked into the doorsill and her knees spread apart. Some things a man just wasn't meant to see. I patted my car and wished him luck in surviving what was going on in his seat.

"God, hurry up. Please." She was sweating hard, her belly skintight. At some point, she'd unlaced the front of her peasant dress and reptilian scars mottled her stomach. Vivid purple on her pale skin, they looked painful to the touch. I would have asked if they were sore, but she didn't seem to be in a talking mood. "Oh God, this hurts."

"Don't faint, Kai," Ryder teased.

"Shut up or I won't share the single-shot whiskey packets I found in the trunk."

"*Chi wo de shi.* Save the whiskey," she snarled at me. Grabbing at my shirt, she screamed, letting pour a wave of curses that would have made Dempsey proud. I tried to imagine my own mother working through my birth, but I failed. "I want some after this."

"Shit." I'd faced down a pack of black dogs, but the mellow woman we'd carried down from Elfhaine was gone. In her place was a frizzy-haired demon I wasn't sure I wanted to come near. "I'm not going close to that. You're on your own."

"Oh no," Ryder said, pulling me toward the car. "We are doing this together. I'm catching. You're tying off. She's doing all the hard work."

Everything became a blur at that point. A bit of screaming, and then a gush of bloody water poured from between Shannon's spread legs. The fluids spilled without warning, splashing over the metal doorsill and washing onto the hut's rough floor. I winced, trying not to pay much notice to the wet soaking into the Mustang's black carpet, reminding myself that my blood, sick, and sweat was all over the car's interior and some of its exterior. Birth debris couldn't be much worse.

How little I knew.

"Baby's coming now," Ryder crooned, rubbing at Shannon's tight belly with his free hand. "Kai, be ready. We're going to have to do this quickly."

"Knife at the ready, your lordship," I said, displaying the Sheffield.

There was a final scream, lingering and sharp, and a pop, leaving me speechless as I stared at what Ryder cradled in his hands.

CHAPTER EIGHTEEN

"THAT'S AN egg," I said.

"Get the knife, Kai," Ryder ordered. "I'll hold it. You'll need to cut through the shell."

"Are you fucking nuts?" I stared down at the watermelon-sized egg, slightly mesmerized by the soft ivory shell. It undulated in Ryder's grasp, slithering wet in his fingers. "Suppose I cut through it? And what the hell is she doing giving birth to... this? Humans don't give birth to eggs! Elfin! They give birth to eggs. What the hell?"

"Cut the shell." He gritted his teeth, growling at me. "There's another one coming."

"Sure. Great. Two." Swallowing, I took a deep breath and carefully placed the knife on the ovum. The metal tip slipped over the rubbery surface as the moist egg dipped and moved under the light pressure. Tightening my grip on the knife, I concentrated on sliding the hook end into the sac. It finally sliced through, splitting apart unevenly under the torrent of sticky white that gushed out.

The inside of the eggshell pulsed with tiny blood vessels, and a long cord connected the petite pale baby to one of the large pieces. Tying a piece of twine around the blood-rich stem, I looped the cord over and tied it off again, hoping the technique would hold up as well as it did for making sausage. Taking the sharp knife, I sliced the cord off the shell just as Shannon's screaming hisses began anew.

"Take the baby." Ryder handed it to me and turned around to press his shoulder against Shannon's knees to prevent her from locking them. "Make sure its mouth is clear. Try to get it crying so we know its lungs are clear."

"How?" I was now certain I'd not be giving back one single cent of my fee.

"Stick your finger in the baby's mouth and make sure the airway is clear." Ryder winced, losing some of his shirt to Shannon's clenched fist. "I need to get the other one out."

The baby's translucent skin beat with faint red lines, a ghostly hexagon pattern ridged over its body. The egg's interior was raised in the same pattern, leaving its mark on the infant as it grew, pressed up against the malleable shell. I watched in horror as the baby struggled, twisting in my hands. Its lips were turning blue, and the strangled noises coming from its mouth bubbled thick clear fluid over its chin. The same gummy fluid clogged its nose, the membrane sucking back in as its tiny nostrils tried to breathe.

"Shit." Another deep breath and I braced myself, promising my throat one of the whiskey shots if I did what I needed to do. *Five*, my mind argued, *at least five*.

Laying my lips tight over the baby's face, I sucked at its membrane-clogged orifices. The albumin hit the roof of my mouth, and I gagged. I spit the mouthful then and sucked again, choking and heaving as my throat filled with the egg's liquid. Steeling myself for another round, I bent over the baby I held in my hands and almost wept with relief as it cried with a beefy howl.

"Okay, Kai," I encouraged myself, "It's just like a puppy. Get it warm and hand it back to the mother."

Dirtying my last clean shirt, I juggled the newborn against my chest. Scrubbing it clean with a ragged car towel, it pinked up nearly immediately, losing the sickly pallor to a healthy glow. I grabbed another cloth then wrapped the baby tightly, swaddling it carefully.

"What is it?" Shannon asked wearily.

Ryder was holding another bundle.

"A baby," I answered, confused. "Oh, um…." I checked under the wrapped towel, tucking the end back into a fold. "It's a girl."

"So is this one. Two girls." Ryder beamed. "They're gorgeous, Shannon. Thank you."

"Here, give me that one," she murmured, touching the baby Ryder had cut free. Cradling the infant, she worked her dress down until one of her breasts swung loose. Stroking the baby's cheek, she placed a nipple in her mouth, getting her to suckle. "Let me feed her first. Then I'll take the other."

Ryder laid a gentle kiss on Shannon's forehead then wiped her brow off with a wet cloth. "Thank you, honey."

"I'll send you the bill," she sighed, settling into the seat sideways.

"I'll write in a big tip." He came in close, wrapping his arms around my waist so the infant was cradled between us. "Thank you, Kai. Thank you very much."

The girls looked alike, ice white blonde sprigs of hair tufting out at the peaks of their heads. The baby I'd helped sighed. Ryder slid the tip of his index finger into her mouth, pressing down on her tongue, and she took a few tentative suckles, quieting her fussing.

Her small hands ended with tiny white tips of fingernails. With the fluids cleaned off her face, her mouth bowed into a butterfly shape, and she blinked, wide deep green eyes flecked with silver and gold. Her ears were tipped, a slight tilt up where they pressed against her skull. I touched her face, stroking the soft down on her cheek, feeling the delicate bones around her wide, slanted eyes.

"She is beautiful. They both are... perfect," Ryder whispered. "I can't thank you enough. Morrígan, I can't repay you for this."

"Sure you can," I said softly so as not to disturb the infant between us. "You can start by telling me how a human woman ended up carrying two sidhe babies. Then you can tell me why they have your eyes."

I SACRIFICED one of the cargo crates from the trunk to serve as a bassinet. Lined with a thin survival blanket and the rest of my clothes, it provided some warmth and protection. We got Shannon settled into the backseat, helping her switch the second born into the makeshift crib. She cradled the first infant to her breast, easing it onto the nipple without a problem.

Leaving Ryder to tuck my last blanket around Shannon, I found the single-shot packets and tore one open. I was on my third by the time Ryder joined me at the back of the car. He lifted his eyebrows at the discarded shot sleeves but didn't say anything, leaning against the open trunk. Rubbing his face, Ryder looked tired, his bright green eyes dulling in the shadowed recess.

"She's a surrogate," he said, bypassing the whiskey in favor of water. He cracked the top open, then guzzled down a mouthful. "The babies were implanted into her womb. They're my sister's children."

"Why the fricking secrets?" I turned too fast, and the world spun. Grabbing at the Mustang, I stayed on my feet. "Why not just tell me?"

The irony of that question didn't escape me. I was merely ignoring it.

"My sister had a healer harvest her ova and fertilize them outside her body." Ryder shoved his hands into his pockets, rocking back on his heels. "She felt pressured to have children. Our House is known for its fertility, and she saw it as the only way."

"Having children doesn't make someone a woman," I scoffed. "Sure, it's got some weight to it, but that's only biological. Some of the best women I know are still male."

"It might not make a woman, but it does make a House. She... needed it."

"So she got a human knocked up?"

"Not at first." He looked away for a moment. "She tried getting pregnant herself, but she lost them. Ciarla and I might not be on the best of terms most of the time, but she's still my sister. I couldn't bear to see her go through that again. With every loss, Ciarla seemed to lose a part of herself as well."

"And that's where Shannon comes in?"

"Ciarla swore the healer to secrecy. I don't want to know how much that cost her, both emotionally and financially," Ryder admitted. "They gambled on a human being able to carry Ciarla's children. No other sidhe would do it. No matter what was promised."

"Why?"

"Any child conceived outside normal means... ordinary means... is considered a violation of nature. Arranging for Shannon, a human, to carry Ciarla's fertilized eggs goes against the most basic tenets of the sidhe culture. Ciarla is risking her position in our House—hell, our Court—by doing this." Ryder sighed. "Which you would know, Kai, if you were one of us."

"One of you?" I snorted. "I'm one of me."

"That's fairly obvious," Ryder said softly. "I thought you were someone young and disaffected by the wars. Your black hair was a rebellious act to separate you from your sidhe blood, but now I know better. The purple is striking. What's your real eye color? Gold? Silver?"

"Does this matter now?" The rock in my stomach sank, hitting me unexpectedly. "What difference does it make what Court I was born to? And what does that have to do with the babies Shannon carried?"

"It doesn't, not now. But I wouldn't have cast the salt binding if I'd known you were Dusk Court. I wouldn't have hurt you. It tore you apart, Kai. It was set to protect us against anything from the unsidhe. I hoped it would keep back the *ainmhí dubh*. I didn't think it would take down my Stalker." The anguish in his voice was real, or Ryder was a better actor than I'd given him credit for. "At least you could have told me before we went into Elfhaine, Kai."

"Not to sound like a nagging boyfriend, but don't turn this around on me," I said, shaking my head. I badly wanted another whiskey shot, because I could still taste the egg membrane in my throat, but instead I went for water. "I'm not anything more than I told you."

"I could have protected you against my grandmother," Ryder said. "I can imagine now what she did to you… in that room. I know what my ancestors built that room for… what's been done in there. It kills me knowing it was done to you."

"Yeah, I wasn't too happy with it either." I shrugged. "We're talking about the babies. What or who I am is my business. Those kids in my backseat, that's my *job*. So leave off me, your lordship, and talk."

"That's it, then? That's where we leave it?"

"That's where I'm leaving it." I cocked my head back and sucked down more water. "Now why the hell did your grandmother want those kids dead? Because Shannon was carrying them or because it would have damaged your Clan's rep?"

"She asked you to kill the babies?" There was shock in his eyes and a tightening of his shoulders. "I…."

"Yeah, sweet grandmother you got there. Reminds me of a gingerbread house witch."

"I didn't think she'd go to that extreme. Not against the children. Against me? Definitely. Maybe even Ciarla, but never the babies."

"She didn't seem all that bothered by it," I said. "But then she didn't seem that bothered by anything she did or said. Strikes me as very much an end justifies the means kind of girl."

"She doesn't see that our people are dying, Kai, or she refuses to," he said softly. "They are dying slowly because we're having fewer and fewer children while holing ourselves up behind high walls. Our traditions say conception should be natural with no outside assistance. Maybe that worked when we were on our own, but now, surrounded by a species more prolific than a parasite, we'll be overrun in no time."

"Wait, so you decided to start up a breeding production line? For what? To have armies to throw against the humans?"

"No." Ryder looked shocked, and he ran his hand through his hair. "I helped so my sister could have children, and if it worked, then others. We have to change, Kai. We have to change our ways if we're going to survive here."

"So you stomped out of your safe little haven up North to form your own club down in San Diego?" The day dragged me down, the whiskey that burned off the taste of baby in my throat now resting in my sour empty stomach. "And let me get this straight, those are pure sidhe babies in there. When you said your sister's, that means they're your nieces. We can't... you know, cross-pollinate, right?"

"We can't," he said. "But, with help from a healer, a human woman can carry our children."

"Huh." I knew I didn't sound convinced. "Why would anyone want to?"

"Because we're people, and a dying one at that," Ryder explained. "An elfin woman ovulates rarely, and if the egg is fertilized, her body treats it as diseased, something to kill off. So our children die before their mother's womb can nurture them. That's why I started looking for human surrogates."

"How many of these wombs do you have lined up?"

"Just Shannon. And whatever untruths I've told you, I wasn't lying when I said she's my sister's friend. She is. They became very close during this experience."

"You're playing God and Goddess," I said. "The damned elfin live for centuries. There are evolutionary reasons they don't breed as often as the humans. How the hell can a planet sustain a race that breeds quickly and doesn't die off?"

"I used to agree with you. Then I compared sidhe births to the deaths we've had since the Merge, and we've fallen far below a zero population," Ryder argued. "The Dawn Court is declining quickly, and the Dusk Court numbers are worse, from what I can tell. It's imperative for our survival to increase our numbers, Kai. Do you think I'd manipulate our bodies and culture just to play God?"

"I don't know," I admitted. "I don't know you."

"And I don't know you," he said softly. "How could I be honest with you until I knew how strongly you felt? What I'm doing—what I've done—will estrange me from most of my Clan and House. Forming a Court in San Diego was my only option. I needed to give Ciarla and her children someplace safe to live in case they're cast out."

"Shit." I exhaled. My body was worn, wrung dry from the day. If I had a choice, I'd crawl into the car and fall asleep, blood and baby goo be damned. "I can't think anymore. Everything's jangled up in my head."

"You've had what? A couple hours of sleep and how much food?" Ryder asked. "Killed a dragon using your car and got caught in two binding circles. Did I forget anything?"

"Babies," I said, saluting him with my water. "Don't forget sucking out and swallowing baby juice. Which I will never ever do again. I'm crossing that off my list of things I'll do on a run. We really should get out of here. I know black dogs. They'll be on our asses soon enough."

"Still trust me enough to drive your car?" he asked.

"Have you seen my car? This was supposed to be a simple run." I ran a hand along the bumper, my fingers tracing the deep bite marks in the steel. "I was going to say forget about paying me, but after the swallowing mouthfuls of uncooked sidhe egg, I'll be sending you a damned huge bill."

CHAPTER NINETEEN

ANY RETORT Ryder had was lost when the hut's steel door rattled, shaking furiously on its skewed rails. In a second, my fatigue burned off, and I headed to the front of the car then reached in to grab my shotguns.

"It's got to be the dogs," I said, loading in iron-packed shells. I was out of slugs, and the most I could hope for would be slowing the black dogs down until we could get onto the road. Something pawed at the door, and I heard it shift on the track, sticking a few inches off the ground.

"We don't know that," he replied, and a howl sliced through his words.

"Nope, those are the dogs," I said.

"We should have locked that behind us." Ryder swore and grabbed at the keys I held out to him.

"It's the only way to get the Mustang out, and we wouldn't get far on foot. Especially not with Shannon and... those things," I replied.

Shannon peered at me, sleep tugging her face down. "Is there something wrong?"

"Stay down," I ordered her. "You're in the safest place we've got. Nothing's going to be able to come through to get you, not without a fight. Ryder, is that circle going to hold? Even if it's not dogs, it could be something else."

"There's no circle. I had to break it, or it would have killed you," he said grimly.

"At least take the Glock." I grabbed the gun from the side of the storage crate. "I'm going to have to flip the engine over. We'll never make it out of here on the electric."

"If the shotgun didn't stop those things, do you think this is going to?" Ryder asked as the door rattled again, rising a bit more.

"In this case, it's not the gun that's going to make the difference, it's the ammo. Nothing I've got left is going to kill them unless they're close in. Just aim in the general direction of anything with teeth and press down on the trigger. I'm going to get the engine switched over." I reached into the trunk, moving the shallow crates aside. "It's not like they have fingers and can open the damned door."

Comprised of a flat generator and engine, the electric system fit up against the backseat, but switching it over was difficult, especially when I was half-dead. Disconnecting the lantern leaders with a grabbing pull, I went to work on the switch sequence. My fingers fumbled. I finally got the combination right, priming the already warmed up gas engine.

"It could be a hermit and not the *ainmhí dubh*." Ryder frowned as I righted myself.

"If it's some lonely guy looking for company and howling for it, then great. We'll pass him some whiskey and head on out," I said. "It doesn't matter who is out there; they're probably not going to like us. I'm going to need you to get into the car."

"I could be the one to open the door." Typical of Ryder, he stood fast, arguing to his last breath. "I'm in better shape to run after you pull the car out."

"We need accurate firepower more than we'll need driving skill." Shutting the trunk, I shot a stern glance at Shannon, who peered out at me through the back window. She dropped her head down before I could say anything.

Ryder didn't have time to respond either. The door blew in, sending long strips of metal flying into the Quonset. I ducked behind the Mustang, and it rocked from the impact. Ryder dove down next to me, curling into a ball with the Glock cradled between his hands. The air smelled of arcane, an oddly curious scent of electrified blood. Pieces of the rolling door came to a violent rest at my feet, the metal scorched and twisted. Something powerful had just smoked the bay door, blowing through the segments.

Rolling out from under the Mustang, I came up on one knee and started firing, both shotguns booming at the *ainmhí dubh* nearly on us.

My first blast hit, tearing into a black dog's shoulder. The creature twisted in midleap, coming down on its three good legs, and howled, rattling my hearing with its piercing cry. Its jaws snapped at my face, barely missing my cheek, and I gagged on the foulness of its carrion-rank breath. The thing moved fast, bouncing away from me as if I'd not just shot it in the haunch.

I heard Ryder firing the Glock. Praying to Dalia's murdered god for safety, I backpedaled a few feet, tracking the large dog as it circled me. With its head reaching my chest, the creature should have been an easy target, but it moved with frightening speed, terrifying me with the bristle of teeth jammed into its mouth. It snapped at my head and nearly connected, shearing off strands of my hair. Getting a taste of me, the dog swallowed and growled low in its throat, sprinting back to make another run.

Tucking down one of the guns, I jacked the other open, popped the shells out, then reloaded. I'd barely brought the muzzle up when the dog was on me again, its acidic spit burning dabs on my neck. As close as the hound was, it was impossible to miss. The trick was not missing well.

Shanks of dirty fur hung from its jowls, making it difficult to find the spot I wanted. Perversely, every one of the damned things was different in shape, some with long sloping heads and compact bodies, while others were stocky and had brick-hard forms. What they had in common was a foul stink and blotchy, oily black marble skin patched over with uneven clumps of spiky fur—and an insatiable desire to rip their prey apart.

This one was no exception. It intended to have me for breakfast, no matter what I had to say about it.

The shotgun's muzzle fit into the *V* of its jaw, and I tilted the stock, aiming for the back of the dog's head. Expelled gunpowder bloomed black roses over me, speckling my skin. A wash of dog blood struck me, some of the bitter fluid splashing into my mouth before I could turn away. It continued to barrel forward, its head, missing half of its skin, flapping out behind it.

I rolled my shoulders out of the way, grabbing the shotgun I'd tucked away, and did a fast reload. Coming to my feet armed, I froze, staring at the long-bodied unsidhe standing amid the carnage of the Quonset's bay door.

His hands were ringed, spiked and gemmed circlets of metal that burned with light. Dressed in midnight blue cotton, he might have been a human dressed in a formal sherwani and slacks, except none of the humans I knew had bone white hair shot through with thick streaks of ebony and sapphire.

His creamy skin fit tight on his bones, his face a rigid mask of control and arrogance. Hook nosed, he looked down its length, piercing me with his metallic gray and blue eyes, and a smile formed on his cold face.

I knew his face. I'd seen it often enough in the darkness of my mind, and my body ached with the memory of the rings he wore on his fingers.

The unsidhe pursed his mouth, whistling to call off the other two dogs pacing near the door. They stalked closer to him, crimson eyes fixed on me. Ryder came up behind me, and a third dog limped toward the unsidhe, its side sticky with blood. The black dogs sniffed at the third, snarling and snapping at its injury, their teeth digging into its ripped skin. The Hunt Master spoke to the dogs with a cutting command, and they separated, sulking and grumbling.

If the Dawn Court spoke in golden ribbons, the Dusk slithered with smoky shadows. Some words were shared between the elfin, but a phrase's meaning often hid cultural references and veiled intimacies. Plainly spoken and kept to the basest inflection, an unsidhe could make himself understood to a sidhe, their exchanges mostly kept to insults during times of diplomacy and death threats in times of war. Regional differences altered the language more, drifting and changing with the land, but the Hunt Master's dialect was too familiar for my nerves.

"I didn't believe my pack when they scratched at this door," the Wild Hunt lord said in accented Singlish, his outstretched hands palms down to keep his lead dogs at bay. Stroking at the largest of the three dogs, he scratched behind one of its ears, flaking off large pieces of dried skin from its diseased-looking head. "Not only do I find the little Golden Lordling with his monsters, but also a wayward little kitten taken from his home."

He studied me, flicking a piece of his long hair from his face. I couldn't read his expression. He'd always been the coldest of my memories, an icy tormentor with a clinical detachment as he inflicted pain.

"What do you want?" Ryder pushed forward, angling to place himself between me and the unsidhe.

"I was sent to kill you, Ryder, Clan Sebac, Third in the House of Devon." The unsidhe sighed, languidly taking a step into the Quonset. His Wild Hunt followed, circling wide around him with long slinking legs. "But then I find with you the sweetest of meat. How I've missed having parts of you on my tongue, *peata*."

I was stronger and probably more stubborn. I also had more to lose. Spitting to clear my throat, I struggled to keep my breathing even. His words raped me, weakening my knees, and I felt spread apart, left wide for his barbs to hook into me. Ryder's grandmother had taken me by surprise, capturing me in her trapdoor spider web, but things were different now. I wasn't bound by sigils and blood.

"Screw you, Lavan," I snarled, shaking my mind free of the unsidhe's hastily muttered casting. "That's your name, right? I couldn't quite make it out between the others' grunting as they had you."

"You've grown teeth, little lizard," he replied, laughing softly. It was a wild sound, tainted with madness and desperation. "Do you even know what you've found, Ryder of the Dead? Do you even know the treasure you stumbled upon as you bumble about to destroy our Races?"

"What the hell are you on about?" Ryder stood at my side. The sidhe's taller form leaned toward me, our shoulders touching. His warmth gave me strength, grounding me against the Hunt Master's commands. "What is he talking about, Kai?"

"I am talking about the one thing Tanic, Lord Master of the Wild Hunt, badly wants returned to him," the Hunt Master said, bowing slightly. "That creature standing next to you is his son, the Chimera."

I winced at the sound of my Singlish name being spoken out loud. It laid me open as neatly as if I'd been carved from my throat down to my crotch with a sharp knife.

So I shot him.

CHAPTER TWENTY

"GET IN the car, Ryder!" I shouted, bringing my other gun up and firing at the black dogs charging forward. "And let's go."

He hesitated, emptying the rest of his clip at the animals. Not stopping to see if any of his shots hit, I vaulted over the back end of the car and tossed one of the shotguns into the front, hooking my hand into the doorframe to slide through the open passenger window.

Reaching under the seat, I fumbled about for the slim ammo cases I'd stashed there, trying not to think about the fluids under my ass. Behind me, Shannon pulled the crate down, lodging it in the gap between the backseat and the after-stock console. Ryder slid into the driver's seat and turned the key.

The engine rumbled, firing up with one pump of the pedal, and Ryder punched the Mustang's accelerator, aiming straight for the black dogs' master. Gray smoke plumed out behind the car as the tires spun on the concrete, cooking thin layers of pungent rubber into the floor. The Mustang spun to the side, hitting the salt. It gained traction and surged forward. Undaunted by the heavy steel carriage, the black dogs were on us, cranking their jaws open wide to snap into the car's metal skin.

An ejected shotgun shell hit my arm as I fired at the misshapen creature trying to claw through the windshield. Its back end scrambled to stay on the hood, and the black dog hooked its front claws over the wiper relays. The glass smoked where the dog's slobber hit it, white frosted trails forming behind the dribbles.

Half leaning out the window, I tried to shoot it off when we hit the unsidhe. The shot went wide, my aim thrown by the impact. A swirl of dark blue cloth shot up over the car, tumbling over the front end and slamming into the windshield before sliding over the edge. The glass gave, overstressed after so much abuse, crackling into minute webs. I'd paid through the teeth to have Kevlar glaze spread over the pane. I'd eaten saimin for a month to scrape up enough money to coat my run-car's glass, and when it counted the sacrifice paid off.

The glass held, suctioned into place by the glaze. Breathing a sigh of relief, I reloaded as we hit weed-choked asphalt, speeding over the uneven road.

"Nice hit. It'll take a while to get up after that," I said, shoving a shell in. The over-under shotguns cost me more than Kevlar, but they loaded quickly, and the spent casings ejected out with a minimum of recoil.

"Get up?" Ryder quickly looked behind him. "Damn. I was hoping the *ainmhí dubh* would...."

A speckled-skin monster caught up with us, its broad shoulders even with the Mustang's open window. The black dog kept its head down, and it twisted, slamming into the car. We skidded, the hit hopscotching us sideways over the road. The suspension groaned, complaining about the abuse, before the gears kicked back in and Ryder got Oketsu back under control.

It struck us again, rattling the car down to its frame. Bearing the gun's muzzle down, I waited until its body shifted again, its high shoulder blades angling as its powerful legs slanted to turn. Ryder's nieces began screaming when I blasted both barrels into the creature. Its angry howls drowned out the babies' cries. Then the beast lunged at me, a wide break of skin and meat flapping over its jowl.

Cracking the shotgun open, I used the other to take a wild shot to the creature's head. With the other stock shucked between me and the seat, I worked in a reload, struggling to keep my balance on the moist leather seat when Ryder veered off the road and onto the ramp leading to the old highway.

"Tell me this road goes somewhere," he said, steering through the overhang of trees crowding in from the hills banking a curve. Dawn was at least an hour away, but the sky was starting to lighten, going pink at the edges and turning a lighter dusky blue overhead. "Kai, do you know where we're going?"

"Sort of. Just drive," I muttered back. The guns were hot, so handling them had to be done carefully. A moving car wasn't my preferred duck blind, but it would have to do, especially when a mangled *ainmhí dubh* bobbed up and down behind Oketsu's trunk. In the distance, another speck was gaining on us, the large black dog's smaller companion joining the hunt.

Leaves cut at my face, blowing through the open window. I tried remembering the lay of the road, its serpentine loops weaving in and out of the low hills. The lanes opened up for a long stretch, low brush and trash-leaf trees turning to bright floral crazy quilt patterned hills, remnants of SoCal's flower industry. Left for fallow, the blooms rose and fell with the seasons, a dizzying vomit of colors spreading over as much land as the Pendle paho'eho'e.

Camouflaged in the blooms, a herd of striped wild horses popped their heads up as we passed, their ears erect with interest. Interbred from the ruined wild animal park's zebras and Mongolian wild horses, the flower-field herds were brown tabby-cat striped, their short black legs perfectly suited for negotiating steppes and sharp valleys.

Even an idiot would have sensed danger when they scattered down the hill and out of sight. The *ainmhí dubh* were behind us, and the wild horses caught the scent of a predator in the air.

"Just the two?" Ryder asked. Forced to steer carefully, he kept the car down to a manageable speed. The powerful engine balked and kicked as the car tucked down tight to take a curve.

"Yeah, just two." Sarcasm filled my voice. "No problem. Why don't you park? I'll get out and take care of this shit."

Shannon screamed when the larger dog landed on the trunk, its claws tearing up what little paint remained on the back panel. It screamed back, spitting at the shrapnel-pocked glass. A bend in the road provided enough momentum to spin the Mustang's back end, and the black dog went flying. In a second, the smaller dog homed in, snapping and snarling at Oketsu's tires.

"Hold him straight," I ordered Ryder.

I slid out of the window opening, hooking my leg around the seat. Praying my perch would hold, I stretched out, unbending my back as far as I could without losing my hold on the leather seat. The air stung through my baby-juiced shirt, the cold biting the tears on my scars.

The second dog was close, near enough to catch its rank smell even with the wind whipping about me. I pulled the trigger, and my aching shoulder twisted from the recoil. The iron-riddled shots hit it square in the forehead, blowing its hard skull into meat mixed with the white powder of shattered bone. Under me, the car bucked, fitting into a bank in the road, and I peeled myself off the roof, nearly losing one of my shotguns when we took the opposite bend.

"Are you trying to kill me?" I shouted into the car, reaching for more shells. The box skittered away, spilling the ammo into the seat's crease. Cursing, I angled in to grab a few when the other dog hit.

Its long teeth burned as they sank into the meat of my thigh. A twist of its head flung me from my seat on the window channel, tumbling me out of the Mustang and onto the broken asphalt. I hit the rough road, the blacktop chewing up my clothes and laying my skin open to the grit. Rolling, I bounced on the road, scraping over the tarmac before momentum carried me over the edge of the hill.

Explosions of flowers followed my roll. Sticks and burrs dug in as I tucked, barely able to wrap my arms around my chest. Thin branches snapped under my windmilling body, and then I slammed to a stop, firework blooms of deep purple rose petals puffing around me.

I tried breathing. My lungs ached, blooming with pain. I sucked in air, unable to get my chest working to pull in enough to keep me conscious. A swirling blackness threatened the edges of my vision. Before I could see how badly I was hurt, the dog was on me, its weight slamming into my torso and pushing me into the line of rose bushes I'd landed in.

I'd lost the shotgun somewhere in the bushes when I didn't clear the rose bramble. No use worrying about it. It was empty, and I had no ammo on me. Dizzy, I ducked under the branches, hoping the thorny mass would give me some kind of cover while I looked for something to hit the dog with.

Above me, the black dog snapped and flailed, turning its head to grab at any part of my body it could reach. Its teeth found my jeans, its sloped body and broad shoulders twisting to yank me out. Taking small snapping bites, its neck heaved back and forth as it dragged me out a few inches at a time. Dried prickly twigs scored tracks on my back and ribs, rose thorns hooking into me like a thousand bee stings.

Then something hard and unyielding jabbed me in the side.

Acid from its spit burned, blistering my exposed leg. I fumbled at the hard length lodged in my side, wrapping my fingers around the shaft of the Ka-Bar Ryder used to open his palm. It was torture to move my arm. Nearly frozen with pain, I kicked at the black dog's chest, pushing it back a step or two with a solid thump.

I heard something carry on the wind, a shout or perhaps another black dog howling to find the Hunt leader, but I wasn't in a position to care. My muscles strained with the effort of unsnapping the sheath, a stinging sweat dripping into my eyes, but it didn't hurt nearly as much as the teasing bites the creature left on me.

The knife came loose and slipped from my fingers. Grabbing at it, it slid around my palm as my hand spasmed. With a lunge, the black dog came back and clamped down on my shoulder, singing a growling hum in its throat as it sank its long fangs into my bones. I felt my collarbone give under its bite, snapping and gouging to break through bruised skin.

Choking on the thin trickle of vomit pushing up from my stomach, I pushed my clenched fist into the dog's head, the knife tilting awkwardly when I brought my arm up. There was no grace in the hit. The stab was desperate, a whining, plunging thrust with little hope of doing anything more than pissing off the black dog determined to eat me whole.

Someone's god apparently had other plans for me.

My knife met a butter-soft resistance, sliding hot into the creature's boiling red eye. It splattered, popping and gushing gore over my hand. The searing liquid cooked my fingers, but I rolled, coming up on one knee to push my weight down on the knife's hilt, hoping I could puncture through the thin bone behind the dog's eye.

The socket broke, and the knife slid down, buried deep into the ruined cavern of the dog's eye. Unable to hold my weight up any longer, my legs buckled, and I slid down the black dog's haunch. It tumbled, convulsing, and its jaws chewed up my upper arm as it died. It gave a final crunch through the remains of my shoulder and toppled, its mouth gaping open.

The sky spun above me, stars turning on a pinwheel course to leave streaks of white light against the pitch black. Metallic silver clouds drifted overhead, lit up bright by the moon. I blinked once; then my eyelids decided it was too much effort to stay open. Agreeing, I let them fall, concentrating more on breathing, with the hitch in my lungs and the radiating pain of my collarbone pricking at my nerves.

The ground quaked, falling away from my split-open back, and the branches hooked into my shirt released me. Warm skin touched my face, and then a voice, soft husky golden in the silvery night, whispered my name and told me to sleep.

"Can't. On a run," I argued. Even to my ringing ears, it sounded like a weak argument. I knew who held me, his vanilla-spiced green tea scent soothing some of the burns in my mind, stroking over the fear and panic of the black dog consuming me bite by bite.

"Please, Kai, let me help you," Ryder begged me in the unseen bobbing world. Taking a final shuddering breath, I rested my head against him and let go.

CHAPTER TWENTY-ONE

TIME PASSES slower in the darkness.

Threads of memories stitch together patchwork monsters that feed on dreams, sometimes even sucking at my marrow when my bones are split apart by careless hands. Parts of me burned, itching fire spreading under and over my skin until I cried, weeping with the need to sleep deeper to escape the anguish. Every part of me hurt. Even the brush of hair at the base of my neck was tender, torn from my scalp by the black dog's shearing teeth.

An engine rumbled somewhere in the distance, a soft roaring noise muffled by the fuzz in my head. Opening my eyes poured hot liquid fire into my brain. I forced my lids apart, and a bright sunlight covered me, cut into squares by the high windows along the west wall. The motor increased its speed, and I felt tiny hooks pierce my shoulder, working in and out of my bare skin.

Groaning, I tried turning my head. My neck ticked off each degree with a crackling sound, and Newt blinked slowly when I made eye contact, his pupils thread-thin in the sunlight. His purring increased, as did the latch hooking, but moving him seemed like too much work. Blinking seemed like too much work, I decided, closing my eyes again.

"Hey, gorgeous," Dalia said softly. Her voice was enough to make me risk the light again, so I peeked. Her smile was tight and didn't hide the worry on her face. It also did nothing to mask the dark circles under her eyes. Leaning over me, her pale face was surrounded by a purple halo, and darker violet strands tickled my nose.

"Hair," I said. Or tried to say. My thick tongue barely moved in my mouth, and it came out a series of clicking hisses. "Shitty color."

"I'm going to put a straw in your mouth." She stroked at my forehead. "See if you can get some water into you. Sip it. Don't gulp."

Sucking in a trickle of water, my throat closed over each drop as if they were precious. Moistened, I tried talking again. "Changed your hair."

151

Trying to sit up was unsuccessful, and Newt complained at being dislodged when my shoulder was no longer flat enough to lie on. Dalia faded from my side, and a pain stabbed through my lungs.

"Lay back, Kai." Ryder appeared in my field of view, pressing his hand on my chest. "You need to rest."

"Hurts," I protested as he slid the straw back into my mouth. Sucking too hard, I got a mouthful of water I couldn't swallow easily and choked, sending waves of agony through my chest. The coughing subsided eventually, leaving me breathless and without any strength. "Go away."

"Still pigheaded, I see." The straw retracted, and I felt what I was lying on give as Ryder sat down next to me. "You've been out for about a week now."

"Get paid?"

"Did you get paid?" He laughed, nodding. "Yes, for the run. I'll need you to work up a bill for damage to your car."

"Good. Get out," I said, struggling against Ryder's hand to sit up. Either he was a lot stronger than I was or my body was refusing to listen to me. "Let go."

"Kai, stop," Ryder whispered into my ear. "You're hurt. Badly. And while you're healing quickly enough, you need to rest."

"Dempsey?" I croaked. The water was a memory in my mouth, and my throat hurt.

"Dalia called him. He said to let him know if you died." Ryder dribbled some water into my parched mouth, using his finger as a stopper as he guided the straw.

"Not getting Oketsu." Newt was back, curled up on the ruin of my collarbone. A thick white bandage speckled with dried blood protected my skin from his claws, but his weight was welcome, as was the heat of his tiny body.

"He didn't want the Mustang." Ryder sounded bitter. "He said he wants your truck."

"Oh," I replied, slipping back into the cradle of darkness. "Okay. That's different, then."

WHEN I resurfaced, I could move, although my muscles felt tender and spongy. All I could do was sit up, and even that left me in a sea of sweat. It was night, from what I could make out from the banks of windows set high in the warehouse walls. To the west, the sky ran blue and orange, reflecting the city's glow. On the east, San Diego dominated the long glass wall, its tall buildings and frantically lit-up billboards selling everything from ramen noodles to used cars.

The swirls of color were the only light downstairs, and I shifted, looking around to make sure I wasn't crowding Newt. The cat was gone, and a futon bed I'd gotten at the swap meet was set up next to the kitchen wall, a makeshift medical bay tucked in around me. As I watched, the glass panes darkened, and the lights I'd set up along the steel support beams flared on.

"Ryder wondered how the hell you slept with all that sparkling into your place. I had to show him how the glass-switch worked." Dalia carried a bowl of something toward me. It smelled delicious, waking my stomach with a fierce growl. "Get some water in you before you eat. I only took the IV out this morning."

I glanced at the inside of my elbow, frowning at a bit of gauze held down by cloth tape. It itched, as did my shoulder blades, but my body only ached instead of screaming in agony when I moved. Taking the water bottle from Dalia, I sipped carefully from the straw, swallowing small drips.

"So I didn't dream about the hair. Purple?" I scratched my face, finding a road rash scab on my cheek. "Where's Shannon? She okay?"

"She's at the Court with the babies. Apparently my looking them over wasn't good enough. Some snot-nosed healer came by to check them out, and they all left together. That bitch wasn't any help. She sniffed at you and said she had other things to do. I wanted to pull her fricking hair out," she said, sitting on a wooden chair I didn't know I owned. "Ryder's sister called. She's coming down to San Diego, but he started speaking sidhe, so I couldn't eavesdrop anymore. I hate when people do that."

"Huh." I left it at that. Maybe things worked differently for the sidhe, but it seemed like the sister should have been here already.

"Here." Dalia drew some soup into a large-bowled spoon, holding it out to me after blowing it cool. "Eat."

The miso was warm, *hondashi*-sweet and shoyu-rich, just the right thing for my tight stomach. I ate half of the bowl, then leaned into the pillows, unable to hold myself up anymore. I peeled back the bandage on my shoulder to inspect the break site and was amused to find the wound stitched together with bright rainbow thread.

"Don't pick at it. All I had was the colored thread I use for kids." She turned her head, but not before I saw the shine in her eyes. "So you're going to be wearing rainbows until you heal up."

"Newt around?" Craning my neck, I tried to do the impossible, see up the wall to the loft where my bed was.

"He's been fed and is probably up on the roof chasing fireflies," Dalia said. "Or crapping. That cat leaves some foul things in the litter box."

"Be glad he decided to start using the litter box," I murmured, debating another mouthful of soup, but fatigue kept me on my back. "You doing okay?"

"You drive me insane, Kai Gracen." Dalia rested her forehead against mine, and I breathed in the sweetness of her breath. "I dyed my hair the same color as your eyes because I wanted something of you with me besides your damned disgusting cat."

"He's pretty disgusting," I agreed. "Probably less than me, though."

"You're an ass sometimes. Did you know that?" Dalia pressed her hands down on my shoulders, and I tried not to wince, failing miserably. "And you're welcome, by the way. I took time off from work to patch you up. I should have left your ass at Medical."

"You know they wouldn't have taken me," I said in a soft voice. "If you'd had your way, I'd *be* in Medical instead of here in my living room with a half-assed triage set up around me."

She couldn't meet my eyes. There was shame in her face, shame for something she had no control over.

"You're a doctor there. In the ER." I wasn't telling her something she didn't already know. Just something she didn't want to hear. "I'm not at Medical because they wouldn't take me. They won't take in a sidhe. Not even when one of their own doctors begs them to."

"Screw you." She blew a raspberry at me, ever the lady.

"I know you, Mick," I said. "You begged for half a minute and then walked out, yelling that you'd treat me at home if those assholes wouldn't help me. Did they suspend you for it?"

"No," she admitted, as subdued as a child caught stealing a cookie. "I have a lot of vacation time built up. Some asshole won't take me to the Bluffs to dragon watch, so I thought I'd take it now."

"Dragons are highly overrated." I laughed, despite the twisting in my heart and guts. "If you really want to go, I'll take you someplace in Pendle. Once Oketsu gets fixed, anyway."

"I don't need to smell them," she sighed. "Just see them. That's the biggest difference between you and me. It's like you have to risk everything just to cross the street. Why can't you for once do things simply?"

"Because that's not me, Dalia," I said, gently pulling her down to sit next to me. "That's something I can't change."

"It's something you won't change, Kai," Dalia insisted. "You don't have to be a Stalker. You're smart, sharper than I am. You could go to school and be something other than…."

"It's all I know, Mick." I broke it to her gently but firmly. "I'm a Stalker. I like it. Even now when I'm wondering whether Ryder picked up all my pieces off the road to put me back together, I like it. You started off as a kid in a family that loves and adores you. That's what you built on. I don't have that. Stalkers raised me. As a Stalker. It's what I am. It's what I'm built on."

"You're more than that," she said. "I'm not taking this *chikusho* you're spooning me and swallowing it."

"Baby, if people find out you're hooked up with me for anything more than borrowing a cup of sugar, your life would be shit. Hell, Dempsey's old lady can't even stand to have me in the house, and I'm sure she makes him bathe right after he touches me. How are you going to be a doctor around that?"

"How I feel about you isn't going to go away, Kai. I *died* a little when they brought you in."

"I'm not worth dying for, Dalia," I said, shrugging.

"Don't say that, you bastard." She hit me again, closer to my collarbone, then looked apologetic before patting the bandage. "I almost got kicked out of Medical because of you."

"I'm definitely not worth that." I teased a smile out of her. Shaking my head sent a wave of hammer falls in my skull, and I waited for the headache to subside. "I wish things were different, Dalia. I do."

"What about Ryder?"

"What about him?"

"Are you going to let him love you? Or do you have a different excuse for him?"

"Honey, Ryder doesn't want to love me. He just wants to fuck me," I replied. "You know I don't have sex with people I know."

"I hate it when you call me honey. It makes me feel like a little kid." Dalia nestled up against me, her arm wrapped over my stomach. A hard squeeze would probably put me into convulsions, but I said nothing when she hugged me gently. "God, I hate you sometimes."

"I hate me sometimes too," I admitted with a nod.

"You want to know what pissed me off the most?"

"What?"

"When Ryder told me about that guy with the dogs, I was jealous." She moved, propping herself up so she could see my face. "I was stitching you up, and he was spewing about some ass hat who knew you from… before."

"That pissed you off? We ran him over with the Mustang."

"It pissed me off because Ryder was there for something so personal, something so intimate that I wanted to punch him in the nose." Dalia pouted and yipped when Newt scrambled up her body to reach me. She let the cat settle before stroking his uneven ears, finding the spot between his shoulders that made him stick his tongue out in pleasure. "He told me the bastard knew your real name; then he shut up. It's a very annoying thing. Shutting up when I want to hear what's next."

"Ryder's good at pissing people off." I shrugged, moving my hand under the cat's chin so Newt had something to sand clean with his tongue. "Shit, his own family seems to be good at it. His grandmother sent the damned Hunt after us. Bitch's got a rock where her heart should be."

"Did seeing that guy make you want to go back to… wherever home is?"

"Not really." Making a face at her, I laughed. "He set his dogs on us. Not exactly a warm and fuzzy homecoming."

"So your name's not Kai."

"It's as much Kai as yours is Dalia." I returned the wrinkled nose she gave me. "And Ryder talks too damned much, especially about crap he should leave alone."

"So what is it?" She stretched up along my ribs to whisper into my ear. "I promise I won't tell anyone else."

"Tanic… my father… called me the Chimera," I said, my worthless brain echoing it in unsidhe. "Kind of a mouthful. Kai's better when filling out paperwork."

"Kai suits you," Dalia said, fighting a yawn. "I'm going to fall asleep now unless you need something."

"Nah, sleep sounds good." I let Newt curl up around my hand, his teeth scrubbing at my nails before he started drooling in his sleep. "And thanks for stitching me up, Michadalia."

"I'm going to kick your ass," she mumbled, biting me lightly on the arm. I guessed she chose someplace less bruised than others because it only stung from the sharp of her teeth. "You will never ever say that aloud again."

"Promise," I said, crossing my heart where I could over the bandage covering my shoulder. "I'll consider my ass prekicked."

I waited until I heard Dalia's breathing deepen, and she turned, a tiny whimpering snore escaping her open mouth. As Newt's purring competed with the pounding of my heart, I risked wrapping my arms around her and held her close, lying with her against me until the sun came up to take it all away.

CHAPTER TWENTY-TWO

"GOT TO tell you, boy," Jonas remarked as he walked around Oketsu's battered shell, "that car looks like it should be shot in the head and left in a swamp someplace to die."

"He's not that bad," I protested weakly. Running my hand over a punctured quarter panel, I refused to admit that Jonas had a point. "He's been worse."

We were in the warehouse's garage bay, directly under the bedroom area, the rolling door open to let the sunlight in. Sitting on the wide cement slab, Oketsu looked like he'd been run through a food processor set on munch. Most of his blood red paint was missing on the passenger side, scraped down to raw steel in some places, and more than one bite had been taken out of his ass end. The front bumper canted inward, distinctively crumpled in a shape vaguely the size of an unsidhe.

Starbursts crackled the front windshield, long lines intersecting and splitting off into different directions, and the back window was pocked with metal shards. Only the thin layers of transparent Kevlar kept the glass in-frame, but the film was shot, too bent and torn up to be repaired. His interior wasn't much better. It stank of blood, puke, and something else I identified as baby gunk combined with other foulness.

"A good cleaning and some steel work, he'll be fine," I said, mourning the ruined line of Oketsu's black leather hardtop. The sections' stitching was ripped apart by claws and teeth. I wasn't certain if the damage had been done by the dragon or black dogs, but I was willing to guess it'd been started by one and finished off by the other.

Jonas reached under the front of the hood to pop it up. He struggled to find the latch under the bent metal, then winced when the distressed springs shrieked. No amount of oil from the workbench would ease that sound, torn metal straining to work against damage. "Damn, Kai. It looks like a war zone in here. There's a strip of fur stuck to the manifold."

158

"Don't say that." Coming around the car, I almost wept with relief at the sight of the bright blue engine. "Quit screwing with me, Jonas. You're going to kill me."

"Considering you're—what?—two weeks dead right now? Just checking if your heart's still beating." He bent into the engine compartment, working at the hoses leading out of the carburetor. "It looks good. Just cosmetic on this end. How's the electric flat running in the back?"

"I don't know yet. This is the first chance I've had to look at him. Dalia wouldn't let me get out of bed." I scooted around the car's fender on my stomach to reach the transmission gauge.

As a bastardized setup, the Mustang ran on a blended system, having to work with both gas and fuel cell engines, so his transmission was usually the first piece to blow if it couldn't handle the shift in power. The dipstick came up a clean, clear pink, adding another positive to the scorecard. I'd have to go underneath to check further, but it was a good sign.

"I'm surprised you're out of the house at all." Ryder's voice drifted down into the engine space, and I nearly slammed the back of my head on the hood. "It's good to see you up and about, Kai. And I have to admit, the view I have of you is sublime."

"Kai, the asshole who tried to kill you is here. Want me to run him off?" Jonas growled, and I lost sight of his feet from my perch under the hood.

"I did not try to kill him," Ryder said as I slid out of the engine space. "No one told him to offer himself up as a sacrifice to the Hunt."

"From where I'm standing, the boy's beating is on you," Jonas said, jutting his wide jaw out and staring down his nose. "Count him as one of my own. Looks a little funny. Could be part Asian, maybe, but as far as I'm concerned, definitely mine. You, on the other hand, I don't know you."

"Jonas." I dusted a bit of grit from my belly and picked off a flower petal lodged in the waistband of my jeans. "There's a drought on. I'd have to wait until sundown to hose him off my driveway if you kill him. Bad enough my car stinks. Don't make my house smell like shit too."

The Stalker gave Ryder one last wicked eyeball, then grabbed me by the back of the neck, wrapping his massive hand nearly all the way around my throat. Shaking me lightly, he bent over and said in a not so quiet whisper, "I've got to head out, but if you need me to come back and shoot this son of a bitch, just let me know."

"I'm good." I let Jonas give me a bear hug, losing my grip on both the Mustang and the ground as he lifted me up. After a few attempts at breathing, I choked out some protest, and he put me down, ruffling my hair. "Thanks for bringing the truck down last week. Tell Briana thanks for the food."

"Not a problem," he grunted, bumping Ryder's shoulder as he passed. Jonas dwarfed him, nearly knocking the sidhe lord off his feet. "You need anything, you call up the house. If I can't come down, I'll get one of the kids to. Some of them should be good for something."

"Some?" Ryder watched Jonas step into the sunlight, then rumble off in his old F-150, its fuel cell convertor working hard to push the heavy steel beast. "How many does he have?"

"I think the last count was seventeen," I said with a shrug. "I've lost track. I know a couple of the wives pretty well. They like feeding me. I like being fed."

"Humans amaze me," he said, exhaling hard. Resting a hand on the front of the Mustang, Ryder looked me up and down, stopping to examine any bruises visible around my tank top. "You look good. The collarbone healed nicely."

"Yeah, Dalia did a good job setting it." I picked up my ink-folio and began to walk around the car, making notes on what I could salvage and what flat-out needed replacing. "Thanks for the money. You sent too much, though. It shouldn't cost that much to fix Oketsu, and to be fair, the dragon's on me."

"Keep it." Ryder followed, tailing me close enough that I could feel his body heat on my skin. "I owe you a lot."

"Hell, you came back for me. You could have kept going. No one would've blamed you. Not with two babies in the car," I said, stopping to inspect a door panel. There was no saving anything above the crease, but the bottom part looked solid. Rubbing at the line, I jotted down the measurements for the steel I'd need before moving down the body. "If anything, I should pay you."

"You still owed me dinner, and now that I know how bloodthirsty your family is, it was in my best interest to go back and get you," he said. "And as lovely as it is to watch you crawl around on your knees, I'm here because I need your help."

"Wasn't the Pendle run the last time I was going to work for you?" His bright green eyes were muted through the uneven bangs Dalia had cut into my hair.

"That's what you wanted but not what I needed." Ryder tried not to look smug as he passed me a slip of clearcoat, activating the liquid ink with a flick of his thumb. "I've contracted you through the Post. Here's the requisition for the job."

"Oh, hell no." I stood too quickly and caught a wave of dizzy. "They can't just assign me work. Stalkers are contract only. I have to accept."

"Actually, it's a government chit commandeering your services," he explained through his wide smile. "As the sidhe High Lord, I have diplomatic status, which includes full cooperation of local and state services. How else do you think I drove your gas-engine-powered monstrosity through San Diego without ending up in jail?"

"I think I hate you," I said, reading through the chit. My name flared through the words, picked out in crimson vivid enough to burn my eyes.

"Don't hate me. I pay better than the Post rates do." Then all teasing drained from his handsome face. "I'm serious, Kai. I need your help. Please."

I loathed hearing *please*, especially from someone I'd as soon tangle my sheets around. Dalia could undo me with a widening of her eyes, and Duffy had me wrapped around her finger when she dropped her voice down to a husky contralto to ask me for anything. My spine rattled under my carved wings, the skin crawling tight along my thighs and belly when I heard Ryder's soft and humble whisper, breaking down any walls I'd built up over the past two weeks.

"I'm to assist the local Court in any way possible?" I waved the chit under his nose. "Now I'm sure I hate you. What the hell is this?"

"Due to your unique position between the elfin and human societies...."

I cut him off. "Unique position? What kind of shit is that? Bent over, you mean."

"How many other elfin Stalkers are there?" he asked, raising an eyebrow at my disgruntled hiss. "None. Only you. Besides, this way I can keep an eye on you."

"I don't need an eye kept on me," I said, stabbing him in the chest with a finger. We were close in height, but I fell short of meeting his gaze straight on by a few inches. "I've got my own eyes on me."

"Can you at least hear me out?"

I slumped against the Mustang, going over the directive chit again. Ryder had effectively tangled up my Stalker license indefinitely. The language was loose, only a directive to assist the Court's successful integration into

San Diego's infrastructure, legal speak for bending over the government's couch. Ryder had me pressed up against a solid bureaucratic wall.

"Fine. Talk."

"Last night, someone broke into the Court's temporary quarters and tried to kill Ciarla's children," he said, nodding when my breath caught in my throat. "They're fine, but it's troubling."

"Your grandmother?" It was a guess on my part, but I couldn't think of anyone else who'd want the children dead. There was a flicker of pissed hovering in my brain. I'd nearly killed myself to see those kids safe.

"I've lodged a formal complaint, but those things take time. I won't know anything for a while." Ryder rocked back and forth on his heels with his fingers tucked into his pants pockets. "I'm making a serious accusation; infanticide is one of the most heinous crimes a sidhe can be charged with. The Justices haven't yet decided if the twins are even elfin."

"Because Shannon carried them?"

"Yes." He nodded. "If they're killed before that decision is handed down, then the accusation goes away, and anyone connected to their deaths walks free. It's as if they never existed."

"That's screwed," I said, nearly spitting in disgust. "Of course they exist. I got baby soup in my lungs because of one of them. What happened?"

"Someone broke in, either a drop onto the roof or through a service entrance—we're not sure which. Alexa opened the door—"

"Wait, Alexa? Your cousin Alexa?"

"She's joined my Court." Ryder nodded. "Alexa, her daughter, and a few of the others from Elfhaine came through the Temecula Pass. She went up to the nursery to see the babies and found Shannon trying to stop Kaia from bleeding."

"Kaia? Really?" I made a face. "What the hell did you name the other one? Ford?"

"No, her name is Rhianna." He shuffled his feet on the cement pad, moving around some of the dirt that had dropped off the Mustang. "You should be happy. It's an honor to have a child named after you."

"No, it sounds like she's going to be called Kayak in school and get into fights," I retorted. "But the kids are okay, right?"

"Shannon said she screamed when she saw someone standing over the crib. She thinks he got frightened and fled down the stairwell."

"How many damned entrances do you have into this building?" So far he'd mentioned at least three, not including the front door. Not a good sign. "And nobody noticed a strange human walking around the place?"

"No one," Ryder admitted reluctantly. He pulled at a shank of hair at his collar, frustration firming his shoulders. "Most of us were either downstairs in the inner courtyard helping the newcomers get settled, or out. Shannon was alone with the babies."

"So why didn't the guy kill her first? It's what I'd do." I grimaced when Ryder gave me a worried glance. "Well, if you were going in to kill a couple of kids, wouldn't you take the adult out first?"

"I don't think he expected her to be in the room or didn't see her come in."

"Pretty crappy assassin, which is a good thing for you but bad for him." I chewed on my lip, trying to imagine the scene. "So what do you think I can do? Sniff him out like a bloodhound?"

"You know San Diego. We don't," Ryder explained. "The elfin at Southern Rise aren't used to *seeing* humans, much less dealing with them on a day to day basis. Many of them never fought in the wars or dealt with the human culture. You look like one of us and act like one of them. I need you in my Court, and if I have to use a human injunction to get you there, then so be it."

"No way in hell's ice tray am I going to join a Court." I shook my head. Closing the hood, I searched my pocket for the keys, wondering if I'd left them in the ignition. "You keep bringing it up, and I keep saying no. I don't know what else to tell you to make you listen."

"Because you're elfin," he murmured, "and I'm the authority over the races here. Technically, anything that happens to you, anything you do, is governed by me and my law. The human government has no say over you. I do."

"Oh, screw that." I turned and gave his shoulder a light shove. "There's an easy way to take care of that. A sharp knife to your ribs and, snick, I'm clear of any elfin authority."

"I said technically. As far as I'm concerned, you're an independent. Until you choose not to be." Ryder slid up next to me, hooking his fingers into my belt loop. "Now I'm merely asking you to help."

"No, you're forcing me to help you," I said, holding up the chit. "This is force, extortion at least. I'm not up on my criminal charges, but at least it's professional blackmail."

"You can walk away," he said. "I wouldn't do anything to make you lose your license. I needed to show you I was serious about needing you."

"Are you?" I turned, still held captive by his fingers. I couldn't break free if I wanted to or tried. Ryder's grip held me firmly in place.

It bothered me that he was stronger. I was too used to humans and their shorter stamina. Another sidhe, brought up fed and at least partially combat trained, was a worry. I'd have to work hard to overcome any physical disadvantages and forget totally about competing against the arcane. I was about as magical as a Chinese finger puzzle.

"Do you have any idea how insane you make me?" Ryder's hand moved from my waist to cup the back of my head. His fingers worked through my hair, tugging at my scalp. A not-so-gentle shove trapped me against the car's fender, and he stepped in close.

"Let go of me," I said, tilting my chin up. Rough didn't bother me. He wouldn't be the first person to bruise me or hold me down, but I liked things on my terms, especially when it looked like it was going to be the only control I had.

"You know, let's do something different," he replied, narrowing his sidhe-emerald eyes. "I'm going to be the one that says no this time."

He bent forward, taking a subtle sip of my mouth. I didn't want the fire that crept along my skin when Ryder touched me, but I did nothing to stop him.

Ryder took my stillness as assent and pushed on, closing over my mouth with an almost punishing possession. When his tongue touched my lips, I gripped his shoulders, then let him in, kissing him deeply. He sucked at me, shoving his tongue deep into my mouth when I parted my lips for him. I took as much as he gave, sliding around his rough tongue. He drew out the kiss, rolling his hips into me with a slow, circular push.

"Don't bite me," he warned, sliding one hand down the back of my neck. "I just need… more."

Pushing up with his thumb, Ryder turned my chin until my head was thrown back and the soft skin under my jaw was exposed to his questing mouth. Trailing a long, slithering kiss down my skin, he stopped long enough to nip affectionately at my neck before tracing a heart with his tongue below it. His teeth nicked my skin there, and I felt tiny red rosettes welting on my throat.

"Ryder...." I needed him to stop. I was drowning in him, and it was a struggle to pull air into my tortured lungs. "Don't...."

"Why?" He kissed his way back up to my mouth, then rested his forehead against mine. We breathed into each other, the air hot between us. "Tell me you don't feel me under your skin. Tell me you can't feel this between us."

"Yeah," I admitted, hooding my eyes from his. Ryder's eyes tore me apart, ripping me open for him to stare down into my soul. "And it pisses me off. This *thing* between us is... chemistry."

"More than that, *áinle*," Ryder teased, stealing his cousin's pet name for me. "But I'll let you believe that for a little while longer." He traced my mouth with his finger, and I bit the tip, warning him away. "I don't want to tame you, Kai. I just want you."

"Yeah, better men have tried," I muttered, cocking my head at him. "Let me go now."

"I still have to know if you'll help me. Help us." He cupped my face, all teasing gone from his eyes. "Please."

Again with the please. Grunting, I pulled away a step, growling under my breath. The air was cold without him against me, and my teeth itched. I wanted to bite into him and leave a mark. I cleared my throat instead. "What happens when your sidhe find out I'm not...."

"Sidhe?"

"Yeah." My breathing was slowly steadying, but my heart beat frantically, and I wondered if Ryder could hear it. I took another step and exhaled slowly. "Yeah, that."

"They won't say anything." Ryder leaned his hand on the seemingly only palm-sized edge of Oketsu's hood that remained unscathed by black dog acid, claws, or dragon sear. "I'm not my grandmother, Kai. I see things differently than she does. I'm not easy on them, but I'm not a tyrant. I demand loyalty and community, not blind devotion."

"I'm not sure I see things the way you do," I admitted.

"That's because you've not been raised by your own kind," he protested. "How did Dempsey get hold of you? The elfin are protective of their children. We don't just let them wander off to be found by a Stalker."

"I've heard different stories about it." Shrugging, I made a face. "Dempsey was bluffing at cards. Tanic's guy cheated, but when it was all said and done, he was the proud owner of one Chimera. Dempsey couldn't pronounce the unsidhe, so he stuck with the Singlish."

"I wondered about that. It's an odd name for a kid," Ryder said softly. His fingers stroked my side. I wanted to pull away, but the touch was comforting despite the strings attached to it.

"I wasn't a kid. Never was." I touched his hand briefly, enough to feel his warmth, then pulled back. "Tanic—my father—had a sidhe woman. I don't know her name. No one ever spoke it near me, but he made sure to let me know what happened to her."

"You don't have to tell me this, Kai. Not if you don't want to." His hands were still on me, burning and comfortable. "If it's too hard...."

"I thought about not telling you, especially after your grandmother's crap, but the more I thought about it, the smarter it seemed, so just shut up and let me talk," I ordered softly. He said nothing but nodded. "Tanic did something to her, my mother. Well, other than the obvious, but whenever she got pregnant, he would... use his power to alter the children before they were born, changing them into... these *things*. She gave birth, I think, four or five times before me, but each baby she had died."

"Died?" Ryder frowned. "From what?"

"Some couldn't breathe or weren't... right. They were hideous—extra legs, or tentacles and twisted. Most didn't live long after they cut open the eggs, but all of them eventually died. Tanic didn't care. He went back to what he was doing. She wasn't anything more than a place to cook his seed."

"Tanic is one of the oldest Hunt Masters from Underhill. He is dedicated to death and suffering. It's what he is. Every sidhe knows of him. Our mothers use him to make us behave," Ryder said, risking another touch on my side. I let him lay his hand there, not moving when he stroked at my spine, traveling down my back until his fingers lay on the rise of my ass. "I'm sorry for that, Kai."

"It's okay." I shook my head when he tried to argue. "No really, it's okay. Or at least now it is. I figure my mother couldn't deal with it anymore. She couldn't give birth to any more of those things, so one night she somehow got ahold of a knife and stabbed herself in the belly. It cut through my egg and severed her spine. She was dead before the guards could open her cell.

"She hated the thought of me so much, Ryder. So much that she wanted to kill both of us," I said, gritting my teeth. The pain I thought I'd tossed off a long time ago came back, kicking me in the heart. "The shell hadn't hardened enough, and I guess I slid out. I don't know much else about it."

"But Tanic… what was he thinking? What did he have to gain from changing the children that way?"

"I don't know, but Tanic kept at it until he got me." I blew a breath out of my pursed mouth. "I came out wrong, both sidhe and unsidhe inside. The healers suspected that maybe I was supposed to be twins, that I hadn't separated or something, but there I was, Tanic's Chimera.

"He couldn't ransom me to her house, not with my blood, and he couldn't keep me as his son, so he had healers age my body, growing me as quickly as they could." I swallowed, remembering the pain of my bones stretching and breaking through skin. "When they were done, I was pretty much as you see me now. Except for my mind. You can't age a mind. I was a baby, stuck in a fully grown body.

"I became something for them to play with, something to practice on." I shrugged at Ryder's murmur. "Then one day, a guard decided he could get some money out of my mother's family, and he stole me. I'm not sure where he was going, but eventually he lost everything he had in a card game to a bunch of humans. That's how I ended up with Dempsey."

"You don't owe Dempsey for that." Ryder's voice trembled, either from shock or horror. I didn't feel brave enough to look at his face.

"Dempsey was saddled with an insane mixed-elfin monster who didn't know enough to unzip before pissing himself. He had to teach me how to eat and to talk. Then he taught me how to shoot and take care of myself. I might be a monkey in a cat suit, but I'm here," I argued, raising my chin to meet Ryder's eyes. "He's not my father. I'd already escaped my father. Dempsey's a frigging saint compared to him."

"You should have been with your own people," he said, touching my cheek with skimming fingers. "You should know what it means to be sidhe."

"No thanks. I've met your grandmother, who I think knows more than she's saying. Hell, she might know Tanic's my father. She knew I was a monster. Even called me one."

"The Sebac's wrong," he finally said, stopping me before I could open my mouth again. Pressing his hand on my back, he pulled me closer, not letting me go until I was up against him. "You're not a monster, Kai. Those little girls aren't monsters. So Tanic found a way to blend our races. So what? I found a way to give the sidhe children their bodies won't kill."

"Are you going to keep doing that?" I asked, looking up at his face. The light hit his cheekbones, brightening the green in his eyes. "Even knowing that Tanic made *things*, do you think that's a good idea?"

"The elfin need to survive, *áinle*," Ryder replied. "We need healthy children, and we need to learn to live with the humans, not kill them. And for the record, I don't think you're a monster. Far from it."

He brushed his mouth against my temple, light enough to be a whispering touch. There was no pressure in it. No promise or entanglement. Just a touch of his lips on my skin. And it was more than enough to leave me stiff and uncomfortable.

And wanting more.

"I don't know if throwing human wombs up for a sidhe free-for-all is right. It's not... how things should be, and I'm not saying that because it's some sacred sidhe dogma. It's... shit, it's not what nature wanted for the sidhe or the unsidhe."

"I can respect that you disagree with me," he said, smirking when I snorted at him. "But that's not the girls' fault. They're innocent in this. Just like you, *áinle*."

"No, you're right there," I agreed. "Crap, Ryder! I wanted to walk away from all this. From anything even connected to the elfin."

"And from me?"

"Especially you. You make me...." I left my sentence unfinished. I didn't want to hear me, and if I said it out loud, I was afraid that what was between us would become more real. My shoulder was beginning to ache, and the previously stitched-up skin over my collarbone itched. I pushed him away again, giving myself some space. "Go home, Ryder."

"Will you be there?" He cocked his head.

"Yeah, I'll head over there. Link me the address. I can at least look at what you've got."

"Thank you, Kai." He touched the small of my back. "I promise, nothing other than business."

Ryder appeared earnest, a sincere honesty painted over his exotic sidhe features. Being an excellent liar myself, I believed him as far as I could toss a dragon. My doubt must have shown on my face. There was only so much a poker face could cover.

"Pfah," I said.

"Too much?"

"Like rolling dog shit in sugar and feeding it to me as chocolate. Get out. I need to close up the garage and then get cleaned up. Give me an hour."

"Okay." Ryder stepped back, probably fearful I'd deal with him the same way we'd done the Hunt Master. Considering the hood was already banged up, it wasn't a bad idea. "Are we going to talk about what my grandmother did to you?"

"Nope," I said.

"Are we ever going to talk about it?"

"Maybe over your grandmother's dead body," I replied. Leaving the garage, I hit the access button and rolled the door sheaves down. "She really screwed me up, bringing a Hunt down on your ass. If he didn't die there, then he's gone back and told Tanic where he saw me. It won't take long before someone comes sniffing around here looking for me."

"I can protect you, Kai," Ryder promised, adding a sidhe sealing ward behind his promise. Predictably, it made me slightly green. He grimaced. "Sorry. I forgot. No spells on you."

"You can't even protect two babies, your lordship," I said as I headed to the front door. "I think your chances of protecting me from my father are about as good as me learning how to pull a unicorn out of my ass."

CHAPTER TWENTY-THREE

A SHOWER took Oketsu's dirt off my skin, washing Pendle grime and oil down the drain. Fairly new black jeans and a T-shirt were the closest things I had to professional. A black leather jacket, old enough to be butter soft, went on last. It would hide any firearms and keep me warm. There was no helping the boots. They were worn in but could take a beating, which seemed to spontaneously occur whenever I went to stick my nose into someone else's business.

I'd not told Dalia I was leaving, and since she was working, I wasn't going to. It seemed safer not to.

The early evening hours were a horrible time to be driving in the center of San Diego. While the upper streets were cramped with traffic, the lower levels were sardined. Tik-tiks flew and dipped as they caught and released overhead cables, and a driver could die of old age waiting for the lights to change as the trolleys filled the underground tunnels. I fought the Broadway lines for almost half an hour before giving up, and stuck my toll pass to the truck's windshield.

"Screw it. Ryder can pay the damned charges." The readout ticked off the amount of a shrimp noodle dinner before I hit the off-ramp to the Cortez district. "He wants me here? He can pay to have me here."

The jacaranda trees left a lavender snow on the streets, their branches twisting up and over the lanes. Walkers trotted behind packs of dogs, stopping to scrape up any feces their furry charges left behind. Overhead, CSiP cops patrolled the air on sleek Spyder Cam-Am. One peeled off, zipping to a side street, the cut-in blue-red lights on his bike flashing as he chased down a speeder. I slowed down, not wanting to be caught driving while elfin. My Stalker creds only got me so far with the local cops, and even closer to nowhere with the CSiP.

While the truck blended on the understreets, above the line it stood out among the sleek-bodied vehicles around me as I drove by. My truck certainly wasn't pretty, not with its mismatched paint and acid-burned sides, but it was a good honest vehicle. I felt rather offended when someone next to me rolled his window up, as if the truck's dents would somehow spill onto his sports car.

"It's okay, old girl," I said, patting the dashboard. "You're a working truck. You've got nothing to be ashamed of."

I found the Court's rented quarters without any trouble. The gated buildings were cordoned off a few hundred yards from the main entrance, mainly to keep the Humans-Only-Earth protesters at bay. Fanatical during the war, their inflamed passions had died down to underhanded petty crimes against elfin or elfin sympathizers. Considering who led Ryder's Clan, I'd be inclined to agree with them.

Stopping at the gate, I rolled the truck window down. My face was enough to pass a bored human security guard. Other cars came through the gates behind me, waved on either from visual recognition or access chips in their consoles. Delivery trucks came through a service entrance, huge lumbering vehicles that could easily hide an entire bloodthirsty anti-sidhe regiment. From the looks of how easily accessible the area was, I was embarrassed at the laziness of the HOE protesters. If they'd been even marginally serious about storming the towers, someone could have walked in with a bazooka hidden in a bouquet of flowers.

"These people suck," I said, parking behind a sidhe transport glider docked against the curb.

A familiar form stepped out of the transport. Alexa straightened and stretched her long body before grabbing a pair of bags from the cargo space. Seeing me, her smile brightened the harsh lines of her face, then wavered, probably dimmed by the memory of serving me up to her grandmother's chewing mandibles.

"Hey," I said, taking the bags from her. We stared at one another. I wasn't sure how to say I was over being pissed off, and was about to make some excuse about not calling sooner when her hands cupped my jaw, and she kissed me.

There was not a shred of softness in the kiss, not at the beginning. She poured her taste into my mouth, drowning me. I grabbed a slice of air into my lungs when Alexa slowed her assault, relaxing into her hands when her tongue rubbed against the roof of my mouth. We slid around each other, a sensual slow dance with slightly rough tongues and nips of our teeth. My jeans tightened over my hips, and her hand slid down to cup my ass. It was harder to pull away from her mouth than it was to kill the black dog that snatched me from Oketsu's window.

"What? Do I look easy today?" I grinned at her, unable to stop a smile from spreading on my face.

"You looked kissable," she said, wiping the edge of my mouth with her thumb. "It is good to see you. You are good to see."

Ryder's flat, chilled voice was like someone threw a bucket of ice water over us.

"Alexa, take your hands off Kai," he said, sliding into view over her shoulder. "Now."

Unlike Alexa, he wore human clothing, a pair of jeans and a dark green button-up shirt. With his rolled-up sleeves and leather loafers, he could almost have passed for one of the affluent from the neighborhood. If it weren't for the metallic gold and bronze streaks in his wheat hair or his gem-colored eyes, I would have mistaken him for human from far away.

"He is not yours, and I am happy to see him," she said, crushing me with strong arms. Her chest was soft, pliable beneath the informal black elfin-cut shirt she wore instead of the uniform I'd last seen her in. There was no mistaking her for anything other than authority, even with her tongue down my throat. If she pulled out a pair of wrist ties and a baton, it would be hard to say no to her, even with my strong dislike of being bound. "You forgive me, then, pretty?"

"Yeah," I replied, smiling at her wide grin. "I thought about it. Figured it was stupid of me to hold your relatives against you."

"Good." Alexa exhaled into my mouth, leaving me with a small taste of her on my lips. "Come along. I will show you where the intruder was."

"I'll do that," Ryder interjected, stepping in to grab my arm. Cocking his head at his cousin, he gave her a cold smile. There was a Newt-like growl under his words, as if someone had poked a paw into his dinner. "Don't you have some unpacking to do?"

"Jealous, cousin?" she replied, standing firm in front of him, her hands on her hips. "Maybe you heard about my offer to make him purple-eyed babies? Maybe he told you he was thinking about it?"

"Standing right here." I waved my hand between the two sidhe. They were close, standing eye to eye and almost snarling at one another. "And no, no babies. Thanks for the offer, though."

"Come on," Ryder said, tugging at me. I stopped and looked at him, silently daring the lord to pull at me again. He released my arm, puffing his cheeks up as he exhaled. "Sorry. Things have been a little tense."

"Not a problem," I replied with a shrug. Stopping at the truck, I retrieved one of my shotguns, sliding extra ammo into my jacket pocket.

"So you really think you'll need that?"

"I'm thinking yes. Especially after not having any weapons the last time I walked into a sidhe Court." I bowed my head, preparing to follow him into the building.

"Is that your vehicle, áinle?" Alexa's wrinkled nose and horrified sniff told me she thought very little of my truck. "What color is that?

"It's not a color. It's primer." The truck had seen better days, certainly, but it was sturdy and durable. It wouldn't make a Pendle run, but it was great for hauling around bounties and skins. "Well, the gray parts are. Most of the rest is just dark brown. Some of it is black dog blood. It eats the paint."

"It is very ugly," she declared, walking around the truck bed. "And it does not suit you. You should be driving something sleek and beautiful. Maybe a little dangerous. Unpredictable—like your pretty red car."

"Let's not talk about Kai's pretty red car," Ryder interrupted.

"Yeah, let's not," I agreed. "See you later, Alexa."

"Of course, áinle." The sidhe warrior gave my truck another indignant sniff before heading back to the transport. "Try not to let my cousin corner you in a hallway."

"Lovely girl. Very shy. She should work on opening up," I said, falling into step behind Ryder. The glass doors swished open for us, parting like beetle wings into the stone sleeves near the entrance. No one stopped me. Someone should have, considering I was following Ryder with a gun near his back. "Your security is horrible. I'm surprised no one's tried to kill you before now."

"Alexa's my security now. Take it up with her," Ryder said, punching in an access code for the lift. "We didn't have any before. We never had a need."

"There are human-only zealots right outside your front door. You didn't think it was necessary?" The sidhe lord boggled my mind. There was arrogance, but this bordered on suicidal. "Are you insane?"

"No. Mostly the local police took care of any problems we had." He shrugged. Letting me into the lift first, he selected a floor near the top. "I didn't anticipate that someone would come into the building to kill the children. It's not something… it's not an elfin thing to do. Killing a child is… unimaginable."

"Well, someone else imagined it pretty good, I think." The elevator clicked off the floors, racing us up to thirty. "You know, you guys aren't living on the yellow brick road anymore."

"It wasn't expected." Ryder stepped out into a plain beige lobby, his tense back muscles hardening his body line. "Alexa being here will help. She has a good reputation. There's a bloc of sidhe soldiers coming here to the Court because she's here."

"Shouldn't they be coming here because of you?" I asked his back as he walked away from me.

Standing in the middle of a sea of dull, Ryder was a vivid line dividing the hallway into shadow and bright, his lean body cutting off the glow from the low-light panels as he walked in front of them. I followed, counting off the number of times the hallways intersected. I'd gotten up to four crisscrosses before we stopped at a door. The place was a maze, and it wasn't hard to imagine losing someone in a foot chase through the sea of dun carpet and wallpaper.

"Gotta admit," I said as I stepped carefully into the room, trying to imagine how the scene played out, "I'm really surprised someone hasn't broken in here and killed all of you in your sleep before now."

The smell of fresh blood was strong. Not human blood but sidhe—the faint snake-scale powdery tinge coupled with copper. I've bled a lot. I know how I smell, and from the overpowering scent, there was a lot of it spilled somewhere in the closed-up rooms.

I went silent, keeping a running string of filth rolling in my throat. Ducking around a narrow wall that blocked my view to the main room, I shoved Ryder behind it. To his credit, he didn't make a sound, letting me stalk farther into the room, the shotgun kept down and cocked at the ready.

Crouching next to a trail of sticky liquid, I skimmed the tip of my finger over the wet on the floor, not surprised to find it was blood. Fat drops shone dull on the wood, spreading out over the pale blue carpet covering the expanse of a living room with windows for walls. The view was expensive, overlooking the ocean and the wide white private beaches maintained for the sector's residents. With the sun falling into the sea, an orange-red glow filled the room, turning the bloodstains on the carpet to mahogany.

The previous owner of the blood lay open-eyed and dead on the floor, partially hidden behind a low couch. Her face was veiled by a curtain of brown-striped wine red hair, a glaze of white already settling into her silver eyes.

Another mouth had been cut into her throat. It was slit so far open that it was uncomfortable to look at her slung-back head. She stared at nothing, her upside-down face slack and white. Clothed in a loose cotton shirt and pants, she lay where she had died, the spray from her throat coating the underside of a glass table. Blood dripped down from the glass and onto the carpet, and up close I could feel some warmth left on her skin.

"Morrígan damned." Ryder swallowed and stopped himself before stepping on the carpet.

"Unsidhe," I said, carefully walking around the edges of the room so I could get a better look at the body. Her blouse was wet from leakage, breasts heavy on her narrow chest. "Odd choice for an assassin. She's milking. I'm guessing she was brought for the babies. Do you know her?"

"No." He followed my footsteps, taking a good look at the woman. "The nursery bedroom is over there."

"I'll go look," I said, giving Ryder a stern frown before he argued. "Stay here."

There was more blood in the hall, drops that got farther apart and tinier as they led to a door. Bringing the gun up, I placed my hand on the latch, keeping to the side as I flung the door open. A hallway dressed in beige lay quiet on the other side. Another door was ajar, and I peeked in, waiting to be jumped. Two elaborate cribs sat against a solid wall, ivory-painted wooden trees cradling soft hammock mattresses. There wasn't any sign of a struggle in the room. Nothing was overturned or looked disturbed. From what I could see through an archway, Shannon slept in an antechamber off the nursery. Or I would have assumed that's where she slept if there'd been any sign left of her in the room.

Drawers were open, left empty of any possessions. She'd only packed a few bags, but the sole trace I found of someone sleeping in the room was the spit of toothpaste in the bathroom sink. Stepping back into the nursery, my stomach sank to my knees, and I was sicker than if the whole building had broken out into a sidhe opera.

"Fuck." Singlish didn't satisfy, so I tried again with better results. *"Diu nei ah seng."*

"Kai?" Ryder's shadow darkened the doorway, and I turned to glare at him.

"Didn't I tell you to stay there?"

"What's going on? I heard you swear."

"Shannon's gone." I padded around the place. The babies were tiny and wouldn't spill a lot of blood. Dark corners lurked in the bedroom, and my stomach clenched in fear. A shadow near a dresser turned out to be a fallen toy rather than what I was scared I'd find. "The girls are gone too. It looks like someone took them."

"Damn it!" Ryder stepped back, searching through the nursery. "Shannon?"

"I'd guess so. Packed up her shit and left. Place is wiped out." I motioned to the bedroom. "I think she's the one who took them, and it wasn't to protect them. If it was, she'd have come and found you."

"She was going to be their nanny until Ciarla and her marriage could take over." He looked shocked and about as sick as I felt. The anger would come later. For right now, he was stunned and guilt-ridden. "What is going on? How did an unsidhe get up here without anyone noticing?"

"I don't know, Ryder." Passing him, I patted his shoulder and activated my phone. "But I think I know someone who can help us find out."

CHAPTER TWENTY-FOUR

RYDER PACED and chewed on the edge of his thumbnail. I put it down as a nervous habit, but the creased line between his eyebrows said something different. He needed to do something. Standing around waiting wasn't a Ryder thing to do.

Standing with me and Alexa, he watched Cari Brent crouch over the dead unsidhe, staring into her open eyes to pull on the memories left behind. I'd grown tired of staring at Cari's butt, and if she suddenly turned and found me checking her out, I'd have to dodge a knife or shoe to my head.

"She's a what?" Ryder asked.

"A *hibiki*." Cupping my hands over the end of my cigarette, I lit the clove, taking a full mouthful of smoke into my chest. It numbed my tongue and pressed the air from my lungs, leaving me with a slight dizziness when I exhaled. "It means echo, kinda. She can look into a dead person's eyes and see their last thoughts. Depending on how fresh the body is."

Most humans refused to believe in things they couldn't see, especially anything dealing with the dead. The elfin spent their lives surrounded by mysteries and magic, so my words got the barest of nods. Alexa murmured something about the skill being useful in investigations, but they seemed to accept Cari's preternatural ability with a shrug of impatience for her to get on with it.

"I would say her last thought was, '*Why am I breathing through my throat?*' or maybe something like that?" Alexa paced off a length of hallway, her hands clenched at her sides. "How long does this take? We should be doing something."

"Nothing to be done," I said, leaning against the wall to get out of her path. "Cari's the best bet. Shannon didn't exactly leave us a note. Besides, Cari's a Stalker. She'll be able to put the things she sees together into something we can use."

"You shouldn't do that here," Ryder said, absently noticing I'd started smoking. For a moment, I thought he was going to join his cousin in measuring out the carpet with his feet, but he remained where he was, splitting his attention between me and Cari. "This is where the babies spend a lot of their time."

"I think smoke and ash aren't high up on your to-be-worried-about list right now." I took another pull, crossing my legs at my ankles. "Finding Shannon and the kids, *that's* what you should be worried about."

"Are we sure that woman took them?" Alexa stopped, pinning me to the wall with a sharp look. "Do we know that?"

"All her stuff is gone, and only the babies were taken from the nursery," I replied. Ryder and I had spent the ten or so minutes before Cari arrived going through the room. He verified that none of the clothing purchased for the infants was gone. Only a few bottles of breast milk and a chiller had been taken. On one hand, I was relieved she took that. It showed she meant to keep the babies alive for a while. On the other hand, it looked like she or someone else killed the wet nurse brought for the girls. "I'm wondering why she gave birth to them at all if she meant to take them. That doesn't make any sense."

"Grandmother," Alexa pronounced. "I will bet she forced the human into something."

"The human?" I cocked my head. "About half an hour ago, she was your buddy Shannon."

"She's violated our trust. Her name's dead to us," Ryder said, turning back to the doorway to watch Cari work. "Just like she'll be dead in body once we find her."

"Can't let you do that," I said softly, shaking my head when the sidhe turned to stare me down. "She's human. She falls under our—human—law. That's the accord. Either a Stalker or an officer of the law can arrest her, but she's got to be handed over to the human authorities."

"I do not like it," Alexa growled. "The human courts will charge her only with kidnapping. They will not understand the—taking—how wrong it is."

"Might help that Ryder's got that diplomatic get-out-of-shit card, but I don't think so." I poked my head in the door, hearing Cari call my name. "Yeah?"

"Come in here," she ordered. "I'm ready for you."

Raised by her Latina mother near the Tijuana-sidhe border while her German-Irish father hunted black dogs and other beasties, Cari was a third-generation Stalker, born into the life with an extra kick of mojo that made her a dangerous woman to cross. Dempsey pissed her off once, and while I wasn't clear on the details, he now avoided Cari Brent like the plague.

Of course, pissing people off was something Dempsey did on a regular basis.

"Stay here," I told Ryder and Alexa. As they pressed up behind me, I didn't have much hope they'd listen to me. All I was hoping for was a manageable distance.

"You ready, *bonito*?" Cari took the clove from my fingers and put it to her mouth. She took a deep slug of smoke, then exhaled slowly up into the air. Passing it back to me after another hit, she shook her arms loose, breathing out a few times to clear her mind. "Finish the rest of that, *bebé*, and let's get started."

I took what I could of the cigarette, bringing it down an inch or more closer to the filter. I pinched the clove out between my fingers, then tossed it into a metal refuse can near the door, hurried by the impatience in her voice. Ryder and Alexa filled the foyer opening. He stood still, with his cousin stalking a few steps back and forth behind him. There was nothing I could say that would make what had happened better or all right. The most I could do for Ryder right now was find out where Shannon went and hope the girls would be alive when we found them.

Other sidhe gathered outside in the hallway, keeping their voices down, but their words floated in, worried and increasingly loud. A silent jerk of Ryder's head toward the door ordered Alexa to close off the hallway, keeping the room quiet. He returned my thanks with a quirk of his mouth.

Cari's fingers worked to loosen her hair, unraveling the thick plait at her back. Strands of gold thread dangled from smaller slender braids hidden within the larger weave. Set free, they fell forward, brushing against her smooth, creamy skin. Her youth had ripened lately, rounding out her curves and layering age into her dark blue eyes. She looked more like her mother than her father, stone-hewn features native to the area, rich with a hot wisdom and a fiery tongue.

I wasn't overly tall by any standard, elfin or human. With her shoes off, Cari came up to my shoulder, but despite the lack of height, there wasn't anything childlike about her. Her eyes were cunningly sharp, and as she lowered herself to the floor, her hips swayed in a way that told men she knew what she could do with them. Crossing her ankles under her, she sat on her legs, wiping her palms on her jeans.

"Good thing you called me before she got deader," she said, her Spanglish rasp roughening her words. "I'll be able to get a lot out of this one."

She needed someone she trusted to help her as she worked, and I made the short list. I'd pitched in for Cari and her mother before and knew that people focused on the oddest things when they died. I could only hope the dead unsidhe woman knew the details of Shannon's flight from the Court's towers.

"Ready?" I asked. I was dreading what was coming, but I was more scared of what we'd find out.

"Yeah, let's screw this bitch," Cari replied.

With the taste of cloves on my tongue, I sipped at the rotgut tequila Cari had brought with her, swishing it around in my mouth. She laid her head back with her face toward the heavens and opened her mouth wide, laying her tongue cupped against her jawbone.

Standing over her with my feet on either side of her thighs, I let the tequila dribble from my mouth into hers, wiping at the splatter on her cheeks. The rotgut agave went down her throat, and Cari choked, coughing around the liquid, but she kept her head back.

I picked up a pair of long tweezers, then dug around in the glass jar she'd opened and placed near us. I fished around the cactus buttons and dried yellow-warty red mushrooms, trying to find what I needed in the milky, clouded tequila. An alcohol-bloated, roasted *gusano* floated by the tines, and I snagged it, careful not to pinch the worm in two.

The worm fit against my lip and teeth, and I held it there while I dug out a few of the buttons. Careful not to swallow the *gusano*, I squashed the cacti down between my molars, then flicked the worm around to add to the mix.

Chewing carefully, I pushed the mash to the front of my mouth, trying not to gag on the bitter, dry potato taste of the buttons. The worm's nuttiness did not mask any of the rancid sourness on my tongue, and when I felt like I couldn't take much more of the taste, it blended together. I pulled my cheeks in to gather the mash up, then spit it past Cari's waiting lips.

She took the mash better than I did, catching it on the flat of her tongue and chewing, sipping at the tequila bottle every few turns to wash the worm-laden buttons down. I left her to swallow, concentrating on extracting three mushrooms from the liquor. The peyote was already working, numbing the skin along my arms and neck.

Struggling to control my fingers' trembling, I found what I needed from the jar and put the caps on my tongue. Using the tips of the tweezers,

I dug under my skin, opening up a gash on my palm. I heard Ryder say something, but I ignored him, concentrating only on the *hibiki*.

Dripping my blood into my mouth, I chewed thoroughly, keeping my tongue pressed up against my throat so I didn't swallow any of the mushrooms. By far they were the worst tasting things in the batch, and I didn't want them anywhere near my throat. Cari grunted as she took the last of the mash down with a mouthful of tequila and laid her head back again, waiting for the rest of it.

I grabbed the jar and filtered the tequila between my teeth, keeping the chewed mushrooms I had on my tongue in and the rest of the jar's contents out. Someone gagged behind me, either Alexa or Ryder. I couldn't guess which. The first time I'd seen the ritual, I emptied my stomach on a pair of new Converses and swore I'd never watch again.

Yet here I was, again chewing up a psychotropic tequila puree.

Spitting the mix into the lid of the jar, I squeezed out a few more drops of blood and lit a lucifer. Setting the flame to the drenched mushrooms and blood, I turned my head as it flared up, bright yellow flames cooking through the chew.

I took the tequila from Cari. I extinguished the flames, then carefully lifted the jar lid from the carpet. Tilting the lid, I poured the still hot fluid, mushrooms, and cooked blood into Cari's mouth, steadying myself when the concoction took her over the edge.

Cari's eyes rolled back, and a film seeped from her lids, covering her corneas with a red-threaded milk. Lifting her arms, she spread her hands out, fingers stiff and bent at the first joint. Bubbling sounds emanated from her open lips, guttural, coarse noises that fought to escape her too-human throat. Her voice settled, changing into a Singlish I could understand. Still accented heavily with her native tongue, it took me a while to focus on what Cari was saying, parsing out the slang into something comprehensible.

"*Oso del chino*," she growled, snapping the words off. "*Blanco y negro*. Black and white bears. They are going to the Towers. Vasco Núñez de Balboa—his towers. They are going to meet a Hunter. One who keeps the madness of the dogs at bay. The human—she is angry—she doesn't believe when the other says that he will pay her. She does not trust him."

"Shannon didn't trust him?" I scoffed. "Who the hell trusted her?"

"Do you know the place she is speaking of?" Alexa shoved past her cousin, her long legs bringing her quickly into the main room. She reeled back when Cari turned her white eyes toward her. Alexa grabbed at the knife hanging from her belt, but Ryder's fingers on her wrist stopped her drawing her weapon.

"Easy, cousin," he rumbled, stroking the inside of her wrist. "The human's gone with an unsidhe?"

"Yes," Cari mumbled, rolling the *S* until it flattened. The white was beginning to bleed from her gaze, returning her eyes to blue. "He killed the unsidhe wet nurse when she tried to stab Shannon—the surrogate. The dead woman was angry, her word challenged. She wanted recompense... from someone. I don't know who."

"And instead she got a knife to the throat," I said, handing Cari a bottle of water. She drank slowly, rinsing the drugs and alcohol from her mouth before swallowing. The numbness was passing from my system, and the edges of my vision were no longer purple-speckled. I couldn't begin to imagine how Cari's smaller body was holding up under the influence of the peyote and mushrooms, but she looked none the worse for wear when she held her hand out for me to help her up. "Balboa's Towers and bears. She's talking about old Balboa Park."

"That's where the Court is going to be established," Ryder said with a nod. "Bears? Was she talking about the pandas?"

"Pandas?" Alexa made a face. "The round, furry cute bears?"

"They are round and furry." Cari wobbled her hand back and forth. "But not so cute; they're very vicious."

"What does this have to do with pandas?" Alexa asked, her bright eyes clouded with confusion. "Are those towers not ours? Where our Court is. Or will be, yes?"

"There are wild pandas roaming through part of the sidhe territory," Ryder explained. "They're from an old pre-Merge conservation program. I agreed to let them remain there. A human woman lives near them. She documents their progress and breeding."

"She's nuts." I snorted. "They don't call her Crazy Gertie because she wears mismatched socks. She'll shoot you if you get near the area."

"I've asked her to stop doing that. The Court will provide protection for her and the animals." Ryder bit his lip, thinking.

"She might have a thing or two to say about that." Stretching my arms out, I shook them, trying to get all the feeling back into my fingers. "Want us to go in and get them, or are you and your great security up to it?"

Ryder didn't answer me. I had no right to care about the babies. Other than sucking out some egg white from one of the girls' nostrils and mouth, I wasn't related to them. Considering the Sebac was their grandmother, the Dusk Court couldn't be that bad in comparison, but I'd be damned if I didn't want them where I could watch them grow up a bit.

"I am very good security. The man before me, we will have to talk to him. Maybe string him up for this, but I am very good," Alexa responded, hitting me lightly on the shoulder. "Besides, you two are Stalkers. This is not your business."

"Kind of is. Shannon is human, and like Kai said, she's ours," Cari admitted with a wry grin. "And the unsidhe bastards have been raiding the *indios* again. Arturo's had his hands full going in to get the kids back. This bitch had a hand in the raids."

"That word—*indios*?" Alexa frowned. "What are those?"

"They are the people who live in the areas outside Tijuana." Cari looked up at Alexa. They were an odd contrast, a tall, muscular flame-headed sidhe and a short, voluptuous brunette, but they both resonated with strength. I pursed my mouth, wondering if bringing them together wasn't the smartest idea I'd ever had. "The Dusk steal *indio* babies and kill the parents. My brothers and father make runs into the *sucio* to bring them back. Sometimes they have too much of a head start and are too deep into their own territory."

"If the Dusk Court steal human children, it is to have a changeling," Alexa growled. "There must be a market for them down there. All the more reason to have a Dawn Court here, cousin."

"Changelings?" Cari cocked her head. "You think the girls were stolen for that?"

"Changelings are more like pets than servants," Ryder said softly, circling us. "Before our worlds collided, the unsidhe stole our children if they could. Some became changelings, while others were raised as unsidhe. They could have taken the twins for either purpose."

I knew all about pets. I didn't need Ryder to fill me in on that little unsidhe tradition.

Most people were motivated by money, regardless of race. Shannon might have carried the girls, but she did it for cash. It wasn't a far stretch for me to think she'd hand them over to someone else for even more.

"I get raising the kids as unsidhe, but why the *indios*? Humans don't live that long, not by elfin standards. Why would you want something that died off quickly?" I shook my head.

"Like he said, pets," Cari replied, crouching back over the dead woman's body. She began going through the woman's clothes, digging into pockets. "You own a cat. He's going to die before you do, but you still own him."

"I've met the cat," Ryder commented darkly. "I would challenge the particulars of who owned whom."

"The Dusk Courts don't just steal children, little Cari," Alexa said, watching Cari thoroughly work over the body for anything else of use. "They take grown sidhe too, make them produce children. It was a way to fund their Courts. A House would give anything to have one of their blood back. Even if the kidnapped sidhe never came back to them, they carried on in their children."

"So elfin *can* breed? With each other?"

"They can have children, but the child will be either sidhe or unsidhe. Our genes… choose which way to go. There are no mingled elfin," Alexa replied.

I said nothing to contradict her. Sometimes keeping my mouth shut was the best course of action.

"Okay, so they're either one or the other." Cari shook her head. "When their sidhe pets got pregnant, they'd ransom those kids back? Like some sort of puppy mill? Why not just keep the kids?"

"If the child was born sidhe, it would be smarter to ransom the child back to the sidhe House," Ryder interjected, crossing his arms and frowning. "Too many sidhe in a Dusk Court would be a problem, especially if they decided to overthrow the adopting House. The House and its properties become a sidhe stronghold, and the Dawn gains in power. That's happened before."

"So they took the girls to be pets or a part of their Court?" I wanted to get the conversation back on track. "That's what we're going with?"

"Their hair is light enough to be turned white if a healer did it," Alexa said. "They could be raised thinking they were unsidhe, especially if that was all they knew. With twins, there would be a problem because they would resonate, bond with each other. If the unsidhe who arranged this is smart, he will separate them. They would be weaker apart and easily controlled."

"They're our bloodline," Ryder reminded his cousin. "They carry the fertility gene. It's as good a reason as any to steal them."

They continued to talk as I walked to the window, avoiding the dead woman in the middle of the room. Outside the glass, San Diego basked under the setting sun. The fading light turned the surrounding towers orange, changing steel and glass into gem monoliths. From where I stood, I could see down the coast and into the fog-drenched shoreline where Tijuana fell to the Merge. It was getting too dark to see more than the misty outline, but beyond it lay a Dusk Court I'd basically ignored.

Cari ran her hand down my back, joining me to stare out the window. She remained silent as the cousins bickered behind us. Others came in, the conversation swaying to sidhe then back to Singlish with a sharp word from Ryder. Her fingers played at the ridges on my shoulder blades, tracing the metacarpal rises under my T-shirt.

"I didn't want to say anything," she whispered, pressing against my back, "but the woman, Shannon, told them about you. The man was very excited, but the dead woman was scared. She thought that you would come after them."

"She's right," I said softly, sparing a glance at the unsidhe's cold body. "Pity her companion got to her before I did."

"She was more frightened of what you were and who you belong to," Cari said, coming around to lean on the windowsill, her fingers wrapping into my shirt. "They're going to meet someone who knows you, someone from before your time with that *ampulla*, Dempsey."

"I don't know why Dempsey rubs people the wrong way," I said, a tight smile on my mouth. "He did fine by me."

"The only reason people give Dempsey half a word is because of you, Kai." She brushed my stomach with her fingers, touching my skin with the heat of her hand. "I'm telling you not to go with the sidhe. Don't chase after those babies. The man they are meeting—they were sure he would give them a lot of money for you, and that's not someone I want you to meet, *bonito*."

"I have to go, Caridad." Murmuring, I kissed the top of her head, resting my chin there for a moment. "It's the right thing to do. I have to go."

"See?" Cari shook her head, slapping my chest with the flat of her hand. "That is why people put up with Dempsey's shit. Somehow he raised you right. I don't know how, because it wouldn't be in him to go after those babies. He wouldn't put himself out that way."

"No, he'd send me." I grinned at her, not ashamed to admit to Dempsey's failings. "But it would still be the right thing to do."

I hugged her as she wrapped her arms around my waist, feeling the strength in her shoulders as she gave me a gentle kiss on the cheek. Letting go, she sighed and found her balance against the windowsill, staring up at me with her large, deep blue eyes.

"Do not get stolen from us," Cari said, waving a finger under my nose. "If you get taken, I will have to go and storm some idiot unsidhe castle and kill everyone inside it. I just had my nails done. I would be very mad."

"Promise. No getting taken or killed," I said, crossing my heart. "Besides, I can't think of anything that would scare a Dusk Court more than a pissed-off Caridad Brent."

"Hah," she snorted, punching my arm. "I am nothing. You get taken from us, and then they will have to deal with Mama. Let us see the unsidhe survive that."

CHAPTER TWENTY-FIVE

NOT MANY people ventured into the Balboa area, and certainly no one sane. The Merge had cracked apart the mesa, filling it in with an ancient sidhe forest while leaving pieces of the old park standing intact. The top of the bell tower crept through the trees, but the area was vast, crowding back the skyscrapers around it. A wide paved road cut through a part of the forest, seeming to start and stop without any rhyme or reason, and several graceful bridges had survived, some spanning the gaps while others rose up from solid ground.

The park used to span a little less than two miles, but the sidhe lands changed all that. Now more than triple its original size, the area was declared sidhe territory following the SoCalGov-Elfin negotiations, but until recently, the Dawn Court from the Underhill left the place alone.

Various animals had taken up residence in the woodlands, mostly fugitives from an old zoo, and a few humans known for having irregular personalities lived at the forest's edges. Crazy Gertie lived somewhere near the 163, a self-appointed caretaker of the giant pandas inhabiting the lower canyons of Balboa, and there was talk of an unwashed hairy man in the south end who ran around naked except for a tinfoil sailor hat—but I didn't know anyone who'd seen him.

Despite all those interesting attractions, I avoided Balboa. The place made my spine shiver every time I went near it.

Standing at the end of old Olive Street looking into the tree line, I didn't see or hear anything to give me the outright creeps. Nothing looked out of place to me. It was the kind of place someone would expect to find a gingerbread house nibbled on by two little children or a lost little girl dressed in a red hooded cape. All perfectly safe and pretty, except for the witch and the wolf lurking just off the page.

"So how exactly are we going to do this?" I asked Ryder, who was also staring into the dark forest.

"How well do you know the place?" He spread a clearcoat sheet over the truck's hood, pressing the activation spot. A map of the territory lit up, distinct areas color coded and annotated with menu bars to zoom in or out for information. "I had the land traced out so we could determine where we wanted to establish the Court, but if you've been inside, that would be helpful."

"I know enough to avoid this place like I'd avoid a diseased hooker," I replied.

"I've noticed a lot of your life is determined by the state or worth of prostitutes."

"It's something I know. Like converting everything into how much rice I can buy," I said, shrugging. "And no, I don't know the place at all. Either the trees will get you or the crazy old panda lady will. There's nothing in there that I'd want to see that badly."

"I'd never have thought of you as cowardly," Ryder commented, poring over his map.

"Low, your lordship." I whistled. "Calling me chicken. What's next? Throwing my cat into Gertie's yard?"

"I wouldn't do that, Ryder," Cari said, tucking a knife into her boot. "He'd just shoot you. He's fond of that mangy cat."

"Thank you," he replied, giving Cari a small bow of his head. "I've been around Kai long enough to witness his problem-solving techniques. It's hard to argue with *shoot first then shoot again*."

"Do I have to stab my cousin for you, Kai?" Alexa bumped my stomach with her hip, craning over Ryder's shoulder to look at the map. "He has always been a problem. Ever since we were young. If you were mine, I would be honor bound to stab him. It is something to think about."

"Ah, how quickly family turns on me because of a pretty ass." Ryder snorted at the small shrug Alexa gave him and pointed out a trail on the flexible sheet. "The river cuts across the end of the old promenade near the towers and curves toward the shore. We can head in through the trees at different points until we reach the river."

"How clear is the ground through there? Can we walk without telling them we're coming?" Cari asked.

"It's sporadic," Ryder said, tapping the map to zoom in. The ground cover seemed minimal, although there appeared to be a few brambles that would cause some trouble. "We'll spread out and walk a line through the area."

"What about link communication?" Cari leaned over the map, tracing a southern route into the promenade. "Still clogged up in there, or did you guys have a chance to clean up the EMI coming from Gertie's jammers?"

"There's too much interference still," Ryder admitted. "I haven't convinced her to shut them all down yet."

"I do not like going in with so few," Alexa grumbled. "If they have more than five, we will run into problems. We should send someone in to scout for numbers."

"No choice. We can't wait for any more help. Jonas is in La Mesa, and everyone else I know is on a run." I pointed at the map, tapping out several spots. "We're talking too much. I've got a full load of ammo. Let's go in."

"Try not to shoot the place up," Cari replied. The sidhe cousins looked at me. "I'll bring in a Glock, but I'm not as good a shot as he is."

"Well then, it's decided. We're going in," Ryder said grimly. "Pray to whichever human god you want to, Kai. We'll need the help."

"Hell, I whore myself out to whatever god is listening," I said, sliding clips into my rig and checking the Ka-Bar I'd fitted into the sheath. "I'll take whatever help I can get."

COMPARED TO Elfhaine's forest, Balboa's woods weren't as bad. I didn't feel like skinning myself the moment I stepped into the deep shadows, and even with the others somewhere nearby, I felt alone when I lost sight of the city streets and was left with the tiny glow on my now useless link. I turned off the light, and the black leather band went matte. I didn't need someone to spot a bobbing blue orb walking through the woods and tag me with a shot.

"Well, no, Kai," I muttered. "What you don't need is for them to see you before you see them."

Enough light seemed to come through the canopy to walk, but some areas were drenched in shadow. I avoided the pockets I couldn't see through and followed the light sketch Ryder drew me on a clearcoat. Approaching the old bell tower from the west was the smartest way in. The Merge-battered structures were close to the city, the land near it stretched out over the highway, enclosing the 163 freeway in a nearly perfect tunnel.

I stopped moving when I hit a stone wall. My knee wasn't very appreciative of the brickwork hidden under ivy and let me know it would be bruising in a few minutes. Rubbing at the injured area, I felt for the end of the wall, crossing over a dip in the stone and past a sheet of greenery blocking my way.

The ground beneath my feet changed from spongy loam to cobblestones, and I stood in a moonlight bath, dwarfed by Balboa's stone towers.

Pressed in by the Merging sidhe territory, Balboa should have fallen, leaving nothing except a memory in old books, but the towers took their existence seriously, refusing to budge under the onslaught of forests and rocks. Most of the outer areas fell, replaced by tall trees and smoother landscape, but the central edifice remained, stretching from the archways to the bell tower and past smaller domes until ending at the round water fountain lying at the far end of a wide brick walkway.

Considering how much time had passed since the Merge, the towers should have been covered by creeping green, but the stonework was clear of obstruction. Many of the museums were gone, taking with them artwork and ancient automobiles. A Japanese garden was untouched, as was the open theater round, but the asphalt around the area was corrupted with weeds and flowers, their sturdy roots cracking the blacktop. I knew there was a pipe organ in there somewhere, but I couldn't see it. People living around the area swore they heard it when the winds were high, and I'd known stranger things to survive the Merge.

A covered walkway provided enough concealment to skulk around the tower. Careful not to trip on the ropy vines crossing the walk, I crept forward. Keeping to the shadows, I passed the tallest tower. I couldn't see the bell hanging there, but I did hear the wind whistle in the cutaway through the middle, the night air catching on the balcony frame and carrying the tower's keening wail through the forest.

Footsteps echoed on the promenade, and Shannon emerged from the darkness. A thin cry leaked from the soft-sided basket she clutched by the handle, and her knuckles were white, paler than her face when she saw me. The unsidhe leading her stopped at the end of the archway, holding his arm out to prevent her from entering the courtyard. I couldn't see much of his face from where I stood. Partially hidden in shadow, he lingered, unsure about walking forward.

"Are you Valin? Valin cuid Anbhás?" he asked. His unsidhe was odd in my ears, the accent choppy and uneven. "I have the children."

Valin. They were looking for Valin cuid Anbhás. The name chilled my blood to ice. My brother. Our father's favorite son. The son he treasured and educated. The son he let practice on me whenever the mood struck him.

I hadn't consciously thought of Valin in years, but he dropped by regularly in my nightmares. The sound of his name made me want to curl up into a ball. I could still feel his fingers working to loosen the skin on my stomach and chest. He couldn't be talking about the same Valin, but I wasn't going to take the chance. I doubted my brother missed me as much as our father did, but I wasn't going to bet on it.

"That's not him! He's Ryder's!" I heard Shannon yell, and the unsidhe growled, pushing her to the side and swearing hotly under his breath.

I couldn't think about Valin, not when I needed my focus. It was hard to pull back into the game, and by the time I'd shaken Valin out of my thoughts, Shannon had plunged into the bushes with the babies, letting the darkness swallow them whole.

I pulled both Glocks from my rig, then brought the guns down, taking aim as I launched into a run. The unsidhe shouted after her and turned toward me, raising a crossbow, its sleek lines glittering with a drawn bolt. The fletched slender spear could pierce my chest or head. I knew the model. It was one of Dempsey's favorites. There'd be no healing up from that if it caught me.

I shot at the unsidhe as I dodged down into a clump of overgrown papyrus. The reedy plants were too thin to keep me hidden, but they were the closest cover I had, and I ate wet dirt, moist from the runoff from the overhang above the walkway. Scrambling on my knees, I kept the guns off the damp ground and fired again.

Keeping my head down, I half crouched and half ran back around to the walkway. From somewhere in the forest, a Wild Hunt belled, the black dogs calling out to one another. My stomach clenched, twisting and folding with fear. I could handle the dogs. It was their Master that kept me moving.

"It could be anyone," I growled at my stomach. "Valin isn't the only one with a Hunt. Maybe that guy just *thought* he was meeting Valin."

You're right, he's not, the wicked, evil part of my brain whispered. *Your father also has a Hunt. Several, in fact.*

The pack's rage covered any sound I made coming through the bushes, their howls ripping away any silence left in the forest. Their cries echoed and bounced, surrounding me as they drew nearer. I couldn't stay near the towers much longer, not with a Hunt closing in.

Creeping up on where I'd seen the unsidhe, I stood up carefully, keeping the guns' muzzles trained down.

The unsidhe lay on his back, mouth open and filling with blood. His eyes were still sharp gold, and a tuft of electric blue hair escaped the hoodie he wore to hide among the humans. I paused long enough to make sure he was dead, checking the star pattern puncturing his face; then I sprinted down the long walkway. I didn't remember hitting the trigger that many times, but it didn't matter. He was dead, and Shannon was long gone.

CHAPTER TWENTY-SIX

"OKAY, SO she can't ditch the kids. They're all she's got left." I scrambled through the bushes, trying to see any trail she might have left behind. The babies were her only bargaining chip at this point, but then any woman willing to piss off an entire race probably didn't have a lot of common sense to begin with.

Farther away from the old tower, I stopped, trying to listen for sounds of someone thrashing through the forest. My heartbeat and the rush of blood in my ears made it hard to hear. My link was useless; Gertie's jammers took care of any signal. All I'd get would be an earful of noise.

"God, I'm going to shoot her for making me run through this damned forest," I seethed, trying to keep my breathing steady. "Calm down, Kai. Focus. Listen. And stop talking to yourself."

Turning slowly, I listened, hoping to hear any motion among the bushes. A shuffling sound came from my right, and then I heard a very thin wail.

Breaking into a hard run, I headed toward the sound and away from the towers. It would only be a matter of time before the Hunt caught my scent and headed after me. The thought of Valin finding me almost broke me from following Shannon.

"Don't be his bitch before he finds you." Cursing, I avoided the bramble of thorns in my path. "You're not that kid anymore, Kai. Get your shit together."

The sound of someone's flailing grew louder, and for a moment I panicked, wondering if I wasn't chasing down one of Crazy Gertie's bears, but a splash of rainbow skirts slipped through the bushes, the colors bright even in the dimness of the closed-in forest. I was rewarded with another thin cry and then a woman's startled scream.

Branches sliced my face, and the slap of leaves against my cheek stung welts on my neck and chin. I almost lost one of the Glocks against a tree, hitting it hard enough to rattle my teeth when I skidded on a patch of mud. The night-drenched forest was difficult to see through, casting shadowy illusions of trees that weren't there and hiding ones that were. My arm hurt, throbbing where I'd struck the tree, and the tingle reached my fingers, deadening them as I tightly clenched the gun. I couldn't lose a gun, not with the *ainmhí dubh* around.

The forest went numb with the sound of rushing water. I tried to remember where the brackish river was on the map Ryder had shown me and got hit in the face by a sapling I'd not seen. It whipped across my face, blinding me for a moment. I blinked at the tears forming in my eyes, trying to wash out the pieces of bark and dust left behind.

I lost my footing again on a bed of ground moss, my heels digging in as I slid forward across the blanketed shore. I'd come out of the forest line, skidding across wet shale and dirt. A flock of something took off from across the river, dark shapes winging up from the canopy.

The water raged, cutting through heavy rock crags on either side. Ten feet across at the most, the river was small but made up for its width with a fierce whitewater that glowed under the night sky. It was a good drop, about my height from the stony shoreline, and the river gave way around large peaked boulders, their battered sides smoothed by the torrent.

Shannon stood a few yards upriver from me, her arms tight around the bassinet. The terror in her face bleached her skin to white, and her eyes stood out dark and wide as I found my footing and approached her.

Fear threaded through my rage, but my anger won out. Close by, the Hunt howled as one. If Valin was as good a Master as our father, he might be able to glean an image from his lead bitch's mind if she hit on my scent. All Tanic's dogs knew what I smelled like. Hell, most of them knew what I tasted like. It wouldn't be difficult for them to know who they were chasing. I'd been fed to them often enough.

I was reasonably sure Valin wouldn't kill me. Tanic would want me back, and he'd have ample opportunity to make me suffer for any *ainmhí dubh* I might kill. Shannon was expendable, especially after fleeing with his newest toys. I knew it, and so did she. The black dogs' belling sent her into a wild panic, and she took a few steps toward the river.

"Get away from the edge, Shannon," I said, tucking the Glocks into my back holsters, hoping she'd feel safer if she didn't see weapons in my hands. Creaking, the leather rig adjusted around my shoulder blades, fitting into the curves of my back and chest. I slipped my jacket off and dropped it to the ground. If Shannon did something stupid like run, I wanted to be able to draw out my guns without the jacket hanging me up. "You don't want to fall in."

"Stay back!" she shouted over the river's roar, her voice rough and hoarse. Her chest heaved with the effort of running through the tight woods, and small cuts bled on her face. I'm sure I bore similar wounds. Ryder's forest seemed filled with razor-sharp leaves thirsty for blood.

"Think this through, Shannon." I spoke calmly, as if talking to one of Jonas's Chihuahuas when it reached its frenzy point.

Hoping it worked better than it did on the tiny dogs with their needle-sharp teeth, I took a step closer, stopping when she leaned over the river and dangled the basket above the water. The bassinet's pale weave darkened quickly, its fibers soaking in the river's thick spray. She held on tight to the basket's creaking handles. One of the twins cried, a pitiful, kittenish wail.

"I'll throw them in!" Her nostrils flared, and the whites of her eyes swallowed up more space around her irises. The woman's shortened breath neared panic, and I stopped, holding perfectly still as she stared at me. "I mean it, Kai. I'll throw them in!"

"Why would you do that?" I tried smiling, hoping I was hiding the tips of my *ainmhí dubh*-sharp canines behind my lips. "You gave birth to them. They're a part of you, right?"

"Don't give me that tree-hugging, otter-scrubbing crap," Shannon snapped. "I carried them because I was paid to. It was supposed to be an easy fricking job. I'd carry them until I showed, and then a healer was supposed to make sure I lost the babies someplace public. It wasn't supposed to happen like this. I wasn't supposed to give birth to these damned things in the front seat of some damned piece of shit."

Bathed in light from the half moon and the city, Shannon should have looked ethereal and motherly, a full-breasted human woman in the glow of mothering, but to me she only looked bat-shit crazy. I wondered if my mother had felt that way, right before she cut herself open and sprayed her guts over Tanic's floor.

I didn't hear the dog. It was too quiet and cunning. It stole upon us with a stealth I would have admired had we not been its target. The only clue I had of its presence was the crash of its body coming through the brush. It shattered a thicket, sending sharp splinters flying across the rocky shelf. I fired, but it moved too quickly, an immature yearling eager to bring something back to its master.

Shannon screamed, a short and piercing sound, and that was enough to draw the dog to her.

Leaping up to grab her throat, the *ainmhí dubh* took her down. Closing its jaws around the slender column, it crunched down, crushing the scream she'd gathered in her chest. Toppling back, Shannon was dead before the black dog's back feet left the stony riverside, her tongue lolling under the gurgle of blood pouring past her open lips. I only had time to take a breath before the dog and woman fell over the rocky edge, and the bassinet tumbled in midair, heading straight for the water.

I launched myself up, my fingers barely brushing the bottom of the basket as it fell, a tiny pale hand rising above the soft pink blankets lining the carrier. The basket hit the water with a soft splash, barely audible over the rapids' churning cries.

Plunging into the cold brackish rush of water after it, I remembered I couldn't swim well when the water covered my head.

Foamy water filled my mouth and nostrils, drowning me. Coughing, I tried pushing up to the surface, but the river fought me, shoving me back down. Slamming into a rock took my breath, and I felt my ribs crack. My chest threatened to burst if I didn't get air soon when the river flung me up above the surface long enough to gasp in a breath, and then I was under again.

Kicking hard, I straightened out and swirled up, caught in the current. The salty taint in the water sucked the moisture from my mouth. It tasted of seaweed and fish with an underlying sweet of fresh water, enough to fool my tongue.

"Where the hell are you?" I took in mouthfuls of air, dragging with the pain stitching up my side. Panic took over; then I spotted it.

The basket dipped and swirled in front of me. An end caught on a tree, holding it steady for a moment before the river took it again. I was close enough to hear the babies screaming and then a heart-stopping silence when the bassinet hit a rock sticking up out of the water. The soft sound sickened me, more than the water I was swallowing. Scissoring against the current, I fought to get closer to the basket.

I caught on the same branch, tearing the back of my shirt. The rig constricted my arm movements a bit, but it was too late to do anything about it. The leather chafed and rubbed, squeaking as it soaked in more and more water. Another rock sprouted in front of me, and I hit it hard, striking first with my shoulder and then my face. Pushing against it with my hands, I launched back into the river flow, straightening out my body.

The basket's edge was bloody, a crimson foam tipping what I could see of the pink blanket. I reached for the handle and lost it when the river dipped, carrying me farther away. Captured in a swirl, the bassinet spun in place, making a few revolutions before its weight threw it out of synch with the circular flow.

"Okay, get to it." I heaved in another breath and stretched.

With the basket slightly behind me, I reached out to grab at anything I could to stop me from traveling farther away. My fingers stung when I tried to grab the edge of a rock, scraping off some skin on my palm. The salt in the water stung the exposed flesh, and my fingers started to spasm. The water's chill finally hit my bones, and I started shuddering. Trying to control my shivering body, I spat out another mouthful of water. Spotting a boulder on the near side of the river's edge, I relaxed my limbs and let the current take me.

I struck hard, tasting blood, and my right lung spurred with pain. Stars filled my eyes, burning and blinding me. I blinked, scared I'd blacked out and missed the baby carrier. My stomach churned, twisting like the river as I searched the foam for any sign of the twins' basket.

Finally, I spotted the damned thing.

The handles bobbed above the water line, and then the rest of the basket ripped free of the river, spiraling toward me on an eddy. Quickening with the river's flow, the basket's course dipped and wove around, stalling when it hit a dead spot. Then it turned, shifted by the twins' uneven weight.

I made a grab for it, losing my hold on the rock. The handles were slippery, and I lost my grip on them almost immediately. The edge of the basket scraped my battered hand, and I winced when the weave sliced into the torn skin. I snatched at the end, then held on tight, grunting when I lost another couple of ribs to a rock hidden under the water and spat out yet another mouthful of diluted blood.

Sucking in air, my chest whistled and ached. Trying to slow down my breathing, I turned midstream, letting the river carry us for a few feet. I needed to rest long enough to make it to shore. Holding the basket, I fell down a small drop, but the water slowed slightly, letting me take a breath. The current was too rushed for me to fully check on the twins, but I felt inside the basket, glad to find them still warm and cradled in tight wraps. One of the girls gurgled at me, spitting out water, but the other lay quiet, her eyes closed. A thin stream of blood spotted her forehead. She moved, straining against the blankets, but then stilled as the water caught us up again.

"Just a bit longer, okay?" I patted the blankets, wondering if the babies could hear me. "Let me find someplace where we can get out."

The river sank down deeper between two rocky cliffs, and as we passed a curve, the waters slowed their pounding. I fought the current, trying to hold the basket up above my shoulders. I ached. Bruises stung as I moved, and the rig tightened further, cutting into my arms.

Rock spires littered the river. I took a few hits on my shoulders and thighs, then saw stars again when my forehead made contact with a jut I didn't see in a crest. With my ears ringing from the impact, I almost missed the drop in the rock walls ahead. They were still high, but it looked promising. I couldn't tell how far I'd come downriver. It could have been a few hundred yards or a few feet, but I knew I had to get out soon. My fingertips were turning blue, and I couldn't feel my feet. The girls would be frozen through in a few minutes.

Timing a kick away from the current, I floated to the edge, grabbing at a crevice with one hand. Breathing hard, I let my body rest for a moment and looked up. It might have only been a few feet, but it seemed like miles, especially with the tired creeping through my limbs. I set the basket's handle between my teeth and took a short breath, inhaling pieces of wet reed.

"No problem." I choked slightly on the feel of my tongue pressing against the back of my throat. "Can do this. Easy."

My fingers left bloody marks behind on the rock, and I strained to pull us up. I couldn't find a decent grip with my heels, and my feet were barely moving. It was so cold, and the wind found me, biting at the wet and leaving its sharp teeth in my muscles until I could barely pull up the rock face.

Unable to see much above me, I slapped at the rock, hoping to find something to hold onto, but my fingers suddenly met air. My back muscles clenched, locking in place, and I forced myself to lift my arms again, finding the edge of the rock face with my palm. Despite the weight of the babies pulling down my jaw, I wanted to bawl with relief. Still choking on the wet basket handles, I took another breath and heaved myself up, catching my stomach on the edge.

And stared into the roiling crimson eyes of an *ainmhí dubh*.

CHAPTER TWENTY-SEVEN

THE CREATURE easily outweighed me by a hundred or so pounds, and from the curled-back frill of its head, it was pissed off something fierce. Hanging onto the cliff edge by the flat of my hands, my palms abused from the river rock, it would have been easy enough to drop back into the safety of water. If only I wasn't holding my babies' carrier between my clenched teeth.

Guns were out, and so was the knife. I couldn't grab either one without dropping the girls, and there was no guarantee that the Glocks would work after the bashing they took against the river's rocks. Leaning all my weight on one hand, I lifted my arm and punched the black dog in the nose, nearly losing my grip on the ledge. I fell back down, slamming my chest on the rock, and my teeth jumped on the handle, the basket precariously close to falling from my mouth. There was a squawk from one of the girls and then a sorrowful cry when my chin jammed the basket against the rocks.

Tilting my head back, I looked up to see the dog shaking its head. A splatter of drool dripped from its mouth, striking my cheekbone, and I winced when the acid burned my skin. Tightening my jaw, I relaxed and as the basket swung back and forth, I took a quick inventory. My hand throbbed, warning me of a break in one or two of my fingers, and I felt the dig of a rib into my lung, but I'd live through that. The hardest part would be getting past that dog.

Trying to breathe through the grit falling from the edge of the cliff, I looked down, wondering if we could survive another dip, but the basket wouldn't hold, and the cold water would probably kill them if we went back in. With no other choice but to hang on, I hoped to get another shot at the dog's face before it bit me. Straining to hold my weight with one hand, I balled my fist and punched up again, striking the dog's mouth and cracking one of its teeth.

Swearing, I almost lost the basket, and I bit down hard as blood poured over my knuckles. The burn along the cuts in my skin was disheartening.

The dog howled and took a step forward, rearing its head back. Mucus and blood dripped from its injured nose, and I felt a small ember of satisfaction that I'd at least pissed the thing off enough to kill me, because I'd be damned if I was going to be dragged back to my father's playroom. I'd at least injured the thing. We all might be destined for its belly, but I was going to make it work for it. Grabbing the cliffside, I lost my grip and swung wildly, desperately windmilling until my feet found purchase and I stopped swaying.

I was waiting for the top of my head to be bitten off when a metal spear sprouted from the black dog's head, piercing its forehead. The triangular tip dripped with blood and bits of bone. Shattered from behind, its skull wobbled under its skin and gave way, bursting out of its eye sockets. Somewhere inside its cranium, it began to lose function, synapses breaking apart, and then it tumbled, still growling and hungry to snap my head off.

Its weight carried it over the edge, and it bounced, first against my shoulder and then a couple of times on the cliff. Its body dropped, flipping in an arc before it splashed into the river, and I saw it catch on a rock. Then it was gone, carried off into the white waters.

I started when a thick-fingered hand gripped my nerveless wrist, and I stared up at Dempsey's rough face, a scrabble of beard darkening his jaw and a sneer twisting his mouth.

"Good to see your ugly face, boy," Dempsey spat. "Jonas told me you probably needed some help."

I took the bassinet from my teeth, closed my stiff fingers around the handle, then lifted it up. My arm protested, creaking and straining, but I forced it up, shivering in the wind.

"Basket," I stammered, cold down to my spine. I stretched to pass the bassinet up to Dempsey, and my shoulders shook with the effort to hold it aloft. "Heavy."

"Drop it and give me your hand," he replied, clenching my wrist tighter. "I can't hold onto you much longer, boy."

"Take the damned basket!" I croaked out. The numbness in my hands began to travel up to my elbows.

"I'm going to kick your ass if you fall." He looked disgusted and grabbed the carrier. I lost sight of him for too long a moment. Then he returned and grabbed me by the wrists. "Bad enough the rest of those idiots that came with you are wandering around like they've lost their dicks. Worst trackers ever and you left a fucking trail a blind slug could follow. Where'd you be if Cari hadn't called me down to save your scrawny butt?"

Straining, he heaved, dragging me up over the edge. Stones dug into my belly, and I scraped along, leaving a layer of skin behind, but he eventually managed to lift me up, dropping onto one knee to leverage me over the edge. He tossed me onto the ground, then left me there to pant as he looked down the river and swore loudly.

"Forget you can't swim good, boy? Or that you hate water deeper than a few feet?" Giving me a stern look, Dempsey grunted and stood, lighting a cigar stump with his ancient Zippo. "That was a damned big dog too. Could have gotten a lot of money for that hide. Almost had wings too. You could see the stumps starting. Don't see many of those."

"You should have tried harder to kill it so it fell down on the ledge instead of over the side," I groaned, stretching out fully onto the mossy flat. I needed to get up and check on the babies, but I was too tired, and my brain was overloaded. "Thanks for grabbing me."

"Don't thank me just yet. You still have to walk out. I'll be damned if I'm carrying you out of here. You're like a drunk giraffe to carry, flailing and all legs." Dempsey kicked at my ribs with the steel toe of his boot and tossed my jacket over my face. "You left that upstream. You know better about taking care of your gear, and you could have ruined your damned guns too."

"What was I going to do? Let them drown?" I grumbled and got to my feet, pulling my guns out and giving them a quick glance. The Glocks looked okay considering the bath they'd taken, but I'd have to check them over to see if they'd taken any damage from the rocks. The knife would be okay in the rig's wet leather. Its coating would protect it until I could wipe off the water. "I've got to get the girls warm."

"Wouldn't have screwed up your guns if you didn't go in after them." He exhaled up, the cigar smoke fouling the air, and grabbed my arm. "And I've helped all the elfin I'm ever going to help when I took you in. Don't even know why I did that."

"Leave off." I shook him off and took an unsteady step. My teeth chattered as I spoke, but I was more concerned with the girls. "They'll freeze. We've got to get them out of the basket. We can use my jacket to wrap them up."

I looked into the basket, relieved when both girls responded to my touch. Choosing spinal injuries over hypothermia, I lifted them out carefully, then handed one to Dempsey. He balked for a second, then took her after I glared at him. When the second one squirmed in my hands, my heart flipped over, and I found myself finally breathing.

I peeled apart the blankets to check on the babies, and they mewled and kicked, grateful to be out of the soaked fabric. The one bleeding would have a scar on her forehead, or not, depending on how well it healed. It was probably Kayak, already burdened with bad luck from my name.

Dempsey made quick work of undressing the infants and swaddling them both in the flannel shirt he wore over his T-shirt. My leather jacket went over them next, giving them another warm layer. They pinked up quickly, and I swiped at the cut on the girl's forehead, watching it clot and start to seal.

"You ain't getting cash for this run, are you?" Dempsey asked, chewing around his cigar. He'd slung his crossbow across his back and picked up a sawed-off shotgun from the ground.

"Things can't always be about money, Dempsey," I replied. I hurt, but I'd be damned if I wasn't going to walk out on my own two feet, especially in front of Dempsey.

"Sure it is, boy. It's always about the money," he said, resting the shotgun against his shoulder. The cigar worked from one side of his mouth to the other, a sure sign he was thinking up numbers in his head. "Take your gear up, and let's see about getting paid."

"Perhaps you should rethink that. Those children are mine, and so is the monster standing next to you." The voice was familiar, and even in accented Singlish I knew who he was. His words stopped me cold, and fear prickled a path up my spine when Valin stepped out of the forest line, smiling wickedly as his eyes roamed over my body. "Hello, little brother. Are you ready to come home?"

CHAPTER TWENTY-EIGHT

IT HAD seemed like I rode the river for miles, but I'd only been carried a few hundred yards. I saw the old towers rising above the canopy, and the forest barely hid a stone arch, faded pre-Merge letters blackening the curve. Standing beneath the crumbling archway was a man wearing my face.

Now that I knew what I looked like, I knew we had the same face. I didn't back...then.

It was odd to see what I only saw in a mirror. Even stranger to see it with metallic brandy eyes and gold-streaked black hair. He stood taller than me, broader in the shoulder, although our legs were the same length. Dressed in durable black cotton pants and a pale shirt, he could blend into a crowd of humans, except for the liquid feline grace of his movements and the pair of long daggers he had sheathed at his hips.

I was not happy to see my brother, Valin. Even less happy to see the Hunt with him.

The shadows moved around Valin, their eyes opening to gleam crimson at me. Rising, the mature black dogs dwarfed me from their position on the steps, massive shoulders settling and flexing before they shook, opening their enormous wings. Watching them, my back itched with the memory of the lengths of iron and hot spatulas working my skin loose to create the scar work on my back.

When Ryder believed my scars to be homage to the Dusk Court's pearl black dragon, I hadn't bothered to correct him. If my wings were a dragon's, they'd at least be a tie to some legacy, some bloodline, but the scars on my back marked me as Tanic's. More importantly, as his property. His house sigil was an *ainmhí dubh* wingspan, taken from the nightmares he created and ruled over. Since anyone encountering Tanic's ancient black dogs didn't usually live long enough to talk about it, much less describe their wings, it didn't seem important at the time.

I couldn't explain the pang of regret I had for not telling Ryder I liked his kiss or that my wings were something I sometimes wished I could scrape off. It felt like something I could have given him, something he could have kept once Valin took me.

My brother moved closer, looming over me. Four of his Hunt flanked him, skulking back and forth, their sparse fur ruffling with anxious aggression. The largest wore a thin red collar, marking her as the pack's alpha. Her teats were tight up against her belly, probably within a day or two of her breeding season. Unless I was off, the second smaller of the males was her mate, his face nearly unmarked despite a chewed-apart ear and a grayish hair patch over a healed wound on his side. The male muscled in past the others, standing at the female's right.

Serpentine and long, Tanic's creatures were more lizards than dogs, their squat bodies moving with the oddly jointed locomotion of a reptile. The female's tongue licked out, slowly tasting the air in front of it. I caught a glimpse of her fangs, ancient yellow and caked with old poison. Spittle threads strung between her jaws as she opened her mouth wider, webbing wet links between her upper and lower teeth. Any fur covering her body was patchy, as if fighting a losing battle with the scaly dry areas running over her rib cage, belly, and back.

"Give him the brats and let's make a run for it, kid," Dempsey muttered behind me. "If we throw them at the dogs, they'll take the easy bait before they run us down."

"It's a good plan, brother." Valin smiled, showing me his teeth. I knew he spoke in Singlish for Dempsey's sake. He loved toying with his prey before he took small bites out of their flesh. "Perhaps you should let him throw the babies to my pets."

"Shut up, Dempsey." I didn't look back at him, letting my tone drop to tell him I was serious. Hoping my whisper was loud enough for him to hear, I said, "Run if you get the chance. Ryder'll pay you for their return."

Both of us running would be useless. The dogs would sniff me out and would take down Dempsey in a single bite. The children weren't even big enough to stick in the black dogs' teeth. They were an old Hunt, creatures forged from skilled and ancient magic. Originally one of my father's packs, it wasn't a surprise to see my brother commanding them now. I found my hate for him undiminished by time.

"I didn't believe it when my spies told me they'd found you, much less that they could deliver you." Valin walked across to stand in front of me, keeping the hounds back with a single wave of his hand. His Singlish was smooth despite his unsidhe accent, a rough suede purr. "And yet, here you are."

I swallowed the sick rising from my belly, refusing to let the burning ember get past my throat. Schooling my face, I did my best to mask my emotions, pretending I was bluffing my way through a poker game with the Brent brothers and Jonas. I bent my head slightly, keeping my eyes fixed on his face. It was an ancient gesture of recognition, one I couldn't be certain I performed properly, but I gave it my best go.

"Well done, little brother. You mimic your betters well." Valin returned the formal nod.

My brother reached out to touch my face, and I flinched. Valin's long-fingered hands were one of my worst terrors, more than the *ainmhí dubh*. The dogs were temporary demons, flesh I knew I could at least maim, provided I could get past the bony armor plates protecting their vital organs. Valin was different. He haunted me when I closed my eyes at night—when I blinked too long and the shadows clung to my lashes before I could shake them off. He was there in my darkness when I slept and lurking at the edge of my vision while I was awake.

He lived in the mirror every time I stared at my own reflection.

His teeth once left marks and bruises I swore I still felt under my healed skin. My right shoulder ached where he'd slipped when Tanic coached him on how to effectively separate skin from flesh. The dig of the razor spatula sliced through the muscle and severed the nerves before hitting bone.

They'd continued Valin's training once the healer sealed my torn muscles together, patching my skin into a solid piece again. Valin took forever to learn, his hands trembling with excitement as our father's low, purring voice coaxed him along. Now I wasn't sure how much of his clumsiness was lack of grace or a glut of sadism.

Those fingers tightened the nut on the bolt that pierced my left shoulder blade, cracking that bone when he turned one too many times. Tanic left it as it was, taking the time to show his son the difference between the left and the right.

"The iron pin turns easier on the right," our father said, demonstrating between the two as I hung naked from chains set into the room's low ceiling beams. "This is important, because we'll need the anchor to turn with the swivel and hoop that will cap the bolt. Try once more, Valin. You'll get it."

And it began again.

I'd kept the iron pieces and the rebar, leaving them on the coffee table in my warehouse to remind me of my family. The iron was rusted in places, turned black where it had cut through bone. Visitors played with the pieces, picking up the curved bars and handling the iron between careless fingers, sometimes dropping them on the floor.

Ryder had no idea what he'd touched the day he came over; besides me, only Dempsey knew where those pieces came from. He'd been there when they were cut out of me. I rejected his suggestion to melt the bars down, but he thought I was sick for displaying them in my living room. For me, there was no sweeter sound in the world than the ping of bloodstained iron hitting hard cement. I'd wept the first time I heard it.

That was not the life I wanted for the girls. Not if I could help it.

"You're looking well, *dearthái*r," Valin said, walking around me. The black dogs paced in time to his movements, and the female's falling drool left smoking divots on the old stone cliff. Valin knew he could control me with a few command words. They were one of his first lessons. His choice of Singlish was nothing more than a cat playing with its prey before it snapped the rodent's neck.

I didn't trust myself to say anything, and Valin didn't expect me to respond. The last time he'd seen me, my communication skills were subpar at best. I understood unsidhe but could barely speak it. Seeing him brought back floods of remembered pain and whispers of conversations my father and his companions had over my body. I was surprised at how much unsidhe I could recall, especially considering my attention was on screaming at the time.

I wasn't going to let Valin lead me back into that darkness, lit only by the watery white glow leaking in through the cracks in the door.

"Don't you speak fluent Singlish, little brother?" Valin cocked his head, inspecting my face. "I can't imagine you'd be comfortable speaking our tongue. Or did your master only teach you simple words? Although I am touched you remembered my name."

"I remembered your smell." I sneered. "People always remember the smell of dog shit they step into."

"Ah, it talks. Praise the Goddess. I'd begun to think we'd somehow damaged that tiny brain of yours," my brother said, sliding his hands into his pants pockets. The dogs shifted. Losing sight of their master's hands made them anxious, and their wings rubbed together, keening a soft dirge. "Those are nice guns—very monkey of you. But they don't work when they're wet, do they?"

"Let the human go with the children, and I'll stay," I offered.

"Are you stupid, boy?" Dempsey spat behind me. "We dump the kids and take off. How much can he pay me to make up for this shit?"

"A lot—a hell of a lot," I mumbled at him before turning my attention back to my brother. "Just let them go, Valin. What good are they to you?"

"Why would I want to do that, Chimera? That's what you are in Singlish, aren't you?" Valin asked, ignoring Dempsey. "I can have both you and the children."

"I'm worth more to you than they are. You said it yourself: Tanic wants me back." I stepped between Dempsey and the dogs. "They don't mean anything to you."

"Ah, my little brother, they do mean something to me," he replied softly. "They are my daughters, and I have plans for them."

"Daughters?" I frowned. Dempsey always accused me of being slow, but I'd always put that down to him being a grumpy asshole. He was being grumpy right now, edging back behind me and mumbling. "They're sidhe. Their mother is Ryder's sister, Ciarla."

"Oh, *deartháir*, Ciarla maneuvered Ryder into this. She just had to arrange matters so Ryder is held responsible for their conception. He is Ciarla's only competition to be heir." Valin stroked my cheek with the back of his hand, and I trembled, forcing myself not to pull away. "Who would be better as the Sebac than the contrite sister of a renegade?"

"You expect me to believe she let you be the father of her children?" I replied. "You're fucking nuts. No sidhe woman would let you touch her."

"I didn't need to be there. They were created in a small dish of cold plastic—enough of a violation of the natural order to make most elfin vomit in their shoes. Using a monkey to carry them? That was sheer brilliance." Valin removed his hand from his pocket and stretched out his fingers. The female shimmered, shuddering into a streak of black in the air as she surged forward to crouch beneath his hand. Her crimson eyes boiled with a low hatred, her stare following every tiny shift of my body. "It was enough to make me wish Ciarla was Dusk Court."

"Is this where you spend the next five minutes telling me about your evil plan?" I mocked, straining to keep my voice even. "Don't you keep up with the evil overlord newsletter? Ranting monologues are cliché now."

"I'll enjoy beating that attitude out of you," he said with a chill in his voice. "You were boring after a while, mewling and crying as Father worked on you, but now you'll be much more interesting."

"The only one crying was you when I bit you in the balls and choked on the foul taste. I can't eat turkey gizzards without being reminded of you."

I swallowed my fear, forcing myself to remain still as Valin circled me, his shoulder brushing the scarification under my shirt. Gritting my teeth, I narrowed my eyes, meeting his steady gaze. If I was going to walk away with anything, it would be my dignity. I'd fought hard to gain it. I wasn't going to let Valin pry it from me with a few sharp words.

"Maybe I'll teach one of the girls like Father taught me. And hang the other one up next to you. Wouldn't that be lovely? Tell me, Chimera, which one should I choose? Maybe I'll raise them side by side until one disappoints me, and that'll be the one who will keep you company."

"You can't do that if you're dead," I growled. Catching Dempsey's gaze, I flicked my eyes toward the forest line, silently telling him to make a run for it if he got the chance. The babies would slow him down, but not as much as his bum knee. I'd have to give Valin enough trouble to keep his mind off Dempsey until he got clear. "You cut me easily enough when I was hanging there. How about you try it now that I've got my hands free?"

"How I've missed your taste," Valin purred in my ear, and his tongue lapped at my cheek. I held my breath, reminding myself that I had to wait it out. Dempsey moved silently, edging away with his arms around my baby-filled jacket. My lip curled, and Valin's low chuckle pushed warm air over my wet face. "Even rolled in shit, you always tasted sweet."

The *ainmhí dubh* female snuffled at my legs, running her flaring nostrils up my shin and over my thigh. She snorted, as if remembering my scent or perhaps even the taste of my meat. Tanic raised dozens of the things, and they'd all had a turn at me. The others shifted back and forth, their talons flexing over the stone. They were getting anxious, drooling as their blood ran hot with the need to hunt. Valin didn't seem to notice. It looked like keeping the female at his side controlled the males, and she was focused on his every word and gesture.

"I'm guessing there was no first intruder. Shannon was trying to kill them when Alexa came in," I said. My breath raised a pink flush on his jaw, hot in the cool night air. He turned toward the warmth, seeking me out.

"That ape should have done what your mother did," Valin purred over the female's croon, his fingers scratching at her neck. "One slice of a knife to her belly before the shells hardened and this would have been done, but I suppose cowardice is the human way. Your mother at least had the guts to try to kill the thing she carried. I will give her that."

"At least I know I had an elfin mother," I replied. "Too bad Tanic has a hard time telling his bitches apart, or you'd know which one he bred to get you."

I saw stars when he hit me, the signet ring on his index finger catching the edge of my mouth. Tasting blood, I took a step back, grateful for the pain and the space now between us. I spit at the dog's feet, clearing my mouth, then smiled at my brother, pulling my lips back until my canines glistened.

"Maybe I'll tell Father you ran." Valin sucked at his knuckle. He'd caught my teeth, tearing open his skin. "That way, I can let the dogs have you. I imagine you miss them."

"Are you so used to Daddy's sloppy seconds, Valin—" Snarling, I nearly closed the gap between us, but I stopped, shifting my weight. "—that you'd rather go after his dogs than be first?"

He cursed, a string of hot unsidhe meant to unnerve me, but it only served to agitate the *ainmhí dubh*. Tightening his fist, Valin moved in to strike me again when the bushes rustled, bringing the black dogs' ears up.

Dempsey was gone, and he'd taken the children with him. I'd gambled on his avarice to carry the babies out, and I knew I'd hit pay dirt with his greed sooner or later.

"Wait here for me, little brother." Valin's hand settled on my chest, stroking at the spot above my heart. I felt his cold flesh, even through my T-shirt, probably imagined, but I wasn't going to argue with my body. "It won't take my boys long to hunt down a crippled monkey. I'm going to get my daughters, and then all of us can go home."

"Do you think I'm just going to stand here like a sheep waiting to be slaughtered?" I said through my teeth.

"Yes, because you've bleated like a sheep under me so many times before," Valin whispered into my ear. "I'm leaving Misneach with you, in case you decide to run."

The bitch let loose a slithering growl as Valin told her to wait, slicing his hand down his side and pointing at me. If I took a too big of a step, the female would be on me, using her weight to hold me down until her Master came back. I had no doubt his pet lizard-dog would keep me rooted to one spot even if she had to kill me to do it.

A mewling cry came from the woods, and the dogs jerked to attention. Their mouths hung open, saliva dripping from hunger. The female's eyes burned as she watched me, held back by a vocal leash. I didn't know the commands and certainly didn't hold the bitch's respect.

"Time to go on a hunt, my babies," Valin murmured. "Wait if you don't want Misneach to have a nibble, little brother. I'll be back to deal with you after I retrieve my daughters."

I shifted and hit something with my foot, hearing the scrape of metal against rock. Glancing down, I spotted Dempsey's shotgun and a scatter of shells lying on the ground against my foot. He'd taken the crossbow with him, but that was fine by me. I preferred the blast of gunpowder to a bolt any day of the week.

"Thanks, old man." I grinned, hooked my foot under the stock's curve, and kicked up, tossing the sawed-off shotgun into the air. Moving my hand slightly, I caught the weapon and fired, praying to any deity bored enough to listen.

The deafening booms from Dempsey's sawed-off echoed, catching Valin in midstride before he disappeared into the darkened woods. Aiming as well as I could, the shots were a near perfect hit, the slugs slamming into the lead male's skull and ripping through his bony forehead.

The slugs' momentum was strong enough to tear out the back of the dog's head, sharp bone cutting from the inside out. The creature's scaly black skin flew out behind it in long uneven ribbons, and pink sponge grew out the exit hole where the dog's brain wrapped around pieces of shot and followed along for the ride.

The male was graceful as he died, surprising considering they were built for speed and endurance rather than looks, but still, his death throes were a ballet.

His wings hung in the air, spreading out as if to catch the wind one final time before the earth commanded his body to rest. The red light in his eyes flared, angry and helpless as his systems began to shut down, his brain kicking in along his trained nerves to attack and frustrated that his legs weren't responding. His chest hit the ground, driven down by the weight of his body. For its loose reptilian look, a black dog was still a densely packed bag of muscle and bone, and when it fell, it fell hard.

Valin howled and broke into a run, but I wasn't waiting for him to get to me.

Dempsey had come prepared for my kind, leaving me slugs packed with a hard iron core. They were more for taking down older dogs or unsidhe than fighting off a full Hunt, but it would do in a pinch. These weren't simply older black dogs breeding out in the wild. Valin's Hunt were seasoned and centuries old.

But when it was all said and done, they were still animals.

CHAPTER TWENTY-NINE

I DIDN'T have enough time to slide in new shells, so I pulled the stock around, flipping the shotgun against my forearm, and cracked it open as if to reload. Slamming the wood piece down on the female's forehead, I cut open her skin. The splash of her hot blood was all I needed. Its sour-rich scent carried in the death-bitter air, and she shook her head, splattering the ground around her.

Growling, the *ainmhí dubh* leaped at me with her mouth open wide enough to swallow my head. Her teeth scraped open my arm, twisting my elbow around before I could move. Desperate, I jammed the broken-open shotgun into her mouth, forcing it in to wedge between her open jaws.

The impact of her slamming into me rattled my shoulders and spine. I was pushed back a few feet, dangerously close to the edge of the ravine, but I shoved back as hard as I could until the short end of the shotgun's V touched the back of her throat.

Angry and frustrated, the female bit down, clamping the shotgun's wedge tight against the roof of her mouth. Her shark-rowed teeth hooked on the muzzle and stock, catching on the tiny metal and wood trims on the gun's edges. Spit dripped on me, and I turned my face, not wanting to risk being blinded if the acidic saliva hit my eyes. My arm burned where she'd bitten it, the tips of her canines slicing into my skin, but it wasn't anything I couldn't shake off. I could absorb the poison, even though it burned. Now I was more concerned about getting away than the bubbling on my skin.

Valin started yelling, and things slowed down, the world ticking off each movement with a molasses drop. The female's blood wasn't the scent of her breeding, but it would hopefully be enough to anger the males into thinking she was hurt badly. I didn't need the other black dogs to frenzy. I just needed them to be distracted long enough for Dempsey to get as far away as possible.

Violence erupted on the stone cliff, a loud battle of snarls and screams as the Hunt tore into the alpha male's fallen body. With their main competition dead or dying, the others drove into one another, slamming their broad

212

chests against anything they could reach in the hopes of knocking their target down. I heard one of the *ainmhí dubh* howl, a high-pitched shriek, and the skirmish became an all-out war.

Then Valin shouted something at me, and ice crackled in my blood. I hit the ground hard, scraping open my palms as I tried to catch myself. Landing on my hands and knees, I choked and my breath hitched, unable to breathe around the magic-infused words binding me in place.

My father's training bred obedience into me, and the unsidhe command froze me stiff. My body rebelled against the magic holding me taut, and I puked, an inglorious emptying of the nothing in my stomach, but thankfully the dogs' screaming hiked up, drowning my brother out. Slivers of words hit me, leaving dizziness along my brain, but it wasn't enough to paralyze. I rolled over onto my side and kicked out, hitting the female square in the chest, and got to my feet.

I knew the spell he was casting at me. It was the soundtrack to my night terrors. Valin intended to bind me where I stood.

My brother came at me, spitting out hot words, and I staggered, trying to remain on my feet. Time hiccupped for me, then sped up. Frenzied, the Hunt continued to tear into each other, bleeding rivers, and the stink of smoking fur and skin overwhelmed their oily scent. Trying to hold back the battle raging among his Hunt while keeping me still, Valin screamed commands at me and the dogs. Sweat beaded on his upper lip with the effort, and his hands shook as he grabbed an *ainmhí dubh*, pulling the massive creature off the fallen male.

"Go to hell, Valin," I spat, tasting my sick on my tongue when my brother reached my side. "Stronger than that now. You can't hold me. I won't let you."

"How much of Father's conditioning do you think you shook off, *arracht*?" Valin asked, keeping his shoulders down as he skulked closer. "Or do you even know? Let's find out, shall we? I'm guessing the old bindings will still hold."

He tested my responses, feinting to one side to see if I would fall for his movements, but I held steady, watching him carefully. The dogs would remain on hold unless he ordered them to strike, and I'd only have enough time to see him flick his fingers before they attacked. I kept my shoulders angled so I could keep half of my attention on the female. For all Valin's boasting and the *ainmhí dubh* responsiveness, I was beginning to think he didn't have as much command over them as he thought. He'd needed the female to bring the males back in line.

Keep talking, I rambled to myself. *Keep your mind off the fear in your belly*. It would have been harder to cheer myself on if I didn't know what waited for me in Tanic's cellars, and my brain seemed to have it in for me, tossing up memories from the darkest corners of my mind, as if I needed incentive.

"Didn't you have six dogs when you started? One went over the cliffs with Shannon, and the other was skewered by Dempsey," I prodded, swallowing to moisten my mouth. "I've got you down to three who don't look good."

"I don't need the *ainmhí dubh* to help me take you down, *dearthár*."

"You sure?" I squared off my hips, giving him a smaller target to hit in case he could throw the daggers he had hanging at his sides. I didn't know how good he was with his knives when I wasn't trussed up like a roasting chicken.

"I have all I need, little brother," he said, inhaling sharply, drawing one of his long weapons. "All I need. I'm going to enjoy spilling your blood to close the final seal on your body. I just have to choose where to start cutting. So many choices."

The words Valin spoke in a hissing breath meant nothing to my ears, but to my body, they were iron bands wrapped around my joints and muscles. Forcing myself to remain standing, I fought the wave of sick crawling through my innards. Valin continued his hissing, taking a step closer to me with his dagger tilted up. The point touched my throat, and I fought to push my head back, willing my body to respond to anything as he began to weave another layer of binding around me.

"*Iallach a chur ar dhuine rud a dhéanamh….*" Tanic's original bindings echoed with bits and pieces of Old Earth's languages, stinking of clover and green. I didn't understand most of it, but the words I did were ominous. I'd been worked over by the spell before, so many times before that I could practically recite it in my sleep. Valin let the working settle over me, cockily winking at me as he moved closer, lifting my shirt with his fingers and rubbing the back of his hand against my stomach.

"Can you feel your blood stirring, my little monster?" Valin slithered around me, catching my hips with his palms. His breath was hot on my face, tinged with mint and something sour. His fingers roamed, catching the hem of my T-shirt. With a quick, flicking upward slice, the dagger in his hand made short work of my shirt, parting it away from my chest. Working the tip of his weapon through one of my nipple rings, he tugged on the gold circle. "Shall I continue, *dearthái̇r*?"

"Fuck you." I strained against the binding. My limbs tugged free, and I jerked forward, bringing my fist up to hit Valin's chin. He easily moved aside, laughing as he ran one hand over the female's broad head.

"Let's finish this, little brother, and then I can take you home. I can always come back for the girls. They won't be going anywhere," Valin said. "Father will be so very happy to see you again."

"*Adar llwch gwin*...." The binding curled, snapping around me. The words licked and bit, sinking down into my bones. Valin continued, spooling out the names given to me in the depths of our father's dungeons. "*Madra... arracht... gan iarraid*...." Valin nicked my chest and ground out the final phrase to bind me. "*Cheannsa.*"

The words ignited my marrow, splintering my bones with pain. A tingle raged along my body, working under every inch of skin. The sensation bit and scraped along my nerves until I wanted to walk through a fire for relief. I waited for the tightening against my mind, bracing for the lessening of my self until there was nothing but a whimpering animal left behind my face.

Then it whispered away, leaving me empty and numb. Ryder's grandmother did worse to me in her chamber of horrors.

His spell shriveled away, leaving me untouched and unbound.

"You've got a problem," I said softly, taking a step forward. "Your binding didn't work, brother. I don't think your names work for me anymore."

The ground under my feet rumbled with the sound of the dogs' fighting, and I tasted blood before I felt the pain of Valin's hand across my face. He hit me hard and fast, one punch after another, until my vision blurred. Swallowing, I bent over, curling into a ball and reaching for my rig. My Ka-Bar slid out of its sheath with a hitch. The damp leather was tight around the blade, but a yank on its hilt jerked it free.

I wasn't surprised when he unsheathed his second dagger. He'd never been one for a fair fight. Valin had the *ainmhí dubh* and magic; why not add two knives to the mix?

"Are you going to stab me, *arracht*?" Valin mocked me, grabbing a handful of my shredded T-shirt to drag me to my feet. The edge of his dagger skipped over my throat, beading a line of pain on my skin, and I went limp, letting him pull me close. "Is that what you're going to do with your tiny knife?"

"Damned going to try." I gritted my teeth and stabbed up into Valin's ribs. The angle was wrong to gut him, but the knife nicked something bony under his skin, probably a rib. Valin let me go, holding his side as blood crept out between his fingers.

"You're going to pay for that, *arracht*." My brother hawked, and the wet hit my face. I half expected it to burn like *ainmhí dubh* spit. "I'm going to make you...."

"Talk too damned much, brother," I grunted, digging the knife in again. He stumbled, gasping for breath. I heard the wheeze of his lungs working to pull in air with the delicate off-balance shushing noise of a gaping wound. I tried to go in again, but he dodged, bringing his fist up to hook me across the jaw.

The punch rattled my eyes and teeth, and I staggered back, trying to shake off the bells ringing in my ears.

Tickles of fear edged into my mind. Valin was stronger than I was. He had the advantage of better food and not being hung up by his wrists after being grown out like an avocado pit. For all the stretching they did to my body, it didn't make me as tall as he was or give me his reach. My mistake was thinking that because we shared the same face, we shared the same body. I'd need more distance between strikes. I told my terror to go suck itself.

"You're quick." He grinned, and I felt a sting of pride at the blood turning his teeth red. "Maybe when I get you home, I'll have to spend more time with you loose. It's a welcome change."

"Only way you're dragging me back to Tanic is dead." Valin tilted his head, staring at me with a bemused smile on his face. "Even then, it'll be in pieces."

"I think you are serious, *dearthár*," he purred, stepping around me until his back was to the river.

"I'm very serious, brother," I said, smiling back at him. The dogs' fighting was dropping to a low rumbling, and a quick glance toward the remains of the pack gave me a little hope.

The female's mouth was loose, but as she growled the remaining males into submission, her yawning maw was speckled with bloody drool, and one of her long canines was broken off nearly down to the root. The two males weren't doing much better. Long gashes marred fur and skin along one's rump, and the bigger male's throat was punctured through, the flesh around the bite marks blackened from the other male's acidic saliva. The larger male limped slowly, reluctant to put weight on his front paw, but the smaller, sleeker male moved even slower, his molting wings tucked tight against his rib cage. The unevenness of his gait could have been another foot injury, but I was betting he'd been bitten across the spine. Neither one of the males would be up for an intense fight.

Dempsey's shotgun was a lost cause. It lay in a crumpled pretzel of wood and metal on the ground, not far from the fallen male, and the female stalked back and forth. Her mouth had to be causing her intense pain, but Tanic's training held her firm. Valin took a few steps away from me, motioning the female black dog forward. The *ainmhi dubh* moved in behind me, blocking an escape into the woods, and the males collapsed into ebony sphinxes, their dark red eyes slitted and watchful. The female remained standing. She'd not let me get past her unless it was over her dead body.

I'd be happy to help her out with that if given the chance.

The river's mist was cool on my bare skin, rising up from the ravine and beading on my face. Standing close to the rock shelf's edge, Valin quickly came forward a few steps to give himself distance from the cliff. I let the Ka-Bar drop and drew my Glocks, aiming at Valin's face and chest.

"You took a bath in the river, little *arracht*." He sneered. "Did you forget that your little metal toys won't work now?"

The guns felt good in my hands, their familiar weight fitting into my palms. I loved the feel of metal against my skin, at the moment, even more than I loved the sound of a full-throated engine on an open road.

"Yeah, that's a myth, Valin." I grinned, teeth bared and threatening. "Just like you're going to be in a few seconds."

The right Glock jammed, beaten too hard when I'd hit the rocks below, but the left shot fine. I aimed and fired, moving quickly as Valin's arms came up, either to defend himself or throw his daggers. Red streams burst across his chest, and he stumbled back, arms flailing with the force of the bullets cutting through him.

Snarling, the *ainmhi dubh* were on me, and I emptied the rest of my clip into their rushing black bodies. Curled in a tight spin, the smaller male caught my leg, taking me down with his weight. Nearly crushed under his chest, I rolled, using his body as cover while I ejected the other gun's clip and scrambled to reload the working Glock. Teeth caught my shoulder, and my right arm went numb before my nerves caught on fire as the dog's saliva entered my bloodstream. The stink of his skin made me retch, but I swallowed hard, concentrating on what I had to do. I was too far away from his head to do a kill shot, and firing into the thing's belly would be a waste of a bullet, but he gave me enough shelter to reload and come back up shooting.

Tucking my elbow against my stomach, I fired at Valin again, catching his shoulder. He jerked, and blood bubbled out of his mouth. Screaming the names our father gave me, he caught his foot on the edge of the cliff and he tumbled back, punching a hole in the mists rising from the river below. Valin reached out, and his fingers caught the rocky edge. Then they too disappeared from view, pulling down a fall of pebbles.

I couldn't hear the splash of his body hitting the water. The ravine was too far up for the sound to carry, but the males bounded up, snarling and snapping at one another as they looked to the female for direction. The large black dog stared me down, mantling her wings and puffing up her spine.

She didn't need to make herself larger to intimidate me. I was already plenty scared down to my ankles as the *ainmhí dubh* wove around one another on the cliff flat. Her gaze rolled over me, taking every inch into her memory. Her bright crimson eyes burned with intelligence, and the warning in her stiff, angry shape was clear: the next time she saw me, I'd be meat she would leave for the scavengers to pick through.

With a shake of her wings and bloodied fur, the *ainmhí dubh* launched herself up, catching air before cutting down into the mists. She left swirls of droplets behind her and disappeared into the ravine after her master. The males hesitated, torn between having me for an easy meal or following their alpha.

A piercing scream from downriver helped them make up their minds. The tinier male dug into the rocky precipice and strained to leap as high as his weight would allow, spreading his span taut before taking a beat to lift him higher. The larger, older male took a running leap and went aloft with a few flaps, gouging the rock face as he ran. The furrows he left behind were nearly an inch deep, dragging marks turning a patch of moss black where his poisonous claws scored down through to stone.

It was hard to stand, so I let myself fall. Now alone, the fear hit full force and crimped me into a ball. My lungs ached, and I took shuddering breaths, forcing my body to respond to the most basic of things. Cold, acid burned, and frightened, I wanted to crawl under a rock and stay there until the world forgot I existed.

"Pity it doesn't work like that," I mumbled, shaking some sense into my thoughts. "Too much shit to do, Kai. Get up and get moving."

I stumbled as I got to my feet, nearly falling flat on my face again. My cut-open shirt flapped as I walked, the rig holding it in place. Stopping to pick up my knife from the ground, I looked over at the *ainmhí dubh* lying near the forest's edge. Shimmying my T-shirt off around my harness, I sliced it in two, wrapping the pieces around my hands as much as I could and leaving my fingers free. The leather straps of my rig rubbed against my bruised skin, but it wasn't a bad pain. It was enough of a sting to let me know I was alive.

Crouching was painful but necessary. I picked up the black dog's back leg and made the first cut, sliding my wrapped hand under its skin, separating the meat from its hide.

"Screw it. I killed it. I'm taking it," I muttered, wincing at the burn to my fingers and wrists. "And if Ryder wants the meat out, the bastard can come get it."

EPILOGUE

I LIT a kretek, inhaling the sweet sting of cloves. My lungs hurt, despite Ryder's healer fixing a puncture I'd gotten from one of my broken ribs. She had to be coaxed into it, nearly defying her High Lord's command, but I understood. She could barely stand to touch me and did the minimum before fleeing the room. The woman left me with my tapestry of bruises but removed the breaks. It was more than I'd hoped for. I pretended to think it was because I stank of the river and *ainmhí dubh* blood, but I'm sure she felt Tanic on me. She'd have been a fool not to.

Standing on the roof of my warehouse, I watched the lights of the boats move around the bay as people took advantage of the pleasant evening air for a nighttime sail. I'd left the rooftop door open, listening to the others laugh below. Cari's voice carried up, bringing with it a story about an Arizona run.

Alexa's questions stalled the tale, but the sidhe liked the idea of earning money outside the Court, and even against Ryder's protests, she wondered aloud about becoming a Stalker. Ryder's snarls became growling threats when Cari offered to show her the ropes. I left them to argue about it, needing some air to clear the tangle in my head.

"I thought I'd find you up here," Ryder said, stepping onto the roof. I turned from my sailboat watching and waited for him to join me. Sniffing at the fragrant smoke, he wrinkled his nose slightly, smiling unevenly at me. "Those smell like you taste."

"I like them better than other cigarettes," I replied, taking a small puff. Motioning him closer, I leaned in and breathed into his mouth, brushing my lips against his. Ryder choked and then gulped, rapping his own chest to stop from coughing, but he steadied his breathing and shook his head at me.

"That's a very dangerous thing to do, Kai," he said in between small gasps. "You're tempting my control."

"Yeah, probably." I shrugged and turned around to lean my elbows on the high ledge. "But according to Dalia, I've got a death wish."

He took the kretek from my fingers and drew a small sip from its filter, handing it back to me as he entered another fit. I tried not to smile when he gave me a dirty look. Catching his voice, Ryder choked out, "Nope, don't like it."

"Good. They're bad for you."

"I cut Dempsey a payment," he said when I turned to look at him. "Even if I wanted to kill him for leaving you behind, he got the girls out. I'd pay you if I didn't think you'd shoot me."

"You're right," I agreed. "I'd shoot you. Or maybe let Alexa gut you. Either would work."

"You are always threatening to shoot me." Ryder laughed. It echoed a bit, then faded, lost in the sounds of the ocean and the tolling bells on the bay buoys. "That *ainmhí dubh* was the largest I've ever seen. I heard they had wings, but I always imagined them differently."

"They get bigger. The wings and the dogs." My shoulder blades itched, and Ryder's face was touched with a fleeting sadness. I didn't need to tell him about wearing Tanic's mark on my back. He'd seen the winged pelt I dragged out of Balboa. "If I was going to make you pay for something, it would be for going into that damned river. That water was cold."

"You didn't have to jump in. I know you felt like you needed to, but you didn't."

"I did," I said quietly, watching the clove's tip flare red when I took another hit. "And you're welcome."

His laugh was as sweet as the smoke in my lungs. "Thank you. My mother would be appalled at my manners."

"Valin, the girls' father? You should know that he's my... brother." It weighed on me, settling hard in my chest, and I needed to tell him, even if it cracked what I had with Ryder. "We share a father.... Tanic. Well, our bodies share a father."

He let that sink in, saying nothing as he watched me intently. I couldn't tell what he was thinking, and when he shifted his hip to lean against the roof wall, my nerves chewed themselves apart.

"That's all you share," he said gently. "It doesn't change anything, not for us, maybe for the girls, but not us. I still want you, Kai. I'm honest about that. That hasn't changed. I don't think that is ever going to change. There's something about you that makes me want you, and I like getting what I want."

I snorted. "That sounds like a threat."

"It sounds like a promise to me," he replied.

"They're not going to stop coming, you know," I said. I tried not to let fear into my voice, but I heard the tremble and shut it down as quickly as I could. "They'll send someone else, or Valin will come back."

"Are you so certain he's alive? You shot him in the chest."

"We're hard to kill, remember?" I was grateful he didn't say *brother*. "And if he'd died, his black dogs would have attacked me. There'd be nothing to hold them. No, the female was still bound to him. That's why she went into the river."

"So he'll come back for you and the girls," Ryder said. His face was hard to read in the shadows, but I heard the weariness in his voice. "And maybe with others."

"It all depends on if he tells Tanic. He'd be stupid to say anything about what happened. Our... his father doesn't like failure."

"I won't let him touch you," he murmured. "I'll kill anyone who comes for you. Maybe one day you'll believe that."

"I'd die before I'd let him take those kids. I know what Tanic would do to them. I'm not letting that happen," I said, staring off into nothing. "Hell, I'd kill myself before I let him touch me again."

"Mind if I touch you?" Ryder asked, and I looked at him sharply. Laughing, he grinned at me. "So they're your nieces as much as they are mine?"

"Yeah," I said. "Guess so."

We left it there, not speaking for a while. Then he shifted against the ledge, drawing up close to my shoulder until we touched. The tingle of his closeness ran up my battered side, and I closed my eyes, wishing the clove would numb more than my lips.

"Ciarla is claiming I conned her into providing eggs for Shannon to carry," Ryder whispered. "She's refusing to raise them, says they're abominations. Alexa's pissed and is taking the girls."

"Scarily enough, Alexa seems like a good mother."

"She is. No one will be able to come near the girls without crossing her first."

"We don't know if Valin's telling the truth. No one's done any genetic testing on the elfin, but we might find out for sure," I said. "Ciarla's your sister. This really all could be a lie."

"I believe it *because* she is my sister," he said bitterly. "I agreed to this because she came to *me*. Those little girls deserve better than Ciarla for a mother, even if she wanted them. Alexa can give that to them unless you want to."

"Raise them?" I rasped. "Are you crazy? I'm surprised I haven't accidently killed my cat. Besides, look around you. Do you really think this is any way a kid should be brought up?"

"You turned out okay." He poked my ribs, and I winced when he found a bruise. "Except for that stubborn streak and maybe the lack of common sense."

"No, I didn't. Not really," I replied. "Dempsey tried his best, you know?"

"I wouldn't give that man credit for how you turned out."

"You've got to. He's all I had." Keeping my face turned to the ocean, I let the clove smolder.

"I'm here now, and the others. Dempsey isn't the only person you have," Ryder suggested, sliding his palm over my side, cupping my rib cage. "Besides, would you let Dempsey do this?"

San Diego blurred behind him, steel structures dotted with lit constellations hidden behind the fog coming in. His tongue raked over the inside of my lower lip, tracing its pout. I was shocked to hear a sigh of surrender pour from my throat. I tried to swallow it, but Ryder caught it in his mouth, teasing it away from me.

Pressing further, Ryder coaxed me with long, even strokes of his fingers along my back, arching me into him. Moving until his thighs touched the short wall, he trapped my legs between his, bending down to deepen the kiss. His tongue tickled the palate ridges in my mouth, and I gave in, sucking at Ryder's heat with a fierceness I only had for good whiskey and fine chocolate.

Kissing Ryder didn't seem to be quenching the need in my body. If anything, it was like pouring kerosene on a wildfire. I felt like dying under his hands and not caring because I wanted him that badly. My common sense, already threadbare, strained as my body reacted to Ryder's touch, and I drew in long heaves of the night air to cool me off.

"Nope," I said, shaking my head and hoping Ryder didn't see the trembling in my hands. "I'd kill Dempsey if he tried that. Still might kill you for it."

"It might be worth dying for, Kai," Ryder said into my hair. "The offer still stands, you know. You are always welcome in my Court."

"Answer's still no," I scoffed, pushing him away. I put the burned-out clove into a can of sand I'd left near the roof's ledge. I needed some space or less space. Distance seemed safer, but up close would have been more satisfying. "You just want me in your bed."

"Not a bad thing," he said, leering at me. "I'm pretty good in bed."

"I only have your word for it," I replied, stepping back toward the door. "I know how good I am. You could suck big time, and then where would I be? Stuck with you when I could have had Alexa."

"Ah, *áinle*." I was nearly at the stairs when Ryder stopped me with his soft whisper, "What makes you think I wouldn't share?"

RHYS FORD is an award-winning author with several long-running LGBT+ mystery, thriller, paranormal, and urban fantasy series and is a two-time LAMBDA finalist with her *Murder and Mayhem* novels. She is also a 2017 Gold and Silver Medal winner in the Florida Authors and Publishers President's Book Awards for her novels *Ink and Shadows* and *Hanging the Stars*. She is published by Dreamspinner Press and DSP Publications.

She shares the house with Harley, a gray tuxedo with a flower on her face, Badger, a disgruntled alley cat who isn't sure living inside is a step up the social ladder, as well as a ginger cairn terrorist named Gus. Rhys is also enslaved to the upkeep of a 1979 Pontiac Firebird and enjoys murdering make-believe people.

Rhys can be found at the following locations:
Blog: www.rhysford.com
Facebook: www.facebook.com/rhys.ford.author
Twitter: @Rhys_Ford

BOOK TWO IN THE KAI GRACEN SERIES

RHYS FORD

MAD LIZARD MAMBO

"Visceral urban fantasy…set in a fascinating
world peopled by compelling characters."
— The Novel Approach

The Kai Gracen Series: Book Two

Kai Gracen has no intention of being anyone's pawn. A pity Fate and SoCalGov have a different opinion on the matter.

Licensed Stalkers make their living hunting down monsters and dangerous criminals… and their lives are usually brief, brutal, and thankless. Despite being elfin and cursed with a nearly immortal lifespan, Kai didn't expect to be any different. Then Ryder, the High Lord of the Southern Rise Court, arrived in San Diego, and Kai's not-so-mundane life went from mild mayhem to full-throttle chaos.

Now an official liaison between the growing Sidhe Court and the human populace, Kai is at Ryder's beck and call for anything a High Lord might need a Stalker to do. Unfortunately for Kai, this means chasing down a flimsy rumor about an ancient lost Court somewhere in the Nevada desert—a court with powerful magics that might save Ryder's—and Kai's—people from becoming a bloody memory in their Merged world's violent history.

The race for the elfin people's salvation opens unwelcome windows into Kai's murky past, and it could also slam the door on any future he might have with his own kind and Ryder.

www.dsppublications.com

RHYS FORD

JACKED CAT JIVE

The Kai Gracen Series: Book Three

Stalker Kai Gracen knew his human upbringing would eventually clash with his elfin heritage, but not so soon. Between Ryder, a pain-in-his-neck Sidhe Lord coaxing him to join San Diego's Southern Rise Court, and picking up bounties for SoCalGov, he has more than enough to deal with. With his loyalties divided between the humans who raised him and the Sidhe Lord he's befriended and sworn to protect, Kai finds himself standing at a crossroads.

When a friend begs Kai to rescue a small group of elfin refugees fleeing the Dusk Court, he's pulled into a dangerous mission with Ryder through San Diego's understreets and the wilderness beyond. Things go from bad to downright treacherous when Kerrick, Ryder's cousin, insists on joining them, staking a claim on Southern Rise and Kai.

Burdened by his painful past, Kai must stand with Ryder against Kerrick while facing down the very Court he fears and loathes. Dying while on a run is expected for a Stalker, but Kai wonders if embracing his elfin blood also means losing his heart, soul, and humanity along the way.

www.dsppublications.com

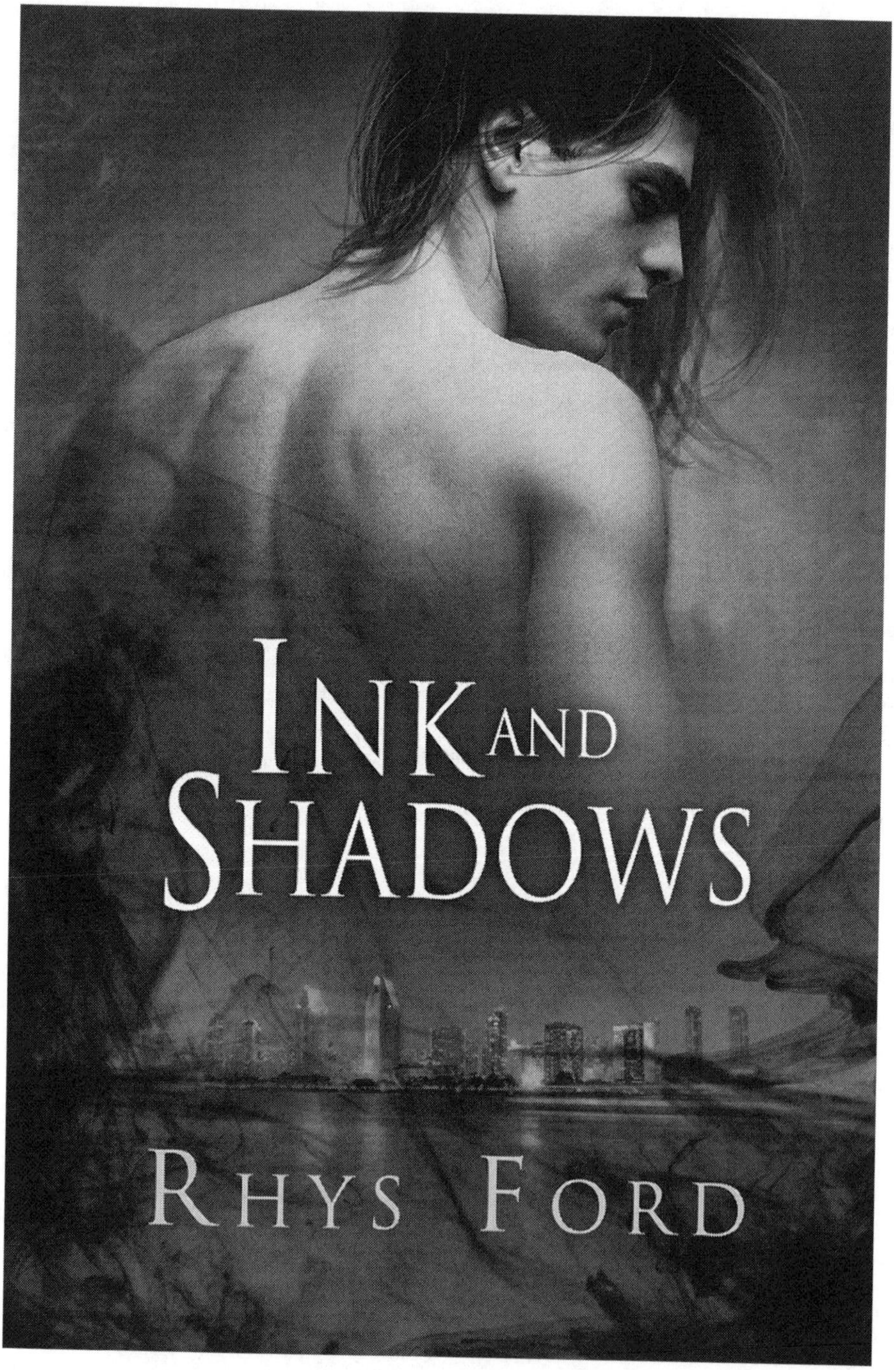
INK AND SHADOWS
RHYS FORD

Ink and Shadows: Book One

Kismet Andreas lives in fear of the shadows.

For the young tattoo artist, the shadows hold more than darkness. He is certain of his insanity because the dark holds creatures and crawling things only he can see—monsters who hunt out the weak to eat their minds and souls, leaving behind only empty husks and despair.

And if there's one thing Kismet fears more than being hunted—it's the madness left in its wake.

The shadowy Veil is Mal's home. As Pestilence, he is the youngest—and most inexperienced—of the Four Horsemen of the Apocalypse, immortal manifestations resurrected to serve—and cull—mankind. Invisible to all but the dead and insane, the Four exist between the Veil and the mortal world, bound to their nearly eternal fate. Feared by other immortals, the Horsemen live in near solitude but Mal longs to know more than Death, War and Famine.

Mal longs to be… more human. To interact with someone other than lunatics or the deceased.

When Kismet rescues Mal from a shadowy attack, Pestilence is suddenly thrust into a vicious war—where mankind is the prize, and the only one who has faith in Mal is the human the other Horsemen believe is destined to die.

www.dsppublications.com